JOANNA GODDEN

Other Virago Modern Classics published by The Dial Press

ANTONIA WHITE
Frost in May
The Lost Traveller
The Sugar House
Beyond the Glass
Strangers

RADCLYFFE HALL
The Unlit Lamp

REBECCA WEST
Harriet Hume
The Judge
The Return of the Soldier

F. TENNYSON JESSE
The Lacquer Lady

SARAH GRAND
The Beth Book

BARBARA COMYNS
The Vet's Daughter
Our spoons came
*   from Woolworths*

HENRY HANDEL RICHARDSON
The Getting of Wisdom
Maurice Guest

MARY WEBB
Gone to Earth
Precious Bane

EMILY EDEN
The Semi-Attached Couple
*   & The Semi-Detached House*

MARGARET KENNEDY
The Ladies of Lyndon
Together and Apart

MAY SINCLAIR
Mary Olivier: A Life

ADA LEVERSON
The Little Ottleys

E. ARNOT ROBERTSON
Ordinary Families

ELIZABETH TAYLOR
Mrs. Palfrey at the Claremont
The Sleeping Beauty
The Soul of Kindness
In a Summer Season

ROSAMOND LEHMANN
A Note in Music
The Weather in the Streets

ROSE MACAULAY
Told by an Idiot

MAUREEN DUFFY
That's How it Was

Sheila Kaye-Smith

JOANNA GODDEN

With a new introduction by
RACHEL ANDERSON

The Dial Press
DOUBLEDAY & COMPANY, INC.
GARDEN CITY, NEW YORK
1984

Published by The Dial Press

First published in Great Britain by Cassell & Co. Ltd. 1921

Library of Congress Cataloging in Publication Data

Kaye-Smith, Sheila, 1887-1956.
Joanna Godden.

Originally published: London: Cassell, 1921.
I. Title.
PR6021.A8J6 1984   823′.912   83-45194
ISBN 0-385-27959-0

To
W. L. GEORGE

CONTENTS

New Introduction by Rachel Anderson   xi

PART I
SHEPHERD'S HEY   1

PART II
FIRST LOVE   59

PART III
THE LITTLE SISTER   129

PART IV
LAST LOVE   214

INTRODUCTION

"My happiness comes from three things—the country, my writing, and my religion. The country and my writing are really two different parts of the same thing . . . They are so interwoven that I cannot separate them. And as for religion, that is the third strand in the shining cord." Sheila Kaye-Smith in *Three Ways Home*, a spiritual autobiography (1937).

The love of countryside was, from an early age, such a strong feature in the shining cord of her life that "merely to smell the grass and soil, to see the night sky brushing down over the fields" was her heart's delight. Later, the urge expressed itself in a lyrical adoration of all that was rustic. Meticulously, Sheila Kaye-Smith recorded speech patterns of Sussex and Kent. She viewed, with regret, the disappearance of old-fashioned customs in favour of agricultural advance. She admired horse-drawn ploughs, sullen skies and, above all, the benefits of soil. She showed, for example, how simply to be in the calm presence of our "good moist earth" could offer relief to a grieving father after the death of his son. The man lay on the ground dragging out bunches of tender, growing things . . .

> He began to smell the sweetness of their roots, to feel the budding springing things, growing out of deadness. He gave a little piteous thrill of joy which broke into the stillness and strength of her scene and moisture and green life struggling out of earth . . . Even in the Valley of Shadow of Death, the earth had not failed him (*Little England* [1918].)

Introduction

Sheila Kaye-Smith was not, however, a country girl by birth or upbringing, but was the product of a genteel South Coast resort, St. Leonard's-on-Sea, and her lived experience of her heart's delight was an annual summer holiday on a farm with her sister. In her later teens she was able to make day trips on foot, bike or horse into the land beyond St. Leonard's and Hastings, though by that age, on her own reckoning, she had already been conditioned.

> Compton Mackenzie has stated somewhere that the whole of an author's stock-in-trade is laid in before he is twenty-one. After that he can only develop and rearrange impressions already in store. Personally I should reduce this figure by reversing it, and say that an author is conditioned by the time he is twelve. Certainly, it was the first twelve years of my life that made me a Sussex novelist.

The habit of writing was, similarly, rooted early and she was enormously prolific. As well as over fifty published books—novels, poems, country lore, and a philosophical cookbook—she produced in her childhood thirteen unpublished novels, and forty-two verbally "composed" novels which, instead of writing down, she recited out loud.

The third strand of her life, religion, was also present early on and what began as an adolescent flirtation with Anglo-Catholicism, lead her in her forties, to be received into the Catholic Church. As a schoolgirl, she made furtive forays to the nearest high church where she was stirred by "the warm incense-smelling shadows, the winking red lights, the atmosphere ten times more catholic than that of any catholic church". Always she sought the exotic, the sentimental, and the foreign-sounding. Briefly, at fifteen, she became an atheist having just discovered the meaning of the word. She reconverted at sixteen, when she watched, though did not participate in, an Anglican communion service which "gave me back my perception of what has been called the numinous side of religion—the shining cloud, the Shekinah, without which the Temple is merely a heap of stones—the gleam".

Religion as it features in her writing closely parallels the quasi-religious themes and messages of the popular romantic novelists of her time. Just as in the romances of Florence Barclay, Elinor Glyn or Ethel M. Dell, in her novels too, we see

Introduction

men and women being stirred up by enthusiasms, moods and passions which are of both an earthly and a heavenly nature. As the *Publisher's Circular* had declared twenty years earlier, "Of all forms of fiction, the semi-religious is the most popular."

"Actually," wrote Sheila Kaye-Smith,

> religion provides nearly as many good situations as the sex-instinct—there are endless combinations, permutations, frustrations and deviations which the novelist can use, and its effect on character (either by its growth or by its thwarting) makes something new in the way of psychological interest.

Nowhere are the plots of her novels as silly as those of Ethel M. Dell or Florence Barclay though her use of a restricted emotional vocabulary—thrill, throb, mother, breast, heart and home—to convey emotional or spiritual intensity, is similar. Nor was she the first popular writer to be driven by her evangelising zeal to place God as a character in a novel. God, angels, divine phallic visions, had all been used to effect in Marie Corelli's erotic-spiritual quests. However, Sheila Kaye-Smith was the first to allow the Almighty to speak in a specially reconstructed Sussex idiom: "I am your God—döan't you know Me?" the Almighty calls down to an agricultural worker about to commit suicide in *Green Apple Harvest* (1920).

> "Did you think I was away up in heaven, watching you from a gurt way off? Didn't you know that I've bin with you all the time?—that every time you looked out on the fields or into your kind brother's eyes or at your baby asleep in his bed you looked on Me? . . . Why wöan't you look and see how beautiful and homely and faithful and loving I am?"

In these displays of respectable moral passion, her aim was to be "challenging and proclaiming". She was writing, not of pantheism, or nature worship, but about "Catholicism—God in all things, no matter how simple and seemingly insufficient. It is the ground of the sacramental system, through which by the operation of the Holy Ghost nature gives birth to that which the whole world cannot contain."

Lack of a sense of proportion is, paradoxically, her biggest limitation as she sows the seeds of her great themes across huge

Introduction

literary fields. Most writers get to a point where they realise that there is something that they cannot achieve. Bad and middling writers don't have this limitation, for the genuine desire to improve the world combines with an unswerving belief that, by the power of their pens, they are doing so.

As in the case of any writer who hovers uncertainly on the borderline between being a good bad writer, and a bad good writer, the critics of the time couldn't make up their minds about her. Frank Swinnerton said *Tamarisk Town* (1919) was "a noble failure". Another critic concluded that though she had the power to present sometimes masterly prose "yet greatness is excepted" while, in contrast, the *Westminster Gazette* confirmed, in 1924, that she was "one of the very few novelists now writing who have quite definitely achieved greatness".

She would have agreed. Although she didn't go as far as Elinor Glyn who saw her works as being inspired by the divinity, nor as Hall Caine and Marie Corelli who both claimed to be the new Shakespeare of the prose form, she did rate her own literary success highly, explaining how the effects of her wide reading of the Bible, Brontë, Jane Austen, William Blake, Richardson, Fielding, *et al*, could be clearly seen to have influenced her work.

Joanna Godden (1921) was sometimes cited as an example of the good books Sheila Kaye-Smith wrote before being overtaken and spoilt by religion. She was at pains to point out that her religious viewpoint, though less explicit and dominating than in subsequent books, was already perfectly apparent in *Joanna Godden*, in such details, she said, as "the sympathetic pen-portrait" of Father Lawrence, the Anglican monk. Like its predecessors, *Sussex Gorse* (1916) and *Tamarisk Town*, it is the study of an ambitious landowner but, unusually, she is a woman—a sheepfarmer on the Romney and Walland Marshes in Kent. The conception of the story was not, she freely admitted, her own but was generously suggested by another popular novelist. When she was about to write a story set in the Channel Isles, W. L. George strongly advised her not to give up writing about Sussex just when she was beginning to be *known* as a Sussex novelist. "The only way to success," he said, "is to fit into a definite pigeon-hole in the public mind. If you're always

Introduction

changing, they'll change too. You want to be labelled—then they won't forget you." He suggested that the heroine's rustic nature, and the sound of her name, must be similar to the "Hannah Iden" of Sheila Kaye-Smith's previous novel, *Green Apple Harvest*. From Hannah Iden, it was a short step to Joanna Godden. Sheila Kaye-Smith still resisted, insisting that she didn't want to spend six months in female company while writing the story.

> Writing as I did from imagination rather than observation, a man presented no more difficulties than a woman, and I definitely preferred a man's society. It was not so much that I doubted my ability to write about Joanna, as that I did not want to. I thought she would bore me.

Willy George sent her copious notes, outlining the heroine's character. She was to hold splendid notions, to be reckless, strong, and above all, barbaric, but with a warm heart. "I never discussed the book with Willy once it had been started," she said. "He did not like it when it was finished, he said I had made Joanna too much of a virago."

She herself was oddly petulant about the book's success. "I do not wish to appear ungrateful, but when one has written more than twenty novels, it is sometimes trying to be known as the author of only one of them." Nonetheless, she took so well to the idea of the unconventional, over-sized girl with the touch of the barbarian about her, that she went on to produce more damn fine women of this type. Three years after Joanna came, for instance, "big, golden, lovely" Belle Munk, a girl who was "somehow immense" so that when her lover kissed her he experienced "a sensation of drawing bigness from her bigness, and strength from her strength".

Popular romantic heroines of the twenties, whether large or small, were uncertain whether they wished to be liberated from man or dominated by him; to choose true love inevitably meant to choose male domination. Joanna Godden, though she yearned for love, though she dreamed of a giant shepherd surrounded by giant sheep, who would seize hold of her and crush her, was not in her waking mind able to accept such a domination.

xv

Introduction

She is an unsophisticated woman who has never been as far as London. Her trials of courtship are acted out within the narrow confines of the gaunt, wind-bitten marshland, beneath doom-laden skies, on soggy soil. Sheila Kaye-Smith writes untiringly about fogs, mists, smoke, water, mud and wind. She writes about sheep-tick, sheep-dipping and root crops. The descriptive prose is tight-packed with swarth, swart, sward, tussocks, shards, lumps of marl and wealden clay. The rustic oafs, whose curious but authentic names the author selected from local tombstones and parish registers, stumble about a landscape spattered with genuine place-names and locations which the author took from the map. There is, however, something more powerful about the novel than the author's fascination for the ring of ancient surnames, and her passing interest in quaint country customs.

A story, as E. M. Forster coldly pointed out in a lecture in 1927 (*Aspects of the Novel*), can have only one merit—that of making the audience want to know what happens next, and conversely only one fault: that of making the audience not want to know what happens next. In *Joanna Godden*, even if we are unmoved by the author's sanctimonious generalisations about life and death, we are nonetheless driven to turn the pages of her story. We must know how Joanna will secure the future she deserves. As she rejects or mislays suitor after suitor, we begin to grow restless. Is the author stringing us along to a predictable conclusion of early spinsterhood?

Then, Sheila Kaye-Smith delivers her surprise. She makes Joanna do something completely out of character so that even as the novel ends on its ambiguous note, we are once more wondering what on earth will happen next to this impossible woman. For Joanna is caught up in a universal dilemma which the passage of forty years, and a women's liberation, can do little to resolve.

As a reasonably well-off (though not well-to-do) landowner, Joanna was free, as are most women today, to choose between domestic or professional fulfilment. She was, however, limited to one or other of these options, not both. She attempted to enter and succeed in a traditional man's world. Thus, she is not a

Introduction

colleague in farming, but a competitor. As a woman, she must work harder, must succeed more remarkably, than any of her fellows. "'Oh God!' She mourned to herself—'why didn't you make me a man?'" Today, the dilemma Joanna faces still faces many women who attempt to succeed with a traditional masculine career. Total fulfilment of a business ambition does not allay the yearnings for maternal fulfilment.

Possibly, the heroine's inability to settle to any man reflected the author's own ignorance of men and marriage. At any rate, at the time of writing *Joanna Godden*, Sheila Kaye-Smith was thirty-four and single, and she conveys with tenderness and conviction, the pain and indeed the actual physical ache of Joanna's unresolved desires. As many women do, Joanna misinterprets her broodiness as a succession of minor and major ailments, from rheumatism to consumption and cancer, before recognising her real problem. The evocation of the middle-aged virgin, waiting in bed in her sensible cotton nightgown buttoned to the neck, is fresh, vital and, in its prudish way, even erotic.

Middling bad writers may fail in their more grandiose schemes to explain and resolve the whole human condition. But in communicating some of the personal anguish of women, they manage to write with intensity, passion and above all honesty. As Virginia Woolf, in defence of women writers, explained in a lecture in 1929:

> The whole character of women's fiction at the present moment is courageous; it is sincere; it keeps closely to what women feel. It is not bitter. It does not insist upon its femininity. These qualities are much commoner than they were, and they give even to second- and third-rate work the value of truth and the interest of sincerity.

Like her heroine, Sheila Kaye-Smith took time to find her marital bliss. At thirty-seven she married an Anglican vicar. Five years after *Joanna Godden*, she was driven by popular demand to write its sequel which took the form of a novella, published in a volume with some shorter stories. But she was not entirely happy with it. In this follow-up, she felt that she had failed to recapture Joanna's original fire and spirit. She believed

Introduction

that, with increased age and maturity, her heroine would have lost much of that bravura which made her such an outstanding figure in the first book.

Unless otherwise specified, all quotations are from Sheila Kaye-Smith's autobiography, *Three Ways Home*.

Rachel Anderson, Canterbury, 1982

NOTE

Though local names, both of places and people, have been used in this story, the author states that no reference is intended to any living person.

JOANNA GODDEN

PART I

SHEPHERD'S HEY

§ 1

THREE marshes spread across the triangle made by the Royal Military Canal and the coasts of Sussex and Kent. The Military Canal runs from Hythe to Rye, beside the Military Road; between it and the flat, white beaches of the Channel lie Romney Marsh, Dunge Marsh and Walland Marsh, from east to west. Walland Marsh is sectored by the Kent Ditch, which draws huge, straggling diagrams here, to preserve ancient rights of parishes and the monks of Canterbury. Dunge Marsh runs up into the apex of the triangle at Dunge Ness, and adds to itself twenty feet of shingle every year. Romney Marsh is the sixth continent and the eighth wonder of the world.

The three marshes are much alike; indeed to the foreigner they are all a single spread of green, slatted with watercourses. No river crosses them, for the Rother curves close under Rye Hill, though these marshes were made by its ancient mouth, when it was the River Limine and ran into the Channel at Old Romney. There are a few big watercourses—the New Sewer, the Yokes Sewer, the White Kemp Sewer—there are a few white roads, and a great many marsh villages—Brenzett, Ivychurch, Fairfield, Snargate, Snave—each little more than a church with a farmhouse or two. Here and there little deserted chapels lie out on the marsh, officeless since the days of the monks of Canterbury; and everywhere there are farms, with hundreds of sheep grazing on the thick pastures.

Little Ansdore Farm was on Walland Marsh, three miles from Rye, and about midway between the villages of Brodnyx and Pedlinge. It was a sea farm. There were no hop-gardens, as on the farms inland, no white-cowled oasts, and scarcely more than twelve acres under the plough. Three hundred acres of pasture spread round Ansdore, dappled over with the big Kent sheep—the road from Pedlinge to Brodnyx went through them, curling and looping and doubling to the demands of the dykes. Just beyond Pedlinge it turned northward and crossed the South Eastern Railway under the hills that used to be the coast of England, long ago when the sea flowed up over the marsh to the walls of Lympne and Rye; then in less than a mile it had crossed the line again, turning south; for some time it ran seawards, parallel with the Kent Ditch, then suddenly went off at right angles and ran straight to the throws where the Woolpack Inn watches the roads to Lydd and Appledore.

On a dim afternoon towards the middle of October in the year 1897, a funeral procession was turning off this road into the drive of Little Ansdore. The drive was thick with shingle, and the mourning coaches lurched and rolled in it, spoiling no doubt the decorum of their occupants. Anyhow, the first two to get out at the farmhouse door had lost a little of that dignity proper to funerals. A fine young woman of about twenty-three, dressed handsomely but without much fashion in black crape and silk, jumped out with a violence that sent her overplumed black hat to a rakish angle. In one black kid-gloved hand she grasped a handkerchief with a huge black border, in the other a Prayer Book, so could not give any help to the little girl of ten who stumbled out after her, with the result that the child fell flat on the doorstep and cut her chin. She immediately began to cry.

"Now be quiet, Ellen," said the elder roughly but not unkindly, as she helped her up, and stuffing the black-bordered handkerchief into her pocket, took out the everyday one which she kept for use. "There, wipe your eyes, and be a stout gal. Don't let all the company see you crying."

The last injunction evidently impressed Ellen, for she

stopped at once. Her sister had wiped the grit and the little smear of blood off her chin, and stood in the doorway holding her hand while one by one the other carriages drew up and the occupants alighted. Not a word was spoken till they had all assembled, then the young woman said : " Please come in and have a cup of tea," and turning on her heel led the way to the dining-room.

" Joanna," said little Ellen in a loud whisper, " may I take off my hat ? "

" No, that you mayn't."

" But the elastic's so tight—it's cutting my chin. Why mayn't I ? "

" You can't till the funeral's over."

" It is over. They've put father in the ground."

" It isn't over till we've had tea, and you keep your hat on till it's over."

For answer Ellen tore off her pork-pie hat and threw it on the floor. Immediately Joanna had boxed her unprotected ears, and the head of the procession was involved in an ignominious scuffle. " You pick up that hat and put it on," said Joanna, " or you shan't have any nice tea." " You're a beast ! You're a brute," cried Ellen, weeping loudly. Behind them stood two rows of respectable marsh-dwellers, gazing solemnly ahead as if the funeral service were still in progress. In their hearts they were thinking that it was just like Joanna Godden to have a terrification like this when folk were expected to be serious. In the end Joanna picked up Ellen's hat, crammed it down ruthlessly on her head, hind part before, and heaving her up under her arm carried her into the dining-room. The rest of the company followed, and were ushered into their places to the accompaniment of Ellen's shrieks, which they pretended not to hear.

" Mr. Pratt, will you take the end of the table ? " said Joanna to the scared little clergyman, who would almost have preferred to sit under it rather than receive the honour which Miss Godden's respect for his cloth dictated. " Mr. Huxtable, will you sit by me ? " Having thus settled her aristocracy she turned to her equals and allotted places to Vine of Birdskitchen, Furnese of Misleham, Southland of Yokes Court, and their wives. " Arthur Alce, you take my left," and a tall young man with red hair, red whiskers, and a face covered with freckles and tan, came sidling to her elbow.

In front of Joanna a servant-girl had just set down a huge black teapot, which had been stewing on the hob ever since the funeral party had been sighted crossing the railway line half a mile off. Round it were two concentric rings of teacups—good old Worcester china, except for a common three which had been added for number's sake, and which Joanna carefully bestowed upon herself, Ellen, and Arthur Alce. Ellen had stopped crying at the sight of the cakes and jam and pots of " relish " which stretched down the table in orderly lines, so the meal proceeded according to the decent conventions of silence. Nobody spoke, except to offer some eatable to somebody else. Joanna saw that no cup or plate was empty. She ought really to have delegated this duty to another, being presumably too closely wrapped in grief to think of anybody's appetite but her own, but Joanna never delegated anything, and her " A little more tea, Mrs. Vine ? "—" Another of these cakes, Mr. Huxtable ? "—" Just a little dash of relish, Mr. Pratt ? " were constantly breaking the stillness, and calling attention to her as she sat behind the teapot, with her plumed hat still a little on one side.

She was emphatically what men call a " fine woman," with her firm, white neck, her broad shoulders, her deep bosom and strong waist ; she was tall, too, with large, useful hands and feet. Her face was brown and slightly freckled, with a warm colour on the cheeks ; the features were strong, but any impression of heaviness was at once dispelled by a pair of eager, living blue eyes. Big jet earrings dangled from her ears, being matched by the double chain of beads that hung over her crape-frilled bodice. Indeed, with her plumes, her earrings, her necklace, her frills, though all were of the decent and respectable black, she faintly shocked the opinion of Walland Marsh, otherwise disposed in pity to be lenient to Joanna Godden and her ways.

Owing to the absence of conversation, tea was not as long drawn-out as might have been expected from the appetites. Besides, everyone was in a hurry to be finished and hear the reading of old Thomas Godden's will. Already several interesting rumours were afloat, notably one that he had left Ansdore to Joanna only on condition that she married Arthur Alce within the year. " She's a mare that's never been präaperly broken in, and she wants a strong hand to do it." Thus unchoicely Furnese of Misleham had expressed the wish that fathered such a thought.

So at the first possible moment after the last munch and loud swallow with which old Grandfather Vine, who was unfortunately the slowest as well as the largest eater, announced repletion, all the chairs were pushed back on the drugget and a row of properly impassive faces confronted Mr. Huxtable the lawyer as he took his stand by the window. Only Joanna remained sitting at the table, her warm blue eyes seeming to reflect the evening's light, her arm round little Ellen, who leaned against her lap.

The will was, after all, not so sensational as had been hoped. It opened piously, as might have been expected of Thomas Godden, who was as good an old man as ever met death walking in a cornfield unafraid. It went on to leave various small tokens of remembrance to those who had known him—a mourning ring to Mr. Vine, Mr. Furnese and Mr. Southland, his two volumes of Robertson's Sermons, and a book called " The Horse in Sickness and in Health," to Arthur Alce, which was a disappointment to those who had expected the bequest to be his daughter Joanna. There was fifty pounds for Mr. Samuel Huxtable of Huxtable, Vidler and Huxtable, Solicitors, Watchbell Street, Rye, five pounds each for those farm hands in his employment at the time of his death, with an extra ten pounds to " Nathan Stuppeny, my carter, on account of his faithful services both to me and to my father. And I give, devise and bequeath the residue of my property, comprising the freehold farm of Little Ansdore, in the parish of Pedlinge, Sussex, with all lands and live and dead stock pertaining thereto to my daughter Joanna Mary Godden. And I appoint the said Joanna Mary Godden sole executrix of this my will."

When the reading was over the company remained staring for a minute as decency required, then the door burst open and a big servant-girl brought in a tray set with glasses of whisky and water for the men and spiced wine for the women. These drink-offerings were received with a subdued hum of conversation—it was impossible to hear what was said or even to distinguish who was saying it, but a vague buzzing filled the room, as of imprisoned bees. In the midst of it Ellen's voice rose suddenly strident.

" Joanna, may I take off my hat now ? "

Her sister looked doubtful. The funeral was not ceremonially complete till Grandfather Vine had done choking over his heel-taps, but Ellen had undoubtedly endured a good deal with remarkable patience—her virtue ought in justice to be rewarded. Also Joanna noticed for the first time that she was looking grotesque as well as uncomfortable, owing perhaps to the hat being still on hind part before. So the necessary dispensation was granted, and Ellen further refreshed by a sip of her sister's wine.

The guests now took their departure, each being given a memorial card of the deceased, with a fine black edge and the picture of an urn upon it. Ellen also was given one, at her urgent request, and ran off in excitement with the treasure. Joanna remained with Mr. Huxtable for a final interview.

§ 2

"Well," he said, " I expect you'll want me to help you a bit, Miss Joanna."

Joanna had sat down again at the end of the table—big, tousled, over-dressed, alive. Huxtable surveyed her approvingly. " A damn fine woman," he said to himself, " she'll marry before long."

" I'm sure I'm much obliged to you, Mr. Huxtable," said Joanna, " there's many a little thing I'd like to talk over with you."

" Well, now's your time, young lady. I shan't have to be home for an hour or two yet. The first thing is, I suppose, for me to find you a bailiff for this farm."

" No, thank you kindly. I'll manage that."

" What ! Do you know of a man ? "

"No—I mean I'll manage the farm."

"You! My dear Miss Joanna . . . ."

"Well, why not? I've been bred up to it from a child. I used to do everything with poor father."

As she said the last word her brightness became for a moment dimmed, and tears swam into her eyes for the first time since she had taken the ceremonial handkerchief away from them. But the next minute she lighted up again.

"He showed me a lot—he showed me everything. I could do it much better than a man who doesn't know our ways."

"But—" the lawyer hesitated, "but it isn't just a question of knowledge, Miss Joanna; it's a question of —how shall I put it?—well, of authority. A woman is always at a disadvantage when she has to command men."

"I'd like to see the man I couldn't make mind me."

Huxtable grinned. "Oh, I've no doubt whatever that you could get yourself obeyed; but the position— the whole thing—you'd find it a great strain, and people aren't as a rule particularly helpful to a woman they see doing what they call a man's job."

"I don't want anyone's help. I know my own business and my poor father's ways. That's enough for me."

"Did your father ever say anything to you about this?"

"Oh no—he being only fifty-one and never thinking he'd be took for a long while yet. But I know it's what he'd have wanted, or why did he trouble to show me everything? And always talked to me about things as free as he did to Fuller and Stuppeny."

"He would want you to do the best for yourself— he wouldn't want you to take up a heavy burden just for his sake."

"Oh, it ain't just for his sake, it's for my own. I don't want a strange man messing around, and Ansdore's mine, and I'm proud of it."

Huxtable rubbed his large nose, from either side of which his sharp eyes looked disapprovingly at Joanna. He admired her, but she maddened him by refusing to see the obvious side of her femininity.

"Most young women of your age have other things to think of besides farming. There's your sister, and then—don't tell me that you won't soon be thinking of getting married."

"Well, and if I do, it'll be time enough then to settle about the farm. As for Ellen, I don't see what difference she makes, except that I must see to things for her sake as well as mine. It wouldn't help her much if I handed over this place to a man who'd muddle it all up and maybe bring us to the Auctioneer's. I've known . . . I've seen . . . they had a bailiff in at Becket's House and he lost them three fields of lucerne the first season, and got the fluke into their sheep. Why, even Sir Harry Trevor's taken to managing things himself at North Farthing after the way he saw they were doing with that old Lambarde, and what he can do I can do, seeing I wasn't brought up in a London square."

As Joanna's volubility grew, her voice rose, not shrilly as with most women, but taking on a warm, hoarse note— her words seemed to be flung out hot as coals from a fire. Mr. Huxtable grimaced. "She's a virago," he thought to himself. He put up his hand suavely to induce silence, but the eruption went on.

"I know all the men, too. They'd do for me what they wouldn't do for a stranger. And if they won't, I know how to settle 'em. I've been bursting with ideas about farming all my life. Poor Father said only a week before he was taken 'Pity you ain't a man, Joanna, with some of the notions you've got.' Well, maybe it's a pity and maybe it isn't, but what I've got to do now is to act up proper and manage what is mine, and what you and other folks have got to do is not to meddle with me."

"Come, come, my dear young lady, nobody's going to meddle with you. You surely don't call it 'meddling' for your father's lawyer, an old man who's known you all your life, to offer you a few words of advice. You must go your own way, and if it doesn't turn out as satisfactorily as you expect, you can always change it."

"Reckon I can," said Joanna, "but I shan't have to. Won't you take another whisky, Mr. Huxtable?"

The lawyer accepted. Joanna Godden's temper might

be bad, but her whisky was good. He wondered if the one would make up for the other to Arthur Alce or whoever had married her by this time next year.

§3

Mr. Huxtable was not alone in his condemnation of Joanna's choice. The whole neighbourhood disapproved of it. The joint parishes of Brodnyx and Pedlinge had made up their minds that Joanna Godden would now be compelled to marry Arthur Alce and settle down to mind her own business instead of what was obviously a man's ; and here she was, still at large and her business more a man's than ever.

"She's a mare that's never been präaperly broken in, and she wants a strong man to do it," said Furnese at the Woolpack. He had repeated this celebrated remark so often that it had almost acquired the status of a proverb. For three nights Joanna had been the chief topic of conversation in the Woolpack bar. If Arthur Alce appeared a silence would fall on the company, to be broken at last by some remark on the price of wool or the Rye United's last match. Everybody was sorry for Alce, everybody thought that Thomas Godden had treated him badly by not making his daughter marry him as a condition of her inheritance.

"Three times he's asked her, as I know for certain," said Vennal, the tenant of Beggar's Bush.

"No, it's four," said Prickett, Joanna's neighbour at Great Ansdore, "there was that time coming back from the Wild Beast Show."

"I was counting that," said Vennal ; "that and the one that Mr. Vine's looker heard at Lydd market, and then that time in the house."

"How do you know he asked her in the house ?—that makes five."

"I don't get that—once indoors and twice out, that's three."

"Well, anyways, whether it's three or four or five, he's asked her quite enough. It's time he had her now."

B

" He won't get her. She'll fly higher'n him now she s
got Ansdore. She'll be after young Edward Huxtable, or
maybe Parson himself, him having neglected to keep
himself married."

" Ha ! Ha ! It ud be valiant to see her married to
liddle Parson—she'd forget herself and pick him up
under her arm, same as she picks up her sister. But
anyways I don't think she'll get much by flying high,
It's all fine enough to talk of her having Ansdore, but
whosumdever wants Ansdore ull have to take Joanna
Godden with it, and it isn't every man who'd care to do
that."

" Surelye. She's a mare that's never bin präaperly
broken in. D'you remember the time she came prancing
into church with a bustle stuck on behind, and everyone
staring and fidgeting so as pore Mus' Pratt lost his place
in the Prayers and jumped all the way from the Belief
to the Royal Family ? "

" And that time as she hit Job Piper over the head
wud a bunch of osiers just because he'd told her he knew
more about thatching than she did."

" Surelye, and knocked his hat off into the dyke, and
then bought him a new one, with a lining to it."

" And there was that time when——"

Several more anecdotes to the point were contributed
by the various patrons of the bar, before the conversation,
having described a full circle, returned to its original
starting point, and then set off again with its vitality
apparently undiminished. It was more than a week
before the summons of Mr. Gain, of Botolph's Bridge,
for driving his gig without a light ousted Joanna from her
central glory in the Woolpack's discussions.

At Ansdore itself the interest naturally lasted longer.
Joanna's dependents whether in yard or kitchen were
resentfully engrossed in the new conditions.

" So Joanna's going to run our farm for us, is she ? "
said the head man, old Stuppeny, " that'll be valiant,
wud some of the notions she has. She'll have our pläace
sold up in a twelve-month, surelye. Well, well, it's time
maybe as I went elsewheres—I've bin long enough at
this job."

Old Stuppeny had made this remark at intervals

for the last sixty years, indeed ever since the day he had first come as a tow-headed boy to scare sparrows from the fields of Joanna's grandfather; so no one gave it the attention that should have been its due. Other people aired their grievances instead.

"I wöan't stand her meddling wud me and my sheep," said Fuller, the shepherd.

"It's her sheep, come to that," said Martha Tilden the chicken-girl.

Fuller dealt her a consuming glance out of his eyes, which the long distances of the marsh had made keen as the sea wind.

"She döan't know nothing about sheep, and I've been a looker after sheep since times when you and her was in your cradles, so I wöan't taake sass from neither of you."

"She'll meddle wud you, Martha, just as she'll meddle wud the rest of us," said Broadhurst, the cowman.

"She's meddled wud me for years—I'm used to it. It's you men what's going to have your time now. Ha! Ha! I'll be pleased watching it."

Martha's short, brightly-coloured face seemed ready to break in two as she laughed with her mouth wide open.

"When she's had a terrification wud me and said things as she's sorry for, she'll give me a gownd of hers or a fine hat. Sometimes I think as I make more out of her tempers than I do out of my good work what she pays me wages for."

"Well, if I wur a decent maid I'd be ashamed to wear any of her outlandish gowns or hats. The colours she chooses! Sometimes when I see her walking through a field near the lambing time, I'm scared for my ewes, thinking they'll drop their lambs out of fright. I can't help being thankful as she's in black now for this season, though maybe I shudn't ought to say it, seeing as we've lost a good mäaster, and one as we'll all be tediously regretting in a week or two if we äun't now. You take my word, Martha—next time she gives you a gownd, you give it back to her and say as you don't wear such things, being a respectable woman. It äun't right, starting you like that on bad ways."

§ 4

There was only one house in the joint parishes where Joanna had any honourable mention, and that was North Farthing House on the other side of the Kent Ditch. Here lived Sir Harry Trevor, the second holder of a title won in banking enterprises, and lately fallen to low estate. The reason could perhaps be seen on his good-looking face, with its sensual, humorous mouth, roving eyes, and lurking air of unfulfilled, undefeated youth. The taverns of the Three Marshes had combined to give him a sensational past, and further said that his two sons had forced him to settle at Brodnyx with a view to preserving what was left of his morals and their inheritance. The elder was in Holy Orders, and belonged to a small community working in the East End of London ; he seldom came to North Farthing House. The younger, Martin, who had some definite job in the city, was home for a few days that October. It was to him his father said :

" I can't help admiring that girl Joanna Godden for her pluck. Old Godden died suddenly two weeks ago, and now she's given out that she'll run the farm herself, instead of putting in a bailiff. Of course the neighbours disapprove, they've got very strict notions round here as to woman's sphere and all that sort of thing."

" Godden ? Which farm's that ? "

" Little Ansdore—just across the Ditch, in Pedlinge parish. It's a big place, and I like her for taking it on."

" And for any other reason ? "

" Lord, no ! She isn't at all the sort of woman I admire—a great big strapping wench, the kind this marsh breeds twelve to the acre, like the sheep. Has it ever struck you, Martin, that the women on Romney Marsh, in comparison with the women one's used to and likes, are the same as the Kent sheep in comparison with Southdowns—admirably hardy and suited to the district and all that, but a bit tough and coarse-flavoured ? "

" I see that farming has already enlarged and refined your stock of similes. I hope you aren't getting tired of it."

" No, not exactly. I'm interested in the place now I manage it without that dolt Lambarde, and Hythe isn't too far for the phaeton if I want to See Life. Besides, I haven't quite got over the thrill of not being in debt and disgrace "—he threw Martin a glance which might have come from a rebellious son to a censorious father. " But sometimes I wish there was less Moated Grange about it all. Damn it, I'm always alone here! Except when you or your reverend brother come down to see how I'm behaving."

" Why don't you marry again ? "

" I don't want to marry. Besides, whom the devil should I marry round here ? There's mighty few people of our own class about, and those there are seem to have no daughters under forty."

Martin looked at him quizzically.

" Oh yes, you young beast—I know what you're thinking. You're thinking that forty's just the right age for me. You're reminding me that I'm a trifle *passé* myself and ought to marry something sere and yellow. But I tell you I don't feel any older than twenty-five— never have, it's my affliction—while you've never been younger than forty in all your life. It's you who ought to marry middle-age "—and he grimaced at Martin.

§ 5

Joanna rather enjoyed being the centre of discussion. She had none of the modest shrinking from being talked about which might have affected some young women. She was glad when Martha Tilden or another of the girls brought her any overheard scraps. " Oh, that's what they say, is it ? " and she would laugh a big jolly laugh like a boy's.

So far she had enjoyed being " Mäaster " of Little Ansdore. It meant a lot of work and a lot of thought and a lot of talking and interference, but Joanna shrank from none of these things. She was healthy and vigorous and intelligent, and was, moreover, quite unhampered by any diffidence about teaching their work to people who had been busy at it before she was born.

Still it was scarcely more than a fortnight since she had taken on the government, and time had probably much to show her yet. She had a moment of depression one morning, rising early as she always must, and pulling aside the flowered curtain that covered her window. The prospect was certainly not one to cheer ; even in sunshine the horizons of the marsh were discouraging with their gospel of universal flatness, and this morning the sun was not yet up, and a pale mist was drifting through the willows, thick and congealed above the watercourses, thinner on the grazing lands between them, so that one could see the dim shapes of the sheep moving through it. Even in clear weather only one other dwelling was visible from Little Ansdore, and that was its fellow of Great Ansdore, about half a mile away seawards. The sight of it never failed to make Joanna contemptuous— for Great Ansdore had but fifty acres of land compared with the three hundred of its Little neighbour. Its Greatness was merely a matter of name and tradition, and had only one material aspect in the presentation to the living of Brodnyx-with-Pedlinge, which had been with Great Ansdore since the passing of the monks of Canterbury.

To-day Great Ansdore was only a patch of grey rather denser than its surroundings, and failed to inspire Joanna with her usual sense of gloating. Her eyes were almost sad as she stared out at it, her chin propped on her hands. The window was shut, as every window in every farm and cottage on the marsh was shut at night, though the ague was now little more than a name on the lips of grand-fathers. Therefore the room in which two people had slept was rather stuffy, though this in itself would hardly account for Joanna's heaviness, since it was what she naturally expected a bedroom to be in the morning. Such vague sorrow was perplexing and disturbing to her practical emotions ; she hurriedly attributed it to " poor father," and the propriety of the sentiment allowed her the relief of a few tears.

Turning back into the room she unbuttoned her turkey-red dressing-gown, preparatory to the business of washing and dressing. Then her eye fell on Ellen still asleep in her little iron bedstead in the corner, and a glow of tenderness passed like a lamp over her face. She went across to where her sister slept, and laid her face for a moment beside hers on the pillow. Ellen's breath came regularly from parted lips—she looked adorable cuddled there, with her red cheeks, like an apple in snow. Joanna, unable to resist the temptation, kissed her and woke her.

" Hullo, Jo—what time is it ? " mumbled Ellen sleepily.

" Not time to get up yet. I'm not dressed."

She sat on the edge of the bed, stooping over her sister, and her big rough plaits dangled in the child's face.

" Hullo, Jo—hullo, old Jo," continued the drowsy murmur.

" Go to sleep, you bad girl," said Joanna, forgetting that she herself had roused her.

Ellen was not wide enough awake to have any conflicting views on the subject, and she nestled down again with a deep sigh. For the next ten minutes the room was full of small sounds—the splashing of cold water in the basin, the shuffle of coarse linen, the click of fastening stays, the rhythmic swish of a hair brush. Then came two silent minutes, while Joanna knelt with closed eyes and folded hands beside her big, tumbled bed, and said the prayers that her mother had taught her eighteen years ago—word for word as she had said them when she was five, even to the " make me a good girl " at the end. Then she jumped up briskly and tore the sheet off the bed, throwing it with the pillows on the floor, so that Grace Wickens the servant should have no chance of making the bed without stripping it, as was the way of her kind.

Grace was not up yet, of course. Joanna hit her door a resounding thump as she passed it on her way to the kitchen. Here the dead ashes had been raked out overnight, and the fire laid according to custom. She lit the fire and put the kettle on to boil ; she did not consider it beneath her to perform these menial offices. She knew that every hand was needed for the early morning work of a farm. By the time she had finished both Grace and Martha were in the room, yawning and rubbing their eyes.

" That'll burn up nicely now," said Joanna, surveying

the fire. "You'd better put the fish-kettle on too, in case Broadhurst wants hot water for a mash. Bring me out a cup of tea as soon as you can get it ready—I'll be somewhere in the yard."

She put on an old coat of her father's over her black dress, and went out, her nailed boots clattering on the cobble-stones. The men were up—they should have been up an hour now—but no sounds of activity came from the barns. The yard was in stillness, a little mist floating against the walls, and the pervading greyness of the morning seemed to be lit up by the huge blotches of yellow lichen that covered the slated roofs of barns and dwelling—the roofs were all new, having only for a year or two superseded the old roofs of osier thatch, but that queer golden rust had almost hidden their substance, covering them as it covered everything that was left exposed to the salt-thick marsh air.

Joanna stood in the middle of the yard looking keenly round her like a cat, then like a cat she pounced. The interior of the latest built barn was dimly lit by a couple of windows under the roof—the light was just enough to show inside the doorway five motionless figures, seated about on the root-pile and the root-slicing machine. They were Joanna's five farm-men, apparently wrapped in a trance, from which her voice unpleasantly awoke them.

"Here, you—what d'you think you're doing?"

The five figures stiffened with perceptible indignation, but they did not rise from their sitting posture as their mistress advanced—or rather swooped—into their midst. Joanna did not expect this. She paid a man fifteen shillings a week for his labour and made no impossible demands of his prejudices and private habits.

"I've been up an hour," she said, looking round on them, "and here I find all of you sitting like a lot of sacks."

"It's two hours since I've bin out o' my warm bed," said old Stuppeny reproachfully.

"You'd be as much use in it as out, if this is how you spend your time. No one's been to the pigs yet, and it wants but half an hour to milking."

"We wur setting around for Grace Wickens to bring us out our tea," said Broadhurst.

" You thought maybe she wouldn't know her way across the yard if you was on the other side of it ? The tea ain't ready yet—I tell you I haven't had any. It's a fine sight to see a lot of strong, upstanding men lolling around waiting for a cup of tea."

The scorn in Joanna's voice was withering, and a resentful grumble arose, amidst which old Stuppeny's dedication of himself to a new sphere was hoarsely discernible. However the men scrambled to their feet and tramped off in various directions ; Joanna stopped Fuller, the shepherd, as he went by.

" You'll be taking the wethers to Lydd this morning ? "

" Surelye."

" How many are you taking ? "

" Maybe two score."

" You can take the lot. It'll save us their grazing money this winter, and we can start fattening the tegs in the spring."

" There's but two score wethers fit for market."

" How d'you mean ? "

" The others äun't fatted präaperly."

" Nonsense—you know we never give 'em cake or turnips, so what does it matter ? "

" They äun't fit."

" I tell you they'll do well enough. I don't expect to get such prices for them as for that lot you've kept down in the New Innings, but they won't fetch much under, for I declare they're good meat. If we keep them over the winter we'll have to send them inland and pay no end for their grazing—and then maybe the price of mutton ull go down in the Spring."

" It ud be a fool's job to täake them."

" You say that because you don't want to have to fetch them up from the Salt Innings. I tell you you're getting lazy, Fuller."

" My old mäaster never called me that."

" Well, you work as well for me as you did for him, and I won't call you lazy, neither."

She gave him a conciliatory grin, but Fuller had been too deeply wounded for such easy balm. He turned and walked away, a whole speech written in the rebellious hunch of his shoulders.

" You'll get them beasts," she called after him.

" Surelye "—came in a protesting drawl. Then
" Yup!—Yup! " to the two sheep dogs couched on the
doorstep.

§ 6

What with supervising the work and herding slackers,
getting her breakfast and packing off Ellen to the little
school she went to at Rye, Joanna found all too soon
that the market hour was upon her. It did not strike
her to shirk this part of a farmer's duty—she would drive
into Rye and into Lydd and into Romney as her father
had always driven, inspecting beasts and watching prices.
Soon after ten o'clock she ran upstairs to make herself
splendid, as the occasion required.

By this time the morning had lifted itself out of the
mist. Great sheets of blue covered the sky and were
mirrored in the dykes—there was a soft golden glow about
the marsh, for the vivid green of the pastures was filmed
over with the brown of the withering seed-grasses, and
the big clumps of trees that protected every dwelling
were richly toned to rust through scales of flame. Already
there were signs that the day would be hot, and Joanna
sighed to think that approaching winter had demanded
that her new best black should be made of thick materials.
She hated black, too, and grimaced at her sombre frills,
which the mourning brooch and chain of jet beads could
only embellish, never lighten. But she would as soon have
thought of jumping out of the window as of discarding
her mourning a day before the traditions of the Marsh
decreed. She decided not to wear her brooch and chain
—the chain might swing and catch in the beasts' horns
as she inspected them, besides her values demanded that
she should be slightly more splendid in church than at
market, so her ornaments were reserved as a crowning
decoration, all except her mourning ring made of a lock
of her father's hair.

It was the first time she had been to market since
his death, and she knew that folks would stare, so she
might as well give them something to stare at. Out-

side the front door, in the drive, old Stuppeny was holding
the head of Foxy, her mare, harnessed to the neat trap
that Thomas Godden had bought early the same year.

" Hullo, Stuppeny—you ain't coming along like that ! "
and Joanna's eye swept fiercely up and down his manure-
caked trousers.

" I never knew as I wur coming along anywheres,
Miss Joanna."

" You're coming along of me to the market. Surely
you don't expect a lady to drive by herself ? "

Old Stuppeny muttered something unintelligible.

" You go and put on your black coat," continued
Joanna.

" My Sunday coat ! " shrieked Stuppeny.

" Yes—quick ! I can't wait here all day."

" But I can't put on my good coat wudout cleaning
myself, and it'll täake me the best part o' the marnun to
do that."

Joanna saw the reasonableness of his objection.

" Oh, well, you can leave it this once, but another
time you remember and look decent. To-day it'll do if
you go into the kitchen and ask Grace to take a brush
to your trousers—and listen here ! " she called after him
as he shambled off—" if she's making cocoa you can ask
her to give you a cup."

Grace evidently was making cocoa—a habit she had
whenever her mistress's back was turned—for Stuppeny
did not return for nearly a quarter of an hour. He looked
slightly more presentable as he climbed into the back
of the trap. It struck Joanna that she might be able to
get him a suit of livery secondhand.

" There isn't much he's good for on the farm now at
his age, so he may as well be the one to come along of
me. Broadhurst or Luck ud look a bit smarter, but it
ud be hard to spare them . . . . Stuppeny ud look
different in a livery coat with brass buttons . . . I'll
look around for one if I've time this afternoon."

It was nearly seven miles from Ansdore to Lydd,
passing the Woolpack, and the ragged gable of Midley
Chapel—a reproachful ruin among the reeds of the Wheels-
gate Sewer. Foxy went smartly, but every now and then
they had to slow down as they overtook and passed flocks

of sheep and cattle being herded along the road by drovers and shepherds in dusty boots, and dogs with red, lolling tongues. It was after midday when the big elm wood which had been their horizon for the last two miles suddenly turned, as if by an enchanter's wand, into a fair-sized town of red roofs and walls, with a great church tower raking above the trees.

Joanna drove straight to the Crown, where Thomas Godden had "put up" every market day for twenty years. She ordered her dinner—boiled beef and carrots, and jam roll—and walked into the crowded coffee room, where farmers from every corner of the three marshes were already at work with knife and fork. Some of them knew her by sight and stared, others knew her by acquaintance and greeted her, while Arthur Alce jumped out of his chair, dropping his knife and sweeping his neighbour's bread off the table. He was a little shocked and alarmed to see Joanna the only woman in the room ; he suggested that she should have her dinner in the landlady's parlour —"you'd be quieter like, in there."

"I don't want to be quiet, thank you," said Joanna.

She felt thankful that none of the few empty chairs was next Alce's—she could never abide his fussing. She sat down between Cobb of Slinches and a farmer from Snargate way, and opened the conversation pleasantly on the subject of liver fluke in sheep.

When she had brought her meal to a close with a cup of tea, she found Alce waiting for her in the hotel entrance.

"I never thought you'd come to market, Joanna."

"And why not, pray ? "

The correct answer was—" Because you don't know enough about beasts," but Alce had the sense to find a substitute.

"Because it ain't safe or seemly for a woman to come alone and deal with men."

"And why not, again ? Are all you men going to swindle me if you get the chance ? "

Joanna's laugh always had a disintegrating effect on Alce, with its loud warm tones and its revelation of her pretty teeth—which were so white and even, except the small pointed canines. When she laughed she opened her mouth wide and threw back her head on her

short white neck. Alce gropingly put out a hairy hand
towards her, which was his nearest approach to a caress.
Joanna flicked it away.

"Now a-done do, Arthur Alce"—dropping in her
merriment into the lower idiom of the Marsh—" a-done
do with your croaking and your stroking both. Let me
go my own ways, for I know 'em better than you can."

"But these chaps—I don't like it—maybe, seeing
you like this amongst them, they'll get bold with you."

"Not they! How can you mention such a thing?
There was Mr. Cobb and Mr. Godfrey at dinner, talking to
me as respectful as churchwardens, all about liver fluke
and then by way of rot in the oats, passing on natural
and civil to the Isle of Wight disease in potatoes—if you
see anything bold in *that* . . . well then you're an old
woman as sure as I ain't."

A repetition of her laugh completed his disruption,
and he found himself there on the steps of the Crown
begging her to let him take over her market day discussions as her husband and deputy.

"Why should you go talking to farmers about Isle
of Wight disease and liver fluke, when you might be talking to their wives about making puddings and stuffing
mattresses and such-like women's subjects."

"I talk about them too," said Joanna, "and I can't
see as I'd be any better for talking of nothing else."

What Alce had meant to convey to her was that he
would much rather hear her discussing the ailments of
her children than of her potatoes, but he was far too
delicate-minded to state this. He only looked at her
sadly.

Joanna had not even troubled to refuse his proposal
—any more than a mother troubles to give a definite
and reasoned refusal to the child who asks for the moon.
Finding him silent, and feeling rather sorry for him,
she suggested that he should come round with her to the
shops and carry some of her parcels.

§ 7

She went first of all to a firm of house-painters, for
she meant to brighten up Ansdore. She disliked seeing

the place with no colour or ornament save that which
the marsh wind gave it of gold and rust. She would
have the eaves and the pipes painted a nice green, such
as would show up well at a distance. There was plenty
of money, so why should everything be drab? Alce
discouraged her as well as he was able—it was the wrong
time of year for painting, and the old paint was still
quite good. Joanna treated his objections as she had
treated his proposal—with good-humoured, almost tender,
indifference. She let him make his moan at the house-
painter's, then carelessly bore him on to the furnishers',
where she bought brightly-flowered stuff for new curtains.
Then he stood by while at an outfitter's she inspected
coats for Stuppeny, and finally bought one of a fine mulberry colour with brass buttons all down the front.

She now returned to the market-place, and sought
out two farmers from the Iden district, with whom she
made arrangements for the winter keep of her lambs.
Owing to the scanty and salt pastures of winter, it had
always been the custom on the marsh to send the young
sheep for grazing on upland farms, and fetch them back
in the spring as tegs. Joanna disposed of her young
flock between Relf of Baron's Grange and Noakes of
Mockbeggar, then, still accompanied by Alce, strolled down
to inspect the wethers she had brought to the market.

On her way she met the farmer of Picknye Bush.

"Good day, Miss Godden—I've just come from buying
some tegs of yourn."

"My looker's settled with you, has he?"

"He said he had the power to sell as he thought
proper—otherways I was going to ask for you."

An angry flush drowned the freckles on Joanna's
cheek.

"That's Fuller, the obstinate, thick-headed old
man . . ."

Bates's round face fell a little.

"I'm sorry if there's bin any mistääke. After all,
I äun't got the beasts yet—thirty shillings a head is the
price he asked and I paid. I call it a fair price, seeing
the time of year and the state of the meat market But
if your looker's bin presuming and you äun't pleased,
then I wöan't call it a deal."

" I'm pleased enough to sell you my beasts, and thirty shillings is a fairish price. But I won't have Fuller fixing things up over my head like this, and I'll tell him so. How many of 'em did you buy, Mr. Bates ? "

" I bought the lot—two score."

Joanna made a choking sound. Without another word, she turned and walked off in the direction of the hurdles where her sheep were penned, Bates and Alce following her after one disconcerted look at each other. Fuller stood beside the wethers, his two shaggy dogs couched at his feet—he started when he suddenly saw his mistress burst through the crowd, her black feathers nodding above her angry face.

" Fuller ! " she shouted, so loud that those who were standing near turned round to see—" How many wether-tegs have you brought to Lydd ? "

" Two score."

" How many did I tell you to bring ? "

" The others wurn't fit, surelye."

" But didn't I tell you to bring them ? "

" You did, but they wurn't fit."

" I said you were to bring them, no matter if you thought 'em fit or not."

" They wurn't fit to be sold as meat."

" I tell you they were."

" No one shall say as Tom Fuller döan't bring fit meat to market."

" You're an obstinate old fool. I tell you they were first-class meat."

Men were pressing round, farmers and graziers and butchers, drawn by the spectacle of Joanna Godden at war with her looker in the middle of Lydd market. Alce touched her arm appealingly—

" Come away, Joanna," he murmured.

She flung round at him.

" Keep clear—leave me to settle my own man."

There was a titter in the crowd.

" I know bad meat from good, surelye," continued Fuller, feeling that popular sentiment was on his side— " I should ought to, seeing as I wur your father's looker before you wur your father's daughter."

" You were my father's looker, but after this you

shan't be looker of mine. Since you won't mind what I say or take orders from me, you can leave my service this day month."

There was a horror-stricken silence in the crowd—even the lowest journeyman butcher realized the solemnity of the occasion.

" You understand me ? " said Joanna.

" Yes, ma'am," came from Fuller in a crushed voice.

§ 8

By the same evening the news was all over Lydd market, by the next it was all over the Three Marshes. Everyone was repeating to everyone else how Joanna Godden of Little Ansdore had got shut of her looker after twenty-eight years' service, and her father not been dead a month. " Enough to make him rise out of his grave," said the Marsh.

The actual reasons for the turning away were variously given—" Just because he spuck up and told her as her pore father wudn't hold wud her goings on," was the doctrine promulgated by the Woolpack ; but the general council sitting in the bar of the Crown decreed that the trouble had arisen out of Fuller's spirited refusal to sell some lambs that had tic. Other pronouncements were that she had sassed Fuller because he knew more about sheep than she did—or that Fuller had sassed her for the same reason—that it wasn't Joanna who had dismissed him, but he who had been regretfully obliged to give notice, owing to her meddling—that all the hands at Ansdore were leaving on account of her temper.

" He'll never get another pläace agäun, will pore old Fuller—he'll end in the Union and be an everlasting shame to her."

There was almost a feeling of disappointment when it became known that Fuller—who was only forty-two, having started his career at an early age—had been given a most satisfactory job at Arpinge Farm inland, and something like consternation when it was further said and confirmed by Fuller himself that Joanna had given him an excellent character.

" She'll never get another looker," became the changed burden of the Marsh.

But here again prophecy failed, for hardly had Joanna's advertisement appeared simultaneously in the *Rye Observer* and the *Kentish Express* than she had half a dozen applications from likely men. Martha Tilden brought the news to Godfrey's Stores, the general shop in Brodnyx.

" There she is, setting in her chair, talking to a young chap what's come from Botolph's Bridge, and there's three more waiting in the passage—she told Grace to give them each a cup of cocoa when she was making it. And what d'you think? Their looker's come over from Old Honeychild, asking for the place, though he was sitting in the Crown at Lydd only yesterday, as Sam Broadhurst told me, saying as it was a shame to get shut of Fuller like that, and as how Joanna deserved never to see another looker again in her life."

" Which of the lot d'you think she'll take? " asked Godfrey.

" I dunno. How should I say? Peter Relf from Old Honeychild is a stout feller, and one of the other men told me he'd got a character that made him blush, it was that fine and flowery. But you never know with Joanna Godden—maybe she'd sooner have a looker as knew nothing, and then she could teach him. Ha! Ha!"

Meanwhile Joanna sat very erect in her kitchen chair, interviewing the young chap from Botolph's Bridge.

" You've only got a year's character from Mr. Gain? "

" Yes, missus . . ." a long pause during which some mental process took place clumsily behind this low, sunburnt forehead . . . " but I've got these."

He handed Joanna one or two dirty scraps of paper on which were written " characters " from earlier employers.

Joanna read them. None was for longer than two years, but they all spoke well of the young man before her.

" Then you've never been on the Marsh before you came to Botolph's Bridge? "

c

" No, missus."

" Sheep on the Marsh is very different from sheep inland."

" I know, missus."

" But you think you're up to the job."

" Yes, missus."

Joanna stared at him critically. He was a fine young fellow—slightly bowed already though he had given his age as twenty-five, for the earth begins her work early in a man's frame, and has power over the green tree as well as the dry. But this stoop did not conceal his height and strength and breadth, and somehow his bigness, combined with his simplicity, his slow thought and slow tongue, appealed to Joanna, stirred something within her that was almost tender. She handed him back his dirty " characters."

" Well, I must think it over. I've some other men to see, but I'll write you a line to Botolph's Bridge and tell you how I fix. You go now and ask Grace Wickens, my gal, to give you a cup of hot cocoa."

Young Socknersh went, stooping his shock-head still lower as he passed under the worn oak lintel of the kitchen door. Joanna interviewed the shepherd from Honeychild, a man from Slinches, another from Anvil Green inland, and one from Chilleye, on Pevensey marsh beyond Marlingate. She settled with none, but told each that she would write. She spent the evening thinking them over. .

No doubt Peter Relf from Honeychild was the best man—the oldest and most experienced—but on the other hand he wanted the most money, and probably also his own way. After the disastrous precedent of Fuller, Joanna wasn't going to have another looker who thought he knew better than she did. Now, Dick Socknersh, he would mind her properly, she felt sure . . . Day from Slinches had the longest " character "—fifteen years man and boy ; but that would only mean that he was set in their ways and wouldn't take to hers—she wasn't going to start fattening her sheep with turnips, coarsening the meat, not to please anyone . . . . Now, Socknersh, having never been longer than two years in a place wouldn't have got fixed in any bad habits . . . . As for Jenkins

and Taylor, they weren't any good—just common Southdown men—she might as well write off to them at once.
Her choice lay between Relf and Day and Socknersh.
She knew that she meant to have Socknersh—he was
not the best shepherd, but she liked him the best, and
he would mind her properly and take to her ways . . . .
for a moment he seemed to stand before her, with his
head stooping among the rafters, his great shoulders
shutting out the window, his curious, brown, childlike
eyes fixed upon her face. Day was a scrubby little fellow,
and Relf had warts all over his hands . . . But she
wasn't choosing Socknersh for his looks ; she was choosing
him because he would work for her the best, not being
set up with " notions." Of course she liked him the best,
too, but it would be more satisfactory from every practical
point of view to work with a man she liked than with a
man she did not like—Joanna liked a man to look a man,
and she did not mind if he was a bit of a child too. . . .
Yes, she would engage Socknersh ; his " characters,"
though short, were most satisfactory—he was " good
with sheep and lambs," she could remember—" hard-
working "—" patient " . . . She wrote to Botolph's
Bridge that evening, and engaged him to come to her at
the end of the week.

§ 9

Nothing happened to make her regret her choice.
Socknersh proved, as she had expected, a humble, hard-
working creature, who never disputed her orders, indeed
who sometimes turned to her for direction and advice.
Stimulated by his deference, she became even more of
an oracle than she had hitherto professed. She looked
up " The Sheep " in her father's " Farmer's Encyclopædia "
of the year 1861, and also read one or two more books
upon his shelves. From these she discovered that there
was more in sheep breeding than was covered by the lore
of the Three Marshes, and her mind began to plunge
adventurously among Southdowns and Leicesters, Black-
faced, Blue-faced, and Cumberland sheep. She saw
Ansdore famous as a great sheep-breeding centre, with

many thousands of pounds coming annually to its mistress from meat and wool.

She confided some of these ideas to Arthur Alce and a few neighbouring farmers. One and all discouraged her, and she told herself angrily that the yeomen were jealous—as for Alce, it was just his usual silliness. She found that she had a more appreciative listener in Dick Socknersh. He received all her plans with deep respect, and sometimes an admiring "Surelye, missus," would come from his lips that parted more readily for food than for speech. Joanna found that she enjoyed seeking him out in the barn, or turning off the road to where he stood leaning on his crook with his dog against his legs.

"You'd never believe the lot there is in sheep-keeping, Socknersh; and the wonders you can do if you have knowledge and information. Now the folks around here, they're middling sensible, but they ain't what you'd call clever. They're stuck in their ways, as you might say. Now if you open your mind properly, you can learn a lot of things out of books. My poor father had some wonderful books upon his shelves, that are mine to read now, and you'd be surprised at the lot I've learned out of 'em, even though I've been sheep-raising all my life."

"Surelye, missus."

"Now I'll tell you something about sheep-raising that has never been done here, all the hundreds of years there's been sheep on the Marsh. And that's the proper crossing of sheep. My book tells me that there's been useful new breeds started that way and lots of money made. Now, would you believe it, they've never tried crossing down here on the Marsh, except just once or twice with Southdowns?—And that's silly, seeing as the Southdown is a smaller sheep than ours, and I don't see any sense in bringing down our fine big sheep that can stand all waters and weathers. If I was to cross 'em, I'd sooner cross 'em with rams bigger than themselves. I know they say that small joints of mutton are all the style nowadays, but I like a fine big animal—besides, think of the fleeces."

Socknersh apparently thought of them so profoundly that he was choked of utterance, but Joanna could tell that he was going to speak by the restless moving of his eyes under their strangely long dark lashes, and by the little husky sounds he made in his throat. She stood watching him with a smile on her face.

" Well, Socknersh—you were going to say . . ."

" I wur going to say, missus, as my mäaster up at Garlinge Green, whur I wur afore I took to the Marsh at Botolph's Bridge—my mäaster, Mus' Pebsham, had a valiant set of Spanish ship, as big as liddle cattle ; you shud ought to have seen them."

" Did he do any crossing with 'em ? "

" No, missus—leastways not whiles I wur up at the Green."

Joanna stared through the thick red sunset to the horizon. Marvellous plans were forming in her head— part, they seemed, of the fiery shapes that the clouds had raised in the west beyond Rye hill. Those clouds walked forth as flocks of sheep—huge sheep under mountainous fleeces, the wonder of the Marsh and the glory of Ansdore . . . .

" Socknersh . . . ."

" Yes, missus."

She hesitated whether she should share with him her new inspiration. It would be good to hear him say " Surelye, missus " in that admiring, husky voice. He was the only one of her farm-hands who, she felt, had any deference towards her—any real loyalty, though he was the last come.

" Socknersh, d'you think your master up at Garlinge would let me hire one or two rams to cross with my ewes ? —I might go up and have a look at them. I don't know as I've ever seen a Spanish sheep . . . Garlinge is up by Court-at-Street, ain't it ? "

" Yes, missus. 'Tis an unaccountable way from here."

" I'd write first. What d'you think of the notion, Socknersh ? Don't you think that a cross between a Spanish sheep and a Kent sheep ud be an uncommon fine animal ? "

" Surelye, missus."

That night Joanna dreamed that giant sheep as big as bullocks were being herded on the Marsh by a giant shepherd.

Spring brought a blooming to Ansdore as well as to
the Marsh. Joanna had postponed, after all, her house-
painting till the winter months of rotting sea mists were
over. But in April the ladders striped her house-front,
and soon her windows and doors began to start luridly
out of their surroundings of mellowed tiles and brick.
After much deliberation she had chosen yellow for her
colour, tastefully picked out with green. She had always
been partial to yellow—it was a colour that " showed up "
well, and she was also influenced by the fact that there
was no other yellow-piped dwelling on the Marsh.

Her neighbours disapproved of her choice for the
same reasons that had induced her to make it. They
were shocked by the fact that you could see her front
door from half a mile off on the Brodnyx Road ; it was
just like Joanna Godden to choose a colour that shrieked
across the landscape instead of merging itself unobtrusively
into it. But there was a still worse shock in store for
public opinion, and that was when she decided to repaint
her waggons as well as her house.

Hitherto there had been only one shape and colour
of waggon on the Marsh—a plain low-sided trough of
deep sea-blue. The name was always painted in white
on a small black wooden square attached to the side.
Thomas Godden's waggons had been no departure from
this rule. It was left to his daughter to flout tradition,
and by some obscure process of local reasoning, bring
discredit to her dead father by painting her waggons
yellow instead of blue. The evil went deeper than mere
colour. Joanna was a travelled woman, having once
been to the Isle of Wight, and it suddenly struck her
that, since she was repainting, she might give her three
waggons the high gondola-shaped fronts that she had
admired in the neighbourhood of Shanklin and Ventnor.
These she further beautified with a rich, scrolled design,
and her name in large, ornate lettering—" Joanna Godden.
Little Ansdore. Walland Marsh "—so that her waggons
went forth upon the roads very much as the old men
o' war of King Edward's fleet had sailed over that same
country when it was fathoms deep under the seas of

Rye Bay . . . With their towering, decorated poops
they were more like mad galleys of a bygone age than
sober waggons of a nineteenth century farm.

Her improvements gave her a sense of adventurous
satisfaction—her house with its yellow window frames and
doors, with its new curtains of swaggering design—her
high-pooped waggons—the coat with the brass buttons
that old Stuppeny wore when he drove behind her to
market—her dreams of giant sheep upon her innings—
all appealed to something fundamental in her which was
big and boastful. She even liked the gossip with which
she was surrounded, the looks that were turned upon
her when she drove into Rye or Lydd or New Romney
—the " there goes Joanna Godden " of folk she passed.
She had no acute sense of their disapproval ; if she became
aware of it she would only repeat to herself that she would
" show 'em the style "—which she certainly did.

§ 11

Arthur Alce was very much upset by the gossip about
Joanna.

" All you've done since you started running Ansdore
is to get yourself talked about," he said sadly.

" Well, I don't mind that."

" No, but you should ought to. A woman should
ought to be modest and timid and not paint her house
so's it shows up five mile off—first your house, and then
your waggons—it'll be your face next."

" Arthur Alce, you're very rude, and till you learn
to be civil you can keep out of my house—the same as
you can see five mile off."

Alce, who really felt bitter and miserable, took her
at her word and kept away for nearly a fortnight. Joanna
was not sorry, for he had been highly disapproving on
the matter of the Spanish sheep, and she was anxious
to carry out her plan in his absence. A letter to Garlinge
Green had revealed the fact that Socknersh's late master
had removed to a farm near Northampton ; he still bred
Spanish sheep, but the risk of Joanna's venture was
increased by the high price she would have to pay for

railway transport as well as in fees. However, once she
had set her heart on anything, she would let nothing
stand in her way. Socknersh was inclined to be aghast
at all the money the affair would cost, but Joanna soon
talked him into an agreeable " Surelye."

" We'll get it all back," she told him. " Our lambs
ull be the biggest at market, and ull fetch the biggest
prices too."

It pleased Joanna to talk of Socknersh and herself
as " we," though she would bitterly have resented any
idea of joint responsibility in the days of Fuller. The
rites of lambing and shearing had not dimmed her faith
in the high priest she had chosen for Ansdore's most
sacred mysteries. Socknersh was a man who was automatically " good with sheep." The scared and trembling
ewes seemed to see in him a kind of affinity with themselves, and lay still under his big, brown, quiet hands.
He had not much " head," but he had that queer inward
kinship with animals which is sometimes found in intensely
simple natures, and Joanna felt equal to managing the
" head " part of the business for both. It pleased her
to think that the looker—who is always the principal
man on a farm such as Ansdore, where sheep-rearing is
the main business—deferred to her openly, before the
other hands, spoke to her with drawling respect, and for
ever followed her with his humble eyes.

She liked to feel those eyes upon her. All his strength
and bigness, all his manhood, huge and unaware, seemed
to lie deep in them like a monster coiled up under the sea.
When he looked at her he seemed to lose that heavy
dumbness, that inarticulate stupidity which occasionally
stirred and vexed even her good disposition ; his mouth
might still be shut, but his eyes were fluent—they told
her not only of his manhood but of her womanhood
besides.

Socknersh lived alone in the looker's cottage which
had always belonged to Ansdore. It stood away on the
Kent Innings, on the very brink of the Ditch, which here
gave a great loop, to allow a peninsula of Sussex to claim
its rights against the Kentish monks. It was a lonely
little cottage, all rusted over with lichen, and sometimes
Joanna felt sorry for Socknersh away there by himself

beside the Ditch. She sent him over a flock mattress
and a woollen blanket, in case the old ague-spectre of
the Marsh still haunted that desolate corner of water
and reeds.

§ 12

Towards the end of that autumn, Joanna and Ellen
Godden came out of their mourning. As was usual on
such occasions, they chose a Sunday for their first appearance in colours. Half mourning was not worn on the
Marsh, so there was no interval of grey and violet between
Joanna's hearse-like costume of crape and nodding feathers
and the tan-coloured gown in which she astonished the
twin parishes of Brodnyx and Pedlinge on the first Sunday
in November. Her hat was of sage green and contained
a bird unknown to natural history. From her ears swung
huge jade earrings, in succession to the jet ones that had
dangled against her neck on Sundays for a year—she
must have bought them, for everyone knew that her
mother, Mary Godden, had left but one pair.

Altogether the sight of Joanna was so breathless,
that a great many people never noticed Ellen, or at best
only saw her hat as it went past the tops of their pews.
Joanna realized this, and being anxious that no one should
miss the sight of Ellen's new magenta pelisse with facings
of silver braid, she made her stand on the seat while the
psalms were sung.

The morning service was in Brodnyx church—in the
evening it would be at Pedlinge. Brodnyx had so far
escaped the restorer, and the pews were huge wooden boxes,
sometimes fitted with a table in the middle, while Sir
Harry Trevor's, which he never occupied, except when
his sons were at home, was further provided with a stove
—all the heating there was in the three aisles. There
was also a two-decker pulpit at the east end and over
the dim little altar hung an escutcheon of Royal George
—the lion and the unicorn fighting for the crown amid
much scroll-work.

Like most churches on the Marsh it was much too
big for its parish, and if the entire population of Brodnyx

and Pedlinge had flocked into it, it would not have been full. This made Joanna and Ellen all the more conspicuous—they were alone in their great horse-box of a pew, except for many prayer books and hassocks— There were as many hassocks in Brodnyx church as there were sheep on the Brodnyx innings. Joanna, as usual, behaved very devoutly, and did not look about her. She had an immense respect for the Church, and always followed the service word for word in her huge calf-bound prayer book, expecting Ellen to do the same—an expectation which involved an immense amount of scuffling and angry whispering in their pew.

However, though her eyes were on her book, she was proudly conscious that everyone else's eyes were on her. Even the rector must have seen her—as indeed from his elevated position on the bottom deck of the pulpit he could scarcely help doing—and his distraction was marked by occasional stutters and the intrusion of an evening Collect. He was a nervous, deprecating little man, terribly scared of his flock, and ruefully conscious of his own shortcomings and the shortcomings of his church. Visiting priests had told him that Brodnyx church was a disgrace, with its false stresses of pew and pulpit and the lion and the unicorn dancing above the throne of the King of kings. They said he ought to have it restored. They did not trouble about where the money was to come from, but Mr. Pratt knew he could not get it out of his congregation, who did not like to have things changed from the manner of their fathers—indeed there had been complaints when he had dislodged the owls that had nested under the gallery from an immemorial rector's day.

The service came to an end with the singing of a hymn to an accompaniment of grunts and wheezes from an ancient harmonium and the dropping of pennies and threepenny bits into a wooden plate. Then the congregation hurried out to the civilities of the churchyard.

From outside, Brodnyx Church looked still more Georgian and abandoned. Its three aisles were without ornament or architecture ; there was no tower, but beside it stood a peculiar and unexplained erection, shaped like a pagoda, in three tiers of black and battered tar-boarding. It had a slight cant towards the church, and suggested nothing so much as a disreputable Victorian widow, in tippet, mantle and crinoline, seeking the support of a stone wall after a carouse.

In the churchyard, among the graves, the congregation assembled and talked of or to Joanna. It was notice-able that the women judged her more kindly than the men.

" She can't help her taste," said Mrs. Vine, " and she's a kind-hearted thing."

" If you ask me," said Mrs. Prickett, " her taste ain't so bad, if only she'd have things a bit quieter. But she's like a child with her yallers and greens."

" She's more like an organist's monkey," said her husband. " What ud I do if I ever saw you tricked out like that, Mrs. Prickett ? "

" Oh, I'd never wear such clothes, master, as you know well. But then I'm a different looking sort of woman. I wouldn't go so far as to say them bright colours don't suit Joanna Godden."

" I never thought much of her looks."

" Nor of her looker—he ! he ! " joined in Furnese with a glance in Joanna's direction.

She was talking to Dick Socknersh, who had been to church with the other hands that could be spared from the farm. She asked him if he had liked the sermon, and then told him to get off home quickly and give the tegs their swill.

" Reckon he don't know a teg from a tup," said Furnese.

" Oh, surelye, Mr. Furnese, he äun't a bad looker. Jim Harmer said he wur just about wonderful with the ewes at the shearing."

" Maybe—but he'd three sway-backed lambs at Rye market on Thursday."

" Sway-backs ! "

" Three. 'Twas a shame."

" But Joanna told me he was such a fine, wonderful man with the sheep—as he got 'em to market about half as tired and twice as quick as Fuller used to in his day."

" Ah, but then she's unaccountable set on young Socknersh. He lets her do what she likes with her sheep, and he's a stout figure of a man, too. Joanna Godden always was partial to stout-looking men."

" But she'd never be such a fool as to git sweet on her looker."

" Well, that's wot they're saying at the Woolpack."

" The Woolpack! Did you ever hear of such a talk-hole as you men get into when you're away from us! They say some unaccountable fine things at the Wool-pack. I tell you, Joanna ain't such a fool as to get sweet on Dick Socknersh."

" She's been fool enough to cross Spanish sheep with her own. Three rams she had sent all the way from furrin parts by Northampton. I tell you, after that, she'd be fool enough for anything."

" Maybe she'll do well by it."

" Maybe she'll do well by marrying Dick Socknersh. I tell you, you döan't know näun about it, missus. Who-sumdever heard of such an outlandish, heathen, foolish notion ? "

On the whole Joanna was delighted with the success of her appearance. She walked home with Mrs. Southland and Maggie Furnese, bridling a little under their glances, while she discussed servants, and food-prices, and a new way of pickling eggs.

She parted from them at Ansdore, and she and Ellen went in to their Sunday's dinner of roast beef and York-shire pudding. After this the day would proceed accord-ing to the well-laid ceremonial that Joanna loved. Little Ellen, with a pinafore tied over her Sabbath splendours, would go into the kitchen to sit with the maids—get into their laps, turn over their picture Bibles, examine their one or two trinkets and strings of beads which they always brought into the kitchen on Sunday. Meanwhile Joanna would sit in state in the parlour, her feet on a footstool, on her lap a volume of Spurgeon's sermons. In the old days it had always been her father who read sermons, but now he was dead she had taken over this part of his duties with the rest, and if the afternoon gener-ally ended in sleep, sleep was a necessary part of a well-kept Sabbath day.

§ 13

When Christmas came that year, Joanna was inspired to celebrate it with a party. The Christmas before she had been in mourning, but in her father's day it had been usual to invite a few respectable farmers to a respectable revel, beginning with high tea, then proceeding through whist to a hot supper. Joanna would have failed in her duty to " poor father " if she had not maintained this custom, and she would have failed in consistency with herself if she had not improved upon it—embellished it with one or two ornate touches, which lifted it out of its prosaic rut of similarity to a dozen entertainments given at a dozen farms, and made it a rather wonderful and terrible occasion to most dwellers on the Marsh.

To begin with, the invitations were not delivered, according to custom, verbally in the churchyard after Morning Prayer on Sunday—they were written on cards, as Mrs. Saville of Dungemarsh Court wrote them, and distributed through the unwonted and expensive medium of the post. When their recipients had done exclaiming over the waste of a penny stamp, they were further astonished to see the word " Music " written in the corner— Joanna had stuck very closely to her Dungemarsh Court model. What could the music be ? Was the Brodnyx Brass Band going to play ? Or had Joanna hired Miss Patty Southland, who gave music lessons on the Marsh ?

She had done neither of these things. When her visitors assembled, stuffed into her two parlours, while the eatables were spread in a kitchen metamorphosed with decorations of crinkled paper, they found, buttressed into a corner by the freshly tuned piano, the Rye Quartet, consisting of the piano-tuner himself, his wife, who played the 'cello, and his two daughters with fiddles and white piqué frocks. At first the music was rather an embarrassment, for while it played eating and conversation were alike suspended, and the guests stood with open mouths and cooling cups of tea till Mr. Plummer's final chords released their tongues and filled their mouths with awkward simultaneousness. However, after a time the general awe abated, and soon the Rye Quartet was swamped in a terrific noise of tongues and mastication.

Everyone was staring at Joanna's dress, for it was
Low—quite four inches of her skin must have shown
between its top most frill and the base of her sturdy throat.
The sleeves stopped short at the elbow, showing a very
soft, white forearm, in contrast with brown, roughened
hands.   Altogether it was a daring display, and one or
two of the Miss Vines and Southlands and Furneses
wondered " how Joanna could do it."

Proudly conscious of the eyes fixed upon her, she
moved—or rather, it must be confessed, squeezed—about
among her guests.   She had put on new manners with
her new clothes, and was full of a rather mincing civility.

" Pray, Mrs. Cobb, may I get you another cup of
tea ? "—" Just one more piece of cake, Mr. Alce ? "—
" Oh, please, Miss Prickett—just a leetle bit of ham."

Ellen followed her sister about, pulling at her skirt.
She was dressed in white, and her hair was crimped, and
tied with pink ribbons.   At eight o'clock she was ordered
up to bed and there was a great uproar, before, striking
out in all directions, she was carried upstairs under
Joanna's stalwart arm.   The Rye Quartet tactfully
started playing to drown her screams, which continued
for some time in the room overhead.

The party did not break up till eleven, having spent
five hours standing squeezed like herrings under the
Ansdore beams, eating and drinking and talking, to the
strains of " The Blue Danube " and " See Me Dance the
Polka."   Local opinion was a little bewildered by the
entertainment—it had been splendid, no doubt, and high-
class to an overwhelming degree, but it had been dis-
tinctly uncomfortable, even tiresome, and a great many
people were upset by eating too much, since the refresh-
ments had been served untiringly from six to eleven,
while others had not had enough, being nervous of eating
their food so far from a table, and clinging throughout
the evening to their first helpings.

To Joanna, however, the evening was an uncriticized
success, and she was inspired to repeat it on a humbler
scale for the benefit of her servants.   She knew that at
big houses there was often a servants' ball at Christmas,
and though she had at present no definite ambition to
push herself into the Manor Class, she was anxious that

Ansdore should have every pomp and that things should
be " done proper." The mere solid comfort of prosperity
was not enough for her—she wanted the glitter and glamour
of it as well, she wanted her neighbours not only to realize
it but to exclaim about it.

Thus inspired she asked Prickett, Vine, Furnese and
other yeomen and tenants of the Marsh to send their
hands, men and maids, to Ansdore, for dancing and supper
on New Year's Eve. She found this celebration even
more thrilling than the earlier one. Somehow these
humbler preparations filled more of her time and thought
than when she had prepared to entertain her peers. She
would not wear her low dress, of course, but she would
have her pink one " done up "—a fall of lace and some
beads sewn on, for she must look her best. She saw herself
opening the ball with Dick Socknersh, her hand in his,
his clumsy arm round her waist . . . Of course old
Stuppeny was technically the head man at Ansdore,
but he was too old to dance—she would see he had plenty
to eat and drink instead—she would take the floor with
Dick Socknersh, and all eyes would be fixed upon her.

They certainly were, except when they dropped for
a wink at a neighbour. Joanna waltzing with Socknersh
to the trills of Mr. Elphick, the Brodnyx schoolmaster,
seated at the tinkling, ancient Collard, Joanna in her
pink gown, close fitting to her waist and then abnormally
bunchy, with her hair piled high and twisted with a strand
of ribbon, with her face flushed, her lips parted and her
eyes bright, was a sight from which no man and few women
could turn their eyes. Her vitality and happiness seemed
to shine from her skin, almost to light up the dark and
heavy figure of Socknersh in his Sunday blacks, as he
staggered and stumbled, for he could not dance. His
big hand pawed at her silken waist, while the other held
hers crumpled in it—his hair was greased with butter,
and his skin with the sweat of his endeavour as he turned
her round.

That was the only time Joanna danced that night.
For the rest of the evening she went about among her
guests, seeing that all were well fed and had partners.
As time went on, gradually her brightness dimmed, and
her eyes became almost anxious as she searched among

the dancers. Each time she looked she seemed to see the same thing, and each time she saw it, it was as if a fresh veil dropped over her eyes.

At last, towards the end of the evening, she went up again to Socknersh.

"Would you like me to dance this polka with you that's coming?"

"Thank you, missus—I'd be honoured, missus—but I'm promised to Martha Tilden."

"Martha!—You've danced with her nearly all the evening."

"She's bin middling kind to me, missus, showing me the steps and hops."

"Oh, well, since you've promised you must pay."

She turned her back on him, then suddenly smarted at her own pettishness.

"You've the makings of a good dancer in you, if you'll learn," she said over her shoulder. "I'm glad Martha's teaching you."

§ 14

Lambing was always late upon the Marsh. The wan film of the winter grasses had faded off the April green before the innings became noisy with bleating, and the new-born lambs could match their whiteness with the first flowering of the blackthorn.

It was always an anxious time—though the Marsh ewes were hardy—and sleepless for shepherds, who from the windows of their lonely lambing huts watched the yellow spring-dazzle of the stars grow pale night after night. They were bad hours to be awake, those hours of the April dawn, for in them, the shepherds said, a strange call came down from the country inland, straying scents of moss and primroses reaching out towards the salt sea, calling men away from the wind-stung levels and the tides and watercourses, to where the little inland farms sleep in the sheltered hollows among the hop-bines, and the sunrise is warm with the scent of hidden flowers.

Dick Socknersh began to look wan and large-eyed under the strain—he looked more haggard than the shepherd of Yokes Court or the shepherd of Birdskitchen, though they kept fast and vigil as long as he. His mistress, too, had a fagged, sorrowful air, and soon it became known all over the Three Marshes that Ansdore's lambing that year had been a gigantic failure.

"It's her own fault," said Prickett at the Woolpack, "and serve her right for getting shut of old Fuller, and then getting stuck on this furrin heathen notion of Spanish sheep. Anyone could have told her as the lambs ud be too big and the ewes could never drop them safe—she might have known it herself, surelye."

"It's her looker that should ought to have known better," said Furnese. "Joanna Godden's a woman, fur all her man's ways, and you can't expéct her to have präaper know wud sheep."

"I wonder if she'll get shut of him after this," said Vine.

"Not she! She don't see through him yet."

"She'll never see through him," said Prickett solemnly. "The only kind of man a woman ever sees through is the kind she don't like to look at."

Joanna certainly did not "see through" Dick Socknersh. She knew that she was chiefly to blame for the tragedy of her lambing, and when her reason told her that her looker should have discouraged instead of obeyed and abetted her, she rather angrily tossed the thought aside. Socknersh had the sense to realize that she knew more about sheep than he, and he had not understood that in this matter she was walking out of her knowledge into experiment. No one could have known that the scheme would turn out so badly—the Spanish rams had not been so big after all, only a little bigger than her ewes . . . . if anyone should have foreseen trouble it was the Northampton farmer who knew the size of Spanish lambs at birth, and from his Kentish experience must also have some knowledge of Romney Marsh sheep.

But though she succeeded in getting all the guilt off her looker and some of it off herself, she was nevertheless stricken by the greatness of the tragedy. It was not only the financial losses in which she was involved, or the derision of her neighbours, or the fulfilment of their

prophecy—or even the fall of her own pride and the shattering of that dream in which the giant sheep walked—
there was also an element of almost savage pity for the
animals whom her daring had betrayed. Those dead
ewes, too stupid to mate themselves profitably and now
the victims of the farm-socialism that had experimented
with them . . . . At first she ordered Socknersh to
save the ewes even at the cost of the lambs, then when
in the little looker's hut she saw a ewe despairingly lick
the fleece of its dead lamb, an even deeper grief and pity
smote her, and she burst suddenly and stormily into
tears.

Sinking on her knees on the dirty floor, she covered
her face, and rocked herself to and fro. Socknersh sat
on his three-legged stool, staring at her in silence. His
forehead crumpled slightly and his mouth twitched, as
the slow processes of his thought shook him. The air
was thick with the fumes of his brazier, from which an
angry red glow fell on Joanna as she knelt and wept.

§ 15

When the first sharpness of death had passed from
Ansdore, Joanna's sanguine nature, her hopeful bump-
tiousness, revived. Her pity for the dead lambs and her
fellow-feeling of compassion for the ewes would prevent
her ever dreaming of a new experiment, but already
she was dreaming of a partial justification of the old one
—her cross-bred lambs would grow so big both in size
and price that they would, even in their diminished numbers
pay for her daring and proclaim its success to those who
jeered and doubted.

Certainly those lambs which had survived their birth
now promised well. They were bigger than the pure-
bred Kent lambs, and seemed hardy enough. Joanna
watched them grow, and broke away from Marsh tradition
to the extent of giving them cake—she was afraid they
might turn bony.

As the summer advanced she pointed them out triumphantly to one or two farmers. They were fine animals,
she said, and justified her experiment, though she would

never repeat it on account of the cost ; she did not expect
to do more than cover her expenses.

" You'll be lucky if you do that," said Prickett rather
brutally, " they look middling poor in wool."

Joanna was not discouraged, nor even offended, for
she interpreted all Prickett's remarks in the light of
Great Ansdore's jealousy of Little Ansdore.

Later on Martha Tilden told her that they were saying
much the same at the Woolpack.

" I don't care what they say at the Woolpack," cried
Joanna, " and what business have you to know what
they say there ? I don't like my gals hanging around
pubs."

" I didn't hang aräound, ma'am. 'Twas Socknersh
töald me."

" Socknersh had no business to tell you—it's no
concern of yours."

Martha put her hand over her mouth to hide a grin,
but Joanna could see it in her eyes and the dimples of
her cheeks.

A sudden anger seized her.

" I won't have you gossiping with Socknersh, neither
—you keep away from my men. I've often wondered
why the place looks in proper need of scrubbing, and
now I know. You can do your work or you can pack
off. I won't have you fooling around with my men."

" I döan't fool aräound wud your men," cried Martha
indignantly. She was going to add " I leave that to
you," but she thought better of it, because for several
reasons she wanted to keep her place.

Joanna flounced off, and went to find Socknersh at
the shearing. In the shelter of some hurdles he and
one or two travelling shearers were busy with the ewes'
fleeces. She noticed that the animal Socknersh was working on lay quiet between his feet, while the other men
held theirs with difficulty and many struggles. The July
sunshine seemed to hold the scene as it held the Marsh
in a steep of shining stillness. The silence was broken
by many small sounds—the clip of the shears, the panting
of the waiting sheep and of the dogs that guarded them,
and every now and then the sudden scraping scuttle of
the released victim as it sprang up from the shearer's

feet and dashed off to where the shorn sheep huddled naked and ashamed together. Joanna watched for a moment without speaking; then suddenly she broke out :

"Socknersh, I hear it's said that the new lambs ull be poor in wool."

"They're saying it, missus, but it äun't true."

"I don't care if it's true or not. You shouldn't ought to tell my gal Martha such things before you tell me."

Socknersh's eyes opened wide, and the other men looked up from their work.

"Seemingly," continued Joanna, "everyone on this farm hears everything before I do, and it ain't right. Next time you hear a lot of tedious gossip, Dick Socknersh, you come and tell me, and don't waste it on the gals, making them idle."

She went away, her eyes bright with anger, and then suddenly her heart smote her. Suppose Socknersh took offence and gave notice. She had rebuked him publicly before the hired shearers—it was enough to make any man turn. But what should she do if he went?—He must not go. She would never get anyone like him. She almost turned and went back, but had enough sense to stop—a public apology would only make a worse scandal of a public rebuke. She must wait and see him alone . . . . the next minute she knew further that she must not apologize, and the minute after she knew further still—almost further than she could bear—that in denying herself an apology she was denying herself a luxury, that she wanted to apologize, to kneel at Socknersh's clay-caked feet and beg his forgiveness, to humble herself before him by her penitence so that he could exalt her by his pardon . . . .

"Good sakes ! Whatever's the matter with me ? " thought Joanna.

§ 16

Her apology took the discreet form of a side of bacon, and Socknersh did not give notice—had evidently never thought of it. Of course the shearers spread the story of

Joanna's outburst when they went on to Slinches and Birdskitchen and other farms, but no one was surprised that the shepherd stayed on.

" He'd never be such a fool as to give up being looker a day before she makes him master," said Cobb of Slinches.

" And when he's master," said Mrs. Cobb, " he'll get his own back for her sassing him before Harmer and his men."

A few weeks later Socknersh brought the first of the cross-bred lambs to market at Rye, and Joanna's wonderful sheep-breeding scheme was finally sealed a failure. The lambs were not only poor in wool, but coarse in meat, and the butchers would not deal, small mutton being the fashion. Altogether they fetched lower prices than the Kent lambs, and the rumour of Ansdore's losses mounted to over four hundred pounds.

Rumour was not very wide of the fact—what with hiring fees, railway expenses, the loss of ewes and lambs at the lambing, and the extra diet and care which panic had undertaken for the survivors, the venture had put about two hundred and sixty pounds on the debit side of Joanna's accounts. She was able to meet her losses —her father had died with a comfortable balance in Lewes Old Bank, and she had always paid ready money, so was without any encumbrance of debt—but Ansdore was bound to feel the blow, which had shorn it of its fleece of pleasant profits. Joanna was for the first time confronted by the need for economy, and she hated economy with all the lavish, colour-loving powers of her nature. Even now she would not bend herself to retrenchment—not a man less in the yard, not a girl less in the kitchen, as her neighbours had expected.

But the failure of the cross-bred lambs did not end the tale of Ansdore's misadventures. There was a lot of dipping for sheep-scab on the Marsh that August, and it soon became known that several of Joanna Godden's sheep and lambs had died after the second dip.

" That's her valiant Socknersh again," said Prickett —" guv 'em a double arsenic dip. Good sakes ! That woman had better be quick and marry him before he does any more harm as her looker."

" There's more than he gives a double arsenic dip,
surelye."

" Surelye—but they mixes the can a bit. Broadhurst says as Socknersh's second dip was as strong as
his first."

The feeling about Socknersh's incapacity reached
such a point that more than one warning was given Joanna
for her father's sake, and one at least for her own, from
Arthur Alce.

" I shouldn't say it, Joanna, if it wasn't true, but a
man who puts a sheep into poison-wash twice in a fortnight isn't fit to be anyone's looker."

" But we were dipping for sheep-scab—that takes
something stronger than Keatings."

" Yes, but the point is, d'you see, that you give 'em
the first dip in arsenic stuff, and the next shouldn't ought
to be poison at all—there's a lot of good safe dips on the
market, that ull do very well for a second wash."

" Socknersh knows his business."

" He don't—that's why I'm speaking. Fuller ud
never have done what he's done. He's lost you a dozen
prime sheep on the top of all your other losses."

The reference was unfortunate. Joanna's cheekbones
darkened ominously.

" It's all very well for you to talk, Arthur Alce, for
you think no one can run Ansdore except yourself who'll
never get the chance. It's well known around, in spite
of what you say, that Socknersh is valiant with sheep—
no one can handle 'em as he can ; at the shearing Harmer
and his men were full of it—how the ewes ud keep quiet
for him as for nobody else—and 'twas the same at the
lambing. It wasn't his fault that the lambs died, but
because that chap at Northampton never told us what
he should ought . . . . I tell you, I've never had
anyone like him for handling sheep—they're quite different
with him from what they were with that rude old Fuller,
barking after 'em like a dog along the Brodnyx road
and bringing 'em up to Rye all raggled and draggled and
dusty as mops . . . . he knows how to manage sheep—
he's like one of themselves."

" That's just about it—he's like another sheep, so they
ain't scared of him, but he can do no more for 'em than

another sheep could, neither. He's ignorant—he's got no sense nor know, or he'd never have let you breed with them Spanishes, or given 'em a poisonous double-dip—and he's always having sway-backs up at market, too, and tic and hoose and fluke . . . Oh, Joanna, if you're any bit wise you'll get shut of him before he messes you all up. And you know what folks say—they say you'd have got shut of him months agone if you hadn't been so unaccountable set on him, so as they say—yes, they say one day you'll marry him and make him master of Ansdore."

Alce's face flamed as red as his whiskers and nearly as red as Joanna's cheeks. For a moment she faced him speechless, her mouth open.

" Oh, that's what they say, is it ! " she broke out at last. " They say I'd marry Dick Socknersh, who looks after my sheep, and who's like a sheep himself. They think I'd marry a man who's got no more'n two words on his tongue and half that number of ideas in his head —who can't think without its giving him a headache— who comes of no class of people—his father and mother were hedge people up at Anvil Green—who gets eighteen bob a week as my looker—who——"

" Don't get so vrothered, Joanna. I'm only telling you what folk say, and if you'll stop and think you'll see they've got some reason. Your looker's done things that no farmer on this Marsh ud put up with a month, and yet you keep him on, you with all your fine ideas about farming and running Ansdore as your poor father ud have had it . . . and then he's a well set-up young man too, nice-looking and stout as I won't deny, and you're a young woman that I'd say was nice-looking too, and it's only natural folks should talk when they see a pretty woman hanging on to a handsome chap in spite of his having half bust her."

" He hasn't half bust me, nor a quarter, neither— and I ain't hanging on to him, as you're elegant enough to say. I keep him as my looker because he's valiant with the sheep and manages 'em as if born to it, and because he minds what I say and doesn't sass me back or meddle, as some I could name. As for being set on him, I'm not so far below myself as all that. You must think unaccountable low of me, Arthur Alce, if you figure I'd get sweet on a man who's courting my chicken-gal, which is what Dick Socknersh is doing."

" Courting Martha Tilden ? "

" Yes, my chicken-gal. And you think I'd look at him !—I ! . . . You must think middling low of me, Arthur Alce . . . a man who's courting my chicken-gal."

" I'd always thought as Martha Tilden—but you must know best. Well, if he's courting her I hope as he'll marry her soon and show folks they're wrong about him and you."

" They should ought to be ashamed of themselves to need showing. I look at a man who's courting my chicken-gal !—I never ! I tell you what I'll do—I'll raise his wages, so as he can marry her at once—my chicken-gal—and so as folk ull know that I'm satisfied with him as my looker."

And Joanna marched off up the drive, where this conversation had taken place.

§ 17

She raised Socknersh's wages to twenty shillings the next day, and it was not due to any wordy flow of his gratitude that the name of Martha Tilden was not mentioned between them. " Better leave it," thought Joanna to herself, " after all, I'm not sure—and she's a slut. I'd sooner he married a cleaner, steadier sort of gal."

Grace Wickens had already departed, her cocoa-making tendencies having lately passed into mania—and her successor was an older woman, a widow, who had fallen on evil days. She was a woman of few words, and Joanna wondered a little when one afternoon she said to her rather anxiously : " I'd lik to speak to you, ma'am—in private, if you please."

They went into the larder and Mrs. Tolhurst began : " I hardly lik to say it to you, Miss Joanna, being a single spinster . . ."

This was a bad beginning, for Joanna flamed at once

at the implication that her spinsterhood put her at any disadvantage as a woman of the world.

" Don't talk nonsense, Mrs. Tolhurst ; I may be unwed as yet, but I'm none of your Misses."

" No, ma'am—well, it's about this Martha Tilden——" Joanna started.

" What about her ? "

" Only, ma'am, that she's six months gone."

" There was no chair in the larder, or Joanna would have fallen into it—instead she staggered back against the shelves, with a great rattle of crockery. Her face was as white as her own plates, and for a moment she could not speak.

" I made bold to tell you, Miss Joanna, for all the neighbourhood's beginning to talk—and the gal getting near her time and all . . . I thought maybe you'd have noticed . . . . Don't be in such a terrification about it, Miss Joanna . . . I'm sorry I told you—maybe I shud ought to have spuck to the gal fust . . ."

" Don't be a fool . . . the dirty slut !—I'll learn her . . . under my very roof——"

" Oh, no, ma'am, 'twasn't under your roof—we shouldn't have allowed it. She used to meet him in the field down by Beggar's Bush . . ."

" Hold your tongue."

Mrs. Tolhurst was offended ; she thought her mistress's behaviour unwarranted either by modesty or indignation. There were burning tears in Joanna's eyes as she flung herself out of the room. She was blind as she went down the passage, twisting her apron furiously in her hands.

" Martha Tilden ! " she called—" Martha Tilden ! "

" Oh," she thought in her heart, " I raised his wages so's he could marry her—for months this has been going on . . . the field down by Beggar's Bush . . . Oh, I could kill her ! " Then shouting into the yard—" Martha Tilden ! Martha Tilden ! "

" I'm coming, Miss Joanna," Martha's soft drawly voice increased her bitterness ; her own, compared with it, sounded harsh, empty, inexperienced. Martha's voice was full of the secrets of love—the secrets of Dick Socknersh's love.

" Come into the dairy," she said hoarsely.

Martha came and stood before her. She evidently knew what was ahead, for she looked pale and a little scared, and yet she had about her a strange air of confidence . . . though not so strange, after all, since she carried Dick Socknersh's child, and her memory was full of his caresses and the secrets of his love . . . thus bravely could Joanna herself have faced an angry world . . .

" You leave my service at once," she said.

Martha began to cry.

" You know what for?"

" Yes, Miss Joanna."

" I wonder you've had the impudence to go about as you've done—eating my food and taking my wages, while all the time you've been carrying on with my looker."

" Your looker?—No, Miss Joanna."

" What d'you mean?"

" I don't know what *you* mean, miss—I've never had näun to do wud Dick Socknersh if it's him you're thinking of."

" Not Socknersh, but I . . . who *is* the man, then? "

" Well, it äun't no secret from anyone but you, Miss Joanna, so I döan't mind telling you as my boy is Peter Relf, their looker at Old Honeychild. We've bin walking out ever sinst the day he came after your pläace as looker here, and we'd be married now if he hadn't his old mother and dad to keep, and got into some nasty silly trouble wud them fellers wot put money on horses they've never seen . . . . He döan't get more'n fifteen bob a week at Honeychild, and he can't keep the old folk on less than eight, them being always filling themselves with doctor's stuff . . . . "

Joanna was not listening to her—she sat amazed and pale, her heart beating in heavy thuds of relief. Mixed with her happiness there was a little shame, for she saw that the mistake had arisen from her putting herself too realistically in Martha's place. Why had she jumped to the conclusion that the girl's lover was Socknersh? It is true that he had danced with her very often at the Christmas party nine months ago, and once since then she had

scolded him for telling the chicken-woman some news
he ought first to have told the mistress . . . but that
was very little in the way of evidence, and Martha had
always been running after boys . . .

Seeing her still silent, Martha began to cry again.

" I'm sure I'm unaccountable sorry, Miss Joanna,
and what's to become of me I don't know, nuther. Maybe
I'm a bad lot, but it's hard to love and wait on and on
for the wedding . . . and Pete was sure as he could
do summat wud a horse running in the Derby race, and at
the Woolpack they told him it wur bound to win . . .
I've always kept straight up till this, Miss Joanna, and a
virtuous virgin for all I do grin and laugh a lot . . . .
and many's the temptation I've had, being a lone gal
wudout father or mother . . ."

" Keep quiet, Martha, and have done with so much
excuse. You've been a very wicked gal, and you shouldn't
ought to think any different of yourself. But maybe
I was too quick, saying you were to go at once. You
can finish your month, seeing as you were monthly hired."

" Thank you, Miss Joanna, that'll give me time to
look around for another plääce ; though—" bursting
out crying again—"I don't see what good that'll do me,
seeing as my time's three months from hence."

A great softness had come over Joanna. There were
tears in her eyes as she looked at Martha, but they were
no longer tears of anger."

" Don't cry, child," she said kindly, " I'll see you
don't come to want."

" Oh, thank you, Miss Joanna . . . it's middling
good of you, and Pete will repay you when we're married
and have sääved some tin."

" I'll do my best, for you've worked well on the whole,
and I shan't forget that Orpington hen you saved when
she was egg-bound. But don't you think, Martha," she
added seriously, " that I'm holding with any of your
goings-on. I'm shocked and ashamed at you, for you've
done something very wicked—something that's spoken
against in the Bible, and in church too—it's in the Ten
Commandments. I wonder you could kneel in your
place and say ' Lord have mercy upon us,' knowing what
you'd been up to "—Martha's tears flowed freely—" and

it's sad to think you've kept yourself straight for years
as you say, and then gone wrong at last, just because
you hadn't patience to wait for your lawful wedding . . .
and all the scandal there's been and ull be, and folks
talking at you and at me . . . and you be off now,
and tell Mrs. Tolhurst you're to have the cream on your
milk and take it before it's skimmed."

§ 18

For the rest of the day Joanna was in a strange fret
—dreams seemed to hang over life like mist, there was
sorrow in all she did, and yet a queer, suffocating joy.
She told herself that she was upset by Martha's revelation, but at the same time she knew it had upset her not
so much in itself as in the disturbing new self-knowledge
it had brought. She could not hide from herself that
she was delighted, overjoyed to find that her shepherd
did not love her chicken-girl, that the thoughts she had
thought about them for nine months were but vain
thoughts.

Was it true, then, that she was moving along that
road which the villages had marked out for her—the
road which would end before the Lion and the Unicorn
in Brodnyx church, with her looker as her bridegroom?
The mere thought was preposterous to her pride. She,
her father's daughter, to marry his father's son!—the
suspicion insulted her. She loved herself and Ansdore
too well for that . . . and Socknersh, fine fellow as he
was, had no mind and very little sense—he could scarcely
read and write, he was slow as an ox, and had common
ways and spoke the low Marsh talk—he drank out of
his saucer and cut his bread with his pocket-knife—he
spat in the yard. How dared people think she would
marry him?—that she was so undignified, infatuated
and unfastidious as to yoke herself to a slow, common
boor? Her indignation flamed against the scandal-
mongers . . . that Woolpack! She'd like to see their
licence taken away, and then perhaps decent women's
characters would be safe . . . .

But folk said it was queer she should keep on Socknersh when he had done her such a lot of harm—they made sure there must be something behind it. For the first time Joanna caught a glimpse of his shortcomings as a looker, and in a moment of vision asked herself if it wasn't really true that he ought to have known about that dip. Was she blinding herself to his incapacity simply because she liked to have him about the place— to see his big stooping figure blocked against the sunset —to see his queer eyes light up with queer thoughts that were like a dog's thoughts or a sheep's thoughts . . . to watch his hands, big and heavy and brown, with the earth worked into the skin . . . and his neck, when he lifted his head, brown as his hands, and like the trunk of an oak with roots of firm, beautiful muscle in the field of his broad chest?

Then Joanna was scared—she knew she ought not to think of her looker so; and she told herself that she kept him on just because he was the only man she'd ever had about the place who had minded her properly . . . .

When evening came, she began to feel stifled in the house, where she had been busy ironing curtains, and tying on her old straw hat went out for a breath of air on the road. There was a light mist over the watercourses, veiling the pollards and thorn trees and the reddening thickets of Ansdore's bush—a flavour of salt was in it, for the tides were high in the channels, and the sunset breeze was blowing from Rye Bay. Northward, the Coast—as the high bank marking the old shores of England before the flood was still called—was dim, like a low line of clouds beyond the marsh. The sun hung red and ray-less above Beggar's Bush, a crimson ball of frost and fire.

A queer feeling of sadness came to Joanna—queer, unaccountable, yet seeming to drain itself from the very depths of her body, and to belong not only to her flesh but to the marsh around her, to the pastures with their tawny veil of withered seed-grasses, to the thorn-bushes spotted with the red haws, to the sky and to the sea, and the mists in which they merged together . . . .

" I'll get shut of Socknersh," she said to herself— " I believe folks are right, and he's too like a sheep him-self to be any real use to ther "

She walked on a little way, over the powdery Brodnyx road.

"I'm silly—that's what I am. Who'd have thought it? I'll send him off—but then folks ull say I'm afraid of gossip."

She chewed the bitter cud of this idea over a hurrying half mile, which took her across the railway, and then brought her back, close to the Kent Ditch.

"I can't afford to let the place come to any harm— besides, what does it matter what people think or say of me? I don't care . . . . But it'll be a mortal trouble getting another looker and settling him to my ways—and I'll never get a man who'll mind me as poor Socknersh does. I want a man with a humble soul, but seemingly you can't get that through advertising . . ."

She had come to the bridge over the Kent Ditch, and Sussex ended in a swamp of reeds. Looking south-ward she saw the boundaries of her own land, the Kent Innings, dotted with sheep, and the shepherd's cottage among them, its roof standing out a bright orange under the fleece of lichen that smothered the tiles. It suddenly struck her that a good way out of her difficulty might be a straight talk with Socknersh. He would probably be working in his garden now, having those few evening hours as his own. Straining her eyes into the shining thickness of mist and sun, she thought she could see his blue shirt moving among the bean-rows and hollyhocks around the little place.

"I'll go and see him and talk it out—I'll tell him that if he won't have proper sense he must go. I've been soft, putting up with him all this time."

Being marsh bred, Joanna did not take what seemed the obvious way to the cottage, across the low pastures by the Kent Ditch; instead, she went back a few yards to where a dyke ran under the road. She followed it out on the marsh, and when it cut into another dyke she followed that, walking on the bank beside the great teazle. A plank bridge took her across between two willows, and after some more such movements, like a pawn on a chess-board, she had crossed three dykes and was at the shepherd's gate.

He was working at the farther side of the garden

and did not see her till she called him. She had been
to his cottage only once before, when he complained of
the roof leaking, but Socknersh would not have shown
surprise if he had seen Old Goodman of the marsh tales
standing at his door. Joanna had stern, if somewhat
arbitrary, notions of propriety, and now not only did
she refuse to come inside the gate, but she made him come
and stand outside it, among the seed-grasses which were
like the ghost of hay.

It struck her that she had timed her visit a little
too late. Already the brightness had gone from the sunset, leaving a dull red ball hanging lustreless between
the clouds. There was no wind, but the air seemed to
be moving slowly up from the sea, heavy with mist and
salt and the scent of haws and blackberries, of dew-soaked
grass and fleeces . . . . Socknersh stood before her
with his blue shirt open at the neck. From him came
a smell of earth and sweat . . . . his clothes smelt
of sheep . . .

She opened her mouth to tell him that she was highly
displeased with the way he had managed her flock since
the shearing, but instead she only said :

" Look ! "

Over the eastern rim of the Marsh the moon had
risen, a red, lightless disk, while the sun, red and lightless
too, hung in the west above Rye Hill. The sun and the
moon looked at each other across the marsh, and midway between them, in the spell of their flushed, haunted
glow, stood Socknersh, big and stooping, like some lonely
beast of the earth and night . . . . A strange fear
touched Joanna—she tottered, and his arm came out
to save her . . . .

It was as if Marsh itself enfolded her, for his clothes
and skin were caked with the soil of it . . . She opened
her eyes, and looking up into his, saw her own face, infinitely white and small, looking down at her out of them.
Joanna Godden looked at her out of Socknersh's eyes.
She stirred feebly, and she found that he had set her a
little way from him, still holding her by the shoulders,
as if he feared she would fall.

" Do you feel better, missus ? "

" I'm all right," she snapped.

" I beg your pardon if I took any liberty, missus. But I thought maybe you'd turned fainty-like."

" You thought wrong "—her anger was mounting— " I trod on a mole-hill. You've messed my nice alpaca body—if you can't help getting dirt all over yourself you shouldn't ought to touch a lady even if she's in a swound."

" I'm middling sorry, missus."

His voice was quite tranquil—it was like oil on the fire of Joanna's wrath.

" Maybe you are, and so am I. You shouldn't ought to have cotched hold of me like that. But it's all of a match with the rest of your doings, you great stupid owl. You've lost me more'n a dozen prime sheep by not mixing your dip proper—after having lost me the best of my ewes and lambs with your ignorant notions—and now you go and put finger marks over my new alpaca body, all because you won't think, or keep yourself clean. You can take a month's notice."

Socknersh stared at her with eyes and mouth wide open.

" A month's notice," she repeated, " it's what I came here to give you. You're the tale of all the parish with your ignorance. I'd meant to talk to you about it and give you another chance, but now I see there'd be no sense in that, and you can go at the end of your month."

" You'll give me a character, missus ? "

" I'll give you a prime character as a drover or a ploughman or a carter or a dairyman or a housemaid or a curate or anything you like except a looker. Why should I give you eighteen shillun a week as my looker —twenty shillun, as I've made it now—when my best wether could do what you do quite as well and not take a penny for it ? You've got no more sense or know than a tup . . ."

She stopped, breathless, her cheeks and eyes burning, a curious ache in her breast. The sun was gone now, only the moon hung flushed in the foggy sky. Socknersh's face was in darkness as he stood with his back to the east, but she could see on his features a look of surprise and dismay which suddenly struck her as pathetic in its helpless stupidity. After all, this great hulking

man was but a child, and he was unhappy because he
must go, and give up his snug cottage and the sheep he
had learned to care for and the kind mistress who gave
him sides of bacon . . . . There was a sudden strangling
spasm in her throat, and his face swam into the sky on
a mist of tears, which welled up in her eyes as without
another word she turned away.

His voice came after her piteously—

" Missus—missus—but you raised my wages last
week."

§ 19

Her tears were dry by the time she reached home,
but in the night they flowed again, accompanied by angry
sobs, which she choked in her pillow, for fear of waking
little Ellen.

She cried because she was humbled in her own eyes.
It was as if a veil had been torn from the last two years,
and she saw her motives at last. For two years she had
endured an ignorant, inefficient servant simply because
his strength and good looks had enslaved her susceptible
womanhood. . . .

Her father would never have acted as she had done ;
he would not have kept Socknersh a single month ; he
would not have engaged him at all—both Relf of Honeychild and Day of Slinches were more experienced men,
with better recommendations ; and yet she had chosen
Socknersh—because his brown eyes had held and drowned
her judgment, as surely as they had held her image, so
dwindled and wan, when she looked into them that evening, between the setting sun and the rising moon.

Then, after she had engaged him, he had shown just
enough natural capacity for her to blind herself with—
his curious affinity with the animals he tended had helped
her to forget the many occasions on which he had failed
to rise above them in intelligence. It had been left to
another to point out to her that a man might be good with
sheep simply because he was no better than a sheep himself.

And now she was humbled—in her own eyes, and also

in the eyes of her neighbours. She would have to confess herself in the wrong. Everyone knew that she had just raised Socknersh's wages, so there would be no good pretending that she had known his shortcomings from the first, but had put up with them as long as she could. Everyone would guess that something had happened to make her change her mind about him . . . there would be some terrible talk at the Woolpack.

And there was Socknersh himself, poor fellow—the martyr of her impulses. She thrust her face deep into the pillow when she thought of him. She had given him as sharp a blow as his thick hide would ever let him suffer. She would never forget that last look on his face. . . .

Then she began wondering why this should have come upon her. Why should she have made a fool of herself over Socknersh, when she had borne unmoved the court-ship of Arthur Alce for seven years? Was it just because Alce had red whiskers and red hands and red hair on his hands, while Socknersh was dark and sweet of face and limb? It was terrible to think that mere youth and comeliness and virility should blind her judgment and strip her of common sense. Yet this was obviously the lesson she must learn from to-day's disgrace.

Hot and tear-stained, she climbed out of bed, and paced across the dark room to the grey blot of the window. She forgot her distrust of the night air in all her misery of throbbing head and heart, and flung back the casement, so that the soft marsh wind came in, with rain upon it, and her tears were mingled with the tears of the night.

" Oh God ! " she mourned to herself—" why didn't you make me a man ? "

PART II

FIRST LOVE

§ 1

It took Joanna nearly two years to recover from the losses of her sheep. Some people would have done it earlier, but she was not a clever economist. Where many women on the Marsh would · have thrown themselves into an orgy of retrenchment—ranging from the dismissal of a dairymaid to the substitution of a cheaper brand of tea—she made no new occasions for thrift, and persevered but lamely in the old ones. She was fond of spending—liked to see things trim and bright ; she hated waste, especially when others were guilty of it, but she found a positive support in display.

She was also generous. Everybody knew that she had paid Dick Socknersh thirty shillings for the two weeks that he was out of work after leaving her—before he went as cattleman to an inland farm—and she had found the money for Martha Tilden's wedding, and for her lying-in a month afterwards, and some time later she had helped Peter Relf with ready cash to settle his debts and move himself and his wife and baby to West Wittering, where he had the offer of a place with three shillings a week more than they gave at Honeychild.

She might have indulged herself still further in this way, which gratified both her warm heart and her proud head, if she had not wanted so much to send Ellen to a good school. The school at Rye was all very well, attended by the daughters of tradesmen and farmers, and taught by women whom Joanna recognized as ladies ; but she had long dreamed of sending her little sister to a really good school at Folkestone—where Ellen would wear a ribbon round her hat and go for walks in a long procession of two-and-two, and be taught wonderful, showy and intricate things by ladies with letters after their names—whom Joanna despised because she felt sure they had never had a chance of getting married.

She herself had been educated at the National School, and from six to fourteen had trudged to and fro on the Brodnyx road, learning to read and write and reckon and say her catechism . . . But this was not good enough for Ellen. Joanna had made up her mind that Ellen should be a lady; she was pretty and lazy and had queer likes and dislikes—all promising signs of vocation. She would never learn to care for Ansdore, with its coarse and crowding occupations, so there was no reason why she should grow up like her sister in capable commonness. Half unconsciously Joanna had planned a future in which she ventured and toiled, while Ellen wore a silk dress and sat on the drawing-room sofa— that being the happiest lot she could picture for anyone, though she would have loathed it herself.

In a couple of years Ansdore's credit once more stood high at Lewes Old Bank, and Ellen could be sent to a select school at Folkestone—so select indeed that there had been some difficulty about getting her father's daughter into it. Joanna was surprised as well as disgusted that the schoolmistress should give herself such airs, for she was very plainly dressed, whereas Joanna had put on all her most gorgeous apparel for the interview; but she had been very glad when her sister was finally accepted as a pupil at Rose Hill House, for now she would have as companions the daughters of clergymen and squires, and learn no doubt to model herself on their refinement. She might even be asked to their homes for her holidays, and, making friends in their circle, take a short cut to silken immobility on the drawing-room sofa by way of marriage . . . . Joanna congratulated herself on having really done very well for Ellen, though during the first weeks she missed her sister terribly. She missed their quarrels and caresses—she missed Ellen's daintiness at meals, though she had often smacked it—she missed her strutting at her side to church on Sunday—she missed her noisy, remonstrant setting out to school every morning

and her noisy affectionate return—her heart ached when
she looked at the little empty bed in her room, and being
sentimental she often dropped a tear where she used to
drop a kiss on Ellen's pillow.

Nevertheless she was proud of what she had done
for her little sister, and she was proud too of having restored Ansdore to prosperity, not by stinging and paring,
but by her double capacity for working hard herself and
for getting all the possible work out of others. If no one
had gone short under her roof, neither had anyone gone
idle—if the tea was strong and the butter was thick and
there was always prime bacon for breakfast on Sundays,
so was there also a great clatter on the stairs at five o'clock
each morning, a rattle of brooms and hiss and slop of
scrubbing-brushes—and the mistress with clogs on her
feet and her father's coat over her gown, poking her head
into the maids' room to see if they were up, hurrying the
men over their snacks, shouting commands across the
yard, into the barns or into the kitchen, and seemingly
omnipresent to those slackers who paused to rest or chat
or "put their feet up."

That time had scarred her a little—put some lines
into the corners of her eyes and straightened the curling
corners of her mouth, but it had also heightened the rich
healthy colour on her cheeks, enlarged her fine girth,
her strength of shoulder and depth of bosom. She did
not look any older, because she was so superbly healthy
and superbly proud. She knew that the neighbours were
impressed by Ansdore's thriving, when they had foretold
its downfall under her sway . . . . She had vindicated
her place in her father's shoes, and best of all, she had
expiated her folly in the matter of Socknersh, and restored
her credit not only in the bar of the Woolpack but in
her own eyes.

§ 2

One afternoon, soon after Ellen had gone back to
school for her second year, when Joanna was making plum
jam in the kitchen, and getting very hot and sharp-tongued
in the process, Mrs. Tolhurst saw a man go past the window
on his way to the front door.

" Lor, miss ! There's Parson ! " she cried, and the next minute came sounds of struggle with Joanna's rusty door-bell.

" Go and see what he wants—take off that sacking apron first—and if he wants to see me, put him into the parlour."

Mr. Pratt lacked " visiting " among many other accomplishments as a parish priest—the vast, strewn nature of his parish partly excused him—and a call from him was not the casual event it would have been in many places, but startling and portentous, requiring fit celebration.

Joanna received him in state, supported by her father's Bible and stuffed owls. She had kept him waiting while she changed her gown, for like many people who are sometimes very splendid she could also on occasion be extremely disreputable, and her jam-making costume was quite unfit for the masculine eye, even though negligible. Mr. Pratt had grown rather nervous waiting for her—he had always been afraid of her, because of her big, breathless ways, and because he felt sure that she was one of the many who criticized him.

" I—I've only come about a little thing—at least it's not a little thing to me, but a very big thing—er—er——"

" What is it ? " asked Joanna, a stuffed owl staring disconcertingly over each shoulder.

" For some time there's been complaints about the music in church. Of course I'm quite sure Mr. Elphick does wonders, and the ladies of the choir are excellent—er—gifted . . . I'm quite sure. But the harmonium—it's very old and quite a lot of the notes won't play . . . and the bellows . . . Mr. Saunders came from Lydd and had a look at it, but he says it's past repair—er—satisfactory repair, and it ud really save money in the long run if we bought a new one."

Joanna was a little shocked. She had listened to the grunts and wheezes of the harmonium from her childhood, and the idea of a new one disturbed her—it suggested sacrilege and ritualism and the moving of landmarks.

" I like what we've got very well," she said truculently—" It's done for us properly this thirty year."

" That's just it," said the Rector, " it's done so well

that I think we ought to let it retire from business, and appoint something younger in its place . . . he! he!"
He looked at her nervously to see if she had appreciated the joke, but Joanna's humour was not of that order.

" I don't like the idea," she said.

Mr. Pratt miserably clasped and unclasped his hands. He felt that one day he would be crushed between his parishioners' hatred of change and his fellow-priests' insistence on it—rumour said that the Squire's elder son, Father Lawrence, was coming home before long, and the poor little rector quailed to think of what he would say of the harmonium if it was still in its place.

" I—er—Miss Godden—I feel our reputation is at stake. Visitors, you know, come to our little church, and are surprised to find us so far behind the times in our music. At Pedlinge we've only got a piano, but I'm not worrying about that now. . . . Perhaps the harmonium might be patched up enough for Pedlinge, where our services are not as yet Fully Choral . . . . it all depends on how much money we collect."

" How much do you want ? "

" Well, I'm told that a cheap, good make would be thirty pounds. We want it to last us well, you see, as I don't suppose we shall ever have a proper organ."

He handed her a little book in which he had entered the names of subscribers.

" People have been very generous already, and I'm sure if your name is on the list they will give better still."

The generosity of the neighbourhood amounted to five shillings from Prickett of Great Ansdore, and half-crowns from Vine, Furnese, Vennal, and a few others. As Joanna studied it she became possessed of two emotions —one was a feeling that since others, including Great Ansdore, had given, she could not in proper pride hold back, the other was a queer savage pity for Mr. Pratt and his poor little collection—scarcely a pound as the result of all his begging, and yet he had called it generous . . . .

She immediately changed her mind about the scheme, and going over to a side table where an ink-pot and pen reposed on a woolly mat, she prepared to enter her name in the little book.

" I'll give him ten shillings," she said to herself—" I'll
have given the most."

Mr. Pratt watched her. He found something stimu-
lating in the sight of her broad back and shoulders, her
large presence had invigorated him—somehow he felt
self-confident, as he had not felt for years, and he began
to talk, first about the harmonium, and then about himself—he was a widower with three pale little children,
whom he dragged up somehow on an income of two
hundred a year.

Joanna was not listening. She was thinking to herself—" My cheque-book is in the drawer. If I wrote
him a cheque, how grand it would look."

Finally she opened the drawer and took the cheques
out. After all, she could afford to be generous—she
had nearly a hundred pounds in Lewes Old Bank,
put aside without any scraping for future " improvements." How much could she spare ? A guinea—that
would look handsome, among all the miserable half-
crowns. . . .

Mr. Pratt had seen the cheque-book, and a stutter
came into his speech—

" So good of you, Miss Godden . . . to help me . . .
encouraging, you know . . . been to so many places,
a tiring afternoon . . . feel rewarded."

She suddenly felt her throat grow tight ; the queer
compassion had come back. She saw him trotting for-
lornly round from farm to farm, begging small sums from
people much better off than himself, receiving denials
or grudging gifts . . . . his boots were all over dust,
she had noticed them on her carpet. Her face flushed,
as she suddenly dashed her pen into the ink, wrote out
the cheque in her careful, half-educated hand, and gave
it to him.

" There—that'll save you tramping any further."

She had written the cheque for the whole amount.

Mr. Pratt could not speak. He opened and shut his
mouth like a fish. Then suddenly he began to gabble,
he poured out thanks and assurances and deprecations
in a stammering torrent. His gratitude overwhelmed
Joanna, disgusted her. She lost her feeling of warmth
and compassion—after all, what should she pity him for

now that he had got what he wanted, and much more
easily than he deserved?

" That's all right, Mr. Pratt. I'm sorry I can't wait
any longer now. I'm making jam."

She forgot his dusty boots and weary legs that had
scarcely had time to rest, she forgot that she had meant
to offer him a cup of tea.

" Good afternoon," she said, as he rose, with apologies
for keeping her.

She went with him to the door, snatched his hat off
the peg and gave it to him, then crashed the door behind
him, her cheeks burning with a queer kind of shame.

§ 3

For the next few days Joanna avoided Mr. Pratt;
she could not tell why her munificence should make her
dislike him, but it did. One day as she was walking
through Pedlinge she saw him standing in the middle of
the road, talking to a young man whom on approach
she recognized as Martin Trevor, the Squire's second son.
She could not get out of his way, as the Pedlinge dyke
was on one side of the road and on the other were some
cottages. To turn back would be undignified, so she
decided to pass them with a distant and lordly bow.

Unfortunately for this, she could not resist the temptation to glance at Martin Trevor—she had not seen him
for some time, and it was surprising to meet him in the
middle of the week, as he generally came home only for
week-ends. That glance was her undoing—a certain
cordiality must have crept into it, inspired by his broad
shoulders and handsome, swarthy face, for Mr. Pratt was
immediately encouraged, and pounced. He broke away
from Trevor to Joanna's side.

" Oh, Miss Godden . . . . so glad to meet you.
I—I never thanked you properly last week for your generosity — your munificence. Thought of writing, but
somehow felt that — felt that inadequate . . . . Mr.
Trevor, I've told you about Miss Godden . . . our
harmonium . . . ."

He had actually seized Joanna's hand. She pulled

it away. What a wretched undersized little chap he was. She could have borne his gratitude if only he had been a real man, tall and dark and straight like the young fellow who was coming up to her.

" Please don't, Mr. Pratt. I wish you wouldn't make all this tedious fuss."

She turned towards Martin Trevor with a greeting in her eyes. But to her surprise she saw that he had fallen back. The Rector had fallen back too, and the two men stood together, as when she had first come up to them.

Joanna realized that she had missed the chance of an introduction. Well, it didn't matter. She really couldn't endure Mr. Pratt and his ghastly gratitude. She put her stiffest bow into practice and walked on.

For the rest of the day she tried to account for young Trevor's mid-week appearance. Her curiosity was soon satisfied, though she was at a disadvantage in having no male to bring her news from the Woolpack. However, she made good use of other people's males, and by the same evening was possessed of the whole story. Martin Trevor had been ill in London with pleurisy, and the doctor said his lungs were in danger and that he must give up office work and lead an open-air life. He was going to live with his father for a time, and help him farm North Farthing House—they were taking in a bit more land there, and buying sheep.

§ 4

That October the Farmers' Club Dinner was held as usual at the Woolpack. There had been some controversy about asking Joanna—there was controversy every year, but this year the difference lay in the issue, for the ayes had it.

The reasons for this change were indefinite—on the whole, no doubt, it was because people liked her better. They had grown used to her at Ansdore, where at first her mastership had shocked them ; the scandal and contempt aroused by the Socknersh episode were definitely dead, and men took off their hats to the strenuousness

with which she had pulled the farm together, and faced
a crisis that would have meant disaster to many of her
neighbours. Ansdore was one of the largest farms of
the district, and it was absurd that it should never be
represented at the Woolpack table merely on the ground
that its master was a woman.

Of course many women wondered how Joanna could
face such a company of males, and suggestions were made
for admitting farmers' wives on this occasion. But
Joanna was not afraid, and when approached as to whether
she would like other women invited, or to bring a woman
friend, she declared that she would be quite satisfied with
the inevitable presence of the landlord's wife.

She realized that she would be far more imposing as
the only woman guest, and made great preparations for
a proper display. Among these was included the buying
of a new gown at Folkestone. She thought that Folkestone, being a port for the channel steamers, would be
more likely to have the latest French fashions than the
nearer towns of Bulverhythe and Marlingate. My!
But she would make the Farmers' Club sit up.

The dressmaker at Folkestone tried to persuade her
not to have her sleeves lengthened or an extra fold of
lace arranged along the top of her bodice.

"Madam has such a lovely neck and arms—it's a
pity to cover them up—and it spoils the character of the
gown. Besides, madam, this gown is not at all extreme
—demi-toilet is what it really is."

"I tell you it won't do—I'm going to dine alone with
several gentlemen, and it wouldn't be seemly to show
such a lot of myself."

It ended, to the dressmaker's despair, in her draping
her shoulders in a lace scarf and wearing kid gloves to
her elbow ; but though these pruderies might have spoilt
her appearance at Dungemarsh Court, there was no doubt
as to its effectiveness at the Woolpack. The whole room
held its breath as she sailed in, with a rustle of amber
silk skirts. Her hair was piled high against a tortoise-
shell comb, making her statelier still.

Furnese of Misleham, who was chairman that year,
came gaping to greet her. The others stared and stood
still. Most of them were shocked, in spite of the scarf

and the long gloves, but then it was just like Joanna Godden to swing bravely through an occasion into which most women would have crept. She saw that she had made a sensation, which she had expected and desired, and her physical modesty being appeased, she had no objection to the men's following eyes. She saw that Sir Harry Trevor was in the room, with his son Martin.

It was the first time that the Squire had been to the Farmers' Club Dinner. Up till then no one had taken him seriously as a farmer. For a year or two after his arrival in the neighbourhood he had managed the North Farthing estate through a bailiff, and on the latter's turning out unsatisfactory, had dismissed him, and at the same time let off a good part of the land, keeping only a few acres for cow-grazing round the house. Now, on his son's coming home and requiring an outdoor life, he had given a quarter's notice to the butcher-grazier to whom he had sub-let his innings, had bought fifty head of sheep, and joined the Farmers' Club—which he knew would be a practical step to his advantage, as it brought certain privileges in the way of marketing and hiring. Joanna was glad to see him at the Woolpack, because she knew that there was now a chance of the introduction she had unfortunately missed in Pedlinge village a few weeks ago. She had a slight market-day acquaintance with the Old Squire—as the neighbourhood invariably called him, to his intense annoyance—and now she greeted him with her broad smile.

" Good evening, Sir Harry."

" Good evening, Miss Godden. I'm pleased to see you here. You're looking very well."

His bold tricky eyes swept over her, and somehow she felt more gratified than by all the bulging glances of the other men.

" I'm pleased to see you, too, Sir Harry. I hear you've joined the Club."

" Surelye—as a real farmer ought to say; and so has my son Martin—he's going to do most of the work. Martin, you've never met Miss Godden. Let me introduce you."

Joanna's welcoming grin broke itself on the young man's stiff bow. There was a moment's silence.

" He doesn't look as if a London doctor had threatened

him with consumption," said the Squire banteringly.
" Sometimes I really don't think I believe it—I think he's
only come down here so as he can look after me."

Martin made some conventional remark. He was a
tall, broadly built young man, with a dark healthy skin
and that generally robust air which sometimes accompanies
extreme delicacy in men.

" The doctor says he's been overworking," continued
his father, " and that he ought to try a year's outdoor
life and sea air. If you ask me, I should say he's overdone
a good many things besides work—" he threw the boy
a defiant, malicious glance, rather like a child who gets
a thrust into an elder—" but Walland Marsh is as good
a cure for over-play as for over-work. Not much to
keep him up late hereabouts, is there, Miss Godden?"

" I reckon it'll be twelve o'clock before any of us
see our pillows to-night," said Joanna.

" Tut ! Tut ! What terrible ways we're getting into,
just when I'm proposing the place as a rest-cure. How
do you feel, Miss Godden, being the only woman guest ? "

" I like it."

" Bet you do—so do we."

Joanna laughed and bridled. She felt proud of her
position—she pictured every farmer's wife on the Marsh
lying awake that night so that she could ask her husband
directly he came upstairs how Joanna Godden had looked,
what she had said, and what she had worn.

§ 5

At dinner she sat on the Chairman's right. On her
other side, owing to some accident of push and shuffle,
sat young Martin Trevor. At first she had not thought
his place accidental, in spite of his rather stiff manner
before they sat down, but after a while she realized with
a pang of vexation that he was not particularly pleased
to find himself next her. He replied without interest
to her remarks and then entered into conversation with
his right-hand neighbour. Joanna was annoyed—she could
not put down his constraint to shyness, for he did not
at all strike her as a shy young man. Nor was he being

ungracious to Mr. Turner of Beckett's House, though
the latter could not talk of turnips half so entertainingly
as Joanna would have done. He obviously did not want
to speak to her. Why? Because of what had happened
in Pedlinge all that time ago? She remembered how he
had drawn back . . . he had not liked the way she had
spoken to Mr. Pratt. She had not liked it herself by the
time she got to the road's turn. But to think of him
nursing his feelings all this time . . . and something
she had said to Mr. Pratt . . . considering that she had
bought them all a new harmonium . . . . the lazy,
stingy louts with their half-crowns . . . .

She had lost her serenity, her sense of triumph—she
felt vaguely angry with the whole company, and snapped
at Arthur Alce when he spoke to her across the table.
He had asked after Ellen, knowing she had been to Folkestone.

" Ellen's fine—and learning such good manners as
it seems a shame to bring her into these parts at Christmas
for her to lose 'em."

" On the other hand, Miss Godden, she might impart
them to us," said the Squire from a little farther down.

" She's learning how to dance and make curtsies right
down to the floor," said Joanna.

" Then she's fit to see the Queen. You really mustn't
keep her away from us at Christmas—on the contrary, we
ought to make some opportunities for watching her dance ;
she must be as pretty as a sprite."

" That she is," agreed Joanna, warming and mollified,
" and I've bought her a new gown that pulls out like an
accordion, so as she can wave her skirts about when she
dances."

" Well, the drawing-room at North Farthing would
make an excellent ball-room . . . . we must see about
that—eh, Martin ? "

" It'll want a new floor laid down—there's rot under
the carpet," was his son's disheartening reply. But
Joanna had lost the smarting of her own wound in the glow
of her pride for Ellen, and she ate the rest of her dinner
in good-humoured contempt of Martin Trevor.

When the time for the speeches came her health was
proposed by the Chairman.

" Gentlemen," he said, " let us drink to—the Lady."

The chivalry of the committee had prompted them to offer her Southland to respond to this toast. But Joanna had doubts of his powers as an orator, whereas she had none of her own. She stood up, a glow of amber brightness above all the black coats, and spoke of her gratification, of her work at Ansdore and hopes for south-country farming. Her speech, as might have been expected, was highly dogmatic. She devoted her last words to the Marsh as a grain-bearing district—on one or two farms, where pasture had been broken, the yield in wheat had been found excellent. Since that was so, why had so few farms hitherto shown enterprise in this direction? There was no denying that arable paid better than pasture, and the only excuse for neglecting it was poverty of soil. It was obvious that no such poverty existed here—on the contrary, the soil was rich, and yet no crops were grown in it except roots and here and there a few acres of beans or lucerne. It was the old idea, she supposed, about breaking up grass. It was time that old idea was bust—she herself would lead the way at Ansdore next spring.

As she was the guest of the evening, they heard her with respect, which did not, however, survive her departure at the introduction of pipes and port.

" Out on the rampage again, is she ? " said Southland to his neighbour.

" Well, if she busts that ' old idea ' same as she bust the other ' old idea ' about crossing Kent sheep, all I can say is that it's Ansdore she'll bust next."

" Whosumdever breaks pasture shall himself be broke," said Vine oracularly.

" Surelye—surelye," assented the table.

" She's got pluck all the same," said Sir Harry.

But he was only an amateur.

" I don't hold for a woman to have pluck," said Vennal of Beggar's Bush, " what do you say, Mr. Alce ? "

" I say nothing, Mr. Vennal."

" Pluck makes a woman think she can do without a man," continued Vennal, " when everyone knows, and it's in Scripture, that she can't. Now Joanna Godden should ought to have married drackly minute Thomas

Godden died and left her Ansdore, instead of which she's
gone on plunging like a heifer till she must be past eight
and twenty as I calculate——"

"Now, now, Mr. Vennal, we mustn't start anything
personal of our lady guest," broke in Furnese from the
Chair, "we may take up her ideas or take 'em down,
but while she's the guest of this here Farmers' Club,
which is till eleven-thirty precise, we mustn't start arguing
about her age or matrimonious intentions. Anyways,
I take it, that's a job for our wives."

"Hear, hear," and Joanna passed out of the conversation, for who was going to waste time either taking
up or taking down a silly, tedious, foreign, unsensible
notion like ploughing grass? . . . .

Indeed, it may be said that her glory had gone up
in smoke—the smoke of twenty pipes.

She had been obliged to leave the table just when it
was becoming most characteristic and convivial, and to
retire forlorn and chilly in her silken gown to the Woolpack
parlour, where she and the landlady drank innumerable
cups of tea. It was an unwelcome reminder of the fact
that she was a woman, and that no matter how she might
shine and impress the company for an hour, she did not
really belong to it. She was a guest, not a member, of
the Farmers' Club, and though a guest has more honour,
he has less fellowship and fun. It was for fellowship
and fun that she hungrily longed as she sat under the
green lamp-shade of the Woolpack's parlour, and dis-
coursed on servants and the price of turkeys with Mrs.
Jupp, who was rather constrained and absent-minded
owing to her simultaneous efforts to price Miss Godden's
gown. Now and then a dull roar of laughter came to
her from the Club room. What were they talking about,
Joanna wondered. Had there been much debate over
her remarks on breaking pasture? . . .

§6

On the whole, the Farmers' Club Dinner left behind
it a rankling trail—for one thing, it was not followed
as she had hoped and half expected by an invitation

to join the Farmers' Club. No, they would never have
a woman privileged among them—she realized that,
in spite of her success, certain doors would always be
shut on her. The men would far rather open those doors
ceremonially now and then than allow her to go freely
in and out. After all, perhaps they were right—hadn't
she got her own rooms that they were shut out of ? . . . .
Women were always different from men, even if they did
the same things . . . . she had heard people talk of
"woman's sphere." What did that mean ? A husband
and children, of course—any fool could tell you that.
When you had a husband and children you didn't go round
knocking at the men's doors, but shut yourself up snugly
inside your own . . . you were warm and cosy, and the
firelight played on the ceiling . . . But if you were
alone inside your room—with no husband or child to keep
you company . . . . then it was terrible, worse than
being outside . . . . and no wonder you went round
to the men's doors, and knocked on them and begged
them to give you a little company, or something to do
to help you to forget your empty room . . . .

"Well, I could marry Arthur Alce any day I liked," she
thought to herself.

But somehow that did not seem any solution to the
problem.

She thought of one or two other men who had approached her, but had been scared off before they had
reached any definite position of courtship. They were
no good either—young Cobb of Slinches had married
six months ago, and Jack Abbot of Stock Bridge belonged
to the Christian Believers, who kept Sunday on Saturday,
and in other ways fathered confusion. Besides, she
didn't want to marry just anyone who would have her
—some dull yeoman who would take her away from Ansdore, or else come with all his stupid, antiquated, man-
made notions to sit for ever on her enterprising acres. She
wanted her marriage to be some big, neighbour-startling
adventure—she wanted either to marry someone above
herself in birth and station, or else very much below. She
had touched the fringe of the latter experience and found
it disappointing, so she felt that she would now prefer
the other—she would like to marry some man of the

upper classes, a lawyer or a parson or a squire. The two first were represented in her mind by Mr. Huxtable and Mr. Pratt, and she did not linger over them, but the image she had put up for the third was Martin Trevor—dark, tall, well-born, comely and strong of frame, and yet with that hidden delicacy, that weakness which Joanna must have in a man if she was to love him. . . .

She had been a fool about Martin Trevor—she had managed to put him against her at the start. Of course it was silly of him to mind what she said to Mr. Pratt, but that didn't alter the fact that she had been stupid herself, that she had failed to make a good impression just when she most wanted to do so. Martin Trevor was the sort of man she felt she could " take to," for in addition to his looks he had the quality she prized in males—the quality of inexperience; he was not likely to meddle with her ways, since he was only a beginner and would probably be glad of her superior knowledge and judgment. He would give her what she wanted— his good name and his good looks and her neighbours' envious confusion—and she would give him what he wanted, her prosperity and her experience. North Farthing House was poorer than Ansdore in spite of late dinners and drawing-rooms—the Trevors could look down on her from the point of view of birth and breeding but not from any advantage more concrete.

As for herself, for her own warm, vigorous, vital person—with that curious simplicity which was part of her unawakened state, it never occurred to her to throw herself into the balance when Ansdore was already making North Farthing kick the beam. She thought of taking a husband as she thought of taking a farm hand—as a matter of bargaining, of offering substantial benefits in exchange for substantial services. If in a secondary way she was moved by romantic considerations, that was also true of her engagement of her male servants. Just as she saw her future husband in his possibilities as a farm-hand, in his relations to Ansdore, so she could not help seeing every farm-hand in his possibilities as a husband, in his relations to herself.

§ 7

Martin Trevor would have been surprised had he known himself the object of so much attention. His attitude towards Joanna was one of indifference based on dislike—her behaviour towards Mr. Pratt had disgusted him at the start, but his antipathy was not all built on that foundation. During the weeks he had been at home, he had heard a good deal about her—indeed he had found her rather a dominant personality on the Marsh—and what he had heard had not helped turn him from his first predisposition against her.

As a young boy he had shared his brother's veneration of the Madonna, and though, when he grew up, his natural romanticism had not led him his brother's way, the boyish ideal had remained, and unconsciously all his later attitude towards women was tinged with it. Joanna was certainly not the Madonna type, and all Martin's soul revolted from her broad, bustling ways—everywhere he went he heard stories of her busyness and her bluff, of " what she had said to old Southland," or " the sass she had given Vine." She seemed to him to be an arrant, pushing baggage, running after notoriety and display. Her rudeness to Mr. Pratt was only part of the general parcel. He looked upon her as sexless, too, and he hated women to be sexless —his Madonna was not after Memling but after Raphael. Though he heard constant gossip about her farming activities and her dealings at market, he heard none about her passions, the likelier subject. All he knew was that she had been expected for years to marry Arthur Alce, but had not done so, and that she had also been expected at one time to marry her looker, but had not done so. The root of such romances must be poor indeed if this was all the flower that gossip could give them.

Altogether he was prejudiced against Joanna Godden, and the prejudice did not go deep enough to beget interest. He was not interested in her, and did not expect her to be interested in him ; therefore it was with great surprise, not to say consternation, that one morning at New Romney Market he saw her bearing down upon him with the light of battle in her eye.

" Good morning, Mr. Trevor."

" Good morning, Miss Godden."

" Fine weather."

" Fine weather."

He would have passed on, but she barred the way, rather an imposing figure in her bottle-green driving coat, with a fur toque pressed down over the flying chestnut of her hair. Her cheeks were not so much coloured as stained deep with the sun and wind of Walland Marsh, and though it was November, a mass of little freckles smudged and scattered over her sk; . It had not occurred to him before that she was even a good-looking creature.

" I'm thinking, Mr. Trevor," she said deliberately, " that you and me aren't liking each other as much as we should ought."

" Really, Miss Godden. I don't see why you need say that."

" Well, we don't like each other, do we ? Leastways, you don't like me. Now "—lifting a large, well-shaped hand—" you needn't gainsay me, for I know what you think. You think I was middling rude to Mr. Pratt in Pedlinge street that day I first met you—and so I think myself, and I'm sorry, and Mr. Pratt knows it. He came around two weeks back to ask about Milly Pump, my chicken-gal, getting confirmed, and I told him I liked him and his ways so much that he could confirm the lot, gals and men—even old Stuppeny who says he's been done already, but I say it don't matter, since he's so old that it's sure to have worn off by this time."

Martin stared at her with his mouth open.

" So I say as I've done proper by Mr. Pratt," she continued, her voice rising to a husky flurry, " for I'll have to give 'em all a day off to get confirmed in, and that'll be a tedious affair for me. However, I don't grudge it, if it'll make things up between us—between you and me, I'm meaning."

" But, I—I—that is, you've made a mistake—your behaviour to Mr. Pratt is no concern of mine."

He was getting terribly embarrassed—this dreadful woman, what would she say next ? Unconsciously yielding to a nervous habit, he took off his cap and violently rubbed up his hair the wrong way. The action somehow appealed to Joanna.

" But it is your concern, I reckon—you've shown me plain that it is. I could see you were offended at the Farmers' Dinner."

A qualm of compunction smote Martin.

" You're showing me that *I*'ve been jolly rude."

" Well, I won't say you haven't," said Joanna affably. " Still you've had reason. I reckon no one ud like me better for behaving rude to Mr. Pratt . . . ."

" Oh, damn Mr. Pratt ! " cried Martin, completely losing his head—" I tell you I don't care tuppence what you or anyone says or does to him."

" Then you should ought to care, Mr. Trevor," said Joanna staidly, " not that I've any right to tell you, seeing how I've behaved. But at least I gave him a harmonium first—it's only that I couldn't abide the fuss he made of his thanks. I like doing things for folks, but I can't stand their making fools of themselves and me over it."

Trevor had become miserably conscious that they were standing in the middle of the road, that Joanna was not inconspicuous, and if she had been, her voice would have made up for it. He could see people—gaitered farmers, clay-booted farm-hands—staring at them from the pavement. He suddenly felt himself—not without justification—the chief spectacle of Romney market-day.

" Please don't think about it any more, Miss Godden," he said hurriedly. " I certainly should never presume to question anything you ever said or did to Mr. Pratt or anybody else. And, if you'll excuse me, I must go on—I'm a farmer now, you know," with a ghastly attempt at a smile, " and I've plenty of business in the market."

" Reckon you have," said Joanna, her voice suddenly falling flat.

He snatched off his cap and left her standing in the middle of the street.

§ 8

He did not let himself think of her for an hour or more —the episode struck him as grotesque and he preferred

not to dwell on it.   But after he had done his business
of buying a farm horse, with the help of Mr. Southland
who was befriending his inexperience, he found himself
laughing quietly, and he suddenly knew that he was laughing over the interview with Joanna.   And directly he
had laughed, he was smitten with a sense of pathos—
her bustle and self-confidence which hitherto had roused
his dislike, now showed as something rather pathetic,
a mere trapping of feminine weakness which would deceive
no one who saw them at close quarters.   Under her loud
voice, her almost barbaric appearance, her queerly tru-
culent manner, was a naïve mixture of child and woman
—soft, simple, eager to please.   He knew of no other
woman who would have given herself away quite so directly
and naturally as she had . . . and his manhood was
flattered.   He was far from suspecting the practical nature
of her intentions, but he could see that she liked him,
and wanted to stand in his favour.   She was not sexless,
after all.

This realization softened and predisposed him ; he
felt a little contrite, too—he remembered how her voice
had suddenly dragged and fallen flat at his abrupt fare-
well . . . . She was disappointed in his reception of
her offers of peace—she had been incapable of appre-
ciating the attitude his sophistication was bound to take
up in the face of such an outburst.   She had proved
herself, too, a generous soul—frankly owning herself
in the wrong and trying by every means to make atone-
ment . . . Few women would have been at once so
frank and so practical in their repentance.   That he suspected the repentance was largely for his sake did not
diminish his respect of it.   When he met Joanna Godden
again, he would be nice to her.

The opportunity was given him sooner than he expected.
Walking up the High Street in quest of some quiet place
for luncheon—every shop and inn seemed full of thick
smells of pipes and beer and thick noises of agricultural
and political discussion conducted with the mouth full
—he saw Miss Godden's trap waiting for her outside
the New Inn.   He recognized her equipage, not so much
from its make or from the fat cob in the shafts, as from
the figure of old Stuppeny dozing at Smiler's head.   Old

Stuppeny went everywhere with Miss Godden, being now quite unfit for work on the farm. His appearance was peculiar, for he seemed, like New Romney church tower, to be built in stages. He wore, as a farm-labourer of the older sort, a semi-clerical hat, which with his long white beard gave him down to the middle of his chest a resemblance to that type still haunting the chapels of marsh villages and known as Aged Evangelist—from his chest to his knees, he was mulberry coat and brass buttons, Miss Joanna Godden's coachman, though as the vapours of the marsh had shaped him into a shepherd's crook, his uniform lost some of its effect. Downwards from the bottom of his coat he was just a farm-labourer, with feet of clay and corduroy trousers tied with string.

His presence showed that Miss Godden was inside the New Inn, eating her dinner, probably finishing it, or he would not have brought the trap round. It was just like her, thought Martin, with a tolerant twist to his smile, to go to the most public and crowded place in Romney for her meal, instead of shrinking into the decent quiet of some shop. But Joanna Godden had done more for herself in that interview than she had thought, for though she still repelled she was no longer uninteresting. Martin gave up searching for that quiet meal, and walked into the New Inn.

He found Joanna sitting at a table by herself, finishing a cup of tea. The big table was edged on both sides with farmers, graziers and butchers, while the small tables were also occupied, so there was not much need for his apologies as he sat down opposite her. Her face kindled at once—

" I'm sorry I'm so near finished."

She was a grudgeless soul, and Martin almost liked her.

" Have you done much business to-day ? "

" Not much. I'm going home as soon as I've had my dinner. Are you stopping long ? "

" Till I've done a bit of shopping "—he found himself slipping into the homeliness of her tongue—" I want a good spade and some harness."

" I'll tell you a good shop for harness . . ." Joanna loved enlightening ignorance and guiding inexperience, and while Martin's chop and potatoes were being brought she held forth on different makes of harness and called spades spades untiringly. He listened without rancour, for he was beginning to like her very much. His liking was largely physical—he wouldn't have believed a month ago that he should ever find Joanna Godden attractive, but to-day the melting of his prejudice seemed to come chiefly from her warm beauty, from the rich colouring of her face and the flying sunniness of her hair, from her wide mouth with its wide smile, from the broad, strong set of her shoulders, and the sturdy tenderness of her breast.

She saw that he had changed. His manner was different, more cordial and simple—the difference between his coldness and his warmth was greater than in many, for like most romantics he had found himself compelled at an early age to put on armour, and the armour was stiff and disguising in proportion to the lightness and grace of the body within. Not that he and Joanna talked of light and graceful things . . . . they talked, after spades and harness, of horses and sheep, and of her ideas on breaking up grass, which was to be a practical scheme at Ansdore that spring in spite of the neighbours, of the progress of the new light railway from Lydd to Appledore, of the advantages and disadvantages of growing lucerne. But the barrier was down between them, and he knew that they were free, if they chose, to go on from horses and sheep and railways and crops to more daring, intimate things, and because of that same freedom they stuck to the homely topics, like people who are free to leave the fireside but wait till the sun is warmer on the grass.

He had begun his apple-tart before she rose.

"Well, I must be getting back now. Good-bye, Mr. Trevor. If you should ever happen to pass Ansdore, drop in and I'll give you a cup of tea."

He was well aware that the whole room had heard this valediction. He saw some of the men smiling at each other, but he was not annoyed. He rose and went with her to the door, where she hugged herself into her big driving coat. Something about her made him feel big enough to ignore the small gossip of the Marsh.

§ 9

He liked her now—he told himself that she was good common stuff. She was like some sterling homespun piece, strong and sweet-smelling—she was like a plot of the marsh earth, soft and rich and alive. He had forgotten her barbaric tendency, the eccentricity of looks and conduct which had at first repelled him—that aspect had melted in the unsuspected warmth and softness he had found in her. He had been mistaken as to her sexlessness—she was alive all through. She was still far removed from his type, but her fundamental simplicity had brought her nearer to it, and in time his good will would bring her the rest of the way. Anyhow, he would look forward to meeting her again—perhaps he would call at Ansdore, as she had proposed.

Joanna was not blind to her triumph, and it carried her beyond her actual attainment into the fulfilment of her hopes. She saw Martin Trevor already as her suitor —respectful, interested, receptive of her wisdom in the matter of spades. She rejoiced in her courage in having taken the first step—she would not have much further to go now. Now that she had overcome his initial dislike, the advantages of the alliance must be obvious to him. She looked into the future, and between the present moment and the consummated union of North Farthing and Ansdore, she saw thrilling, half-dim, personal adventures for Martin and Joanna . . . . the touch of his hands would be quite different from the touch of Arthur Alce's . . . . and his lips—she had never wanted a man's lips before, except perhaps Socknersh's for one wild, misbegotten minute . . . . she held in her heart the picture of Martin's well-cut, sensitive mouth, so unlike the usual mouths of Brodnyx and Pedlinge, which were either coarse-lipped or no-lipped . . . . Martin's mouth was wonderful—it would be like fire on hers . . . .

Thus Joanna rummaged in her small stock of experience, and of the fragments built a dream. Her plans were not now all concrete—they glowed a little, though dimly, for her memory held no great store, and her imagination was the imagination of Walland Marsh, as a barndoor fowl to the birds that fly. She might have dreamed more if her mind had not been occupied with the practical matter of welcoming Ellen home for her Christmas holidays.

Ellen, who arrived on Thomas-day, already seemed in some strange way to have grown apart from the life of Ansdore. As Joanna eagerly kissed her on the platform at Rye, there seemed something alien in her soft cool cheek, in the smoothness of her hair under the dark boater hat with its deviced hat-band.

" Hullo, Joanna," she said.

" Hullo, dearie. I've just about been pining to get you back. How are you?—how's your dancing?"— This as she bundled her up beside her in the trap, while the porter helped old Stuppeny with her trunk.

" I can dance the waltz and the polka."

" That's fine—I've promised the folks around here that you shall show 'em what you can do."

She gave Ellen another warm, proud hug, and this time the child's coolness melted a little. She rubbed her immaculate cheek against her sister's sleeve—

" Good old Jo . . ."

Thus they drove home at peace together.

The peace was shattered many times between that day and Christmas. Ellen had forgotten what it was like to be slapped and what it was like to receive big smacking kisses at odd encounters in yard or passage—she resented both equally. " You're like an old bear, Jo—an awful old bear." She had picked up at school a new vocabulary, of which the word " awful," used to express every quality of pleasure or pain, was a fair sample. Joanna sometimes could not understand her—sometimes she understood too well.

" I sent you to school to be made a little lady of, and here you come back speaking worse than a National child."

" All the girls talk like that at school."

" Then seemingly it was a waste to send you there, since you could have learned bad manners cheaper at home."

" But the mistresses don't allow it," said Ellen, in hasty fear of being taken away, " you get a bad mark if you say ' damn.' "

" I should just about think you did, and I'd give you a good spanking too. I never heard such language—no, not even at the Woolpack."

Ellen gave her peculiar, alien smile.

" You're awfully old-fashioned, Jo."

" Old-fashioned, am I, because I don't go against my Catechism and take the Lord's name in vain ? "

" Yes, you do—every time you say ' Lord sakes ' you take the Lord's name in vain, and it's common into the bargain."

Here Joanna lost her temper and boxed Ellen's ears.

" You dare say I'm common ! So that's what you learn at school ?—to come home and call your sister common. Well, if I'm common, you're common too, since we're the same blood."

" I never said you were common," sobbed Ellen— " and you really are a beast, hitting me about. No wonder I like school better than home if that's how you treat me."

Joanna declared with violence if that was how she felt she should never see school again, whereupon Ellen screamed and sobbed herself into a pale, quiet, tragic state—lying back in her chair, her face patchy with crying, her head falling queerly sideways like a broken doll's— till Joanna, scared and contrite, assured her that she had not meant her threat seriously, and that Ellen should stop at school as long as she was a good girl and minded her sister.

This sort of thing had happened every holiday, but there were also brighter aspects, and on the whole Joanna was proud of her little sister and pleased with the results of the step she had taken. Ellen could not only dance and drop beautiful curtsies, but she could play tunes on the piano, and recite poetry. She could ask for things in French at table, could give startling information about the Kings of England and the exports and imports of Jamaica, and above all these accomplishments, she showed a welcome alacrity to display them, so that her sister could always rely on her for credit and glory.

" When Martin Trevor comes I'll make her say her piece."

§ 10

Martin came on Christmas Day. He knew that the feast would lend a special significance to the visit, but he did not care; for in absence he had idealized Joanna into a fit subject for flirtation. He had no longer any wish to meet her on the level footing of friendship—besides, he was already beginning to feel lonely on the Marsh, to long for the glow of some romance to warm the fogs that filled his landscape. In spite of his father's jeers, he was no monk, and generally had some sentimental adventure keeping his soul alive—but he was fastidious and rather bizarre in his likings, and since he had come to North Farthing, no one, either in his own class or out of it, had appealed to him, except Joanna Godden.

She owed part of her attraction to the surviving salt of his dislike. There was still a savour of antagonism in his liking of her. Also his curiosity was still unsatisfied. Was that undercurrent of softness genuine? Was she really simple and tender under her hard flaunting? Was she passionate under her ignorance and *naïveté*? Only experiment could show him, and he meant to investigate, not merely for the barren satisfaction of his curiosity, but for the satisfaction of his manhood which was bound up with a question.

When he arrived, Joanna was still in church—on Christmas Day as on other selected festivals, she always " stayed the Sacrament," and did not come out till nearly one. He went to meet her, and waited for her some ten minutes in the little churchyard which was a vivid green with the Christmas rains. The day was clear and curiously soft for the season, even on the Marsh where the winters are usually mild. The sky was a delicate blue, washed with queer, flat clouds—the whole country of the Marsh seemed faintly luminous, holding the sunshine in its greens and browns. Beside the dyke which flows by Brodnyx village stood a big thorn tree, still bright with haws. It made a vivid red patch in the foreground, the one touch of Christmas in a landscape which otherwise suggested October—especially in the sunshine, which poured in a warm shower on to the altar-tomb where Martin sat.

He grew dreamy with waiting—his thoughts seemed to melt into the softness of the day, to be part of the still air and misty sunshine, just as the triple-barned church with its grotesque tower was part . . . . He could feel the great Marsh stretching round him, the lonely miles of Walland and Dunge and Romney, once the sea's bed, now lately inned for man and his small dwellings, his keepings and his cares, perhaps one day to return to the same deep from which it had come. People said that the bells of Broomhill church—drowned in the great floods which had changed the Rother's mouth—still rang under the sea. If the sea came to Brodnyx, would Brodnyx bells ring on?—And Pedlinge? And Brenzett? And Fairfield? And all the little churches of Thomas à Becket on their mounds?—What a ringing there would be.

He woke out of his daydream at the sound of footsteps—the people were coming out, and glancing up he saw Joanna a few yards off. She looked surprised to see him, but also she made no attempt to hide her pleasure.

" Mr. Trevor ! You here ? "

" I came over to Ansdore to wish you a happy Christmas, and they told me you were still in church."

" Yes—I stopped for Communion—" her mouth fell into a serious, reminiscent line, " you didn't come to the first service, neither ? "

" No, my brother's at home, and he took charge of my father's spiritual welfare—they went off to church at Udimore, and I was too lazy to follow them."

" I'm sorry you didn't come here—they used my harmonium, and it was valiant."

He smiled at her adjective.

" I'll come another day and hear your valiant harmonium. I suppose you think everybody should go to church ? "

" My father went, and I reckon I'll keep on going."

" You always do as your father did ? "

" In most ways."

" But not in all ?—I hear startling tales of new-shaped waggons and other adventures, to say nothing of your breaking up grass next spring."

" Well, if you don't see any difference between breaking
up grass and giving up church . . . ."

" They are both a revolt from habit."

" Now, don't you talk like that—it ain't seemly.
I don't like hearing a man make a mock of good things,
and going to church is a good thing, as I should ought
to know, having just come out of it."

" I'm sorry," said Martin humbly, and for some reason
he felt ashamed. They were walking now along the
Pedlinge road, and the whole Marsh, so broad and simple,
seemed to join in her rebuke of him.

She saw his contrite look, and repented of her sharpness.

" Come along home and have a bit of our Christmas
dinner."

Martin stuttered—he had not expected such an invitation, and it alarmed him.

" We all have dinner together on Christmas Day,"
continued Joanna, " men and gals, old Stuppeny, Mrs.
Tolhurst, everybody—we'd take it kindly if you'd join us.
But—I'm forgetting—you'll be having your own dinner at
home."

" We shan't have ours till the evening."

" Oh—late dinner "—her tone became faintly rever-
ential—" it ud never do if we had that. The old folk,
like Stuppeny and such, ud find their stomachs keep
them awake. We've got two turkeys and a goose and
plum puddings and mince pies, to say nothing of the
oranges and nuts—that ain't the kind of food to go to
bed with."

" I agree," said Martin, smiling.

" Then you'll come and have dinner at Ansdore ? "

They had reached the first crossing of the railway
line, and if he was going back to North Farthing he should
turn here. He could easily make an excuse—no man
really wanted to eat two Christmas dinners—but his
flutter was gone, and he found an attraction in the communal meal to which she was inviting him. He would
like to see the old folk at their feast, the old folk who had
been born on the Marsh, who had grown wrinkled with its
sun and reddened with its wind and bent with their labours
in its damp soil. There would be Joanna too—he would

get a close glimpse of her. It was true that he would be pulling the cord between them a little tighter, but already she was drawing him and he was coming willingly. To-day he had found in her an unsuspected streak of goodness, a sound, sweet core which he had not looked for under his paradox of softness and brutality . . . . It would be worth while committing himself with Joanna Godden.

§ 11

Dinner on Christmas Day was always in the kitchen at Ansdore. When Joanna reached home with Martin, the two tables, set end to end, were laid—with newly ironed cloths and newly polished knives, but with the second-best china only, since many of the guests were clumsy. Joanna wished there had been time to get out the best china, but there was not.

Ellen came flying to meet them, in a white serge frock tied with a red sash.

"Arthur Alce has come, Jo—we're all waiting. Is Mr. Trevor coming too?" and she put her head on one side, looking up at him through her long fringe.

"Yes, duckie. Mr. Trevor's dropped in to taste our turkey and plum pudding—to see if they ain't better than his own to-night."

"Is he going to have another turkey and plum pudding to-night? How greedy!"

"Be quiet, you sassy little cat"—and Joanna's hand swooped, missing Ellen's head only by the sudden duck she gave it.

"Leave me alone, Joanna—you might keep your temper just for Christmas Day."

"I won't have you sass strangers."

"I wasn't sassing."

"You was."

"I wasn't."

Martin felt scared.

"I hope you don't mean me by the stranger," he said, taking up lightness as a weapon, "I think I know you well enough to be sassed—not that I call that sassing."

"Well, it's good of you not to mind," said Joanna,

" personally I've great ideas of manners, and Ellen's brought back some queer ones from her school, though others she's learned are beautiful. Fancy, she never sat down to dinner without a serviette."

" Never," said Ellen emphatically.

Martin appeared suitably impressed. He thought Ellen a pretty little thing, strangely exotic beside her sister.

Dinner was ready in the kitchen, and they all went in, Joanna having taken off her coat and hat and smoothed her hair. Before they sat down there were introductions to Arthur Alce and to Luck and Broadhurst and Stuppeny and the other farm people. The relation between employer and employed was at once more patriarchal and less sharply defined at Ansdore than it was at North Farthing— Martin tried to picture his father sitting down to dinner with the carter and the looker and the housemaid . . . . it was beyond imagination, yet Joanna did it quite naturally. Of course there was a smaller gulf between her and her people—the social grades were inclined to fuse on the Marsh, and the farmer was only just better than his looker —but on the other hand, she seemed to have far more authority . . . .

" Now, hold your tongues while I say grace," she cried.

Joanna carved the turkeys, refusing to deputise either to Martin or to Alce. At the same time she led a general kind of conversation. The Christmas feast was to be communal in spirit as well as in fact—there were to be no formalities above the salt or mutterings below it. The new harmonium provided a good topic, for everyone had heard it, except Mrs. Tolhurst who had stayed to keep watch over Ansdore, cheering herself with the prospect of carols in the evening.

" It sounded best in the psalms," said Wilson, Joanna's looker since Socknersh's day—" oh, the lovely grunts it made when it said—' Thou art my Son, this day have I begotten thee ! ' "

" So it did," said Broadhurst, " but I liked it best in the Herald Angels."

" I liked it all through," said Milly Pump, the chicken-girl. " And I thought Mr. Elphick middling clever to

make it sound as if it wur playing two different tunes at
the same time."

"Was that how it sounded?" asked Mrs. Tolhurst
wistfully, "maybe they'll have it for the carols to-night."

"Surelye," said old Stuppeny, "you'd never have
carols wudout a harmonister. I'd lik myself to go and
hear it, but doubt if I ull git so far wud so much good
victual inside me."

"No, you won't—not half so far," said Joanna briskly,
"you stop at home and keep quiet after this, or you'll
be having bad dreams to-night."

"I never do but have one kind o' dream," said old
Stuppeny, "I dream as I'm setting by the fire and a young
gal brings me a cup of cocoa. 'Tis but an old dream, but
reckon the Lord God sends the old dreams to the old folk
—all them new dreams that are about on the Marsh,
they goes to the young uns."

"Well, you've no call to complain of your dreams,
Stuppeny," said Wilson, "'tisn't everyone who has the
luck to dream regular of a pretty young gal. Leastways,
I guess she's pretty, though you äun't said it."

"I döan't take much count on her looks—'tis the cocoa
I'm after, though it äun't often as the Lord God lets
the dream stay till I've drunk my cup. Sometimes 'tis
my daughter Nannie wot brings it, but most times 'tis
just some unacquainted female."

"Oh, you sorry old dog," said Wilson, and the table
laughed deep-throatedly, or giggled, according to sex.
Old Stuppeny looked pleased. His dream, for some
reason unknown to himself, never failed to raise a laugh,
and generally produced a cup of cocoa sooner or later
from one of the girls.

Martin did not join in the discussion—he felt that
his presence slightly damped the company, and for him
to talk might spoil their chances of forgetting him. He
watched Miss Godden as she ate and laughed and kept
the conversation rolling—he also watched Arthur Alce,
trying to use this man's devotion as a clue to what was
left of Joanna's mystery. Alce struck him as a dull
fellow, and he put down his faithfulness to the fact that
having once fallen into love as into a rut he had lain
there ever since like a sheep on its back. He could see

that Alce did not altogether approve of his own choice—
her vigour and flame, her quick temper, her free airs—
she was really too big for these people ; and yet she was
so essentially one of them . . . . their roots mingled
in the same soil, the rich, damp, hardy soil of the Marsh.

His attitude towards her was undergoing its second
and final change. Now he knew that he would never
want to flirt with her. He did not want her tentatively
or temporarily. He still wanted her adventurously, but
her adventure was not the adventure of siege and capture
but of peaceful holding. Like the earth, she would give
her best not to the man who galloped over her, but to
the man who chose her for his home and settlement.
Thus he would hold her, or not at all. Very likely after
to-day he would renounce her—he had not yet gone
too far, his eyes were still undazzled, and he could see the
difficulties and limitations in which he was involving
himself by such a choice. He was a gentleman and a
townsman—he trod her country only as a stranger, and
he knew that in spite of the love which the Marsh had
made him give it in the few months of his dwelling, his
thoughts still worked for years ahead, when better health
and circumstances would allow him to go back to the town,
to a quick and crowded life. Could he then swear himself
to the slow blank life of the Three Marshes, where events
move deliberately as a plough ? To the empty landscape,
to the flat miles ? He would have to love her enough
to endure the empty flatness that framed her. He could
never take her away, any more than he could take away
Ansdore or North Farthing. He must make a renunciation for her sake—could he do so ? And after all, she was
common stuff—a farmer's daughter, bred at the National
School. By taking her he would be making just a yokel
of himself . . . . Yet was it worth clinging to his
simulacrum of gentility—boosted up by his father's title
and a few dead rites, such as the late dinner which had
impressed her so much. The only real difference between
the Goddens and the Trevors was that the former knew
their job and the latter didn't.

All this thinking did not make either for much talk
or much appetite, and Joanna was disappointed. She
let fall one or two remarks on farming and outside matters,

thinking that perhaps the conversation was too homely
and intimate for him, but he responded only languidly.

"A penny for your thoughts, Mr. Trevor," said Ellen
pertly.

"You eat your pudding," said Joanna.

It occurred to her that perhaps Martin was disgusted
by the homeliness of the meal—after all, he was gentry,
and it was unusual for gentry to sit down to dinner with
a crowd of farm-hands . . . . No doubt at home he had
wine-glasses, and a servant-girl to hand the dishes. She
made a resolution to ask him again and provide both
these luxuries. To-day she would take him into the parlour
and make Ellen show off her accomplishments, which
would help put a varnish of gentility on the general coarse-
ness of the entertainment. She wished she had asked
Mr. Pratt—she had thought of doing so, but finally decided
against it.

So when the company had done shovelling the Stilton
cheese into their mouths with their knives, she announced
that she and Mr. Trevor would have their cups of tea in
the parlour, and told Milly to go quick and light the
fire.

Ellen was most satisfactorily equal to this part of
the occasion. She recited "Curfew shall not Ring To-
night," and played Haydn's "Gipsy Rondo." Joanna
began to feel complacent once more.

"I made up my mind she should go to a good school,"
she said when her sister had run back to what festivities
lingered in the kitchen, "and really it's wonderful what
they've taught her. She'll grow up to be a lady."

It seemed to Martin that she stressed the last word
rather wistfully, and the next moment she added—

"There's not many of your sort on the Marsh."

"How do you mean—my sort?"

"Gentlefolk."

"Oh, we don't trouble to call ourselves gentlefolk.
My father and I are just plain farmers now."

"But you don't really belong to us—you're the like
of the Savilles at Dungemarsh Court, and the clergy
families."

"Is that where you put us?—We'd find our lives
jolly dull if we shut ourselves up in that set. I can tell

you that I've enjoyed myself far more here to-day than
ever at the Court or the Rectory. Besides, Miss Godden,
your position on Walland Marsh is very much better than
ours. You're a great personage, you know."

"Reckon folks talk about me," said Joanna proudly.
"Maybe you've heard 'em."

He nodded.

"You've heard about me and Arthur Alce?"

"I've heard some gossip."

"Don't you believe it. I'm fond of Arthur, but he
ain't my style—and I could do better for myself . . . ."

She paused—her words seemed to hang in the flickering
warmth of the room. She was waiting for him to speak,
and he felt a little shocked and repelled. She was angling
for him—he had never suspected that.

"I must go," he said, standing up.

"So soon?"

"Yes—tradition sends one home on Christmas Day."

He moved towards the door, and she followed him,
glowing and majestic in the shadows of the firelit room.
Outside, the sky was washed with a strange, fiery green,
in which the new kindled stars hung like lamps.

They stood for a moment on the threshold, the warm,
red house behind them, before them the star-hung width
and emptiness of the Marsh. Martin blocked the sky
for Joanna, as he turned and held out his hand. Then,
on the brink of love, she hesitated. A memory smote
her—of herself standing before another man who blocked
the sky, and in whose eyes sat the small, enslaved image
of herself. Was she just being a fool again?—Ought she
to draw back while she had still the power, before she
became his slave, his little thing, and all her bigness was
drowned in his eyes. She knew that whatever she gave
him now could never be taken back. Here stood the
master of the mistress of Ansdore.

As for Martin, his thoughts were of another kind.

"Good-bye," he said, renouncing her—for her boldness
and her commonness and all that she would mean of
change and of foregoing—"Good-bye, Joanna."

He had not meant to say her name, but it had come,
and with it all the departing adventure of love. She seemed
to fall towards him, to lean suddenly like a tree in a gale

—he smelt a fresh, sweet smell of clean cotton underclothing, of a plain soap, of free unperfumed hair . . . then she was in his arms, and he was kissing her warm, shy mouth, feeling that for this moment he had been born.

§ 12

" Well, where have you been ? " asked Sir Harry, as his son walked in at the hall door soon after six.

" I've been having dinner with Joanna Godden."

" The deuce you have."

" I looked in to see her this morning and she asked me to stay."

" You've stayed long enough—your saintly brother's had to do the milking."

" Where's Dennett ? "

" Gone to the carols with the rest. Confounded nuisance, these primitive religious impulses of an elemental people—always seem to require an outlet at an hour when other people want their meals."

" They'll be back in time for dinner."

" I doubt it, and cook's gone too—and Tom Saville's coming, you know."

" Well, I'd better go and see after the milking."

" Don't worry. I've finished," and a dark round head came round the door, followed by a hunched figure in a cloak, from the folds of which it deprecatingly held out a pint jug.

" What's that ? "

" The results of half an hour's milking. I know I should have got more, but I think the cows found me unsympathetic."

Martin burst out laughing. Ordinarily he would have felt annoyed at the prospect of having to go milking at this hour, but to-night he was expansive and good-humoured towards all beasts and men.

He laughed again—

" I don't know that the cows have any particular fancy for me, but I'll go and see what I can do."

" I'm sorry not to have succeeded better," said his brother.

The elder Trevor was only two years older than Martin, but his looks gave him more. His features were blunter, more humorous, and his face was already lined, while his hands looked work-worn. He wore a rough grey cassock buttoned up to his chim.

" You should have preached to them," said Sir Harry, "like St. Francis of something or other. You should have called them your sisters and they'd have showered down their milk in gallons. What's the good of being a monk if you can't work miracles ? "

" I leave that to St. Francis Dennett—I'm quite convinced that cows are milked only supernaturally, and I find it very difficult even to be natural with them. Perhaps Martin will take me in hand and show me that much."

" I don't think I need. I hear the servants coming in."

" Thank God," exclaimed Sir Harry, " now perhaps we shall get our food cooked. Martin's already had dinner, Lawrence—he had it with Joanna Godden. Martin, I don't know that I like your having dinner with Joanna Godden. It marks you—they'll talk about it at the Woolpack for weeks, and it'll probably end in your having to marry her to make her an honest woman."

" That's what I mean to do—to marry her."

The words broke out of him. He had certainly not meant to tell his father anything just yet. Apart from his natural reserve, Sir Harry was not the man he would have chosen for such confidences till they became inevitable. The fact that his father was still emotionally young and had love affairs of his own gave him feelings of repugnance and irritation—he could have endured the conventionally paternal praise or blame, but he was vaguely outraged by the queer basis of equality from which Sir Harry dealt with his experiences. But now the truth was out. What would they say, these two ?—The old rake who refused to turn his back on youth and love, and the triple-vowed religious who had renounced both before he had enjoyed either.

Sir Harry was the first to speak.

" Martin, I am an old man, who will soon be forced to dye his hair, and really my constitution is not equal

to these shocks. What on earth makes you think you want
to marry Joanna Godden ? "

" I love her."

" A most desperate situation. But surely marriage
is rather a drastic remedy."

" Well, don't let's talk about it any longer. I'm
going to dress—Saville will be here in a quarter of an
hour."

" But I must talk about it. Hang it all, I'm your
father—I'm the father of both of you, though you don't
like it a bit and would rather forget it. Martin, you
mustn't marry Joanna Godden however much you love
her. It would be a silly mistake—she's not your equal,
and she's not your type. Have you asked her ? "

" Practically."

" Oh that's all right, then. It doesn't matter asking
a woman practically as long as you don't ask her liter-
ally."

" Father, please don't talk about it."

" I will talk about it. Lawrence, do you know what
this idiot's letting himself in for ? Have you seen Joanna
Godden ? Why, she'd never do for him ? She's a big,
bouncing female, and her stays creak."

" Be quiet, father. You make me furious."

" Yes, you'll be disrespectful to me in a minute. That
would be very sad, and the breaking of a noble record.
Of course it's presumptuous of me to want a lady for my
daughter-in-law, and perhaps you're right to chuck away
the poor remains of our dignity—they were hardly worth
keeping."

" I've thought over that," said Martin. He saw
now that having recklessly started the subject he could
not put it aside till it had been fought out. " I've thought
over that, and I've come to the conclusion that Joanna's
worth any sacrifice I can make for her."

" But not marriage—why must you ask her to marry
you ? You don't really know her. You'll cool off."

" I shan't."

" What about your health, Martin ? " asked Lawrence,
" are you fit and able to marry ? You know what the
doctor said."

" He said I might go off into consumption if I hung

on in town—that beastly atmosphere at Wright's and all
the racket . . . But there's nothing actually wrong
with me, I'm perfectly fit down here. I'll last for ever
in this place, and I tell you it's been a ghastly thought
till now—knowing that I must either stop here, away
from all my friends and interests, or else shorten my life.
But now, I don't care—when I marry Joanna Godden
I'll take root, I'll belong to the Marsh, I'll be at home.
You don't know Joanna Godden, Lawrence—if you did
I believe you'd like her. She's so sane and simple—she's
so warm and alive; and she's good, too—when I met
her to-day, she had just been to Communion. She'll
help me to live—at last I'll be able to live the best life
for me, body and soul, down here in the sea air, with no
town rubbish . . . ."

" It sounds a good thing," said Lawrence. " After
all, father, there really isn't much use trying to keep up
the state of the Trevors and all that now . . . ."

" No, there isn't — especially when this evening's
guest will arrive in two minutes to find us sitting round
in dirt and darkness and dissension, all because we've
been too busy discussing our heir's betrothal to a neighbouring goose-girl to trouble about such fripperies as
dressing for dinner. Of course now Lawrence elects to
take Martin's part there's no good my trying to stand
against the two of you. I've always been under your
heels, ever since you were old enough to boss me. Let
the state of the Trevors go—Martin, marry Joanna Godden
and we will come to you for our mangolds—Lawrence,
if you were not hindered by your vows, I should suggest
your marrying one of the Miss Southlands or the Miss
Vines, and then we could have a picturesque double wedding.
As for me, I will build on more solid foundations than
either of you, and marry my cook."

With which threat he departed to groom himself.

" He'll be all right," said Martin, " he likes Joanna
Godden really."

" So do I. She sounds a good sort. Will you take
me to see her before I go ? "

" Certainly. I want you to meet her. When you
do you'll see that I'm not doing anything rash, even from
the worldly point of view. She comes of fine old yeoman

stock, and she's of far more consequence on the Marsh than any of us."

" I can't see that the social question is of much importance. As long as your tastes and your ideas aren't too different . . ."

" I'm afraid they are, rather. But somehow we seem to complement each other. She's so solid and so sane—there's something barbaric about her too . . . it's queer."

" I've seen her. She's a fine-looking girl—a bit older than you, isn't she ? "

" Five years. Against it, of course—but then I'm so much older than she is in most ways. She's a practical woman of business—knows more about farming than I shall ever know in my life—but in matters of life and love, she's a child . . ."

" I should almost have thought it better the other way round—that you should know about the business and she about the love. But then in such matters I too am a child."

He smiled disarmingly, but Martin felt ruffled—partly because his brother's voluntary abstention from experience always annoyed him, and partly because he knew that in this case the child was right and the man wrong.

§ 13

In the engagement of Joanna Godden to Martin Trevor Walland Marsh had its biggest sensation for years. Indeed it could be said that nothing so startling had happened since the Rother changed its mouth. The feelings of those far-back marsh-dwellers who had awakened one morning to find the Kentish river swirling past their doors at Broomhill might aptly be compared with those of the farms round the Woolpack, who woke to find that Joanna Godden was not going just to jog on her final choice between Arthur Alce and old maidenhood, but had swept aside to make an excellent, fine marriage.

" She's been working for this all along," said Prickett disdainfully.

" I don't see that she's had the chance to work much,"

said Vine, "she hasn't seen the young chap more than three or four times."

"Bates's looker saw them at Romney once," said Southland, "having their dinner together; but that time at the Farmers' Club he'd barely speak to her."

"Well she's got herself talked about over two men that she hasn't took, and now she's took a man that she hasn't got herself talked about over."

"Anyways, I'm glad of it," said Furnese, "she's a mare that's never been präaperly broken in, and now at last she's got a man to do it."

"Poor feller, Alce. I wonder how he'll take it."

Alce took it very well. For a week he did not come to Ansdore, then he appeared with Joanna's first wedding present in the shape of a silver tea-service which had belonged to his mother.

"Maybe it's a bit early yet for wedding presents. They say you won't be married till next fall. But I've always wanted you to have this tea-set of mother's—it's real silver, as you can see by the lion on it—a teapot and milk jug and sugar bowl; many's the time I've seen you in my mind's eye, setting like a queen and pouring my tea out of it. Since it can't be my tea, it may as well be another's."

"There'll always be a cup for you, Arthur," said Joanna graciously.

"Thanks," said Arthur in a stricken voice.

Joanna could not feel as sorry for Alce as she ought and would have liked. All her emotions, whether of joy or sorrow, seemed to be poured into the wonderful new life that Martin had given her. A new life had begun for her on Christmas Day—in fact, it would be true to say that a new Joanna had begun. Something in her was broken, melted, changed out of all recognition—she was softer, weaker, more excited, more tender. She had lost much of her old swagger, her old cocksureness, for Martin had utterly surprised and tamed her. She had come to him in a scheming spirit of politics, and he had kept her in a spirit of devotion. She had come to him as Ansdore to North Farthing—but he had stripped her of Ansdore, and she was just Joanna Godden who had waited twenty-eight years for love.

Yet, perhaps because she had waited so long, she was now a little afraid. She had hitherto met love only in the dim forms of Arthur Alce and Dick Socknersh, with still more hazy images in the courtships of Abbot and Cobb. Now Martin was showing her love as no dim flicker or candlelight or domestic lamplight but as a bright, eager fire. She loved his kisses, the clasp of his strong arms, the stability of his chest and shoulders—but sometimes his passion startled her, and she had queer, shy withdrawals. Yet these were never more than temporary and superficial ; her own passions were slowly awaking, and moreover had their roots in a sweet, sane instinct of vocation and common sense.

On the whole, though, she was happiest in the quieter ways of love—the meals together, the fireside talks, the meetings in lonely places, the queer, half-laughing secrets, the stolen glances in company. She made a great fuss of his bodily needs—she was convinced that he did not get properly fed or looked after at home, and was always preparing him little snacks and surprises. For her sake Martin swallowed innumerable cups of milk and wrapped his chin in choky mufflers.

She had prouder moments too. On her finger glittered a gorgeous band of diamonds and sapphires which she had chosen for her engagement ring, and it was noticed that Joanna Godden now always drove with her gloves off. She had insisted on driving Martin round the Marsh to call on her friends—to show him to Mrs. Southland, Mrs. Vine, and Mrs. Prickett, to say nothing of their husbands who had always said no man in his senses would marry Joanna Godden. Well, not merely a man but a gentleman was going to do it—a gentleman who had his clothes made for him at a London tailor's instead of buying them ready-made at Lydd or Romney or Rye, who had—he confessed it, though he never wore it—a top hat in his possession, who ate late dinner and always smelt of good tobacco and shaving soap . . . . such thoughts would bring the old Joanna back, for one fierce moment of gloating.

Her reception by North Farthing House had done nothing to spoil her triumph. Martin's father and brother had both accepted her—the latter willingly, since he be-

lieved that she would be a sane and stabilizing influence
in Martin's life, hitherto over-restless and mood-ridden.
He looked upon his brother as a thwarted romantic,
whose sophistication had debarred him from finding
a natural outlet in religion.   He saw in his love for Joanna
the chance of a return to nature and romance, since he
loved a thing at once simple and adventurous, homely
and splendid—which was how religion appeared to Father
Lawrence.   He had liked Joanna very much on their
meeting, and she liked him too, though as she told him
frankly she " didn't hold with Jesoots."

As for Sir Harry, he too liked Joanna, and was too
well-bred and fond of women to show himself ungracious
about that which he could not prevent.

" I've surrendered, Martin. I can't help myself.
You'll bring down my grey hairs in sorrow to the grave,
but I am all beautiful resignation.   Indeed I think I
shall offer myself as best man, and flirt dutifully with
Ellen Godden, who I suppose will be chief bridesmaid.
Your brother shall himself perform the ceremony.   What
could your family do more ? "

" What indeed ? " laughed Martin.   He felt warm-
hearted towards all men now—he could forgive both his
father for having had too much experience and his brother
for having had too little.

§ 14

The actual date of the wedding was not fixed till two
months had run.   Though essentially adult and practical
in all matters of business and daily life, Joanna was still
emotionally adolescent, and her betrothed state satisfied
her as it would never have done if her feelings had been
as old as her years.   Also this deferring of love had helped
other things to get a hold on her—Martin was astonished
to find her swayed by such considerations as sowing and
shearing and marketing—" I can't fix up anything till
I've got my spring sowings done "——" that ud be in
the middle of the shearing "—" I'd sooner wait till I'm
through the autumn markets."

He discovered that she thought " next fall " the best

time for the wedding—" I'll have got everything clear by then, and I'll know how the new ploughs have borne." He fought her and beat her back into June—" after the hay." He was rather angry with her for thinking about these things, they expressed a side of her which he would have liked to ignore. He did not care for a " managing " woman, and he could still see, in spite of her new moments of surrender, that Joanna eternally would " manage." But in spite of this his love for her grew daily, as he discovered daily her warmth and breadth and tenderness, her growing capacity for passion. Once or twice he told her to let the sowings and the shearings be damned, and come and get married to him quietly without any fuss at the registrar's. But Joanna was shocked at the idea of getting married anywhere but in church—she could not believe a marriage legal which the Lion and the Unicorn had not blessed. Also he discovered that she rejoiced in fuss, and thought June almost too early for the preparations she wanted to make.

" I'm going to show 'em what a wedding's like," she remarked ominously—" I'm going to do everything in the real, proper, slap-up style. I'm going to have a white dress and a veil and carriages and bridesmaids and favours—" this was the old Joanna—" you don't mind, do you, Martin ? " this was the new.

Of course he could not say he minded. She was like an eager child, anxious for notice and display. He would endure the wedding for her sake. He also would endure for her sake to live at Ansdore ; after a few weeks he saw that nothing else could happen. It would be ridiculous for Joanna to uproot herself from her prosperous establishment and settle in some new place just because in spirit he shrank from becoming " Mr. Joanna Godden." She had said that " Martin and Joanna Trevor " should be painted on the scrolled name-boards of her waggons, but he knew that on the farm and in the market-place they would not be on an equal footing, whatever they were in the home. As farmer and manager she would outshine him, whose tastes and interests and experiences were so different. Never mind—he would have more time to give to the beloved pursuit of exploring the secret, shy marsh country—he would do all Joan.'s business afield, in the far market towns of New Romney and Dymchurch, and the farms away in Kent or under the Coast at Ruckinge and Warhorne.

Meanwhile he spent a great deal of his time at Ansdore. He liked the life of the place with its mixture of extravagance and simplicity, democracy and tyranny. Fortunately Ellen approved of him—indeed he sometimes found her patronage excessive. He thought her spoilt and affected, and might almost have come to dislike her if she had not been such a pretty, subtle little thing, and if she had not interested and amused him by her sharp contrasts with her sister. He was now also amused by the conflicts between the two, which at first had shocked him. He liked to see Joanna's skin go pink as she faced Ellen in a torment of loving anger and rattled the fierce words off her tongue, while Ellen tripped and skipped and evaded and generally triumphed by virtue of a certain fundamental coolness. " It will be interesting to watch that girl growing up," he thought.

§ 15

As the year slid through the fogs into the spring, he persuaded Joanna to come with him on his rambles on the Marsh. He was astonished to find how little she knew of her own country, of that dim flat land which was once under the sea. She knew it only as the hunting ground of her importance. It was at Yokes Court that she bought her roots, and from Becket's House her looker had come; Lydd and Rye and Romney were only markettowns—you did best in cattle at Rye, but the other two were proper for sheep; Old Honeychild was just a farm where she had bought some good spades and dibbles at an auction; at Misleham they had once had foot-and-mouth disease—she had gone to Picknye Bush for the character of Milly Pump, her chicken-girl . . . .

He told her of the smugglers and owlers who had used the Woolpack as their headquarters long ago, riding by moonlight to the cross-roads, with their mouths full of slang—cant talk of " mackerel " and " fencing " and " hornies " and " Oliver's glim."

" Well, if they talked worse there then than they talk now, they must have talked very bad indeed," was all Joanna found to say.

He told her of the old monks of Canterbury who had covered the Marsh with the altars of Thomas à Becket.

" We got shut of 'em all on the fifth of November," said Joanna, " as we sing around here on bonfire nights —and ' A halfpenny loaf to feed the Pope, a penn'orth of cheese to choke him,' as we say."

All the same he enjoyed the expeditions that they had together in her trap, driving out on some windy-skied March day, to fill the hours snatched from her activities at Ansdore and his muddlings at North Farthing, with all the sea-green sunny breadth of Walland, and still more divinely with Walland's secret places—the shelter of tall reeds by the Yokes Sewer, or of a thorn thicket making a tent of white blossom and spindled shadows in the midst of the open land.

Sometimes they crossed the Rhee Wall on to Romney Marsh, and he showed her the great church at Ivychurch, which could have swallowed up in its nave the two small farms that make the village. He took her into the church at New Romney and showed her the marks of the Great Flood, discolouring the pillars for four feet from the ground.

" Doesn't it thrill you ?—Doesn't it excite you ? " he teased her, as they stood together in the nave, the church smelling faintly of hearthstones.

" How long ago did it happen ? "

" In the year of our Lord twelve hundred and eighty seven the Kentish river changed his mouth, and after swilling out Romney Sands and drowning all the marsh from Honeychild to the Wicks, did make himself a new mouth in Rye Bay, with which mouth he swallowed the fifty taverns and twelve churches of Broomhill, and——"

" Oh, have done talking that silly way—it's like the Bible, only there's no good in it."

Her red mouth was close to his in the shadows of the church—he kissed it . . . .

" Child ! "

" Oh, Martin——"

She was faintly shocked because he had kissed her in church, so he drew her to him, tilting back her chin.

" You mustn't " . . . but she had lost the power of gainsaying him now, and made no effort to release herself. He held her up against the pillar and gave her mouth another idolatrous kiss before he let her go.

" If it happened all that while back, they might at least have got the marks off by this time," she said, tucking away her loosened hair.

Martin laughed aloud—her little reactions of common sense after their passionate moments never failed to amuse and delight him.

" You'd have had it off with your broom, and that's all you think about it. But look here, child—what if it happened again ? "

" It can't."

" How do you know ? "

" It can't—I know it."

" But if it happened then it could happen again."

" There ain't been a flood on the Marsh in my day, nor in my poor father's day, neither. Sometimes in February the White Kemp brims a bit, but I've never known the roads covered. You're full of old tales. And now let's go out, for laughing and love-making ain't the way to behave in church."

" The best way to behave in church is to get married."

She blushed faintly and her eyes filled with tears.

They went out, and had dinner at the New Inn, which held the memory of their first meal together, in that huge, sag-roofed dining-room, then so crowded, now empty except for themselves. Joanna was still given to holding forth on such subjects as harness and spades, and to-day she gave Martin nearly as much practical advice as on that first occasion.

" Now, don't you waste your money on a driller—we don't give our sheep turnips on the Marsh. It's an Inland notion. The grass here is worth a field of roots. You stick to grazing and you'll keep your money in your pocket and never send coarse mutton to the butcher."

He did not resent her advice, for he was learning humility. Her superior knowledge and experience of all practical matters was beginning to lose its sting. She was in his eyes so adorable a creature that he could forgive her for being dominant. The differences in their natures were no longer incompatibilities, but gifts which they brought each other—he brought her gifts of knowledge and imagination and emotion, and she brought him gifts of stability and simplicity and a certain saving commonness And all these gifts were fused in the glow of personality, in a kind bodily warmth, in a romantic familiarity which sometimes found its expression in shyness and teasing.

They loved each other.

§ 16

Martin had always wanted to go out on the cape at Dunge Ness, that tongue of desolate land which rakes out from Dunge Marsh into the sea, slowly moving every year twenty feet towards France. Joanna had a profound contempt of Dunge Ness—" not enough grazing on it for one sheep "—but Martin's curiosity mastered her indifference and she promised to drive him out there some day. She had been once before with her father, on some forgotten errand to the Hope and Anchor inn.

It was an afternoon in May when they set out, bowling through Pedlinge in the dog cart behind Smiler's jogging heels. Joanna wore her bottle green driving coat, with a small, close-fitting hat, since Martin, to her surprise and disappointment, disliked her best hat with the feathers. He sat by her, unconsciously huddling to her side, with his hand thrust under her arm and occasionally pressing it —she had told him that she could suffer that much of a caress without detriment to her driving.

It was a bright, scented day, heavily coloured with green and gold and white ; for the new grass was up in the pastures, releasing the farmer from many anxious cares, and the buttercups were thick both on the grazing lands and on the innings where the young hay stood, still green ; the watercourses were marked with the thick clumpings of the may, walls of green-teased white streaking here and there across the pastures, while under the boughs the thick green water lay scummed with white ranunculus, and edged with a gaudy splashing of yellow irises, torches among the never silent reeds. Above it all the sky was misty and full of shadows, a low soft cloud, occasionally pierced with sunlight.

"It'll rain before night," said Joanna.

"What makes you think that?"

"The way of the wind, and those clouds moving low —and the way you see Rye Hill all clear with the houses on it—and the way the sheep are grazing with their heads to leeward."

"Do you think they know?"

"Of course they know. You'd be surprised at the things beasts know, Martin."

"Well, it won't matter if it does rain—we'll be home before night. I'm glad we're going down on the Ness —I'm sure it's wonderful."

"It's a tedious hole."

"That's what you think."

"I know—I've been there."

"Then it's very sweet of you to come again with me."

"It'll be different with you."

She was driving him by way of Broomhill, for that was another place which had fired his imagination, though to her it too was a tedious hole. Martin could not forget the Broomhill of old days—the glamour of taverns and churches and streets lay over the few desolate houses and ugly little new church which huddled under the battered sea-wall. Great reedy pools still remained from the thirteenth century floods, brackish on the flat seashore, where the staked keddle nets showed that the mackerel were beginning to come into Rye Bay.

"Nothing but fisher-folk around here," said Joanna contemptuously—"you'll see 'em all in the summer, men, women and children, with heaps of mackerel that they pack in boxes for London and such places—so much mackerel they get that there's nothing else ate in the place for the season, and yet if you want fish-guts for manure they make you pay inland prices, and do your own carting."

"I think it's a delicious place," he retorted, teasing her, "I've a mind to bring you here for our honeymoon."

"Martin, you'd never! You told me you were taking me to foreign parts, and I've told Mrs. Southland and Mrs. Furnese and Maudie Vine and half a dozen more all about my going to Paris and seeing the sights and hearing French spoken."

"Yes—perhaps it would be better to go abroad; Broomhill is wonderful, but you in Paris will be more wonderful than Broomhill—even in the days before the flood."

"I want to see the Eiffel Tower—where they make the lemonade—and I want to buy myself something really chick in the way of hats."

"Joanna—do you know the hat which suits you best?"

"Which?" she asked eagerly, with some hope for the feathers.

"The straw hat you tie on over your hair when you go out to the chickens first thing in the morning."

"That old thing! Why! My! Lor! Martin! That's an old basket that I tie under my chin with a neckerchief of poor father's."

"It suits you better than any hat in the Rue St. Honoré—it's brown and golden like yourself, and your hair comes creeping and curling from under it, and there's a shadow on your face, over your eyes—the shadow stops just above your mouth—your mouth is all of your face that I can see clearly, and it's your mouth that I love most . . ."

He suddenly kissed it, ignoring her business with the reins and the chances of the road, pulling her round in her seat and covering her face with his, so that his eyelashes stroked her cheek. She drew her hands up sharply to her breast, and with the jerk the horse stopped.

For a few moments they stayed so, then he released her and they moved on. Neither of them spoke; the tears were in Joanna's eyes and in her heart was a devouring tenderness that made it ache. The trap lurched in the deep ruts of the road, which now had become a mass of shingle and gravel, skirting the beach. Queer sea plants grew in the ruts, the little white sea-campions with their fat seed-boxes filled the furrows of the road as with a foam —it seemed a pity and a shame to crush them, and one could tell by their fresh growth how long it was since wheels had passed that way.

At Jury's Gap, a long white-daubed coastguard station

marked the end of the road. Only a foot-track ran out to the Ness. They left the horse and trap at the station and went afoot.

"I told you it was a tedious place," said Joanna. Like a great many busy people she did not like walking, which she always looked upon as a waste of time. Martin could seldom persuade her to come for a long walk.

It was a long walk up the Ness, and the going was bad, owing to the shingle. The sea-campion grew everywhere, and in sunny corners the yellow-horned poppy put little spots of colour into a landscape of pinkish grey. The sea was the same colour as the land, for the sun had sunk away into the low thick heavens, leaving the sea an unrelieved, tossed dun waste.

The wind came tearing across Rye Bay with a moan, lifting all the waves into little sharp bitter crests.

"We'll get the rain," said Joanna sagely.

"I don't care if we do," said Martin.

"You haven't brought your overcoat."

"Never mind that."

"I do mind."

His robust appearance—his broad back and shoulders, thick vigorous neck and swarthy skin—only magnified his pathos in her eyes. It was pitiful that this great thing should be so frail . . . He could pick her up with both hands on her waist, and hold her up before him, the big Joanna—and yet she must take care of him.

§ 17

An hour's walking brought them to the end of the Ness—to a strange forsaken country of coastguard stations and lonely taverns and shingle tracks. The lighthouse stood only a few feet above the sea, at the end of the point, and immediately before it the water dropped to sinister, glaucous depths.

"Well, it ain't much to see," said Joanna.

"It's wonderful," said Martin—"it's terrible."

He stood looking out to sea, into the Channel streaked with green and grey, as if he would draw France out of

the southward fogs. He felt half-way to France . . . .
here on the end of this lonely crane, with water each side
of him and ahead, and behind him the shingle which was
the uttermost of Kent.

"Joanna—don't you feel it, too?"

"Yes—maybe I do. It's queer and lonesome—I'm
glad I've got you, Martin."

She suddenly came close to him and put out her arms,
hiding her face against his heart.

"Child—what is it?"

"I dunno. Maybe it's this place, but I feel scared.
Oh, Martin, you'll never leave me? You'll always be good
to me? . . ."

"I . . . . oh, my own precious thing."

He held her close to him and they both trembled—
she with her first fear of those undefinable forces and
associations which go to make the mystery of place, he
with the passion of his faithfulness, of his vows of devotion, too fierce and sacrificial even to express.

"Let's go and have tea," she said, suddenly dis-
engaging herself, "I'll get the creeps if we stop out here
on the beach much longer—reckon I've got 'em now,
and I never was the one to be silly like that. I told you
it was a tedious hole."

They went to the Britannia, on the eastern side of
the bill. The inn looked surprised to see them, but agreed
to put the kettle on. They sat together in a little queer,
dim room, smelling of tar and fish, and bright with the
flames of wreckwood. Joanna had soon lost her fears
—she talked animatedly, telling him of the progress of
her spring wheat; of the dead owl that had fallen out
of the beams of Brenzett church during morning prayers
last Sunday, of the shocking way they had managed
their lambing at Beggar's Bush, of King Edward's Corona-
tion that was coming off in June.

"I know of something else that's coming off in June,"
said Martin.

"Our wedding?"

"Surelye."

"I'm going into Folkestone next week, to that shop
where I bought my party gown."

"And I'm going to Mr. Pratt to tell him to put up

our banns, or we shan't have time to be cried three times before the first of June."

" The first !—I told you the twenty-fourth."

" But I'm not going to wait till the twenty-fourth. You promised me June."

" But I shan't have got in my hay, and the shearers are coming on the fourteenth—you have to book weeks ahead, and that was the only date Harmer had free."

" Joanna."

Her name was a summons, almost stern, and she looked up. She was still sitting at the table, stirring the last of her tea. He sat under the window on an old sea-chest, and had just lit his pipe.

" Come here, Joanna."

She came obediently, and sat beside him, and he put his arm round her. The blue and ruddy flicker of the wreckwood lit up the dark day.

" I've been thinking a lot about this, and I know now —there is only one thing between us, and that's Ansdore."

" How d'you mean ? It ain't between us."

" It is—again and again you seem to be putting Ansdore in the place of our love. What other woman on God's earth would put off her marriage to fit in with the sheep-shearing ? "

" I ain't putting it off. We haven't fixed the day yet, and I'm just telling you to fix a day that's suitable and convenient."

" You know I always meant to marry you the first week in June."

" And you know as I've told you, that I can't take the time off then."

" The time off ! You're not a servant. You can leave Ansdore any day you choose."

" Not when the shearing's on. You don't understand, Martin—I can't have all the shearers up and nobody to look after 'em."

" What about your looker ?—or Broadhurst ? You don't trust anybody but yourself."

" You're just about right—I don't."

" Don't you trust me ? "

" Not to shear sheep."

Martin laughed ruefully.

" You're very sensible, Joanna—unshakably so. But
I'm not asking you to trust me with the sheep, but to
trust me with yourself. Don't misunderstand me, dear.
I'm not asking you to marry me at the beginning of the
month just because I haven't the patience to wait till
the end. It isn't that, I swear it. But don't you see
that if you fix our marriage to fit in with the farm-work,
it'll simply be beginning things in the wrong way? As
we begin we shall have to go on, and we can't go on settling
and ordering our life according to Ansdore's requirements
—it's a wrong principle. Think, darling," and he drew
her close against his heart, " we shall want to see our
children—and will you refuse, just because that would
mean that you would have to lie up and keep quiet and
not go about doing all your own business ? "

Joanna shivered.

" Oh, Martin, don't talk of such things."

" Why not ? "

She had given him some frank and graphic details
about the accouchement of her favourite cow, and he
did not understand that the subject became different
when it was human and personal.

" Because I—because we ain't married yet."

" Joanna, you little prude ! "

She saw that he was displeased and drew closer to
him, slipping her arms round his neck, so that he could
feel the roughness of her work-worn hands against it.

" I'm not shocked—only it's so wonderful—I can't
abear talking of it . . . Martin, if we had one . . . I
should just about die of joy . . ."

He gripped her to him silently, unable to speak. Somehow it seemed as if he had just seen deeper into Joanna
than during all the rest of his courtship. He moved his
lips over her bright straying hair—her face was hidden
in his sleeve.

" Then we'll stop at Mr. Pratt's on our way home and
ask him to put up the banns at once ? "

" Oh no—" lifting herself sharply—" I didn't mean
that."

" Why not ? "

" Well, it won't make any difference to our marriage,
being married three weeks later—but it'll make an un-

accountable difference to my wool prices if the shearers don't do their job proper—and then there's the hay."

" On the contrary, child—it *will* make a difference to our marriage. We shall have started with Ansdore between us."

" What nonsense."

" Well, I can't argue with you—you must do as you like. My wife is a very strong-willed person, who will keep her husband in proper order. But he loves her enough to bear it."

He kissed her gently, and they both stood up. At the same time there was a sharp scud of rain against the window.

§ 18

The journey home was quieter and dimmer than the journey out. Their voices and footsteps were muffled in the roar of the wind, which had risen from sorrow to anger. The rain beat in their faces as they walked arm in arm over the shingle. They could not hurry, for at every step their feet sank.

" I said it was a tedious hole," reiterated Joanna, " and now perhaps you'll believe me—the folk here walk with boards on their feet, what they call backstays. Our shoes will be just about ruined."

She was not quite happy, for she felt that Martin was displeased with her, though he made no reproaches. He did not like her to arrange their wedding day to fit in with the shearing. But what else could she do ? If she was away when the shearers came, there'd be no end to their goings on with the girls, and besides, who'd see that the work was done proper and the tegs not scared out of their lives ?

It was only six o'clock, but a premature darkness was falling as the clouds dropped over Dunge Marsh, and the rain hung like a curtain over Rye Bay, blotting out all distances, showing them nothing but the crumbling, uncertain track. In half an hour they were both wet through to their shoulders, for the rain came down with all the drench of May. Joanna could see that Martin was beginning to be worried about himself—he was worried

about her too, but he was more preoccupied with his
own health than other men she knew, the only way in
which he occasionally betrayed the weak foundations
of his stalwart looks.

" The worst of it is, we'll have to sit for an hour in
the dog-cart after we get to Jury's Gap. You'll catch
your death of cold, Joanna."

" Not I! I often say I'm like our Romney sheep—
I can stand all winds and waters. But you're not used
to it like I am—you should ought to have brought your
overcoat."

" How was I to know it would turn out like this ? "

" I told you it would rain."

" But not till after we'd started."

Joanna said nothing. She accepted Martin's rather
unreasonable displeasure without protest, for she felt
guilty about other things. Was he right, after all, when
he said that she was putting Ansdore between them ?
. . . She did not feel that she was, any more than she
was putting Ansdore between herself and Ellen. But she
hated him to have the thought. Should she give in and
tell him he could call on Mr. Pratt on their way home ?
. . . . No, there was plenty of time to make up her
mind about that. To-day was only Tuesday, and any
day up till Saturday would do for putting in notice of
banns . . . she must think things over before committing
herself . . . . it wasn't only the shearers—there was
the hay . . . .

Thus they came, walking apart in their own thoughts,
to Jury's Gap. In a few moments the horse was put to,
and they were lurching in the ruts of the road to Broomhill. The air was full of the sound of hissing rain, as it
fell on the shingle and in the sea and on the great brackish
pools of the old flood. Round the pools were thick beds
of reeds, shivering and moaning, while along the dykes
the willows tossed their branches and the thorn-trees
rattled.

" It'll freshen up the grass," said Joanna, trying to
cheer Martin.

" I was a fool not to bring my overcoat," he grumbled.

Then suddenly her heart went out to him more than
ever, because he was fractious and fretting about himself.

She took one hand off the reins and pressed his as it lay warm between her arm and her side.

"Reckon you're my own silly child," she said in a low voice.

"I'm sorry, Jo," he replied humbly, "I know I'm being a beast and worrying you. But I'm worried about you too—you're as wet as I am."

"No, I'm not. I've got my coat. I'm not at all worried about myself—nor about you, neither." She could not conceive of a man taking cold through a wetting.

She had planned for him to come back to supper with her at Ansdore, but with that fussiness which seemed so strange and pathetic, he insisted on going straight back to North Farthing to change his clothes.

"You get into a hot bath with some mustard," he said to her, meaning what he would do himself.

"Ha! ha!" laughed Joanna, at such an idea.

§ 19

She did not see Martin for the next two days. He had promised to go up to London for the first night of a friend's play, and was staying till Friday morning. She missed him very much—he used to come to Ansdore every day, sometimes more than once, and they always had at least one meal together. She brooded about him too, for she could not rid herself of the thought that she had failed him in her refusal to be married before the shearing. He was disappointed—he could not understand . . .

She looked round on Ansdore almost distrustfully . . . was it true that she loved it too much ? The farm looked very lonely and bare, with the mist hanging in the doorways, and the rain hissing into the midden, while the bush—as the trees were called which sheltered nearly every marsh dwelling—sighed and tossed above the barn-roofs. She suddenly realized that she did not love it as much as she used.

The knowledge came like a slap. She suddenly knew that for the last four months her love for Martin had been eating into her love for Ansdore . . . It was like the sun shining on a fire and putting it out—now that the sun had gone she saw that her hearth was cold. It was for Martin she had sown her spring wheat, for Martin she had broken up twelve acres of pasture by the Kent Ditch, for Martin she would shear her sheep and cut her hay . . .

Then since it was all for Martin, what an owl she was to sacrifice him to it, to put it before his wants and needs. He wanted her, he needed her, and she was offering him bales of wool and cocks of hay. Of course in this matter she was right and he was wrong—it would be much better to wait just a week or two till after the shearing and the hay-making—but for the first time Joanna saw that even right could surrender. Even though she was right, she could give way to him, bend her will to his. After all, nothing really mattered except his love, his good favour—better that she should muddle her shearing and her crops than the first significant weeks of their married life. He should put his dear foot upon her neck —for the last of her pride was gone in that discovery of the dripping day, the discovery that her plans, her ambitions, her life, herself, had their worth only in the knowledge that they belonged to him.

It was on Thursday afternoon that Joanna finally beat Ansdore out of her love. She cried a little, for she wished that it had happened earlier, before Martin went away. Still, it was his going that had shown her at last clearly where she belonged. She thought of writing and telling him of her surrender, but like most of her kind she shrank from writing letters except when direly necessary ; and she would see Martin to-morrow—he had promised to come to Ansdore straight from the station.

So instead of writing her letter, she went and washed the tears off her face over the sink and sat down to a cup of tea and a piece of bread and dripping with Mrs. Tolhurst and Milly Pump. When Ellen was at home Joanna was lofty and exclusive, and had her meals in the dining-room—she did not think it right that her little sister, with all her new accomplishments and elegancies, should lead the common, kitchen life—also, of course, when Martin came they sat down in state, with pink wine-glasses beside their tumblers. But when she was alone she much preferred a friendly meal with Milly and Mrs. Tolhurst—she even joined them in pouring

her tea into her saucer, and sat with it cooling on her
spread fingers, her elbow on the cloth. She unbent from
mistress to fellow-worker, and they talked the scandal
of a dozen farms.

" It's as I said, at Yokes Court," said Mrs. Tolhurst—
" there's no good young Mus' Southland saying as the
girl's mother sent for her—*I* know better."

" I saw Mrs. Lambarde after church on Sunday,"
said Joanna, " and she wasn't expecting Elsie then."

" Elsie went before her box did," said Milly Pump,
" Bill Piper fetched it along after her, as he told me himself."

" I'm sure it's Tom Southland," said Joanna.

" Surelye," said Mrs. Tolhurst, " and all the more
as he's been saying at the Woolpack that the Old Squire's
been hanging around after the girl—which reminds me,
Miss Joanna, as I hear Mus' Martin's back this afternoon."

" This afternoon ! He said to-morrow morning."

" Well, he's come this afternoon. Broadhurst met
him driving from Rye station."

" Then he's sure to be over to-night. You get the
wine-glasses out, Mrs. Tolhurst, and spread in the dining-
room."

She rose up from table, once more apart from her
servants. Her brain was humming with surprised joy
—Martin was back, she would soon see him, he would
be sure to come to her. And then she would tell him
of her surrender, and the cloud would be gone from their
love.

With beating heart she ran upstairs to change her
dress and tidy herself, for he might come at any moment.
There was a red-brown velvet dress he particularly liked—
she pulled it out of her drawer and smoothed its folds.
Her drawers were crammed and heavy with the garments
she was to wear as Martin's wife ; there were silk blouses
bought at smart shops in Folkestone and Marlingate ;
there was a pair of buckled shoes—size eight ; there were
piles of neat longcloth and calico underclothing, demure
nightdresses buttoning to the chin, stiff petticoats, and
what she called " petticoat bodies," fastening down the
front with linen buttons, and with tiny, shy frills of embroidery at the neck and armholes.

She put on the brown dress, and piled up her hair against the big comb. She looked at herself in the glass by the light of the candles she had put to light up the rainy evening. Her cheeks were flushed and her eyes bright, and her hair and her dress were the same soft, burning colour . . . When would Martin come?

Then suddenly she thought of something even better than his coming. She thought of herself going over to North Farthing House and telling him that she had changed her mind and that she was his just as soon as ever he wanted her . . . . Her breath came fast at the inspiration—it would be better than waiting for him here; it gave to her surrender the spectacular touch which hitherto it had lacked and her nature demanded. The rain was coming down the wind almost as fiercely and as fast as it had come on Tuesday night, but Joanna the marsh-born had never cared for weather. She merely laced on her heavy boots and bundled into her father's overcoat. Then she put out a hand for an old hat, and suddenly she remembered the hat Martin had said he liked her in above all others. It was an old rush basket, soft and shapeless with age, and she tied it over her head with her father's red and white spotted handkerchief.

She was now ready, and all she had to do was to run down and tell Mrs. Tolhurst that if Mr. Martin called while she was out he was to be asked to wait. She was not really afraid of missing him, for there were few short cuts on the Marsh, where the long way round of the road was often the only way—but she hoped she would reach North Farthing before he left it; she did not want anything to be taken from her surrender, it must be absolute and complete . . . . the fires of her own sacrifice were kindled and were burning her heart.

§ 20

She did not meet Martin on the Brodnyx Road; only the wind was with her, and the rain. She turned aside to North Farthing between the Woolpack and the village, and still she did not meet him—and now she really thought that she would arrive in time. On either side of the track she followed, Martin's sheep were grazing—that was his land, those were his dykes and willows, ahead of her were the lighted windows of his house. She wondered what he would say when he saw her. Would he be much surprised? She had come to North Farthing once or twice before, but not very often. If he was not surprised to see her, he would be surprised when she told him why she had come. She pictured how he would receive her news —with his arms round her, with his kisses on her mouth.

Her arrival was a check—the formalities of her betrothed's house never failed to upset her. To begin with she had to face that impertinent upstart of a Nell Raddish, all tricked out in a black dress and white apron and cap and collar and cuffs, and she only a cowman's daughter with a face like a plum, and no sense or notions at all till she came to Farthing, since when, as everyone knew, her skirts had grown shorter and her nose whiter and her hair frizzier and her ways more knowing.

" Good evening, Nell," said Joanna, covering her embarrassment with patronage, " is Mr. Martin at home ? "

" Yes, he is," said Nell, " he came back this afternoon."

" I know that, of course. I want to see him, please."

" I'm not sure if he's gone up to bed. Come in, and I'll go and look."

" Up to bed ! "

" Yes, he's feeling poorly. That's why he came home."

" Poorly, what's the matter ? " Joanna pushed past Nell into the house.

" I dunno, a cold or cough. He told me to bring him some tea and put a hot brick in his bed. Sir Harry ain't in yet."

Joanna marched up the hall to the door of Martin's study. She stopped and listened for a moment, but could hear nothing, except the beating of her own heart. Then, without knocking, she went in. The room was ruddy and dim with firelight, and at first she thought it was empty, but the next minute she saw Martin huddled in an armchair, a tea-tray on a low stool beside him.

" Martin ! "

He started up out of a kind of sleep, and blinked at her.

" Jo ! Is that you ? "

"Yes. I've come over to tell you I'll marry you whenever you want. Martin dear, what's the matter? Are you ill?"

"It's nothing much—I've caught cold, and thought I'd better come home. Colds always make me feel wretched."

She could see that he was anxious about himself, and in her pity she forgave him for having ignored her surrender. She knelt down beside him and took both his restless hands.

"Have you had your tea, dear?"

"No. I asked her to bring it, and then I sort of fell asleep . . . ."

"I'll give it to you."

She poured out his tea, giving him a hot black cup, with plenty of sugar, as they liked it on the Marsh. He drank it eagerly, and felt better.

"Jo, how good of you to come over and see me. Who told you I was back?"

"I heard it from Milly Pump, and she heard it from Broadhurst."

"I meant to send a message round to you. I hope I'll be all right to-morrow."

"Reckon you will, dear . . . . Martin, you heard what I said—about marrying you when you want?"

"Do you mean it?"

"Of course I mean it—I came over a-purpose to tell you. While you was away I did some thinking, and I found that Ansdore doesn't matter to me what it used. It's only you that matters now."

She was crouching at his feet, and he stooped over her, taking her in his arms, drawing her back between his knees.

"You noble, beloved thing . . . ."

The burning touch of his lips and face reminded her that he was ill, so the consecration of her sacrifice lost a little of its joy.

"You're feverish—you should ought to go to bed."

"I'm going—when I've had another cup of tea. Will you give me another, child?"

"I've a mind to go home through Brodnyx and ask Dr. Taylor to call round."

" Oh, I don't think I'm bad enough for a doctor—
I catch cold easily, and I was wet through the other
night."

" Was it that ! " Her voice shook with consternation.

" I expect so—but don't fret, darling Jo. It's nothing.
I'll be quite right to-morrow—I feel better already."

" I think you should ought to see a doctor, though.
I'll call in on my way back. I'll call in on Mr. Pratt, too,
and tell him to start crying us next Sunday."

" That's my business—I'll go to-morrow. But are
you sure, darling, you can make such a sacrifice ? I'm
afraid I've been a selfish beast, and I'm spoiling your
plans."

" Oh no, you ain't. I feel now as if I wanted to get
married more'n anything wotsumever. The shearing
ull do proper—the men know their job—and Broadhurst
ull see to the hay. They dursn't muck things up, knowing
as I'll be home to see to it by July."

" To say nothing of me," said Martin, pinching her
ear.

" To say nothing of you."

" Joanna, you've got on the old hat . . ."

"I put it on special."

" Bless you."

He pulled her down to the arm of his chair, and for
a moment they huddled together, cheek on cheek. The
opening of the door made Joanna spring virtuously upright. It was Sir Harry.

" Hullo, Joanna !—you here. Hullo, Martin ! The
lovely Raddish says you've come home middling queer.
I hope that doesn't mean anything serious."

" I've got some sort of a chill, and I feel a beast. So
I thought I'd better come home."

" I've given him his tea," said Joanna, " and now he
should ought to go to bed."

Sir Harry looked at her. She struck him as an odd
figure, in her velvet gown and basket hat, thick boots
and man's overcoat. The more he saw of her, the less
could he think what to make of her as a daughter-in-law ;
but to-night he was thankful for her capable managing
—mentally and physically he was always clumsy with
Martin in illness. He found it hard to adapt himself to

the occasional weakness of this being who dominated him in other ways.

" Do you think he's feverish ? "

Joanna felt Martin's hands again.

" I guess he is. Maybe he wants a dose—or a cup of herb tea does good, they say. But I'll ask Doctor to come around. Martin, I'm going now this drackly minute, and I'll call in at Dr. Taylor's and at Mr. Pratt's."

" Wait till to-morrow, and I'll see Pratt," said Martin, unable to rid himself of the idea that a bride should find such an errand embarrassing.

" I'd sooner go myself to-night. Anyways you mustn't go traipsing around, even if you feel better to-morrow. I'll settle everything, so don't you fret."

She took his face between her hands, and kissed him as if he were a child.

" Good night, my duck. You get off to bed and keep warm."

§ 21

She worked off her fears in action. Having given notice of the banns to Mr. Pratt, sent off Dr. Taylor to North Farthing, put up a special petition for Martin in her evening prayers, she went to bed and slept soundly. She was not an anxious soul, and a man's illness never struck her as particularly alarming. Men were hard creatures—whose weaknesses were of mind and character rather than of body—and though Martin was softer than some, she could not quite discount his broad back and shoulders, his strong, swinging arms.

She drove over to North Farthing soon after breakfast, expecting to find him, in spite of her injunctions, about and waiting for her.

" The day's warm and maybe he won't hurt if he drives on with me to Honeychild "—the thought of him there beside her was so strong that she could almost feel his hand lying pressed between her arm and her heart.

But when she came to the house she found only Sir Harry, prowling in the hall.

" I'm glad you've come, Joanna. I'm anxious about Martin."

" What's the matter ? What did the doctor say ? "

" He said there's congestion of the lung or something. Martin took a fit of the shivers after you'd gone, and of course it made him worse when the doctor said the magic word ' lung.'   He's always been hipped about himself, you know."

" I'd better go and see him."

She hitched the reins, and climbed down out of the trap—stumbling awkwardly as she alighted, for she had begun to tremble.

" You don't think he's very bad, do you ? "

" Can't say.   I wish Taylor ud come.   He said he'd be here again this morning."

His voice was sharp and complaining, for anything painful always made him exasperated.   Martin lying ill in bed, Martin shivering and in pain and in a funk was so unlike the rather superior being whom he liked to pretend bullied him, that he felt upset and rather shocked.   He gave a sigh of relief as Joanna ran upstairs—he told himself that she was a good practical sort of woman, and handsome when she was properly dressed.

She had never been upstairs in North Farthing House before, but she found Martin's room after only one false entry—which surprised the guilty Raddish sitting at Sir Harry's dressing-table and smarming his hair-cream on her ignoble head.   The blinds in Martin's room were down, and he was half-sitting, half-lying in bed, with his head turned away from her.

" That you, father ?—has Taylor come ? "

" No, it's me, dearie.   I've come to see what I can do for you."

The sight of him huddled there in the pillows, rest-less, comfortless, neglected, wrung her heart.   Hitherto her love for Martin had been singularly devoid of intimacy. They had kissed each other, they had eaten dinner and tea and supper together, they had explored the Three Marshes in each other's company, but she had scarcely ever been to his house, never seen him asleep, and in normal circumstances would have perished rather than gone into his bedroom.   To-day when she saw him there, lying on his wide, tumbled bed, among his littered belong-ings—his clothes strewn untidily on the floor, his books on their shelves, his pictures that struck her rigidity as indecent, his photographs of people who had touched his life, some perhaps closely, but were unknown to her, she had a queer sense of the revelation of poor, pathetic secrets. This, then, was Martin when he was away from her—untidy, sensual, forlorn, as all men were . . . . she bent down and kissed him.

"Lovely Jo," . . . he yielded childish, burning lips, then drew away—"No, you mustn't kiss me—it might be bad for you."

"Gammon, dear. 'Tis only a chill."

She saw that he was in a bate about himself, so after her tender beginnings, she became rough. She made him sit up while she shook his pillows, then she made him lie flat and tucked the sheet round him strenuously; she scolded him for leaving his clothes lying about on the floor. She felt as if her love for him was only just beginning —the last four months seemed cold and formal compared with these moments of warm, personal service. She brought him water for his hands, and scrubbed his face with a sponge to his intense discomfort. She was bawling downstairs to the unlucky Raddish to put the kettle on for some herb tea—since an intimate cross-examination revealed that he had not had the recommended dose— when the doctor arrived and came upstairs with Sir Harry.

He undid a good deal of Joanna's good work—he ordered the blind to be let down again, and he refused to back her up in her injunctions to the patient to lie flat—on the contrary he sent for more pillows, and Martin had to confess to feeling easier when he was propped up against them with a rug round his shoulders. He then announced that he would send for a nurse from Rye.

"Oh, but I can manage," cried Joanna—"let me nurse him. I can come and stop here, and nurse him day and night."

"I am sure there is no one whom he'd rather have than you, Miss Godden," said Dr. Taylor gallantly, "but of course you are not professional, and pneumonia wants thoroughly experienced nursing—the nurse counts more than the doctor in a case like this."

"Pneumonia! Is that what's the matter with him?"

They had left Martin's room, and the three of them were standing in the hall.

" I'm afraid that's it—only in the right lung so far."

" But you can stop it—you won't let him get worse. Pneumonia ! . . . ."

The word was full of a sinister horror to her, suggesting suffocation—agony.   And Martin's chest had always been weak—the weak part of his strong body.   She should have thought of that . . . thought of it three nights ago when, all through her, he had been soaked with the wind-driven rain . . . . just like a drowned rat he had looked when they came to Ansdore, his cap dripping, the water running down his neck . . . . No, no, it could not be that—he couldn't have caught pneumonia just through getting wet that time—she had got wet a dunnamany times and not been tuppence the worse . . . . his lungs were not weak in that way—it was the London fogs that had disagreed with them, the doctor had said so, and had sent him away from town, to the Marsh and the rain . . . . He had been in London for the last two days, and the fog had got into his poor chest again, —that was all, and now that he was home on the Marsh he would soon be well—of course he would soon be well —she was a fool to fret.   And now she would go upstairs and sit with him till the nurse came ; it was her last chance of doing those little tender, rough, intimate things for him . . . . till they were married—oh, she wouldn't let him fling his clothes about like that when they were married !   Meantime she would go up, and see that he swallowed every drop of the herb tea—that was the stuff to give anyone who was ill on the Marsh, no matter what the doctor said . . . . rheumatism, bronchitis, colic, it cured them all.

§ 22

Martin was very ill.   The herb tea did not cure him, nor did the stuff the doctor gave him.   Nor did the starched crackling nurse, who turned Joanna out of the room and exasperatingly spoke of Martin as " my patient."

Joanna had lunch with Sir Harry, who in the stress of anxiety was turning into something very like a father, and afterwards drove off in her trap to Rye, having forgotten all about the Honeychild errand. She went to the fruiterers, and ordered grapes and peaches.

"But you won't get them anywhere now, Miss Godden. It's just between seasons—in another month . . . . "

"I must have 'em now," said Joanna truculently, "I don't care what I pay."

It ended in the telephone at the Post Office being put into hysteric action, and a London shop admonished to send down peaches and grapes to Rye station by passenger train that afternoon.

The knowledge of Martin's illness was all over Walland Marsh by the evening. All the Marsh knew about the doctor and the nurse and the peaches and grapes from London. The next morning they knew that he was worse, and that his brother had been sent for—Father Lawrence arrived on Saturday night, driving in the carrier's cart from Rye station. On Sunday morning people met on their way to church, and shook their heads as they told each other the latest news from North Farthing—double pneumonia, an abscess on the lung . . . . Nell Raddish said his face was blue . . . the Old Squire was quite upset . . . the nurse was like a heathen, raging at the cook . . . . Joanna Godden?—she sat all day in Mr. Martin's study, waiting to be sent for upstairs, but she'd only seen him once . . . .

Then, when tongues at last were quiet in church, just before the second lesson, Mr. Pratt read out—

"I publish the banns of marriage between Martin Arbuthnot Trevor, bachelor, of this parish, and Joanna Mary Godden, spinster, of the parish of Pedlinge. This is for the first time of asking. If any of you know any just cause or impediment why these persons should not be joined together in holy matrimony, ye are to declare it."

§ 23

Martin died early on Monday morning. Joanna was with him at the last, and to the last she did not believe that he would die—because he had given up worrying about himself, so she was sure he must feel better. Three hours before he died he held both her hands and looked at her once more like a man out of his eyes . . . . "Lovely Jo," he said.

She had lain down in most of her clothes as usual, in the little spare room, and between two and three o'clock in the morning the nurse had roused her.

"You're wanted . . . but I'm not sure if he'll know you."

He didn't. He knew none of them—his mind seemed to have gone away and left his body to fight its last fight alone.

"He doesn't feel anything," they said to her, when Martin gasped and struggled—"but don't stay if you'd rather not."

"I'd rather stay," said Joanna, "he may know me. Martin . . ." she called to him. "Martin—I'm here—I'm Jo—" but it was like calling to someone who is already far away down a long road.

There was a faint sweet smell of oil in the room—Father Lawrence had administered the last rites of Holy Church. His romance and Martin's had met at his brother's death-bed . . . "Go forth, Christian soul, from this world, in the Name of God—in the name of the Angels and Archangels—in the name of the Patriarchs, Prophets, Apostles, Evangelists, Martyrs, Confessors, Virgins, and of all the Saints of God ; let thine habitation to-day be in peace and thine abode in Holy Sion " . . . "Martin, it's only me, it's only Jo " . . . Thus the two voices mingled, and he heard neither.

The cold morning lit up the window square, and the window rattled with the breeze of Rye Bay. Joanna felt someone take her hand and lead her towards the door. "He's all right now," said Lawrence's voice—"it's over . . ."

Somebody was giving her a glass of wine—she was sitting in the dining-room, staring unmoved at Nell Raddish's guilt revealed in a breakfast-table laid over night. Lawrence and Sir Harry were both with her, being kind to her, forgetting their own grief in trying to comfort her. But Joanna only wanted to go home. Suddenly she felt lonely and scared in this fine house, with its thick carpets and mahogany and silver—now that Martin was not here to befriend her in it. She did not belong—she was an outsider, she wanted to go away.

She asked for the trap, and they tried to persuade her to stay and have some breakfast, but she repeated doggedly, "I want to go." Lawrence went and fetched the trap round, for the men were not about yet. The morning had not really come—only the cold twilight, empty and howling with wind, with a great drifting sky of fading stars.

Lawrence went with her to the door, and kissed her —"Good-bye, dear Jo. Father or I will come and see you soon." She was surprised at the kiss, for he had never kissed her before, though the Squire had taken full advantage of their relationship—she had supposed it wasn't right for Jesoots.

She did not know what she said to him—probably nothing. There was a terrible silence in her heart. She heard Smiler's hoofs upon the road—clop, clop, clop. But they did not break the silence within . . . . oh, Martin, Martin, put your hand under my arm, against my heart—maybe that'll stop it aching.

Thoughts of Martin crowding upon her, filling her empty heart with memories . . . . Martin sitting on the tombstone outside Brodnyx church on Christmas day, Martin holding her in his arms on the threshold of Ansdore . . . Martin kissing her in New Romney church, bending her back against the pillar stained with the old floods . . . that drive through Broomhill— how he had teased her !—" we'll come here for our honeymoon " . . . Dunge Ness, the moaning sea, the wind, her fear, his arms . . . the warm kitchen of the Britannia, with the light of the wreckwood fire, the teacups on the table, " we shall want to see our children " . . . No, no, you mustn't say that—not *now*, not *now* . . . Remember instead how we quarrelled, how he tried to get between me and Ansdore, so that I forgot Ansdore, and gave it up for his sake ; but it's all I've got now. I gave up Ansdore to Martin, and now I've lost Martin and got Ansdore. I've got three hundred acres and four hundred sheep and three hundred pounds at interest in Lewes Old Bank. But I've lost Martin. I've done valiant for Ansdore, better'n ever I hoped—poor father

ud be proud of me. But my heart's broken. I don't
like remembering—it hurts—I must forget.

Colour had come into the dawn. The Marsh was
slowly turning from a strange papery grey to green. The
sky changed from white to blue, and suddenly became
smeared with ruddy clouds. At once the watercourses
lit up, streaking across the green in fiery slats—the shaking
boughs of the willows became full of fire, and at the turn
of the road the windows of Ansdore shone as if it were
burning.

There it stood at the road's bend. Its roofs a fiery
yellow with the swarming sea-lichen, its solid walls flushed
faintly pink in the sunrise, its windows squares of amber
and flame. It was as a house lit up and welcoming.
It seemed to shout to Joanna as she came to it clop, clop
along the road.

"Come back—come home to me—I'm glad to see
you again. You forgot me for five days, but you won't
forget me any more—for I'm all that you've got now."

PART III

THE LITTLE SISTER

§ 1

FOR many months Ansdore was a piece of wreckage to which a drowning woman clung. Joanna's ship had foundered—the high-castled, seaworthy ship of her life—and she drifted through the dark seas, clinging only to this which had once been so splendid in the midst of her decks, but was now mere wreckage, the least thing saved. If she let go she would drown. So she trailed after Ansdore, and at last it brought her a kind of anchorage, not in her native land, but at least in no unkind country of adoption. During the last weeks of Martin's wooing, she had withdrawn herself a little from the business of the farm into a kind of overlordship, from which she was far more free to detach herself than from personal service. Now she went back to work with her hands— she did not want free hours, either for his company or for her own dreams; she rose early, because she waked early and must rise when she waked, and she went round waking the girls, hustling the men, putting her own hand to the milking or the cooking, more sharp-tongued than ever, less tolerant, but more terribly alive, with a kind of burning, consuming life that vexed all those about her.

"She spicks short wud me," said old Stuppeny, "and I've töald her as she mun look around fur a new head man. This time I'm going."

"She's a scold," said Broadhurst, "and reckon the young chap säaved himself a tedious life by dying."

"Reckon her heart's broke," said Mrs. Tolhurst.

"Her temper's broke," said Milly Pump.

129

They were unsympathetic, because she expressed her grief in terms of fierce activity instead of in the lackadaisical ways of tradition. If Joanna had taken to her bed on her return from North Farthing House that early time, and had sent for the doctor, and shown all the credited symptoms of a broken heart, they would have pitied her and served her and borne with her. But, instead, she had come back hustling and scolding, and they could not see that she did so because not merely her heart but her whole self was broken, and that she was just flying and rattling about like a broken thing. So instead of pitying her, they grumbled and threatened to leave her service—in fact, Milly Pump actually did so, and was succeeded by Mene Tekel Fagge, the daughter of Bibliolatious parents at Northlade.

Ansdore throve on its mistress's frenzy. That autumn Joanna had four hundred pounds in Lewes Old Bank, the result of her splendid markets and of her new ploughs, which had borne eight bushels to the acre. She had triumphed gloriously over everyone who had foretold her ruin through breaking up pasture ; strong-minded farmers could scarcely bear to drive along that lap of the Brodnyx road which ran through Joanna's wheat, springing slim and strong and heavy-eared as from Lothian soil—if there had been another way from Brodnyx to Rye market they would have taken it ; indeed it was rumoured that on one occasion Vine had gone by train from Appledore because he couldn't abear the sight of Joanna Godden's ploughs.

This rumour, when it reached her, brought her a faint thrill. It was the beginning of a slow process of re-identification of herself with her own activities, which till then had been as some furious raging outside the house. She began to picture new acts of discomfiting adventure, new roads which should be shut to Vine through envy. Ansdore was all she had, so she must make it much. When she had given it and herself to Martin she had had all the Marsh and all the world to plant with her love ; but since he was gone and had left her gifts behind him, she had just a few acres to plant with wheat—and her harvest should be bread alone.

§ 2

Her black months had changed her—not outwardly very much, but leaving wounds in her heart. Martin had woken in her too many needs for her to be able to go back quietly into the old life of unfulfilled content. He had shown her a vision of herself as complete woman, mother and wife, of a Joanna Godden bigger than Ansdore. She could no longer be the Joanna Godden whose highest ambition was to be admitted member of the Farmers' Club. He had also woken in her certain simple cravings —for a man's strong arm round her and his shoulder under her cheek. She had now to make the humiliating discovery that the husk of such a need can remain after the creating spirit had left it. In the course of the next year she had one or two small, rather undignified flirtations with neighbouring farmers—there was young Gain over at Botolph's Bridge, and Ernest Noakes of Belgar. They did not last long, and she finally abandoned both in disgust, but a side of her, always active unconsciously, was now disturbingly awake, requiring more concrete satisfactions than the veiled, self-deceiving episode of Socknersh.

She was ashamed of this. And it made her withdraw from comforts she might have had. She never went to North Farthing House, where she could have talked about Martin with the one person who—as it happened—would have understood her treacheries. Lawrence came to see her once at the end of September, but she was gruff and silent. She recoiled from his efforts to break the barriers between life and death ; he wanted her to give Martin her thoughts and her prayers just as if he were alive. But she " didn't hold with praying for the dead "—the Lion and the Unicorn would certainly disapprove of such an act ; and Martin was now robed in white, with a crown on his head and a harp in his hand and a new song in his mouth—he had no need of the prayers of Joanna Godden's unfaithful lips. As for her thoughts, by the same token she could not think of him as he was now ; that radiant being in glistening white was beyond the soft approaches of imagination—robed and crowned, he could scarcely be expected to remember himself in

a tweed suit and muddy boots kissing a flushed and hot
Joanna on the lonely innings by Beggar's Bush. No,
Martin was gone—gone beyond thought and prayer—
gone to sing hymns for ever and ever—he who could
never abide them on earth—gone to forget Joanna in the
company of angels—pictured uncomfortably by her as
females, who would be sure to tell him that she had let
Thomas Gain kiss her in the barn over at Botolph's
Bridge . . . .

She could not think of him as he was now, remote
and white, and she could bear still less to think of him
as he had been once, warm and loving, with his caressing
hands and untidy hair, with his flushed cheek pressed
against hers, and the good smell of his clothes—with his
living mouth closing slowly down on hers . . . no,
earth was even sharper than heaven. All she had of
him in which her memory and her love could find rest
were those few common things they keep to remember
their dead by on the Marsh—a memorial card, thickly
edged with black, which she had had printed at her own
expense, since apparently such things were no part of
the mourning of North Farthing House; his photograph
in a black frame; his grave in Brodnyx churchyard, in
the shadow of the black, three-hooded tower, and not
very far from the altar-tomb on which he had sat and
waited for her that Christmas morning.

§ 3

In the fall of the next year, she found that once again
she had something to engross her outside Ansdore. Ellen
was to leave school that Christmas. The little sister
was now seventeen, and endowed with all the grace and
learning that forty pounds a term can buy. During the
last year she and Joanna had seen comparatively little
of each other. She had received one or two invitations
from her school friends to spend her holidays with them
—a fine testimonial, thought Joanna, to her manners
and accomplishments—and her sister had been only too
glad that she should go, that she should be put out of
the shadow of a grief which had grown too black even

for her sentimental schoolgirl sympathy, so gushing and caressing, in the first weeks of her poor Joanna's mourning.

But things were different now—Martin's memory was laid. She told herself that it was because she was too busy that she had not gone as usual to the Harvest Festival at New Romney, to sing hymns beside the pillar marked with the old floods. She was beginning to forget. She could think and she could love. She longed to have Ellen back again, to love and spoil and chasten. She was glad that she was leaving school, and would make no fugitive visit to Ansdore. Immediately her mind leapt to preparations—her sister was too big to sleep any more in the little bed at the foot of her own, she must have a new bed . . . . and suddenly Joanna thought of a new room, a project which would mop up all her overflowing energies for the next month.

It should be a surprise for Ellen. She sent for painters and paper-hangers, and chose a wonderful new wall-paper of climbing chrysanthemums, rose and blue in colour, and tied with large bows of gold ribbon—real, shining gold. The paint she chose was a delicate fawn, picked out with rose and blue. She bought yards of flowered cretonne for the bed and window curtains, and had the mahogany furniture moved in from the spare bedroom. The carpet she bought brand new—it was a sea of stormy crimson, with fawn-coloured islands rioted over with roses and blue tulips. Joanna had never enjoyed herself so much since she lost Martin, as she did now, choosing all the rich colours, and splendid solid furniture. The room cost her nearly forty pounds, for she had to buy new furniture for the spare bedroom, having given Ellen the mahogany.

As a final touch she hung the walls with pictures. There was a large photograph of Ventnor church, Isle of Wight, and another of Furness Abbey in an Oxford frame ; there was " Don't Touch " and " Mother's Boy " from " Pears' Christmas Annual," and two texts, properly expounded with robins. To crown all, there was her father's certificate of enrolment in the Ancient Order of Buffaloes, sacrificed from her own room, and hung proudly in the place of honour over Ellen's bed.

§ 4

Her sister came at Thomas-tide, and Joanna drove
in to meet her at Rye. Brodnyx had now a station of
its own on the new light railway from Appledore to Lydd,
but Joanna was still faithful to Rye. She loved the spanking miles, the hard white lick of road that flew under her
wheels as she drove through Pedlinge, and then, swinging
round the throws, flung out on the Straight Mile. She
trotted under the Land Gate, feeling pleasantly that
all the town was watching her from shop and street.
Her old love of swagger had come back, with perhaps
a slight touch of defiance.

At the station she had to wake old Stuppeny out of
his slumber on the back seat, and put him in his proper
place at Smiler's head, while she went on the platform.
The train was just due, and she had not passed many remarks with the ticket-collector—a comely young fellow
whom she liked for his build and the sauciness of his tongue
—before it arrived. As it steamed in, her heart began
to beat anxiously—she bit her lip, and actually looked
nervous. Ellen was the only person in the world who
could make her feel shy and ill at ease, and Ellen had
only lately acquired this power; but there had been a
constraint about their meetings for the last year. During
the last year Ellen had become terribly good-mannered
and grown up, and somehow that first glimpse of the
elegant maiden whom her toil and sacrifice had built
out of little Ellen Godden of Ansdore, never failed
to give Joanna a queer sense of awkwardness and
inferiority.

To-day Ellen was more impressive, more "different"
than ever. She had been allowed to buy new clothes
before leaving Folkestone, and her long blue coat and
neat little hat made Joanna, for the first time in her
life, feel tawdry and savage in her fur and feathers. Her
sister stepped down from her third-class carriage as a
queen from her throne, beckoned to Rye's one porter, and
without a word pointed back into the compartment, from
which he removed a handbag; whereat she graciously
gave him twopence and proceeded to greet Joanna.

"Dear Jo," she murmured, filling her embrace with

a soft perfume of hair, which somehow stifled the " Hello, duckie " on the other's tongue.

Joanna found herself turning to Rye's one porter with inquiries after his wife and little boy, doing her best to take the chill off the proceedings. She wished that Ellen wouldn't give herself these airs. It is true that they always wore off as Ansdore reasserted itself in old clothes and squabbles, but Joanna resented her first impressions.

However, her sister thawed a little on the drive home —she was curious about the affairs of Brodnyx and Pedlinge, for her time in two worlds was at an end, and Ansdore was henceforth to give her its horizons.

" Will there be any parties at Christmas ? " she asked.

" Sure to be," said Joanna, " I'll be giving one myself, and Mrs. Vine was telling me only yesterday as she's a mind to have some neighbours in for whist."

" Won't there be any dancing ? "

" Oh, it's that what you're after, is it ? " said Joanna proudly.

" Mabel and Pauline are going to heaps of dances this Christmas—and Myra West is coming out. Mayn't I come out, Joanna ? "

" Come out o' what, dearie ? "

" Oh, you know—put up my hair and go to balls,"

" You can put your hair up any day you please—I put mine up at fifteen, and you're turned seventeen now. As for balls . . . "

She broke off, a little at a loss as to how she was to supply this deficiency. It would scarcely be possible for her to break into the enclosures of Dungemarsh Court —especially since she had allowed herself to drop away from North Farthing House . . . she had been a fool to do that—Sir Harry might have helped her now. But then . . . her lips tightened . . . . Anyhow, he would not be at home for Christmas—since Martin's death he had sub-let the farm and was a good deal away ; people said he had " come into " some money, left him by a former mistress, who had died more grateful than he deserved.

" I'll do the best I can for you, duck," said Joanna,

" you shall have your bit of dancing—and anyways I've got a fine, big surprise for you when we're home."

" What sort of a surprise ? "

" That's telling."

Ellen, in spite of her dignity, was child enough to be intensely excited at the idea of a secret, and the rest of the drive was spent in baffled question and provoking answer.

" I believe it's something for me to wear," she said finally, as they climbed out of the trap at the front door—" a ring, Joanna . . . . I've always wanted a ring."

" It's better than a ring," said Joanna, " leastways it's bigger," and she laughed to herself.

She led the way upstairs, while Mrs. Tolhurst and old Stuppeny waltzed recriminatingly with Ellen's box.

" Where are you taking me ? " asked her sister, pausing with her hand on the door-knob of Joanna's bedroom.

" Never you mind—come on."

Would Mene Tekel, she wondered, have remembered to set the lamps, so that the room should not depend on the faint gutter of sunset to display its glories ? She opened the door, and was reassured—a fury of light and colour leapt out—rose, blue, green, buff, and the port-wine red of mahogany. The pink curtains were drawn, but there was no fire in the grate—for fires in bedrooms were unknown at Ansdore ; however, a Christmas-like effect was given by sprigs of holly stuck in the picture-frames, and a string of paper flowers hung from the bed-tester to the top of the big woolly bell-rope by the mantelpiece. Joanna heard her sister gasp.

" It's yours, Ellen—your new room. I've given it to you—all to yourself. There's the spare mahogany furniture, and the best pictures, and poor father's Buffalo certificate."

The triumph of her own achievement melted away the last of her uneasiness—she seized Ellen in her arms and kissed her, knocking her hat over one ear.

" See, you've got new curtains—eighteenpence a yard . . . and that's mother's text—' Inasmuch . . .' and I've bought a new soap-dish at Godfrey's—it doesn't

quite go with the basin, but they've both got roses on
'em . . . and you won't mind there being a few of my
gowns in the wardrobe—only the skirts—I've got room
for the bodies in my drawers . . . that's the basket
armchair out of the dining-room, with a new cover that
Mene Tekel fixed for it . . . the clock's out of the spare
room—it don't go, but it looks fine on the mantelpiece
. . . . Say, duckie, are you pleased?—are you pleased
with your old Jo?"

"Oh, Joanna . . . thank you," said Ellen.

"Well, I'll have to be leaving you now—that gal's
got a rabbit pie in the oven for our tea, and I must go and
have a look at her crust. You unpack and clean yourself—and be careful not to spoil anything."

§ 5

Supper that night was rather a quiet meal. Something about Ellen drove Joanna back into her old sense
of estrangement. Her sister made her think of a lily
on a thundery day. She wore a clinging dress of dull
green stuff, which sheathed her delicate figure like a lily
bract—her throat rose out of it like a lily stalk, and her
face, with its small features and soft skin, was the face
of a white flower. About her clung a dim atmosphere
of the languid and exotic, like the lily's scent which is
so unlike the lily.

"Ellen," broke out Joanna, with a glance down at
her own high, tight bosom, "don't you ever wear stays?"

"No. Miss Collins and the gym mistress both say
it's unhealthy."

"Unhealthy! And don't they never wear none
themselves?"

"Never. They look much better without—besides,
small waists are going out of fashion."

"But . . . Ellen . . . it ain't seemly—to show
the natural shape of your body as you're doing."

"I've been told my figure's a very good one."

"And whoever dared make such a remark to you?"

"It was a compliment."

"I don't call it any compliment to say such things

to a young girl. Besides, what right have you to go
showing what you was meant to hide ? "

" I'm not showing anything I was meant to hide.
My figure isn't nearly so pronounced as yours—if I had
your figure, I couldn't wear this sort of frock."

" My figure is as God made it "—which it certainly
was not—" and I was brought up to be the shape of a
woman, in proper stays, and not the shape of a heathen
statue. I'd be ashamed for any of the folk around
here to see you like that—and if Arthur Alce, or any
other man, came in, I'd either have to send you out or
wrap the table-cover round you."

Ellen took refuge in a haughty silence, and Joanna
began to feel uneasy and depressed. She thought that
Ellen was " fast." Was this what she had learned at
school—to flout the standards of her home ?

§ 6

The next morning Joanna overslept herself, in consequence of a restless hour during the first part of the
night. As a result, it had struck half past seven before
she went into her sister's room. She was not the kind
of person who knocks at doors, and burst in to find Ellen,
inadequately clothed in funny little garments, doing
something very busily inside the cupboard.

" Hullo, duckie ! And how did you sleep in your
lovely bed ? "

She was once more aglow with the vitality and triumph
of her own being, but the next moment she experienced
a vague sense of chill—something was the matter with
the room, something had happened to it. It had lost
its sense of cheerful riot, and wore a chastened, hangdog
air. In a spasm of consternation Joanna realized that
Ellen had been tampering with it.

" What have you done ?—Where's my pictures ?—
Where've you put the window curtains ? " she cried at
last.

Ellen stiffened herself and tried not to look guilty.

" I'm just trying to find room for my own things."

Joanna stared about her.

" Where's father's Buffalo certificate ? "

" I've put it in the cupboard."

" In the cupboard !—father's . . . . and I'm blessed if you haven't taken down the curtains."

" They clash with the carpet—it quite hurts me to look at them. Really, Joanna, if this is my room, you oughtn't to mind what I do in it."

" Your room, indeed !—You've got some sass !—And I spending more'n forty pound fixing it up for you. I've given you new wall paper and new carpet and new curtains and all the best pictures, and took an unaccountable lot of trouble, and now you go and mess it up."

" I haven't messed it up. On the contrary "—Ellen's vexation was breaking through her sense of guilt—" I'm doing the best I can to make it look decent. Since you say you've done it specially for me and spent all that money on it, I think at least you might have consulted my taste a little."

" And what is your taste, ma'am ? "

" A bit quieter than yours," said Ellen saucily. " There are about six different shades of red and pink in this room."

" And what shades would you have chosen, may I be so bold as to ask ? " Joanna's voice dragged ominously with patience—" the same shade as your last night's gownd, which is the colour of the mould on jam ? I'll have the colours I like in my own house—I'm sick of your dentical, die-away notions. You come home from school thinking you know everything, when all you've learned is to despise my best pictures, and say my curtains clash with the carpet, when I chose 'em for a nice match. I tell you what, ma'am, you can just about put them curtains back, and them pictures, and that certificate of poor father's that you're so ashamed of."

" I want to put my own pictures up," said Ellen doggedly—" if I've got to live with your carpet and wallpaper, I don't see why I shouldn't have my own pictures."

Joanna swept her eye contemptuously over " The Vigil," " Sir Galahad," " The Blessed Damozel," and one or two other schoolgirl favourites that were lying on the bed.

" You can stick those up as well—there ain't such a lot."

" But can't you see, Joanna, that there are too many pictures on the wall already ?—It's simply crowded with them. Really, you're an obstinate old beast," and Ellen began to cry.

Joanna fought back in herself certain symptoms of relenting. She could not bear to see Ellen cry, but on the other hand she had " fixed up " this room for Ellen—she had had it furnished and decorated for her—and now Ellen must and should appreciate it. She should not be allowed to disguise and bowdlerize it to suit the unwelcome tastes she had acquired at school. The sight of her father's Buffalo certificate, lying face downwards on the cupboard floor, gave strength to her flagging purpose.

" You pick that up and hang it in its proper place."

" I won't."

" You will."

" I won't! Why should I have that hideous thing over my bed ? "

" Because it was your father's, and you should ought to be proud of it."

" It's some low drinking society he belonged to, and I'm not proud—I'm ashamed."

Joanna boxed her ears.

" You don't deserve to be his daughter, Ellen Godden, speaking so. It's you that's bringing us all to shame—thank goodness you've left school, where you learned all that tedious, proud nonsense. You hang those pictures up again, and those curtains, and you'll keep this room just what I've made it for you."

Ellen was weeping bitterly now, but her sacrilege had hardened Joanna's heart. She did not leave the room till the deposed dynasty of curtains and pictures was restored, with poor father's certificate once more in its place of honour. Then she marched out.

§ 7

The days till Christmas were full of strain. Joanna had won her victory, but she did not find it a satisfying one. Ellen's position in the Ansdore household was that of a sulky rebel—resentful, plaintive, a nurse of hard memories—too close to be ignored, too hostile to be trusted.

The tyrant groaned under the heel of her victim. She was used to quarrels, but this was her first experience of a prolonged estrangement. It had been all very well to box Ellen's ears as a child, and have her shins kicked in return, and then an hour or two later be nursing her on her lap to the tune of " There was an Old Woman," or " Little Boy Blue " . . . . But this dragged out antagonism wore down her spirits into a long sadness. It was the wrong start for that happy home she had planned, in which Ellen, the little sister, was to absorb that overflowing love which had once been Martin's, but which his memory could not hold in all its power.

It seemed as if she would be forced to acknowledge Ellen's education as another of her failures. She had sent her to school to be made a lady of, but the finished article was nearly as disappointing as the cross-bred lambs of Socknersh's unlucky day. If Ellen had wanted to lie abed of a morning, never to do a hand's turn of work, or had demanded a table napkin at all her meals, Joanna would have humoured her and bragged about her. But, on the contrary, her sister had learned habits of early rising at school, and if left to herself would have been busy all day with piano or pencil or needle of the finer sort. Also she found more fault with the beauties of Ansdore's best parlour than the rigours of its kitchen ; there lay the sting—her revolt was not against the toils and austerities of the farm's life but against its glories and comelinesses. She despised Ansdore for its very splendours, just as she despised her sister's best clothes more than her old ones.

By Christmas Day things had righted themselves a little. Ellen was too young to sulk more than a day or two, and she began to forget her grievances in the excitement of the festival. There was the usual communal midday dinner, with Arthur Alce back in his old place at Joanna's right hand. Alce had behaved like a gentleman, and refused to take back the silver tea set, his premature wedding gift. Then in the evening, Joanna gave a party, at which young Vines and Southlands and Fur-

neses offered their sheepish admiration to her sister Ellen.
Of course everyone was agreed that Ellen Godden gave
herself lamentable airs, but she appealed to her neighbours' curiosity through her queer, exotic ways, and the
young men found her undeniably beautiful—she had a
thick, creamy skin, into which her childhood's roses
sometimes came as a dim flush, and the younger genera-
tion of the Three Marshes was inclined to revolt from
the standards of its fathers.

So young Stacey Vine kissed her daringly under the
mistletoe at the passage bend, and was rewarded with
a gasp of sweet scent, which made him talk a lot at the
Woolpack. While Tom Southland, a man of few words,
went home and closed with his father's offer of a partnership in his farm, which hitherto he had thought of setting
aside in favour of an escape to Australia. Ellen was
pleased at the time, but a night's thought made her
scornful.

" Don't you know any really nice people ? " she asked
Joanna. " Why did you send me to school with gentlemen's daughters if you just meant me to mix with common
people when I came out ? "

" You can mix with any gentlefolk you can find to
mix with. I myself have been engaged to marry a gentleman's son, and his father would have come to my party
if he hadn't been away for Christmas."

She felt angry and sore with Ellen, but she was bound
to admit that her grievance had a certain justification.
After all, she had always meant her to be a lady, and now,
she supposed, she was merely behaving like one. She cast
about her for means of introducing her sister into the
spheres she coveted . . . . if only Sir Harry Trevor
would come home !—But she gathered there was little
prospect of that for some time. Then she thought of
Mr. Pratt, the rector . . . It was the first time that
she had ever considered him as a social asset—his poverty,
his inefficiency and self-depreciation had quite outweighed
his gentility in her ideas ; he had existed only as the
Voice of the Church on Walland Marsh, and the spasmodic
respect she paid him was for his office alone. But now
she began to remember that he was an educated man
and a gentleman, who might supply the want in her

sister's life without in any way encouraging those more
undesirable " notions " she had picked up at school.

Accordingly, Mr. Pratt, hitherto neglected, was invited
to Ansdore with a frequency and enthusiasm that completely turned his head. He spoiled the whole scheme
by misinterpreting its motive, and after about the ninth
tea-party, became buoyed with insane and presumptuous
hopes, and proposed to Joanna. She was overwhelmed,
and did not scruple to overwhelm him, with anger and
consternation. It was not that she did not consider
the rectory a fit match for Ansdore, even with only two
hundred a year attached to it, but she was furious that
Mr. Pratt should think it possible that she could fancy
him as a man—" a little rabbity chap like him, turned
fifty, and scarce a hair on him. If he wants another wife
at his age he should get an old maid like Miss Godfrey
or a hopeful widder like Mrs. Woods—not a woman who's
had real men to love her, and ud never look at anything
but a real, stout feller."

However, she confided the proposal to Ellen, for she
wanted her sister to know that she had had an offer from
a clergyman, and also that she was still considered desirable—for once or twice Ellen had thrown out troubling
hints that she thought her sister middle-aged. Of course
she was turned thirty now, and hard weather and other
hard things had made her inclined to look older, by reddening and lining her face. But she had splendid eyes, hair
and teeth, and neither the grace nor the energy of youth
had left her body, which had coarsened into something
rather magnificent, tall and strong, plump without stout-
ness, clean-limbed without angularity.

She could certainly now have had her pick among
the unmarried farmers—which could not have been said
when she first set up her mastership at Ansdore. Since
those times men had learned to tolerate her swaggering
ways, also her love affair with Martin had made her more
normal, more of a soft, accessible woman. Arthur Alce
was no longer the only suitor at Ansdore—it was well
known that Sam Turner, who had lately moved from
inland to Northlade, was wanting to have her, and Hugh
Vennal would have been glad to bring her as his second
wife to Beggar's Bush. Joanna was proud of these attach-

ments, and saw to it that they were not obscure—also, one or two of the men, particularly Vennal, she liked for themselves, for their vitality and " set-upness " ; but she shied away from the prospect of marriage. Martin had shown her all that it meant in the way of renunciation, and she felt that she could make its sacrifices for no one less than Martin. Also, the frustration of her hopes and the inadequacy of her memories had produced in her a queer antipathy to marriage—a starting aside. Her single state began to have for her a certain worth in itself, a respectable rigour like a pair of stays. For a year or so after Martin's death, she had maintained her solace of secret kisses, but in time she had come to withdraw even from these, and by now the full force of her vitality was pouring itself into her life at Ansdore, its ambitions and business, her love for Ellen, and her own pride.

§ 8

Ellen secretly despised Joanna's suitors, just as she secretly despised all Joanna's best and most splendid things. They were a dull lot, driving her sister home on market-day, or sitting for hours in the parlour with Arthur Alce's mother's silver tea-set. It was always " Good evening, Miss Godden," " Good evening, Mr. Turner "— " Fine weather for roots "—" A bit dry for the grazing." It was not thus that Ellen Godden understood love. Besides, these men looked oafs, in spite of the fine build of some of them—they were not so bad in their working clothes, with their leggings and velveteen breeches, but in their Sunday best, which they always wore on these occasions, they looked clumsy and ridiculous, their broad black coats in the cut of yester-year and smelling of camphor, their high-winged collars scraping and reddening their necks . . . . in their presence Ellen was rather sidling and sweet, but away from them in the riotous privacy of her new bedroom, she laughed to herself and jeered.

She had admirers of her own, but she soon grew tired of them—would have grown tired sooner if Joanna had not clucked and shoo'd them away, thus giving them the glamour of the forbidden thing. Joanna looked upon them all as detrimentals, presumptuously lifting up their eyes to Ansdore's wealth and Ellen's beauty.

" When you fall in love, you can take a stout yeoman with a bit of money, if you can't find a real gentleman same as I did. Howsumever, you're too young to go meddling with such things just yet. You be a good girl, Ellen Godden, and keep your back straight, and don't let the boys kiss you."

Ellen had no particular pleasure in letting the boys kiss her—she was a cold-blooded little thing—but, she asked herself, what else was there to do in a desert like Walland Marsh ? The Marsh mocked her every morning as she looked out of her window at the flat miles between Ansdore and Dunge Ness. This was her home—this wilderness of straight dykes and crooked roads, every mile of which was a repetition of the mile before it. There was never any change in that landscape, except such as came from the sky—cloud-shadows shaking like swift wings across the swamp of buttercups and sunshine, mists lying in strange islands by the sewers, rain turning all things grey, and the wind as it were made visible in a queer flying look put on by the pastures when the storms came groaning inland from Rye Bay . . . . with a great wail of wind and slash of rain and a howl and shudder through all the house.

She found those months of spring and summer very dreary. She disliked the ways of Ansdore ; she met no one but common and vulgar people, who took it for granted that she was just one of themselves. Of course she had lived through more or less the same experiences during her holidays, but then the contact had not been so close or so prolonged, and there had always been the prospect of school to sustain her.

But now schooldays were over, and seemed very far away. Ellen felt cut off from the life and interests of those happy years. She had hoped to receive invitations to go and stay with the friends she had made at school ; but months went by and none came. Her school-friends were being absorbed by a life very different from her own, and she was sensitive enough to realize that parents who had not minded her associating with their daughters while they were still at school, would not care for their grown-up lives to be linked together. At first letters were eagerly written and constantly received, but in time even this comfort failed, as ways became still further divided, and Ellen found herself faced with the alternative of complete isolation or such friendships as she could make on the Marsh.

She chose the latter. Though she would have preferred the humblest seat in a drawing-room to the place of honour in a farm-house kitchen, she found a certain pleasure in impressing the rude inhabitants of Brodnyx and Pedlinge with her breeding and taste. She accepted invitations to " drop in after church," or to take tea, and scratched up rather uncertain friendships with the sisters of the boys who admired her.

Joanna watched her rather anxiously. She tried to persuade herself that Ellen was happy and no longer craved for the alien soil from which she had been uprooted. But there was no denying her own disappointment. A lady was not the wonderful being Joanna Godden had always imagined. Ellen refused to sit in impressive idleness on the parlour sofa, not because she disapproved of idleness, but because she disapproved of the parlour and the sofa. She despised Joanna's admirers, those stout, excellent men she was so proud of, who had asked her in marriage, " as no one ull ever ask you, Ellen Godden, if you give yourself such airs." And worst of all, she despised her sister . . . . her old Jo, on whose back she had ridden, in whose arms she had slept . . . . Those three years of polite education seemed to have wiped out all the fifteen years of happy, homely childhood. Sometimes Joanna wished she had never sent her to a grand school. All they had done there was to stuff her head with nonsense. It would have been better, after all, if she had gone to the National, and learned to say her Catechism instead of to despise her home.

§ 9

One day early in October the Vines asked Ellen to go with them into Rye and visit Lord John Sanger's menagerie. Joanna was delighted that her sister should go—a wild beast show was the ideal of entertainment on the Three Marshes.

" You can put on your best gown, Ellen—the blue one Miss Godfrey made you. You've never been to Lord John Sanger's before, have you ? I'd like to go myself, but Wednesday's the day for Romney, and I just about can't miss this market. I hear they're sending up some heifers from Orgarswick, and there'll be sharp bidding . . . . I envy you going to a wild beast show. I haven't been since Arthur Alce took me in '93. That was the first time he asked me to marry him. I've never had the time to go since, though Sanger's been twice since then, and they had Buffalo Bill in Cadborough meadow . . . . I reckon you'll see some fine riding and some funny clowns—and there'll be stalls where you can buy things, and maybe a place where you can get a cup of tea. You go and enjoy yourself, duckie."

Ellen smiled a wan smile.

On Monday night the news came to the Vines that their eldest son, Bill, who was in an accountant's office at Maidstone, had died suddenly of peritonitis. Of course Wednesday's jaunt was impossible, and Joanna talked as if young Bill's untimely end had been an act of pre-meditated spite.

" If only he'd waited till Thursday—even Wednesday morning ud have done . . . the telegram wouldn't have got to them till after they'd left the house, and Ellen ud have had her treat."

Ellen bore the deprivation remarkably well, but Joanna fumed and champed. " I call it a shame," she said to Arthur Alce,—" an unaccountable shame, spoiling the poor child's pleasure. It's seldom she gets anything she likes, with all her refined notions, but here you have, as you might say, amusement and instruction combined. If only I hadn't got that tedious market . . . . but go I must ; it's not a job I can give to Broadhurst, bidding for them heifers—and I mean to have 'em. I hear Furnese is after 'em, but he can't bid up to me."

" Would you like me to take Ellen to the wild beast show ? " said Arthur Alce.

" Oh, Arthur—that's middling kind of you, that's neigh-bourly. But aren't you going into Romney yourself ? '

" I've nothing particular to go for. I don't want to buy. If I went it ud only be to look at stock."

" Well, I'd take it as a real kindness if you'd drive in Ellen to Rye on Wednesday. The show's there only for the one day, and nobody else is going up from these parts save the Cobbs, and I don't want Ellen to go along with them 'cos of that Tom Cobb what's come back and up to no good."

" I'm only too pleased to do anything for you, Joanna, as you know well."

" Yes, I know it well. You've been a hem good neighbour to me, Arthur."

" A neighbour ain't so good as I'd like to be."

" Oh, don't you git started on that again—I thought you'd done."

" I'll never have done of that."

Joanna looked vexed. Alce's wooing had grown stale, and no longer gratified her. She could not help comparing his sandy-haired sedateness with her memories of Martin's fire and youth—that dead sweetheart had made it impossible for her to look at a man who was not eager and virile ; her admirers were now all, except for him, younger than herself. She liked his friendship, his society, his ready and unselfish support, but she could not bear to think of him as a suitor, and there was almost disdain in her eyes.

" I don't like to hear such talk from you," she said coldly. Then she remembered the silver tea-set which he had never taken back, and the offer he had made just now . . . . " Not but that you ain't a good friend to me, Arthur—my best."

A faint pink crept under his freckles and tan.

" Well, I reckon that should ought to be enough for me—to hear you say that."

" I do say it. And now I'll go and tell Ellen you're taking her into Rye for the show. She'll be a happy girl."

§ 10

Ellen was not quite so happy as her sister expected. Her sum of spectacular bliss stood in Shakespearean plays which she had seen, and in "Monsieur Beaucaire," which she had not. A wild beast show with its inevitable accompaniment of dust and chokiness and noise would give her no pleasure at all, and the slight interest which had lain in the escort of the Vines with the amorous Stacey was now removed. She did not want Arthur Alce's company. Her sister's admirer struck her as a dull dog.

"I won't trouble him," she said. "I'm sure he doesn't really want to go."

"Reckon he does," said Joanna. "He wants to go anywhere that pleases me."

This did not help to reconcile Ellen.

"Well, I don't want to be taken anywhere just to please you."

"It pleases you too, don't it?"

"No, it doesn't. I don't care twopence about fairs and shows, and Arthur Alce bores me."

This double blasphemy temporarily deprived Joanna of speech.

"If he's only taking me to please you," continued Ellen, "he can just leave me at home to please myself."

"What nonsense!" cried her sister—"here have I been racking around for hours just to fix a way of getting you to the show, and now you say you don't care about it."

"Well, I don't."

"Then you should ought to. I never saw such airs as you give yourself. Not care about Sanger's World Wide Show!—I tell you, you just about shall go to it, ma'am, whether you care about it or not, and Arthur Alce shall take you."

Thus the treat was arranged, and on Wednesday afternoon Alce drove to the door in his high, two-wheeled dog-cart, and Ellen climbed up beside him, under the supervision of Mrs. Tolhurst, whom Joanna, before setting out for market, had commissioned to "see as she went." Not that Joanna could really bring herself to believe that Ellen was truthful in saying she did not care about the show, but she thought it possible that sheer con-trariness might keep her away.

Ellen was wearing her darkest, demurest clothes, in emphatic contrast to the ribbons and laces in which

Brodnyx and Pedlinge usually went to the fair. Her hair was neatly coiled under her little, trim black hat, and she wore dark suède gloves and buckled shoes. Alce felt afraid of her, especially as during the drive she never opened her mouth except in brief response to some remark of his.

Ellen despised Arthur Alce—she did not like his looks, his old-fashioned side-whiskers and Gladstone collars, or the amount of hair and freckles that covered the exposed portions of his skin. She despised him, too, for his devotion to Joanna; she did not understand how a man could be inspired with a lifelong love for Joanna, who seemed to her unattractive—coarse and bouncing. She also a little resented this devotion, the way it was accepted as an established fact in the neighbourhood, a standing sum to Joanna's credit. Of course she was fond of her sister—she could not help it—but she would have forgiven her more easily for her ruthless domineering, if she had not also had the advantage in romance. An admirer who sighed hopelessly after you all your life was still to Ellen the summit of desire. It was fortunate that she could despise Alce so thoroughly in his person, or else she might have found herself jealous of her sister.

They arrived at Sanger's in good time for the afternoon performance, and their seats were the best in the tent. Alce, ever mindful of Joanna, bought Ellen an orange and a bag of bull's-eyes. During the performance he was too much engrossed to notice her much—the elephants, the clowns, the lovely ladies, were as fresh and wonderful to him as to any child present, though as a busy farmer he had long ago discarded such entertainments and would not have gone to-day if it had not been for Ellen, or rather for her sister. When the interval came, however, he had time to notice his companion, and it seemed to him that she drooped.

" Are you feeling it hot in here ? "

" Yes—it's very close."

He did not offer to take her out—it did not strike him that she could want to leave.

" You haven't sucked your orange—that'll freshen you a bit."

Ellen looked at her orange.

"Let me peel it for you," said Alce, noticing her gloved hands.

"Thanks very much—but I can't eat it here; there's nowhere to put the skin and pips."

"What about the floor? Reckon they sweep out the sawdust after each performance."

"I'm sure I hope they do," said Ellen, whose next-door neighbour had spat at intervals between his knees, "but really, I'd rather keep the orange till I get home."

At that moment the ring-master came in to start the second half of the entertainment, and Alce turned away from Ellen. He was unconscious of her till the band played "God Save the King," and there was a great scraping of feet as the audience turned to go out.

"We'll go and have a cup of tea," said Alce.

He took her into the refreshment tent, and blundered as far as offering her a twopenny ice-cream at the ice-cream stall. He was beginning to realize that she took her pleasures differently from most girls he knew; he felt disappointed and ill at ease with her—it would be dreadful if she went home and told Joanna she had not enjoyed herself.

"What would you like to do now?" he asked when they had emptied their tea-cups and eaten their stale buns in the midst of a great steaming, munching squash—"there's swings and stalls and a merry-go-round—and I hear the Fat Lady's the biggest they've had yet in Rye; but maybe you don't care for that sort of thing?"

"No, I don't think I do, and I'm feeling rather tired. We ought to be starting back before long."

"Oh, not till you've seen all the sights. Joanna ud never forgive me if I didn't show you the sights. We'll just stroll around, and then we'll go to the George and have the trap put to."

Ellen submitted—she was a born submitter, whose resentful and watchful submission had come almost to the pitch of art. She accompanied Alce to the swings, though she would not go up in them, and to the merry-go-round, though she would not ride in it.

"There's Ellen Godden out with her sister's young man," said a woman's voice in the crowd.

"Maybe he'll take the young girl now he can't get the old 'un," a man answered her.

"Oh, Arthur Alce ull never change from Joanna Godden."

"But the sister's a dear liddle thing, better worth having to my mind."

"Still, I'll never believe . . . ."

The voices were lost in the crowd, and Ellen never knew who had spoken, but for the first time that afternoon her boredom was relieved. It was rather pleasant to have anyone think that Arthur Alce was turning to her from Joanna . . . . it would be a triumph indeed if he actually did turn . . . . for the first time she began to take an interest in him.

The crowd was very thick, and Alce offered her his arm.

"Hook on to me, or maybe I'll lose you."

Ellen did as he told her, and after a time he felt her weight increase.

"Reckon you're middling tired."

He looked down on her with a sudden pity—her little hand was like a kitten under his arm.

"Yes, I am rather tired." It was no pretence—such an afternoon, without the stimulant and sustenance of enjoyment, was exhausting indeed.

"Then we'll go home—reckon we've seen everything."

He piloted her out of the crush, and they went to the George, where the trap was soon put to. Ellen sat drooping along the Straight Mile.

"Lord, but you're hem tired," said Alce, looking down at her.

"I've got a little headache—I had it when I started."

"Then you shouldn't ought to have come."

"Joanna said I was to."

"You should have told her about your head."

"I did—but she said I must come all the same. I said I was sure you wouldn't mind, but she wouldn't let me off."

"Joanna's valiant for getting her own way. Still, it was hard on you, liddle girl, making you come—I shouldn't have taken offence."

"I know you wouldn't. But Jo's so masterful.

She always wants me to enjoy myself in her way, and being strong, she doesn't understand people who aren't."

" That's so, I reckon. Still your sister's a fine woman, Ellen—the best I've known."

" I'm sure she is," snapped Ellen.

" But she shouldn't ought to have made you come this afternoon, since you were feeling poorly."

" Don't let out I said anything to you about it, Arthur —it might make her angry. Oh, don't make her angry with me."

§ 11

During the next few weeks it seemed to Joanna that her sister was a little more alert. She went out more among the neighbours, and when Joanna's friends came to see her, she no longer sulked remotely, but came into the parlour, and was willing to play the piano and talk and be entertaining. Indeed, once or twice when Joanna was busy she had sat with Arthur Alce after tea and made herself most agreeable—so he said.

The fact was that Ellen had a new interest in life. Those words sown casually in her thoughts at the show were bearing remarkable fruit. She had pondered them well, and weighed her chances, and come to the conclusion that it would be a fine and not impossible thing to win Arthur Alce from Joanna to herself.

She did not see why she should not be able to do so. She was prettier than her sister, younger, more accomplished, better educated. Alce on his side must be tired of wooing without response. When he saw there was a chance of Ellen, he would surely take it ; and then— what a triumph ! How people would talk and marvel when they saw Joanna Godden's life-long admirer turn from her to her little sister ! They would be forced to acknowledge Ellen as a superior and enchanting person. Of course there was the disadvantage that she did not particularly want Arthur Alce, but her schemings did not take her as far as matrimony.

She was shrewd enough to see that the best way to capture Alce was to make herself as unlike her sister as

possible. With him she was like a little soft cat, languid
and sleek, or else delicately playful. She appealed to
his protecting strength, and in time made him realize
that she was unhappy in her home life and suffered under
her sister's tyranny. She had hoped that this might
help detach him from Joanna, but his affection was of
that passive, tenacious kind which tacitly accepts all the
faults of the beloved. He was always ready to sympathize
with Ellen, and once or twice expostulated with Joanna
—but his loyalty showed no signs of wavering.

As time went on, Ellen began to like him more in
himself. She grew accustomed to his red hair and freckles,
and when he was in his everyday kit of gaiters and breeches
and broadcloth, she did not find him unattractive. Moreover she could not fail to appreciate his fundamental
qualities of generosity and gentleness—he was like a big,
faithful, gentle dog, a red-haired collie, following and
serving.

§ 12

The weeks went by, and Ellen still persevered. But
she was disappointed in results. She had thought that
Alce's subjection would not take very long, she had not
expected the matter to drag. It was the fault of his
crass stupidity—he was unable to see what she was after,
he looked upon her just as a little girl, Joanna's little
sister, and was good to her for Joanna's sake.

This was humiliating, and Ellen fretted and chafed
at her inability to make him see. She was no siren,
and was without either the parts or the experience for
a definite attack on his senses. She worked as an amateur
and a schoolgirl, with only a certain fundamental shrewd-
ness to guide her ; she was doubtless becoming closer
friends with Alce—he liked to sit and talk to her after
tea, and often gave her lifts in his trap—but he used
their intimacy chiefly to confide in her his love and admiration for her sister, which was not what Ellen wanted.

The first person to see what was happening was Joanna
herself. She had been glad for some time of Ellen's
increased friendliness with Alce, but had put it down

to nothing more than the comradeship of that happy day at Lord John Sanger's show. Then something in Ellen's looks as she spoke to Arthur, in her manner as she spoke of him, made her suspicious—and one Sunday evening, walking home from church, she became sure. The service had been at Pedlinge, in the queer barn-like church whose walls inside were painted crimson ; and directly it was over Ellen had taken charge of Alce, who was coming back to supper with them. Alce usually went to his parish church at Old Romney, but had accepted Ellen's invitation to accompany the Goddens that day, and now Ellen seemed anxious that he should not walk with her and Joanna, but had taken him on ahead, leaving Joanna to walk with the Southlands.

The elder sister watched them—Alce a little oafish in his Sunday blacks, Ellen wearing her new spring hat with the daisies. As she spoke to him she lifted her face on her graceful neck like a swan, and her voice was eager and rather secret. Joanna lost the thread of Mrs. Southland's reminiscences of her last dairy-girl, and she watched Ellen, watched her hands, watched the shrug of her shoulders under her gown—the girl's whole body seemed to be moving, not restlessly or jerkily, but with a queer soft ripple.

Then Joanna suddenly said to herself—" She loves him. Ellen wants Arthur Alce." Her first emotion was of anger, a resolve to stop this impudence ; but the next minute she pitied instead—Ellen, with her fragile beauty, her little die-away airs, would never be able to get Arthur Alce from Joanna, to whom he belonged. He was hers, both by choice and habit, and Ellen would never get him. Then from pity, she passed into tenderness—she was sorry Ellen could not get Arthur, could not have him when she wanted him, while Joanna, who could have him, did not want him. It would be a good thing for her, too. Alce was steady and well-established—he was not like those mucky young Vines and Southlands. Ellen would be safe to marry him. It was a pity she hadn't a chance.

Joanna looked almost sentimentally at the couple ahead—then she suddenly made up her mind. " If I spoke to Arthur Alce, I believe I could make him do it."

She could make Arthur do most things, and she did not
see why he should stop at this. Of course she did not
want Ellen to marry him or anybody, but now she had
once come to think of it she could see plainly, in spite
of herself, that marriage would be a good thing for her
sister. She was being forced up against the fact that
her schemes for Ellen had failed—school-life had spoiled
her, home-life was making both her and home miserable.
The best thing she could do would be to marry, but she
must marry a good man and true—Alce was both good
and true, and moreover his marriage would set Joanna
free from his hang-dog devotion, of which she was beginning to grow heartily tired. She appreciated his friendship and his usefulness, but they could both survive,
and she would at the same time be free of his sentimental
lapses, the constant danger of a declaration. Yes, Ellen
should have him—she would make a present of him to
Ellen.

§ 13

" Arthur, I want a word with you."

They were alone in the parlour, Ellen having been
dispatched resentfully on an errand to Great Ansdore.

" About them wethers ? "

" No—it's a different thing. Arthur, have you noticed
that Ellen's sweet on you ? "

Joanna's approach to a subject was ever direct, but
this time she seemed to have taken the breath out of
Arthur's body.

" Ellen . . . . sweet on me ? " he gasped.

" Yes, you blind-eyed owl. I've seen it for a dunnamany weeks."

" But—Ellen ? That liddle girl ud never care an
onion for a dull, dry chap lik me."

" Reckon she would. You ain't such a bad chap,
Arthur, though I could never bring myself to take you."

" Well, I must say I haven't noticed anything, or maybe
I'd have spoken to you about it. I'm unaccountable sorry,
Jo, and I'll do all I can to help you stop it."

" I'm not sure I want to stop it. I was thinking only
to-day as it wouldn't be a bad plan if you married Ellen."

" But, Jo, I don't want to marry anybody but you."

" Reckon that's middling stupid of you, for I'll never marry you, Arthur Alce—*never !* "

" Then I don't want nobody."

" Oh, yes, you do. You'll be a fool if you don't marry and get a wife to look after you and your house, which has wanted new window-blinds this eighteen month. You can't have me, so you may as well have Ellen—she's next best to me, I reckon, and she's middling sweet on you."

" Ellen's a dear liddle thing, as I've always said against them that said otherwise—but I've never thought of marrying her, and reckon she don't want to marry me, she'd sooner marry a stout young Southland or young Vine."

" She ain't going to marry any young Vine. When she marries I'll see she marries a steady, faithful, solid chap, and you're the best I know."

" It's kind of you to say it, but reckon it wouldn't be a good thing for me to marry one sister when I love the other."

" But you'll never get the other, not till the moon's cheese, so there's no sense in vrothering about that. And I want Ellen to marry you, Arthur, since she's after you. I never meant her to marry yet awhiles, but reckon I can't make her happy at home—I've tried and I can't—so you may as well try."

" It ud be difficult to make Ellen happy—she's a queer liddle dentical thing."

" I know, but marriage is a wonderful soberer-down. She'll be happy once she gets a man and a house of her own."

" I'm not so sure. Anyways I'm not the man for her. She should ought to marry a gentleman."

" Well, there ain't none for her to marry, nor likely to be none. She'll go sour if she has to stand . . . . and she wants you, Arthur. I wouldn't be asking you this if I hadn't seen she wanted you, and seen too as the best thing as could happen to her would be for her to marry you."

" I'm sure she'll never take me."

" You can but ask her."

" She'll say ' No.' "

" Reckon she won't—but if she does, there'll be no harm in asking her."

" You queer me, Jo—it seems a foolish thing to marry Ellen when I want to marry you."

" But I tell you, you can never marry me. You're a stupid man, Arthur, who won't see things as they are. You go hankering after whom you can't get, and all the time you might get someone who's hankering after you. It's a lamentable waste, I say, and I'll never be pleased if you don't ask Ellen. It ain't often I ask you to do anything to please me, and this is no hard thing. Ellen's a fine match—a pretty girl, and clever, and well-taught— she'll play the piano to your friends. And I'll see as she has a bit of money with her. You'll do well for yourself by taking her, and I tell you, Arthur, I'm sick and tired of your dangling after me."

§ 14

Joanna had many more conversations with Arthur Alce, and in the end bore down his objections. She used her tongue to such good purpose that by next Sunday he had come to see that Ellen wanted him, and that for him to marry her would be the best thing for everyone —Joanna, Ellen and himself. After all, it wasn't as if he had the slightest chance of Joanna—she had made that abundantly clear, and his devotion did not feed on hope so much as on a stale content in being famous throughout three marshes as her rejected suitor. Perhaps it was not amiss that her sudden call should stir him into a more active and vital service.

In the simplicity of his heart, he saw nothing outrageous in her demands. She was troubled and anxious about Ellen, and had a right to expect him to help her solve this problem in the best way that had occurred to her. As for Ellen herself, now his attention had been called to the matter, he could see that she admired him and sought him out. Why she should do so was as much a mystery as ever—he could not think why so soft and dainty and beautiful a creature should want to marry a homely chap like himself. But he did not doubt the facts, and when, at the beginning of the second week, he proposed to her, he was much less surprised at her acceptance than she was herself.

Ellen had never meant to accept him—all she had wanted had been the mere proclaimable fact of his surrender ; but during the last weeks the focus of her plans had shifted—they had come to mean more than the gratification of her vanity. The denial of what she sought, the dragging of her schemes, the growing sense of hopelessness, had made her see just exactly how much she wanted. She would really like to marry Alce—the slight physical antipathy with which she had started had now disappeared, and she felt that she would not object to him as a lover. He was, moreover, an excellent match— better than any young Vines or Southlands or Furneses ; as his wife she would be important and well-to-do, her triumph would be sealed, open and celebrated . . . She would moreover be free. That was the strong hidden growth that had heaved up her flat little plans of a mere victory in tattle—if she married she would be her own mistress, free for ever of Joanna's tyranny. She could do what she liked with Alce—she would be able to go where she liked, know whom she liked, wear what she liked ; whereas with Joanna all these things were ruthlessly decreed. Of course she was fond of Jo, but she was tired of living with her—you couldn't call your soul your own —she would never be happy till she had made herself independent of Jo, and only marriage would do that. She was tired of sulking and submitting—she could make a better life for herself over at Donkey Street than she could at Ansdore. Of course if she waited she might get somebody better, but she might have to wait a long time, and she did not care for waiting. She was not old or patient or calculating enough to be a really successful schemer ; her plans carried her this time only as far as a triumph over Joanna and an escape from Ansdore.

§ 15

Certainly her triumph was a great one. Brodnyx and Pedlinge had never expected such a thing. Their attitude had hitherto been that of the man at the fair, who would rather distrust appearances than believe Arthur Alce could change from Joanna Godden to her sister Ellen. It would have been as easy to think of the sunset changing from Rye to Court-at-Street.

There was a general opinion that Joanna had been injured—though no one really doubted her sincerity when she said that she would never have taken Arthur. Her evident pleasure in the wedding was considered magnanimous—it was also a little disappointing to Ellen. Not that she wanted Joanna to be miserable, but she would have liked her to be rather more sensible of .her sister's triumph, to regret rather more the honour that had been taken from her. The bear's hug with which her sister had greeted her announcement, the eager way in which she had urged and hustled preparations for the wedding, all seemed a little incongruous and humiliating. . . . . Joanna should at least have had some moments of realizing her fallen state.

However, what she missed at home Ellen received abroad. Some neighbours were evidently offended, especially those who had sons to mate. Mrs. Vine had been very stiff when Ellen called with Alce.

" Well, Arthur "—ignoring the bride-to-be—" I always felt certain you would marry Ansdore, but it was the head I thought you'd take and not the tail."

" Oh, the tail's good enough for me," said Arthur, which Ellen thought clumsy of him.

Having taken the step, Arthur was curiously satisfied. His obedience in renouncing Joanna seemed to have brought him closer to her than all his long wooing. Besides, he was growing very fond of little Ellen—her soft, clinging ways and little sleek airs appealed to him as those of a small following animal would, and he was proud of her cleverness, and of her prettiness, which now he had come to see, though for a long time he had not appreciated it, because it was so different from Joanna's healthy red and brown.

He took her round the farms, not only in her own neighbourhood, but those near Donkey Street, over on Romney Marsh, across the Rhee Wall. In her honour he bought a new trap, and Ellen drove beside him in it, sitting very demure and straight. People said—" There goes Ellen Godden, who's marrying her sister's young man," and sometimes Ellen heard them.

She inspected Donkey Street, which was a low, plain, oblong house, covered with grey stucco, against which flamed the orange of its lichened roof. It had been built in Queen Anne's time, and enlarged and stuccoed over about fifty years ago. It was a good, solid house, less rambling than Ansdore, but the kitchens were a little damp.

Alce bought new linen and new furniture. He had some nice pieces of old furniture too, which Ellen was very proud of. She felt she could make quite a pleasant country house of Donkey Street. In spite of Joanna's protests, Alce let her have her own way about styles and colours, and her parlour was quite unlike anything ever seen on the Marsh outside North Farthing and Dunge-marsh Court. There was no centre table and no cabinet, but a deep, comfortable sofa, which Ellen called a chester-field, and a " cosy corner," and a Sheraton bureau, and a Sheraton china-cupboard with glass doors. The carpet was purple, without any pattern on it, and the cushions were purple and black. For several days those black cushions were the talk of the Woolpack bar and every farm. It reminded Joanna a little of the frenzy that had greeted the first appearance of her yellow waggons, and for the first time she felt a little jealous of Ellen.

She sometimes, too, had moments of depression at the thought of losing her sister, of being once more alone at Ansdore, but having made up her mind that Ellen was to marry Arthur Alce, she was anxious to carry through the scheme as quickly and magnificently as possible. The wedding was fixed for May, and was to be the most wonderful wedding in the experience of the three marshes of Walland, Dunge and Romney. For a month Joanna's trap spanked daily along the Straight Mile, taking her and Ellen either into Rye to the confectioner's—for Joanna had too true a local instinct to do as her sister wanted and order the cake from London—or to the station for Folkestone where the clothes for both sisters were being bought. They had many a squabble over the clothes —Ellen pleaded passionately for the soft, silken undergarments in the shop windows, for the little lace-trimmed drawers and chemises . . . . . it was cruel and bigoted of Joanna to buy yards and yards of calico for nightgowns and "petticoat bodies," with trimmings of untearable embroidery. It was also painful to be obliged to wear a saxe-blue going-away dress when she wanted an olive green, but Ellen reflected that she was submitting for the last time, and anyhow she was spared the worst by the fact that the wedding-gown must be white—not much scope for Joanna there.

§ 16

The day before the wedding Joanna felt unusually nervous and restless. The preparations had been carried through so vigorously that everything was ready—there was nothing to do, no finishing touches, and into her mind came a sudden blank and alarm. All that evening she was unable to settle down either to work or rest. Ellen had gone to bed early, convinced of the good effect of sleep on her complexion, and Joanna prowled unhappily from room to room, glancing about mechanically for dust which she knew could not be there . . . . the farm was just a collection of gleaming surfaces and crackling chintzes and gay, dashing colours. Everything was as she wished it, yet did not please her.

She went into her room. On the little spare bed which had once been Ellen's lay a mass of tissue paper, veiling a marvellous gown of brown and orange shot silk, the colour of the sunburn on her cheeks, which she was to wear to-morrow when she gave the bride away. In vain had Ellen protested and said it would look ridiculous if she came down the aisle with her sister—Joanna had insisted on her prerogative. "It isn't as if we had any he-cousins fit to look at—I'll cut a better figger than either Tom or Pete Stansbury, and what right has either of them to give you away, I'd like to know?" Ellen had miserably suggested Sam Huxtable, but Joanna had fixed herself in her mind's eye, swaggering, rustling and flaming up Pedlinge aisle, with the little drooping lily of the bride upon her arm. "Who giveth this woman to be married to this man ? " Mr. Pratt would say—" I do," Joanna would answer. Everyone would stare at Joanna, and remember that Arthur Alce had loved her for years before he loved her sister—she was certainly " giving " Ellen to him in a double sense.

She would be just as grand and important at this wedding as she could possibly have been at her own, yet to-night the prospect had ceased to thrill her. Was it because in this her first idleness she realized she was giving away something she wanted to keep ? Or because she saw that, after all, being grand and important at another person's wedding is not as good a thing even as being humble at your own ?

" Well, it might have been my own if I'd liked," she said to herself, but even that consideration failed to cheer her.

She went over to the chest of drawers. On it stood Martin's photograph in a black velvet frame adorned with a small metal shield on which were engraved the words " Not lost but gone before." The photograph was a little faded—Martin's eyes had lost some of their appealing darkness and the curves of the mouth she had loved were dim . . . . . She put her face close to the faded face in the photograph, and looked at it. Gradually it blurred in a mist of tears, and she could feel her heart beating very slowly, as if each beat were an effort . . .

Then suddenly she found herself thinking about Ellen in a new way, with a new, strange anxiety. Martin's fading face seemed to have taught her about Ellen, about some preparation for the wedding which might have been left out, in spite of all the care and order of the burnished house. Did she really love Arthur Alce ?—Did she really know what she was doing—what love meant ?

Joanna put down the photograph and straightened her back. She thought of her sister alone for the last time in her big flowery bedroom, lying down for the last time in the rose-curtained, mahogany bed, for her last night's rest under Ansdore's roof. It was the night on which, if she had not been motherless, her mother would have gone to her with love and advice. Surely on this night of all nights it was not for Joanna to shirk the mother's part.

Her heaviness had gone, for its secret cause had been displayed—no doubt this anxiety and this question had lurked with her all the evening, following her from room to room. She did not hesitate, but went down the passage to Ellen's door, which she opened as usual without knocking.

"Not in bed, yet, duckie?"

Ellen was sitting on the bolster, in her little old plain linen nightdress buttoning to her neck, two long plaits hanging over her shoulders. The light of the rose-shaded lamp streamed on the flowery walls and floor of her compulsory bower, showing the curtains and pictures and vases and father's Buffalo certificate—showing also her packed and corded trunks, lying there like big, blobbed seals on her articles of emancipation.

"Hullo," she said to Joanna, "I'm just going to get in." She did not seem particularly pleased to see her.

"You pop under the clothes, and I'll tuck you up. There's something I want to speak to you about if you ain't too sleepy."

"About what?"

"About this wedding of yours."

"You've spoken to me about nothing else for weeks and months."

"But I want to speak to you different and most particular. Duckie, are you quite sure you love Arthur Alce?"

"Of course I'm sure, or I shouldn't be marrying him."

"There's an unaccountable lot of reasons why any gal ud snap at Arthur. He's got a good name and a good establishment, and he's as mild-mannered and obliging as a cow."

Ellen looked disconcerted at hearing her bridegroom thus defined.

"If that's all I saw in him I shouldn't have said 'yes.' I like him—he's got a kind heart and good manners, and he won't interfere with me—he'll let me do as I please."

"But that ain't enough—it ain't enough for you just to like him. Do you love him?—It's struck me all of a sudden, Ellen, I've never made sure of that, and it ud be a lamentable job if you was to get married to Arthur without loving him."

" But I do love him—I've told you. And may I ask, Jo, what you'd have done if I'd said I didn't ? It's rather late for breaking off the match."

Joanna had never contemplated such a thing. It would be difficult to say exactly how far her plans had stretched, probably no further than the argument and moral suasion which would forcibly compel Ellen to love if she did not love already.

" No, no—I'd never have you break it off—with the carriages and the breakfast ordered, and my new gownd, and your troosoo and all . . . But, Ellen, if you *want* to change your mind . . . . I mean, if you feel, thinking honest, that you don't love Arthur . . . for pity's sake say so now before it's too late. I'll stand by you—I'll face the racket—I'd sooner you did anything than——"

" Oh, don't be an ass, Jo. Of course I don't want to change my mind. I know what I'm doing, and I'm very fond of Arthur—I love him, if you want the word. I like being with him, and I even like it when he kisses me. So you needn't worry."

" Marriage is more than just being kissed and having a man about the house."

" I know it is."

Something in the way she said it made Joanna see she was abysmally ignorant.

" Is there anything you'd like to ask me, dearie ? "

" Nothing you could possibly know anything about."

Joanna turned on her.

" I'll learn you to sass me. You dare say such a thing ! "

" Well, Jo—you're not married, and there *are* some things you don't know."

" That's right—call me an old maid ! I tell you I could have made a better marriage than you, my girl . . . . I could have made the very marriage you're making, for the matter of that."

She stood up, preparing to go in anger. Then suddenly as she looked down on Ellen, fragile and lily-white among the bed-clothes, her heart smote her and she relented. This was Ellen's last night at home.

" Don't let's grumble at each other. I know you and I haven't quite hit it off, my dear, and I'm sorry, as I counted a lot on us being at Ansdore together. I thought maybe we'd be at Ansdore together all our lives. How-sumever, I reckon things are better as they are—it was my own fault, trying to make a lady of you, and I'm glad it's all well ended. Only see as it's truly well ended, dear—for Arthur's sake as well as yours. He's a good chap and deserves the best of you."

Ellen was still angry, but something about Joanna as she stooped over the bed, her features obscure in the lamplight, her shadow dim and monstrous on the ceiling, made a sudden, almost reproachful appeal. A rush of genuine feeling made her stretch out her arms.

"Jo . . . ."

Joanna stooped and caught her to her heart, and for a moment, the last moment, the big and the little sister were as in times of old.

§ 17

Ellen's wedding was the most wonderful that Brodnyx and Pedlinge had seen for years. It was a pity that the law of the land required it to take place in Pedlinge church, which was comparatively small and mean, and which indeed Joanna could never feel was so Established as the church at Brodnyx, because it had only the old harmonium, and queer paintings of angels instead of the Lion and the Unicorn.

However, Mr. Elphick ground and sweated wonders out of "the old harmonister" as it was affectionately called by the two parishes, and everyone was too busy staring at the bride and the bride's sister to notice whether angels or King George the Third presided over the altar.

Joanna had all the success that she had longed for and expected. She walked down the aisle with Ellen white and drooping on her arm, like a sunflower escorting a lily. When Mr. Pratt said "Who giveth this woman to be married to this man?" she answered "I do" in a voice that rang through the church. Afterwards, she took her handkerchief out of her pocket and cried a little, as is seemly at weddings.

Turner of Northlade was Arthur Alce's best man, and there were four bridesmaids dressed in pink—Maudie

Vine, Gertrude Prickett, Maggie Southland and Ivy Cobb. They carried bouquets of roses with lots of spiræa, and wore golden hearts " the gift of the bridegroom." Altogether the brilliance of the company made up for the deficiencies of its barn-like setting and the ineffectiveness of Mr. Pratt, who, discomposed by the enveloping presence of Joanna, blundered more helplessly than ever, so that, as Joanna said afterwards, she was glad when it was all finished without anyone getting married besides the bride and bridegroom.

After the ceremony there was a breakfast at Ansdore, with a wedding-cake and ices and champagne, and waiters hired from the George Hotel at Rye. Ellen stood at the end of the room shaking hands with a long procession of Pricketts, Vines, Furneses, Southlands, Bateses, Turners, Cobbs . . . . She looked a little tired and droopy, for she had had a trying day, with Joanna fussing and fighting her ever since six in the morning; and now she felt resentfully that her sister had snatched the splendours of the occasion from her to herself—it did not seem right that Joanna should be the most glowing, conspicuous, triumphant object in the room, and Ellen, unable to protest, sulked languishingly.

However, if the bride did not seem as proud and happy as she might, the bridegroom made up for it. There was something almost spiritual in the look of Arthur Alce's eyes, as he stood beside Ellen, his arm held stiffly for the repose of hers, his great choker collar scraping his chin, lilies of the valley and camellias sprouting from his buttonhole, a pair of lemon kid gloves—split at the first attempt, so he could only hold them—clutched in his moist hand. He looked devout, exalted, as he armed his little bride and watched her sister.

" Arthur Alce looks pleased enough," said Furnese to Mrs. Bates—" reckon he sees he's got the best of the family."

" Maybe he's thankful now that Joanna wouldn't take him."

Neither of them noticed that the glow was in Alce's eyes chiefly when they rested on Joanna.

He knew that to-day he had pleased her better than he had ever pleased her in his life. To-day she had said

to him " God bless you, Arthur—you're the best friend
I have, or am like to have, neither." To-day he had made
himself her kinsman, with a dozen new opportunities
of service. Chief among these was the dear little girl
on his arm—how pretty and sweet she was ! How he
would love her and cherish her as he had promised Mr.
Pratt ! Well, thank God, he had done Joanna one good
turn, and himself not such a bad one, neither. How clever
she had been to think of his marrying Ellen ! He would
never have thought of it himself ; yet now he saw clearly
that it was a wonderful notion—nothing could be better.
Joanna was valiant for notions . . . . Alce had had
one glass of champagne.

At about four o'clock, Joanna dashed into the circle
round the bride, and took Ellen away upstairs, to put
on her travelling dress of saxe-blue satin—the last humiliation she would have to endure from Ansdore. The honeymoon was being spent at Canterbury, cautiously chosen
by Arthur as a place he'd been to once and so knew the
lie of a bit. Ellen had wanted to go to Wales, or to the
Lakes, but Joanna had sternly forbidden such outrageous
pinings—" Arthur's got two cows calving next week—
what are you thinking of, Ellen Godden ? "

The bridal couple drove away amidst much hilarity,
inspired by the unaccustomed champagne and expressed
in rice and confetti. After they had gone the guests still
lingered, feasting at the littered tables or re-inspecting
and re-valuing the presents which had been laid out,
after the best style, in the dining-room. Sir Harry Trevor
had sent Ellen a little pearl pendant, though he had been
unable to accept Joanna's invitation and come to the
wedding himself—he wrote from a London address and
hinted vaguely that he might never come back to North
Farthing House, which had been let furnished. His
gift was the chief centre of interest—when Mrs. Vine had
done comparing her electro-plated cruet most favourably
with the one presented by Mrs. Furnese and the ignoble
china object that Mrs. Cobb had had the meanness to send,
and Mrs. Bates had recovered from the shock of finding
that her tea-cosy was the exact same shape and pattern
as the one given by Mrs. Gain. People thought it odd
that the Old Squire should send pearls to Ellen Godden—

something for the table would have been much more
seemly.

Joanna had grown weary—her shoulders drooped
under her golden gown, she tossed back her head and
yawned against the back of her hand. She was tired of
it all, and wanted them to go. What were they staying
for? They must know the price of everything pretty
well by this time and have eaten enough to save their
suppers. She was no polished hostess, concealing her
boredom, and the company began soon to melt away.
Traps lurched over the shingle of Ansdore's drive, the
Pricketts walked off across the innings to Great Ansdore,
guests from Rye packed into two hired wagonettes, and
the cousins from the Isle of Wight drove back to the
George, where, as there were eight of them and they refused
to be separated, Joanna was munificently entertaining
them instead of under her own roof.

When the last was gone, she turned back into the
house, where Mrs. Tolhurst stood ready with her broom
to begin an immediate sweep-up after the waiters, whom
she looked upon as the chief source of the disorder. A
queer feeling came over Joanna, a feeling of loneliness,
of craving, and she fell in all her glory of feathers and silk
upon Mrs. Tolhurst's alpaca bosom. Gone were those
arbitrary and often doubtful distinctions between them,
and the mistress enjoyed the luxury of a good cry in her
servant's arms.

§ 18

Ellen's marriage broke into Joanna's life quite as
devastatingly as Martin's death. Though for more than
three years her sister had been away at school, with an
ever-widening gulf of temperament between herself and
the farm, and though since her return she had been little
better at times than a rebellious and sulky stranger,
nevertheless she was a part of Ansdore, a part of Joanna's
life there, and the elder sister found it difficult to adjust
things to her absence.

Of course Ellen had not gone very far—Donkey Street
was not five miles from Ansdore, though in a different
parish and a different county. But the chasm between

them was enormous—it was queer to think that a mere
change of roof-tree could make such a difference. No
doubt the reason was that with Ellen it had involved
an entire change of habit. While she lived with Joanna
she had been bound both by the peculiarities of her sister's
nature and her own to accept her way of living. She
had submitted, not because she was weak or gentle-
minded but because submission was an effective weapon
of her welfare ; now, having no further use for it, she ruled
instead and was another person. She was, besides, a
married woman, and the fact made all the difference
to Ellen herself. She felt herself immeasurably older
and wiser than Joanna, her teacher and tyrant. Her
sister's life seemed to her puerile . . . . Ellen had at
last read the riddle of the universe and the secret of wisdom.

The sisters' relations were also a little strained over
Arthur Alce. Joanna resented the authority that Ellen
assumed—it took some time to show her that Arthur
was no longer hers. She objected when Ellen made him
shave off his moustache and whiskers ; he looked ten
years younger and a far handsomer man, but he was
no longer the traditional Arthur Alce of Joanna's history,
and she resented it. Ellen on her part resented the way
Joanna still made use of him, sending him to run errands
and make inquiries for her just as she used in the old
days before his marriage. " Arthur, I hear there's some
good pigs going at Honeychild auction—I can't miss
market at Lydd, but you might call round and have a
look for me." Or " Arthur, I've a looker's boy coming
from Abbot's Court—you might go there for his characters,
I haven't time, with the butter-making to-day and Mene
Tekel such an owl."

Ellen rebelled at seeing her husband ordered about,
and more than once " told off " her sister, but Joanna
had no intention of abandoning her just claims in Arthur,
and the man himself was pig-headed—" I mun do what
I can for her, just as I used." Ellen could make him
shave off his whiskers, she could even make him on occasion young and fond and frolicsome, but she could not
make him stop serving Joanna, or, had she only known
it, stop loving her. Arthur was perfectly happy as Ellen's
husband, and made her, as Joanna had foretold, an ex-

emplary one, but his love for Joanna seemed to grow rather than diminish as he cared for and worked for and protected her sister. It seemed to feed and thrive on his love for Ellen—it gave him a wonderful sense of action and effectiveness, and people said what a lot of good marriage had done for Arthur Alce, and that he was no longer the dull chap he used to be.

§ 19

It had done Ellen a lot of good too. During the next year she blossomed and expanded. She lost some of her white looks. The state of marriage suited her thoroughly well. Being her own mistress and at the same time having a man to take care of her, having an important and comfortable house of her own, ordering about her own servants and spending her husband's money, such things made her life pleasant, and checked the growth of peevishness that had budded at Ansdore.

During the first months of her marriage, Joanna went fairly often to see her, one reason being the ache which Ellen's absence had left in her heart—she wanted to see her sister, sit with her, hear her news. Another reason was the feeling that Ellen, a beginner in the ways of life and household management, still needed her help and guidance. Ellen soon undeceived her on this point. " I really know how to manage my own house, Joanna," she said once or twice when the other commented and advised, and Joanna had been unable to enforce her ideas, owing to the fact that she seldom saw Ellen above once or twice a week. Her sister could do what she liked in her absence, and it was extraordinary how definite and cocksure the girl was about things she should have approached in the spirit of meekness and dependence on her elders.

" I count my linen after it is aired—it comes in at such an inconvenient time that I can't attend to it then. The girls can easily hang it out on the horse—really, Joanna, one must trust people to do something."

" Well, then, don't blame me when you're a pillow-case short."

" I certainly shan't blame you," said Ellen coolly.

Joanna felt put out and injured. It hurt her to see that Ellen did not want her supervision—she had looked forward to managing Donkey Street as well as Ansdore. She tried to get a hold on Ellen through Arthur Alce. " Arthur, it's your duty to see Ellen don't leave the bread-making to that cook-gal of hers. I never heard of such a notion—her laying on the sofa while the gal wastes coal and flour." . . . " Arthur, Ellen needs a new churn —let her get a Wallis. It's a shame for her to be buying new cushions when her churn's an old butter-spoiler I wouldn't use if I was dead—Arthur, you're there with her, and you can make her do what I say."

But Arthur could not, any more than Joanna, make Ellen do what she did not want. He had always been a mild-mannered man, and he found Ellen, in her different way, quite as difficult to stand up to as her sister.

" I'm not going to have Jo meddling with my affairs," she would say with a toss of her head.

§ 20

Another thing that worried Joanna was the fact that the passing year brought no expectations to Donkey Street. One of her happiest anticipations in connexion with Ellen's marriage was her having a dear little baby whom Joanna could hug and spoil and teach. Perhaps it would be a little girl, and she would feel like having Ellen over again.

She was bitterly disappointed when Ellen showed no signs of obliging her quickly, and indeed quite shocked by her sister's expressed indifference on the matter.

" I don't care about children, Jo, and I'm over young to have one of my own."

" Young ! You're rising twenty, and mother was but eighteen when I was born."

" Well, anyhow, I don't see why I should have a child just because you want one."

" I don't want one. For shame to say such things, Ellen Alce."

" You want me to have one, then, for your benefit."

" Don't you want one yourself ? "

"No—not now. I've told you I don't care for children."

"Then you should ought to! Dear little mites! It's a shame to talk like that. Oh, what wouldn't I give, Ellen, to have a child of yours in my arms."

"Why don't you marry and have one of your own?"

Joanna coloured.

"I don't want to marry."

"But you ought to marry if that's how you feel. Why don't you take a decent fellow like, say, Sam Turner, even if you don't love him, just so that you may have a child of your own? You're getting on, you know, Joanna—nearly thirty-four—you haven't much time to waste."

"Well it ain't my fault," said Joanna tearfully, "that I couldn't marry the man I wanted to. I'd have been married more'n five year now if he hadn't been took. And it's sorter spoiled the taste for me, as you might say. I don't feel inclined to get married—it don't take my fancy, and I don't see how I'm ever going to bring myself to do it. That's why it ud be so fine for me if you had a little one, Ellen—as I could hold and kiss and care for and feel just as if it was my own."

"Thanks," said Ellen.

§ 21

The winding up of her plans for her sister made it necessary that Joanna should cast about for fresh schemes to absorb her energies. The farm came to her rescue in this fresh, more subtle collapse, and she turned to it as vigorously as she had turned after Martin's death, and with an increase of that vague feeling of bitterness which had salted her relations with it ever since.

A strong rumour was blowing on the Marsh that shortly Great Ansdore would come into the market. Joanna's schemes at once were given their focus. She would buy Great Ansdore if she had the chance. She had always resented its presence, so inaptly named, on the fringe of Little Ansdore's greatness. If she bought it, she would be adding more than fifty acres to her own, but it was

good land—Prickett was a fool not to have made more
of it—and the possession carried with it manorial rights,
including the presentation of the living of Brodnyx with
Pedlinge.   When Joanna owned Great Ansdore in addition
to her own thriving and established patrimony, she would
be a big personage on the Three Marshes, almost "county."
No tenant or yeoman from Dymchurch to Winchelsea,
from Romney to the coast, would dare withhold his respect
—she might even at last be admitted a member of the
Farmers' Club. . . .

It was characteristic of her that, with this purchase
in view, she made no efforts to save money.   She set out
to make it instead, and her money-making was all of the
developing, adventurous kind—she ploughed more grass,
and decided to keep three times the number of cows and
open a milk-round.

As a general practice only a few cows were kept on
the Marsh farms, for, owing to the shallowness of the dykes,
it was difficult to prevent their straying.   However,
Joanna boldly decided to fence all the Further Innings.
She could spare that amount of grazing, and though she
would have to keep down the numbers of her sheep till
after she had bought Great Ansdore, she expected to make
more money out of the milk and dairy produce—she
might even in time open a dairy business in Rye.   This
would involve the engaging of an extra girl for the dairy
and chickens, and an extra man to help Broadhurst with
the cows, but Joanna was undaunted.   She enjoyed a
gamble, when it was not merely a question of luck, but
also in part a matter of resource and planning and hard
driving pace.

"There's Joanna Godden saving her tin to buy Great
Ansdore," said Bates of Pickuye Bush to Cobb of Slinches,
as they watched her choosing her shorthorns at Romney.
She had Arthur Alce beside her, and he was, as in the
beginning, trying to persuade her to be a little smaller
in her ideas, but, as in the beginning, she would not
listen.

"Setting up cow-keeping now, is she ?—Will she make
as much a valiant wonder of that as she did with her
sheep ?   Ha ! ha !"

"Ha ! ha !"   The two men laughed and winked

and rubbed their noses, for they liked to remember the doleful tale of Joanna's first adventure at Ansdore; it made them able to survey more equably her steady rise in glory ever since.

It was obvious to Walland Marsh that, on the whole, her big ideas had succeeded where the smaller, more cautious ones of her neighbours had failed. Of course she had been lucky—luckier than she deserved—but she was beginning to make men wonder if after all there wasn't policy in paying a big price for a good thing, rather than in obeying the rules of haggle which maintained on other farms. Ansdore certainly spent half as much again as Birdskitchen or Beggar's Bush or Misleham or Yokes Court, but then it had nearly twice as much to show for it. Joanna was not the woman who would fail to keep pace with her own prosperity—her swelling credit was not recorded merely in her pass-book; it was visible, indeed dazzling, to every eye.

She had bought a new trap and mare—a very smart turn-out, with rubber tires and chocolate-coloured upholstery, while the mare herself had blood in her, and a bit of the devil too, and upset the sleepy, chumbling rows of farmers' horses waiting for their owners in the streets of Lydd or Rye. Old Stuppeny had died in the winter following Ellen's marriage, and had been lavishly buried, with a tombstone, and an obituary notice in the *Rye Observer*, at Joanna's expense. In his place she had now one of those good-looking, rather saucy-eyed young men, whom she liked to have about her in a menial capacity. He wore a chocolate-coloured livery made by a tailor in Marlingate, and sat on the seat behind Joanna with his arms folded across his chest, as she spanked along the Straight Mile.

Joanna was now thirty-three years old, and in some ways looked older than her age, in others younger. Her skin, richly weather-beaten into reds and browns, and her strong, well-developed figure in its old-fashioned stays, made her look older than her eyes, which had an expectant, childish gravity in their brightness, and than her mouth, which was still a young woman's mouth, large, eager, full-lipped, with strong, little, white teeth. Her hair was beautiful—it had no sleekness, but, even in its coils, looked rough and abundant, and it had the same rich, apple-red colours in it as her skin.

She still had plenty of admirers, for the years had made her more rather than less desirable in herself, and men had grown used to her independence among them. Moreover, she was a " catch," a maid with money, and this may have influenced the decorous, well-considered offers she had about this time from farmers inland as well as on the Marsh. She refused them decidedly—nevertheless, it was obvious that she was well pleased to have been asked ; these solid, estimable proposals testified to a quality in her life which had not been there before.

Yes—she had done well for herself on the whole, she thought. Looking back over her life, over the ten years she had ruled at Ansdore, she saw success consistently rewarding hard work and high ambition. She saw, too, strange gaps—parts of the road which had grown dim in her memory, parts where probably there had been a turning, where she might have left this well-laid, direct and beaten highway for more romantic field-paths. It was queer, when she came to think of it, that nothing in her life had been really successful except Ansdore, that directly she had turned off her high-road she had become at once as it were bogged and lantern-led. Socknersh . . . . Martin . . . . Ellen . . . . there had been by-ways, dim paths leading into queer unknown fields, a strange beautiful land, which now she would never know.

§ 22

Ellen watched her sister's thriving. " She's almost a lady," she said to herself, " and it's wasted on her." She was inclined to be dissatisfied with her own position in local society. When she had first married she had not thought it would be difficult to get herself accepted as " county " in the new neighbourhood, but she had soon discovered that she had had far more consequence as Joanna Godden's sister than she would ever have as Arthur Alce's wife. Even in those days Little Ansdore had been a farm of the first importance, and Joanna was at least notorious where she was not celebrated ; but Donkey Street held comparatively humble rank in a district overshadowed by Dungemarsh Court, and Arthur was not the man to push himself into consideration, though Ellen had agreed that half her marriage portion should be spent on the improvement of his farm.

No one of any consequence had called upon her, though her drawing-room, with its black cushions and Watts pictures, was more fit to receive the well-born and well-bred than Joanna's disgraceful parlour of oleographs and aspidistras and stuffed owls. The Parson had " visited " Mrs. Alce a few weeks after her arrival, but a " visit " is not a call, and when at the end of three months his wife still ignored her existence, Ellen made Arthur come over with her to Brodnyx and Pedlinge on the Sundays she felt inclined to go to church, saying that she did not care for their ways at Romney, where they had a lot of ceremonial centering round the alms-dish.

It was bitter for her to have to watch Joanna's steady rise in importance—the only respect in which she felt bitter towards her sister, since it was the only respect in which she felt inferior to her. After a time, Joanna discovered this. At first she had enjoyed pouring out her triumphs to Ellen on her visits to Donkey Street, or on the rarer occasions when Ellen visited Ansdore.

" Yes, my dear, I've made up my mind. I'm going to give a dinner-party—a late dinner-party. I shall ask the people to come at seven, and then not have dinner till the quarter, so as there'll be no chance of the food being kept waiting. I shall have soup and meat and a pudding, and wine to drink."

" Who are you going to invite ? " asked Ellen, with a curl of her lip.

" Why, didn't I tell you ? Sir Harry Trevor's coming back to North Farthing next month. Mrs. Tolhurst got it from Peter Crouch, who had it from the Woolpack yesterday. He's coming down with his married sister, Mrs. Williams, and I'll ask Mr. Pratt, so as there'll be two gentlemen and two ladies. I'd ask you, Ellen, only I know Arthur hasn't got an evening suit."

" Thanks. I don't care about dinner-parties. Who's going to do your waiting ? "

" Mene Tekel. She's going to wear a cap, and stand in the room all the time."

" I hope that you'll be able to hear yourselves talk through her breathing."

It struck Joanna that Ellen was not very cordial.

" I believe you want to come," she said, " and I tell you, duckie, I'll try and manage it. It doesn't matter about Arthur not having proper clothes—I'll put ' evening dress optional ' on the invitations. "

" I shouldn't do that," said Ellen, and laughed in a way that made Joanna feel uncomfortable. " I really don't want to come in the least—it would be very dreary driving to and fro."

" Then what's the matter, dearie ? "

" Matter ? There's nothing the matter."

But Joanna knew that Ellen felt sore, and failing to discover the reason herself at last applied to Arthur Alce.

" If you ask me," said Arthur, " it's because she's only a farmer's wife."

" Why should that upset her all of a sudden ? "

" Well, folks don't give her the consequence she'd like ; and now she sees you having gentry at your table. . . . "

" I'd have had her at it too, only she didn't want to come, and you haven't got the proper clothes. Arthur, if you take my advice, you'll go into Lydd this very day and buy yourself an evening suit."

" Ellen won't let me. She says I'd look a clown in it."

" Ellen's getting very short. What's happened to her these days ? "

" It's only that she likes gentlefolk and is fit to mix with them ; and after all, Jo, I'm nothing but a pore common man."

" I hope you don't complain of her, Arthur ? "

" Oh, no—I've no complaints—don't you think it. And don't you go saying anything to her, Jo."

" Then what am I to do about it ? I won't have her troubling you, nor herself, neither. I tell you what I'll do—look here !—I—I—" Joanna gave a loud sacrificial gulp—" I'll make it middle-day dinner instead of late, and then you won't have to wear evening dress, and Ellen can come and meet the Old Squire. She should ought to, seeing as he gave her a pearl locket when she was

married. It won't be near so fine as having it in the
evening, but I don't want neither her nor you to be upset
—and I can always call it ' lunch ' . . . ."

§ 23

As the result of Joanna's self-denial, Ellen and Arthur
were able to meet Sir Harry Trevor and his sister at
luncheon at Ansdore. The luncheon did not differ in
any respect from the dinner as at first proposed. There
was soup—much to Ellen's annoyance, as Arthur had
never been able to master the etiquette of its consumption
—and a leg of mutton and roast fowls, and a large fig
pudding, washed down with some really good wine, for
Joanna had asked the wine-merchant at Rye uncom-
promisingly for his best—" I don't mind what I pay
so long as it's that "—and had been served accordingly.
Mene Tekel waited, with creaking stays and shoes, and
loud breaths down the visitors' necks as she thrust vege-
table dishes and sauce-boats at perilous angles over their
shoulders.

Ellen provided a piquant contrast to her surroundings.
As she sat there in her soft grey dress, with her eyes cast
down under her little town hat, with her quiet voice,
and languid, noiseless movements, anything more unlike
the average farmer's wife of the district was difficult
to imagine. Joanna felt annoyed with her for dressing
up all quiet as a water-hen, but she could see that, in spite
of it, her sacrifice in having her party transferred from
the glamorous evening hour had been justified. Both
the Old Squire and his sister were obviously interested
in Ellen Alce—he in the naïve unguarded way of the
male, she more subtly and not without a dash of
patronage.

Mrs. Williams always took an interest in any woman
she thought downtrodden, as her intuition told her Ellen
was by that coarse, hairy creature, Arthur Alce. She
herself had disposed of an unsatisfactory husband with
great decision and resource, and, perhaps as a thank-
offering, had devoted the rest of her life to woman's
emancipation. She travelled about the country lecturing

for a well-known suffrage society, and was bitterly disappointed in Joanna Godden because she expressed herself quite satisfied without the vote.

" But don't you feel it humiliating to see your carter and your cowman and your shepherd boy all go up to Rye to vote on polling-day, while you, who own this farm, and have such a stake in the country, aren't allowed to do so ? "

" It only means as I've got eight votes instead of one," said Joanna, " and don't have the trouble of going to the poll, neither. Not one of my men would dare vote but as I told him, so reckon I do better than most at the elections."

Mrs. Williams told Joanna that it was such opinions which were keeping back the country from some goal unspecified.

" Besides, you have to think of other women, Miss Godden—other women who aren't so fortunate and independent as yourself."

She gave a long glance at Ellen, whose downcast eyelids flickered.

" I don't care about other women," said Joanna, " if they won't stand up for themselves, I can't help them. It's easy enough to stand up to a man. I don't think much of men, neither. I like 'em, but I can't think any shakes of their doings. That's why I'd sooner they did their own voting and mine too. Now, Mene Tekel, can't you see the Squire's ate all his cabbage ?—You hand him the dish again—not under his chin—he don't want to eat out of it—but low down, so as he can get hold of the spoon . . . ."

Joanna looked upon her luncheon party as a great success, and her pleasure was increased by the fact that soon after it Sir Harry Trevor and his sister paid a ceremonial call on Ellen at Donkey Street.

" Now she'll be pleased," thought Joanna, " it's always what she's been hankering after—having gentlefolk call on her and leave their cards. It ain't my fault it hasn't happened earlier . . . I'm unaccountable glad she met them at my house. It'll learn her to think prouder of me."

§ 24

That spring and summer Sir Harry Trevor was a good deal at North Farthing, and it was rumoured on the Marsh that he had run through the money so magnanimously left him and had been driven home to economize. Joanna did not see as much of him as in the old days—he had given up his attempts at farming, and had let off all the North Farthing land except the actual garden and paddock. He came to see her once or twice, and she went about as rarely to see him. It struck her that he had changed in many ways, and she wondered a little where he had been and what he had done during the last four years. He did not look any older. Some queer, rather unpleasant lines had traced themselves at the corners of his mouth and eyes, but strangely enough, though they added to his characteristic air of humorous sophistication, they also added to his youth, for they were lines of desire, of feeling . . . . perhaps in his four years of absence from the Marsh he had learned how to feel at last, and had found youth instead of age in the commotions which feeling brings. Though he must be fifty-five, he looked scarcely more than forty— and he had a queer, weak, loose, emotional air about him that she found it hard to account for.

In the circumstances she did not press invitations upon him, she had no time to waste on men who did not appreciate her as a woman—which the Squire, in spite of his susceptibility, obviously failed to do. From June to August she met him only once, and that was at Ellen's. Neither did she see very much of Ellen that summer—her life was too full of hard work, as a substitute for economy.

Curiously enough next time she went to see her sister Sir Harry was there again.

"Hullo! I always seem to be meeting you here," she said—"and nowhere else—you never come to see me now."

Sir Harry grinned.

"You're always so mortal busy, Jo—I'd feel in your way. Now this little woman never seems to have much to do. You're a lazy little thing, Ellen—I don't believe you ever move off the sofa, except to the piano."

Joanna was surprised to see him on such familiar terms with her sister—"Ellen," indeed! He'd no right to call her that.

"Mrs. Alce hasn't nothing beyond her housework to do—and any woman worth her keep 'ull get shut of that in the morning. Now I've got everything on my hands—and I've no good, kind Arthur to look after me neither," and Joanna beamed on Arthur Alce as he stirred his tea at the end of the table.

"And jolly thankful you are that you haven't," said the Squire. "Own up, Joanna, and say that the last thing you'd want in life would be someone to look after you."

"Well, it strikes me,' said Joanna, "as most of the people I meet want looking after themselves, and it 'ud be just about waste for any of 'em to start looking after me."

Arthur Alce unexpectedly murmured something that sounded like "Hear, hear."

When Joanna left, he brought round her trap, as the saucy-eyed young groom was having a day off in Rye.

"How've your turnips done?" he asked.

"Not so good as last year, but the wurzels are fine."

"Mine might be doing better"—he stood fumbling with a trace-buckle.

"Has that come loose?" asked Joanna.

"Nun-no. I hope your little lady liked her oats."

"She looks in good heart—watch her tugging. You've undone that buckle, Arthur."

"So I have—I was just fidgeting."

He fastened the strap again, his fingers moving clumsily and slowly. It struck her that he was trying to gain time, that he wanted to tell her something.

"Anything the matter, Arthur?"

"Nothing—why?"

"Oh, it struck me you looked worried."

"What should I be worried about?"

"There's a lot of things you might be worried about. What did you tell me about your wurzels?"

"They're not so bad."

" Then I can't see as there's any need for you to look glum."

" No more there ain't," said Arthur in the voice of a man making a desperate decision.

§ 25

It was not till nearly a month later that Joanna heard that people were " talking " about Ellen and Sir Harry. Gossip generally took some time to reach her, owing to her sex, which was not privileged to frequent the Wool-pack bar, .where rumours invariably had a large private circulation before they were finally published at some auction or market. She resented this disability, but in spite of the general daring of her outlook and behaviour, nothing would have induced her to enter the Woolpack save by the discreet door of the landlady's parlour, where she occasionally sipped a glass of ale. However, she had means of acquiring knowledge, though not so quickly as those women who were provided with husbands and sons. On this occasion Mene Tekel Fagge brought the news, through the looker at Slinches, with whom she was walking out.

" That'll do, Mene," said Joanna to her handmaiden, " you always was the one to pick up idle tales, and Dansay should ought to be ashamed of himself, drinking and talking the way he does. Now you go and tell Peter Crouch to bring me round the trap."

She drove off to Donkey Street, carrying her scandal to its source. She was extremely angry—not that for one moment she believed in the truth of those accusations brought against her sister, but Ellen was just the sort of girl, with her airs and notions, to get herself talked about at the Woolpack, and it was disgraceful to have such things said about one, even if they were not true. There was a prickly heat of shame in Joanna's blood as she hustled the mare over the white loops of the Romney road.

The encounter with Ellen made her angrier still.

" I don't care what they say," said her sister, " why should I mind what a public-house bar says against me ? "

" Well, you should ought to mind—it's shameful."

" They've said plenty against you."

" Not that sort of thing."

" I'd rather have that sort of thing said about me than some."

" Ellen ! "

" Well, the Squire's isn't a bad name to have coupled with mine, if they must couple somebody's."

" I wonder you ain't afraid of being struck dead, talking like that—you with the most kind, good-tempered and lawful husband that ever was."

" Do you imagine that I'm disloyal to Arthur ? "

" Howsumever could you think I'd dream of such a thing ? "

" Well, it's the way you're talking."

" It ain't."

" Then why are you angry ? "

" Because you shouldn't ought to get gossiped about like that."

" It isn't my fault."

" It is. You shouldn't ought to have Sir Harry about the place as much as you do. The last two times I've been here, he's been too."

" I like him—he amuses me."

" I like him too, but he ain't worth nothing, and he's got a bad name. You get shut of him, Ellen—I know him, and I know a bit about him ; he ain't the sort of man to have coming to your house when folks are talking."

" You have him to yours—whenever you can get him."

" But then I'm a single woman, and he being a single man there's no harm in it."

" Do you think that a married woman should know no man but her husband ? "

" What did she marry a husband for ? "

" Really, Joanna . . . . however, there's no use arguing with you. I'm sorry you're annoyed at the gossip, but to keep out of the gossip here one would have to live like a cabbage, You haven't exactly kept out of it yourself."

" Have done, do, with telling me that. They only talk about me because I'm more go-ahead than any of 'em, and make more money. Anyone may talk about you that way and I shan't mind. But to have it said at the Woolpack as you, a married woman, lets a man like Sir Harry be for ever hanging around your house . . . . "

" Are you jealous ? " said Ellen softly. " Poor old Jo—I'm sorry if I've taken *another* of your men."

Joanna opened her mouth and stared at her. At first she hardly understood, then, suddenly grasping what was in Ellen's mind, she took in her breath for a torrential explanation of the whole matter. But the next minute she realized that this was hardly the moment to say anything which would prejudice her sister against Arthur Alce. If Ellen would value him more as a robbery, then let her persist in her delusion. The effort of silence was so great that Joanna became purple and apoplectic —with a wild, grabbing gesture she turned away, and burst out of the house into the drive, where her trap was waiting.

§ 26

The next morning Mene Tekel brought fresh news from the Woolpack, and this time it was of a different quality, warranted to allay the seething of Joanna's moral sense. Sir Harry Trevor had sold North Farthing to a retired bootmaker. He was going to the South of France for the winter, and was then coming back to his sister's flat in London, while she went for a lecturing tour in the United States. The Woolpack was very definitely and minutely informed as to his doings, and had built its knowledge into the theory that he must have had some more money left him.

Joanna was delighted—she forgave Sir Harry, and Ellen too, which was a hard matter. None the less, as November approached through the showers and floods, she felt a little anxious lest he should delay his going or perhaps even revoke it. However, the first week of the month saw the arrival of the bootmaker from Deal, with two van-loads of furniture, and his wife and four grown-up daughters—all as ugly as roots, said the Woolpack. The Squire's furniture was sold by auction at Dover, from which port his sailing was in due course guaranteed by credible eye-witnesses. Joanna once more breathed freely. No one could talk about him and Ellen now—that disgraceful scandal, which seemed to lower Ellen to the level of Marsh dairy-girls in trouble, and had about it too that strange luciferian flavour of " the sins of Society," that scandal had been killed, and its dead body taken away in the Dover mail.

Now that he was gone, and no longer a source of danger to her family's reputation, she found herself liking Sir Harry again. He had always been friendly, and though she fundamentally disapproved of his " ways," she was woman enough to be thrilled by his lurid reputation. Moreover, he provided a link, her last living link, with Martin's days—now that strange women kept rabbits in the backyards of North Farthing and the rooms were full of the Deal bootmaker's resplendent suites, that time of dew and gold and dreams seemed to have faded still further off. For many years it had lain far away on the horizon, but now it seemed to have faded off the earth altogether, and to live only in the sunset sky or in the dim moon-risings, which sometimes woke her out of her sleep with a start, as if she slipped on the verge of some troubling memory.

This kindlier state of affairs lasted for about a month, during which Joanna saw very little of Ellen. She was at rest about her sister, for the fact that Ellen might be feeling lonely and unhappy at the departure of her friend did not trouble her in the least ; such emotions, so vile in their source, could not call for any sympathy. Besides, she was busy, hunting for a new cowman to work under Broadhurst, whose undertakings, since the establishment of the milk-round, had almost come to equal those of the looker in activity and importance.

She was just about to set out one morning for a farm near Brenzett, when she saw Arthur Alce come up to the door on horseback.

" Hullo, Jo ! " he called rather anxiously through the window. " Have you got Ellen ? "

" I ?—No. Why should I have her, pray ? "

" Because I ain't got her."

" What d'you mean ? Get down, Arthur, and come and talk to me in here. Don't let everyone hear you shouting like that."

Arthur hitched his horse to the paling and came in.
"I thought maybe I'd find her here," he said. "I ain't seen her since breakfast."

"There's other places she could have gone besides here. Maybe she's gone shopping in Romney and forgot to tell you."

"It's queer her starting off like that without a word —and she's took her liddle bag and a few bits of things with her too."

"What things?—Arthur! Why couldn't you tell me that before?"

"I was going to. . . . I'm feeling a bit anxious, Jo. . . . I've a feeling she's gone after that Old Squire."

"You dare say such a thing! Arthur, I'm ashamed of you, believing such a thing of your wife and my sister."

"Well, she was unaccountable set on him."

"Nonsense! He just amused her. It's you whose wife she is."

"She's scarce given me a word more'n in the way of business, as you might say, this last three month. And she won't let me touch her."

"Why didn't you tell me this before?"

"I didn't want to trouble you, and I thought maybe it was a private matter."

"You should have told me the drackly minute Ellen started not to treat you proper. I'd have spoken to her . . . . Now we're in for a valiant terrification."

"I'm unaccountable sorry, Jo."

"How long has she been gone?"

"Since around nine. I went out to see the tegs, counting them up to go inland, and when I came in for dinner the gal told me as Ellen had gone out soon after breakfast, and had told her to see as I got my dinner, as she wouldn't be back."

"Why didn't you start after her at once?"

"Well, I made sure as she'd gone to you. Then I began to think over things and put 'em together, and I found she'd taken her liddle bag, and I got scared. I never liked her seeing such a lot of that man."

"Then why didn't you stop it?"

"How could I?"

"I could have—and the way people talked . . . .

I'd have locked her up sooner than . . . . well, it's too late now . . . . the boat went at twelve. Oh, Arthur, why didn't you watch her properly? Why did you let her go like that? Think of it! What's to become of her—away in foreign parts with a man who ain't her husband . . . . my liddle Ellen . . . oh, it's turble— turble——"

Her speech suddenly roughened into the Doric of the Marsh, and she sat down heavily, dropping her head to her knees.

"Joanna—don't, don't . . . . don't take on, Jo."

He had not seen her cry before, and now she frightened him. Her shoulders heaved, and great panting sobs shook her broad back.

"My liddle Ellen . . . . my treasure, my duckie . . . . oh, why have you left us? . . . . You could have come back to me if you didn't like it . . . . Oh, Ellen, where are you? . . . . Come back . . . ."

Arthur stood motionless beside her, his frame rigid, his protuberant blue eyes staring through the window at the horizon. He longed to take Joanna in his arms, caress and comfort her, but he knew that he must not.

"Cheer up," he said at last in a husky voice, "maybe it ain't so bad as you think. Maybe I'll find her at home when I get back to Donkey Street."

"Not if she took her bag. Oh, whatsumever shall we do?—whatsumever shall we do?"

"We can but wait. If she don't come back, maybe she'll send me a letter."

"It queers me how you can speak so light of it."

"I speak light?"

"Yes, you don't seem to tumble to it."

"Reckon I do tumble to it, but what can we do?"

"You shouldn't have left her alone all that time from breakfast till dinner—if you'd gone after her at the start you could have brought her back. You should ought to have kicked Sir Harry out of Donkey Street before the start. I'd have done it surely. Reckon I love Ellen more'n you."

"Reckon you do, Jo. I tell you, I ought never to have married her—since it was you I cared for all along."

" Hold your tongue, Arthur. I'm ashamed of you to choose this time to say such an immoral thing."

" It ain't immoral—it's the truth."

" Well, it shouldn't ought to be the truth. When you married Ellen you'd no business to go on caring for me. I guess all this is a judgment on you, caring for a woman when you'd married her sister."

" You ain't yourself, Jo," said Arthur sadly, " and there's no sense arguing with you. I'll go away till you've got over it. Maybe I'll have some news for you to-morrow morning."

§ 27

To-morrow morning he had a letter from Ellen herself. He brought it at once to a strangely drooping and weary-eyed Joanna, and read it again over her shoulder.

" DEAR ARTHUR," it ran—

" I'm afraid this will hurt you and Joanna terribly, but I expect you have already guessed what has happened. I am on my way to San Remo, to join Sir Harry Trevor, and I am never coming back, because I know now that I ought not to have married you. I do not ask you to forgive me, and I'm sure Joanna won't, but I had to think of my own happiness, and I never was a good wife to you. Believe me, I have done my best—I said ' Good-bye for ever ' to Harry a month ago, but ever since then my life has been one long misery ; I cannot live without him.

" ELLEN."

" Well, it's only told us what we knew already," said Joanna with a gulp, " but now we're sure we can do better than just talk about it."

" What can we do ? "

" We can get the Old Squire's address from somebody —Mrs. Williams or the people at North Farthing House —and then send a telegram after her, telling her to come back."

" That won't be much use."

" It'll be something, anyway. Maybe when she gets out there in foreign parts she won't be so pleased—or maybe he never asked her to come, and he'll have changed his mind about her. We must try and get her back. Where have you told your folk she's gone to ? "

" I've told 'em she's gone to stop with you."

" Well, I can't pretend she's here. You might have thought of something better, Arthur."

" I can't think of nothing else."

" You just about try. If only we can get her somewheres for a week, so as to have time to write and tell her as all will be forgiven and you'll take her back . . . ."

Arthur looked mutinous.

" I don't know as I want her back."

" Arthur, you must. Otherways, everybody ull have to know what's happened."

" But she didn't like being with me, or she wouldn't have gone away."

" She liked it well enough, or she wouldn't have stayed with you two year. Arthur, you must have her back, you just about must. You send her a telegram saying as you'll have her back if only she'll come this once, before folks find out where she's gone."

Arthur's resistance gradually failed before Joanna's entreaties and persuasions. He could not withstand Jo when her blue eyes were all dull with tears, and her voice was hoarse and frantic. For some months now his marriage had seemed to him a wrong and immoral thing, but he rather sorrowfully told himself that having made the first false step he could not now turn round and come back, even if Ellen herself had broken away. He rode off to find out the Squire's address, and send his wife the summoning and forgiving telegram.

§ 28

It was not perhaps surprising that, in spite of a lavish and exceedingly expensive offer of forgiveness, Ellen did not come home. Over a week passed without even an acknowledgment of the telegram, which she must have found reproachfully awaiting her arrival—the symbol of Walland Marsh pursuing her into the remoteness of a new life and a strange country.

As might have been expected Joanna felt this period of waiting and inactivity far more than she had felt the actual shock. She had all the weight on her shoulders of a sustained deception. She and Arthur had to dress up a story to deceive the neighbourhood, and they gave out that Ellen was in London, staying with Mrs. Williams —her husband had forbidden her to go, so she had run away, and now there would have to be some give and take on both sides before she could come back. Joanna had been inspired to circulate this legend by the discovery that Ellen actually had taken a ticket for London. She had probably guessed the sensation that her taking a ticket to Dover would arouse at the local station, so had gone first to London and travelled down by the boat express. It was all very cunning, and Joanna thought she saw the Old Squire's experienced hand in it. Of course it might be true that he had not persuaded Ellen to come out to him, but that she had gone to him on a sudden impulse . . . . But even Joanna's plunging instinct realized that her sister was not the sort to take desperate risks for love's sake, and the whole thing had about it a sly, concerted air, which made her think that Sir Harry was not only privy, but a prime mover.

After some ten days of anxiety, self-consciousness, shame and exasperation, these suspicions were confirmed by a letter from the Squire himself. He wrote from Œpedaletti, a small place near San Remo, and he wrote charmingly. No other adverb could qualify the peculiarly suave, tactful, humorous and gracious style in which not only he flung a mantle of romance over his and Ellen's behaviour (which till then, judged by the standards of Ansdore, had been just drably " wicked "), but by some mysterious means brought in Joanna as a third conspirator, linked by a broad and kindly intuition with himself and Ellen against a censorious world.

" You, who know Ellen so well, will realize that she has never till now had her birthright. You did your best for her, but both of you were bounded north, south, east and west by Walland Marsh. I wish you could see her

now, beside me on the terrace—she is like a little finch
in the sunshine of its first spring day. Her only trouble
is her fear of you, her fear that you will not understand.
But I tell her I would trust you first of all the world to
do that. As a woman of the world, you must realize
exactly what public opinion is worth—if you yourself
had bowed down to it, where would you be now ? Ellen
is only doing now what you did for yourself eleven years
ago."

Joanna's feelings were divided between gratification
at the flattery she never could resist, and a fierce re-
sentment at the insult offered her in supposing she could
ever wink at such "goings on." The more indignant
emotions predominated in the letter she wrote Sir Harry,
for she knew well enough that the flattery was not sincere
—he was merely out to propitiate.

Her feelings towards Ellen were exceedingly bitter,
and the letter she wrote her was a rough one :—

"You're nothing but a baggage. It makes no difference that you wear fine clothes and shoes that he's bought
you to your shame. You're just every bit as low as Martha
Tilden whom I got shut of ten year ago for no worse than
you've done."

Nevertheless, she insisted that Ellen should come home.
She guaranteed Arthur's forgiveness, and—somewhat
rashly—the neighbours' discretion. "I've told them
you're in London with Mrs. Williams. But that won't
hold good much more than another week. So be quick
and come home, before it's too late."

Unfortunately the facts of Ellen's absence were already
beginning to leak out. People did not believe in the
London story. Had not the Old Squire's visits to Donkey
Street been the tattle of the Marsh for six months ? She
was condemned not only at the Woolpack, but at the
three markets of Rye, Lydd and Romney. Joanna was
furious.

"It's that Post Office," she exclaimed, and the remark
was not quite unjust. The contents of telegrams had
always had an alarming way of spreading themselves
over the district, and Joanna felt sure that Miss Godfrey

would have both made and published her own conclusions
on the large amount of foreign correspondence now received at Ansdore.

Ellen herself was the next to write. She wrote im-
penitently and decidedly. She would never come back,
so there was no good either Joanna or Arthur expecting
it. She had left Donkey Street because she could not
endure its cramped ways any longer, and it was unreasonable to expect her to return.

" If Arthur has any feeling for me left, he will divorce
me. He can easily do it, and then we shall both be free
to re-marry."

" Reckon she thinks the old Squire ud like to marry
her," said Alce, " I'd be glad if I thought so well of him."

" He can't marry her, seeing as she's your wife."

" If we were divorced, she wouldn't be."

" She would. You were made man and wife in Pedlinge church, as I saw with my own eyes, and I'll never
believe as what was done then can be undone just by
having some stuff written in the papers."

" It's a lawyer's business," said Arthur.

" I can't see that," said Joanna—" a parson married
you, so reckon a parson must unmarry you."

" He wouldn't do it. It's a lawyer's job."

" I'd thank my looker if he went about undoing my
carter's work. Those lawyers want to put their heads
in everywhere. And as for Ellen, all I can say is, it's
just like her wanting the Ten Commandments altered
to suit her convenience. Reckon they ain't refined and
high-class enough for her. But she may ask for a divorce
till she's black in the face—she shan't get it."

So Ellen had to remain—very much against the grain,
for she was fundamentally respectable—a breaker of the
law. She wrote once or twice more on the subject, appealing to Arthur, since Joanna's reply had shown her exactly
how much quarter she could expect. But Arthur was not
to be won, for apart from Joanna's domination, and his
own unsophisticated beliefs in the permanence of marriage,
his suspicions were roused by the Old Squire's silence
on the matter. At no point did he join his appeals and
arguments with Ellen's, though he had been ready enough
to write to excuse and explain . . . . No, Arthur felt

that love and wisdom lay not in sanctifying Ellen in her
new ways with the blessing of the law, but in leaving
the old open for her to come back to when the new should
perhaps grow hard. " That chap 'ull get shut of her—
I don't trust him—and then she'll want to come back
to me or Jo."

So he wrote with boring reiteration of his willingness
to receive her home again as soon as she chose to return,
and assured her that he and Joanna had still managed
to keep the secret of her departure, so that she need not
fear scornful tongues. They had given the Marsh to
understand that no settlement having been arrived at,
Ellen had accompanied Mrs. Williams to the South of
France, hoping that things would have improved on her
return. This would account for the foreign post-marks,
and both he and Joanna were more proud of their cunning
than was quite warrantable from its results.

§ 29

That winter brought Great Ansdore at last into the
market. It would have come in before had not Joanna
so rashly bragged of her intention to buy it. As it was
—" I guess I'll get a bit more out of the old gal by holding
on," said Prickett disrespectfully, and he held on till
Joanna's impatience about equalled his extremity ; whereupon he sold it to her for not over fifty per cent. more
than he would have asked had he not known of her ambition. She paid the price manfully, and Prickett went
out with his few sticks.

The Woolpack was inclined to be contemptuous.

" Five thousand pounds for Prickett's old shacks,
and his mouldy pastures that are all burdock and fluke.
If Joanna Godden had had any know, she could have
beaten him down fifteen hundred—he was bound to sell,
and she was a fool not to make him sell at her price."

But when Joanna wanted a thing she did not mind
paying for it, and she had wanted Great Ansdore very
much, though no one knew better than she that it was
shacky and mouldy. For long it had mocked with its
proud title the triumphs of Little Ansdore. Now the

whole manor of Ansdore was hers, Great and Little, and with it she held the living of Brodnyx and Pedlinge—it was she, of her own might, who would appoint the next Rector, and for some time she imagined that she had it in her power to turn out Mr. Pratt.

She at once set to work, putting her new domain in order. Some of the pasture she grubbed up for spring sowings, the rest she drained by cutting a new channel from the Kent Ditch to the White Kemp Sewer. She re-roofed the barns with slate, and painted and re-tiled the dwelling-house. This last she decided to let to some family of gentlepeople, while herself keeping on the farm and the barns. The dwelling-house of Little Ansdore, though more flat and spreading, was in every way superior to that of Great Ansdore, which was rather new and inclined to gimcrackiness, having been built on the site of the first dwelling, burnt down somewhere in the eighties. Besides, she loved Little Ansdore for its associations—under its roof she had been born and her father had been born, under its roof she had known love and sorrow and denial and victory ; she could not bear to think of leaving it. The queer, low house, with its mixture of spaciousness and crookedness, its huge, sag-ceilinged rooms and narrow, twisting passages, was almost a personality to her now, one of the Godden family, the last of kin that had remained kind.

Her activities were merciful in crowding what would otherwise have been a sorrowful period of emptiness and anxiety. It is true that Ellen's behaviour had done much to spoil her triumph, both in the neighbourhood and in her own eyes, but she had not time to be thinking of it always. Visits to Rye, either to her lawyers or to the decorators and paper-hangers, the engaging of extra hands, both temporary and permanent, for the extra work, the supervising of labourers and workmen whom she never could trust to do their job without her . . . . all these crowded her cares into a few hours of evening or an occasionally wakeful night.

But every now and then she must suffer. Sometimes she would be overwhelmed, in the midst of all her triumphant business, with a sense of personal failure. She had succeeded where most women are hopeless failures, but where so many women are successful and satisfied she had failed and gone empty. She had no home, beyond what was involved in the walls of this ancient dwelling, the womb and grave of her existence—she had lost the man she loved, had been unable to settle herself comfortably with another, and now she had lost Ellen, the little sister, who had managed to hold at least a part of that over-running love, which since Martin's death had had only broken cisterns to flow into.

The last catastrophe now loomed the largest. Joanna no longer shed tears for Martin, but she shed many for Ellen, either into her own pillow, or into the flowery quilt of the flowery room which inconsequently she held sacred to the memory of the girl who had despised it. Her grief for Ellen was mixed with anxiety and with shame. What would become of her? Joanna could not, would not, believe that she would never come back. Yet what if she came? . . . . In Joanna's eyes, and in the eyes of all the neighbourhood, Ellen had committed a crime which raised a barrier between her and ordinary folk. Between Ellen and her sister now stood the wall of strange, new conditions—conditions that could ignore the sonorous Thou Shalt Not, which Joanna never saw apart from Mr. Pratt in his surplice and hood, standing under the Lion and the Unicorn, while all the farmers and householders of the Marsh murmured into their Prayer Books —" Lord, have mercy upon us, and incline our hearts to keep this law." She could not think of Ellen without this picture rising up between them, and sometimes in church she would be overwhelmed with a bitter shame, and in the lonely enclosure of her great cattle-box pew would stuff her fingers into her ears, so that she should not hear the dreadful words of her sister's condemnation.

She had moments, too, of an even bitterer shame— strange, terrible, and mercifully rare times when her attitude towards Ellen was not of judgment or of care or of longing, but of envy. Sometimes she would be overwhelmed with a sense of Ellen's happiness in being loved, even if the love was unlawful. She had never felt this during the years that her sister had lived with Alce ; the thought of his affection had brought her nothing but happiness and content. Now, on sinister occasions, she would find herself thinking of Ellen cherished and spoiled, protected and caressed, living the life of love—and a desperate longing would come to her to enjoy what her sister enjoyed, to be kissed and stroked and made much of and taken care of, to see some man laying schemes and taking risks for her . . . . sometimes she felt that she would like to see all the fullness of her life at Ansdore, all her honour on the Three Marshes, blown to the winds if only in their stead she could have just ordinary human love, with or without the law.

Poor Joanna was overwhelmed with horror at herself —sometimes she thought she must be possessed by a devil. She must be very wicked—in her heart just as wicked as Ellen. What could she do to cast out this dumb, tearing spirit?—should she marry one of her admirers on the Marsh, and trust to his humdrum devotion to satisfy her devouring need? Even in her despair and panic she knew that she could not do this. It was love that she must have—the same sort of love that she had given Martin; that alone could bring her the joys she now envied in her sister. And love—how shall it be found?—Who shall go out to seek it?

§ 30

Towards the spring, Ellen wrote again, breaking the silence of several weeks. She wrote in a different tone—some change had passed over her. She no longer asked Arthur to divorce her—on the contrary she hinted her thanks for his magnanimity in not having done so. Evidently she no longer counted on marrying Sir Harry Trevor, perhaps, even, she did not wish to. But in one point she had not changed—she was not coming back to her husband.

"I couldn't bear to live that life again, especially after what's happened. It's not his fault—it's simply that I'm different. If he wants his freedom, I suggest that he should let me divorce him—it could easily be arranged. He should go and see a really good lawyer in London."

Yes—Ellen spoke truly when she said that she was

" different." Her cavalier dealings with the situation, the glib way she spoke of divorce, the insult she flung at the respectable form of Huxtable, Vidler and Huxtable by suggesting that Arthur should consult " a really good lawyer in London," all showed how far she had travelled from the ways of Walland Marsh.

" What's she after now ? " asked Joanna.

" Reckon they're getting tired of each other."

" She don't say so."

" No—she wants to find out which way the land lays first."

" I'll write and tell her she can come back and live along of me, if she won't go to you."

" Then I'll have to be leaving these parts—I couldn't be at Donkey Street and her at Ansdore."

" Reckon you could—she can go out of the way when you call."

" It wouldn't be seemly."

" Where ud you go ? "

" I've no notion. But reckon all this ain't the question yet. Ellen won't come back to you no more than she'll come back to me."

" She'll just about have to come if she gets shut of the Old Squire, seeing as she's got no more than twelve pounds a year of her own. Reckon poor father was a wise man when he left Ansdore to me and not to both of us—you'd almost think he'd guessed what she was coming to."

Joanna wrote to Ellen and made her offer. Her sister wrote back at great length, and rather pathetically—" Harry " was going on to Venice, and she did not think she would go with him—" when one gets to know a person, Jo, one sometimes finds they are not quite what one thought them." She would like to be by herself for a bit, but she did not want to come back to Ansdore, even if Arthur went away—" it would be very awkward after what has happened." She begged Jo to be generous and make her some small allowance—" Harry would provide for me if he hadn't had such terrible bad luck—he never was very well off, you know, and he can't manage unless we keep together. I know you wouldn't like me to be tied to him just by money considerations."

Joanna was bewildered by the letter. She could

have understood Ellen turning in horror and loathing from the partner of her guilt, but she could not understand this wary and matter-of-fact separation. What was her sister made of? " Harry would provide for me " . . . . would she really have accepted such a provision ? Joanna's ears grew red. " I'll make her come home," she exclaimed savagely—" she'll have to come if she's got no money."

" Maybe she'll stop along of him," said Arthur.

" Then let her—I don't care. But she shan't have my money to live on by herself in foreign parts, taking up with any man that comes her way ; for I don't trust her now—I reckon she's lost to shame."

She wrote Ellen to this effect, and, not surprisingly, received no answer. She felt hard and desperate—the thought that she was perhaps binding her sister to her misdoing gave her only occasional spasms of remorse. Sometimes she would feel as if all her being and all her history, Ansdore and her father's memory, disowned her sister, and that she could never take her back into her life again, however penitent—" She's mocked at our good ways—she's loose, she's low." At other times her heart melted towards Ellen in weakness, and she knew within herself that no matter what she did, she would always be her little sister, her child, her darling, whom all her life she had cherished and could never cast out.

She said nothing about these swaying feelings to Arthur—she had of late grown far more secretive about herself—as for him, he took things as they came. He found a wondrous quiet in this time, when he was allowed to serve Joanna as in days of old. He did not think of marrying her—he knew that even if it was true that the lawyers could set aside parson's word, Joanna would not take him now, any more than she would have taken him five or ten or fifteen years ago ; she did not think about him in that way. On the other hand she appreciated his company and his services. He called at Ansdore two or three times a week, and ran her errands for her. It was almost like old times, and in his heart he knew and was ashamed to know that he hoped Ellen would never come back. If she came back either to him or to Joanna, these days of quiet happiness would end.

Meantime, he would not think of it—he was Joanna's
servant, and when she could not be in two places at once
it was his joy and privilege to be in one of them. " I
could live like this for ever, surely," he said to himself,
as he sat stirring his solitary cup of tea at Donkey Street,
knowing that he was to call at Ansdore the next morning.

That was the morning he met Joanna in the drive,
hatless, and holding a piece of paper in her hand.

." I've heard from Ellen—she's telegraphed from
Venice—she's coming home."

§ 31

Now that she knew Ellen was coming, Joanna had
nothing in her heart but joy and angry love. Ellen was
coming back, at last, after many wanderings—and she
saw now that these wanderings included the years of her
life with Alce—she was coming back to Ansdore and the
old home. Joanna forgot how much she had hated it,
would not think that this precious return was merely
the action of a woman without resources. She gave
herself up to the joy of preparing a welcome—as splendidly
and elaborately as she had prepared for her sister's return
from school. This time, however, she went further, and
actually made some concessions to Ellen's taste. She
remembered that she liked dull die-away colours " like
the mould on jam," so she took down the pink curtains
and folded away the pink bedspread, and put in their
places material that the shop at Rye assured her was
" art green "—which, in combination with the crimson,
flowery walls and floor contrived most effectually to
suggest a scum of grey-green mould on a pot of especially
vivid strawberry jam.

But she was angry too—her heart burned to think
not only of Ellen's sin but of the casual way in which
she treated it. " I won't have none of her loose notions
here," said Joanna grimly. She made up her mind to
give her sister a good talking to, to convince her of the
way in which her "goings on" struck decent folk ; but she
would not do it at the start—" I'll give her time to settle
down a bit first."

During the few days which elapsed between Ellen's telegram and her arrival, Joanna saw nothing of Alce. She had one letter from him, in which he told her that he had been over to Fairfield to look at the plough she was speaking of, but that it was old stuff and would be no use to her. He did not even mention Ellen's name. She wondered if he was making any plans for leaving Donkey Street—she hoped he would not be such a fool as to go. He and Ellen could easily keep out of each other's way. Still, if Ellen wouldn't stay unless he went, she would rather have Ellen than Alce . . . . He would have to sell Donkey Street, or perhaps he might let it off for a little time.

April had just become May when Ellen returned to Ansdore. It had been a rainy spring, and great pools were on the marshes, overflows from the dykes and channels, clear mirrors green from the grass beneath their shallows and the green rainy skies that hung above them. Here and there they reflected white clumps and walls of hawthorn, with the pale yellowish gleam of the buttercups in the pastures. The two sisters, driving back from Rye, looked round on the green twilight of the Marsh with indifferent eyes. Joanna had ceased to look for any beauty in her surroundings since Martin's days—the small gift of sight that he had given her had gone out with the light of his own eyes, and this evening all she saw was the flooded pastures, which meant poor grazing for her tegs due to come down from the Coast, and her lambs new-born on the Kent Innings. As for Ellen, the Marsh had always stood with her for unrelieved boredom. Its eternal flatness—the monotony of its roads winding through an unvarying landscape of reeds and dykes and grazings, past farms each of which was almost exactly like the one before it, with red walls and orange roofs and a bush of elms and oaks—the wearisome repetition of its seasons —the mists and floods of winter, the may and buttercups of spring, the hay and meadow-sweet and wild carrot of the summer months, the bleakness and winds of autumn —all this was typical of her life there, water-bound, cut off from all her heart's desire of variety and beauty and elegance, of the life to which she must now return because her attempt to live another had failed and left her stranded on a slag-heap of disillusion from which even Ansdore was a refuge.

Ellen sat very trim and erect beside Joanna in the trap. She wore a neat grey coat and skirt, obviously not of local, nor indeed of English, make, and a little toque of flowers. She had taken Joanna's breath away on Rye platform; it had been very much like old times when she came home for the holidays and checked the impulse of her sister's love by a baffling quality of self-containment. Joanna, basing her expectations on the Bible story of the Prodigal Son rather than on the experiences of the past winter, had looked for a subdued penitent, surfeited with husks, who, if not actually casting herself at her sister's feet and offering herself as her servant, would at least have a hang-dog air and express her gratitude for so much forgiveness. Instead of which Ellen had said—" Hullo, Jo—it's good to see you again," and offered her a cool, delicately powdered cheek, which Joanna's warm lips had kissed with a queer, sad sense of repulse and humiliation. Before they had been together long, it was she who wore the hang-dog air—for some unconscionable reason she felt in the wrong, and found herself asking her sister polite, nervous questions about the journey.

This attitude prevailed throughout the evening—on the drive home, and at the excellent supper they sat down to : a stuffed capon and a bottle of wine, truly a genteel feast of reconciliation—but Joanna had grown more aristocratic in her feeding since she bought Great Ansdore. Ellen spoke about her journey—she had had a smooth crossing, but had felt rather ill in the train. It was a long way from Venice—yes, you came through France, and Switzerland too . . . the St. Gothard tunnel . . . . twenty minutes—well, I never ? . . . . Yes, a bit smoky—you had to keep the windows shut . . . . she preferred French to Italian cooking—she did not like all that oil . . . oh yes, foreigners were very polite when they knew you, but not to strangers . . . . just the opposite from England, where people were polite to strangers and rude to their friends. Joanna had never spoken or heard so many generalities in her life.

At the end of supper she felt quite tired, what with saying one thing with her tongue and another in her heart. Sometimes she felt that she must say something to break down this unreality, which was between them like a wall of ice—at other times she felt angry, and it was Ellen she wanted to break down, to force out of her superior refuge, and show up to her own self as just a common sinner receiving common forgiveness. But there was something about Ellen which made this impossible —something about her manner, with its cold poise, something about her face, which had indefinitely changed— it looked paler, wider, and there were secrets at the corners of her mouth.

This was not the first time that Joanna had seen her sister calm and collected while she herself was flustered —but this evening a sense of her own awkwardness helped to put her at a still greater disadvantage. She found herself making inane remarks, hesitating and stuttering —she grew sulky and silent, and at last suggested that Ellen would like to go to bed.

Her sister seemed glad enough, and they went upstairs together. But even the sight of her old bedroom, where the last year of her maidenhood had been spent, even the sight of the new curtains chastening its exuberance with their dim austerity, did not dissolve Ellen's terrible, cold sparkle—her frozen fire.

" Good night," said Joanna.

" Good night," said Ellen, " may I have some hot water ? "

" I'll tell the gal," said Joanna tamely, and went out.

§ 32

When she was alone in her own room, she seemed to come to herself. She felt ashamed of having been so baffled by Ellen, of having received her on those terms. She could not bear to think of Ellen living on in the house, so terribly at an advantage. If she let things stay as they were, she was tacitly acknowledging some indefinite superiority which her sister had won through sin. All the time she was saying nothing she felt that Ellen was saying in her heart—" I have been away to foreign parts, I have been loved by a man I don't belong to, I have Seen Life, I have stopped at hotels, I have met people of a kind you haven't even spoken to . . . ." That was what Ellen was saying, instead of what Joanna thought she ought to say, which was—" I'm no better then a dairy girl in trouble, than Martha Tilden whom you sacked when I was a youngster, and it's unaccountable good of you to have me home."

Joanna was not the kind to waste her emotions in the sphere of thought. She burst out of the room, and nearly knocked over Mene Tekel, who was on her way to Ellen with a jug of hot water.

" Give that to me," she said, and went to her sister's door, at which she was still sufficiently demoralized to knock.

" Come in," said Ellen.

" I've brought you your hot water."

" Thank you very much—I hope it hasn't been a trouble."

Ellen was standing by the bed in a pretty lilac silk wrapper, her hair tucked away under a little lace cap. Joanna wore her dressing-gown of turkey-red flannel, and her hair hung down her back in two great rough plaits. For a moment she stared disapprovingly at her sister, whom she thought looked " French," then she suddenly felt ashamed of herself and her ugly, shapeless coverings. This made her angry, and she burst out—

" Ellen Alce, I want a word with you."

" Sit down, Jo," said Ellen sweetly.

Joanna flounced on to the rosy, slippery chintz of Ellen's sofa. Ellen sat down on the bed.

" What do you want to say to me ? "

" An unaccountable lot of things."

" Must they all be said to-night ? I'm very sleepy."

" Well, you must just about keep awake. I can't let it stay over any longer. Here you've been back five hour, and not a word passed between us."

" On the contrary, we have had some intelligent conversation for the first time in our lives."

" You call that rot about furriners ' intelligent conversation ' ? Well, all I can say is that it's like you—all pretence. One ud think you'd just come back from a pleasure-trip abroad instead of from a wicked life that you should ought to be ashamed of."

For the first time a flush darkened the heavy whiteness of Ellen's skin.

" So you want to rake up the past ? It's exactly like you, Jo—' having things out,' I suppose you'd call it. How many times in our lives have you and I ' had things out ' ?—And what good has it ever done us ? "

" I can't go on all pretending like this—I can't go on pretending I think you an honest woman when I don't —I can't go on saying ' It's a fine day ' when I'm wondering how you'll fare in the Day of Judgment."

" Poor old Jo," said Ellen, " you'd have had an easier life if you hadn't lived, as they say, so close to nature. It's just what you call pretences and others call good manners that make life bearable for some people."

" Yes, for ' some people ' I daresay—people whose characters won't stand any straight talking."

" Straight talking is always so rude—no one ever seems to require it on pleasant occasions."

" That's all nonsense. You always was a squeamish, obstropulous little thing, Ellen. It's only natural that having you back in my house—as I'm more than glad to do—I should want to know how you stand. What made you come to me sudden like that ? "

" Can't you guess ? It's rather unpleasant for me to have to tell you."

" Reckon it was that man "—somehow Sir Harry's name had become vaguely improper, Joanna felt unable to pronounce it—" then you've made up your mind not to marry him," she finished.

" How can I marry him, seeing I'm somebody else's wife ? "

" I'm glad to hear you say such a proper thing. It ain't what you was saying at the start. Then you wanted a divorce and all sorts of foreign notions . . . . what's made you change round ? "

" Well, Arthur wouldn't give me a divorce, for one thing. For another, as I told you in my letter, one often doesn't know people till one's lived with them—besides, he's too old for me."

" He'll never see sixty again."

" He will," said Ellen indignantly—" he was only fifty-five in March."

" That's thirty year more'n you."

" I've told you he's too old for me."

" You might have found out that at the start—he was only six months younger then."

" There's a great many things I might have done at the start," said Ellen bitterly—" but I tell you, Joanna, life isn't quite the simple thing you imagine. There was I, married to a man utterly uncongenial——"

" He wasn't ! You're not to miscall Arthur—he's the best man alive."

" I don't deny it—perhaps that is why I found him uncongenial. Anyhow, we were quite unsuited to each other—we hadn't an idea in common."

" You liked him well enough when you married him."

" I've told you before that it's difficult to know anyone thoroughly till one's lived with them."

" Then at that rate, who's to get married—eh ? "

" I don't know," said Ellen wearily, " all I know is that I've made two bad mistakes over two different men, and I think the least you can do is to let me forget it—as far as I'm able—and not come here baiting me when I'm dog tired, and absolutely down and out . . . . ."

She bowed her face into her hands, and burst into tears. Joanna flung her arms round her——

" Oh, don't you cry, duckie—don't—I didn't mean to bait you. Only I was getting so mortal vexed at you and me walking round each other like two cats and never getting a straight word."

" Jo," . . . . said Ellen.

Her face was hidden in her sister's shoulder, and her whole body had drooped against Joanna's side, utterly weary after three days of travel and disillusioned loneliness.

" Reckon I'm glad you've come back, dearie—and I won't ask you any more questions. I'm a cross-grained, cantankerous old thing, but you'll stop along of me a bit, won't you ? "

" Yes," said Ellen, " you're all I've got in the world."

" Arthur ud take you back any day you ask it," said Joanna, thinking this a good time for mediation.

"'No—no ! " cried Ellen, beginning to cry again— " I won't stay if you try to make me go back to Arthur. If he had the slightest feeling for me he would let me divorce him."

" How could you ?—seeing that he's been a pattern all his life."

" He needn't do anything wrong—he need only pretend to. The lawyers ud fix it up."

Ellen was getting French again. Joanna pushed her off her shoulder.

" Really, Ellen Alce, I'm ashamed of you—that you should speak such words ! What upsets me most is that you don't seem to see how wrong you've done. Don't you never read your Bible any more ? "

" No," sobbed Ellen.

" Well, there's lots in the Bible about people like you—you're called by your right name there, and it ain't a pretty one. Some are spoken uncommon hard of, and some were forgiven because they loved much. Seemingly you haven't loved much, so I don't see how you expect to be forgiven. And there's lots in the Prayer Book too . . . . the Bible and the Prayer Book both say you've done wrong, and you don't seem to mind—all you think of is how you can get out of your trouble. Reckon you're like a child that's done wrong and thinks of nothing but coaxing round so as not to be punished."

" I have been punished."

" Not half what you deserve."

" It's all very well for you to say that—you don't understand ; and what's more, you never will. You're a hard woman, Jo—because you've never had the temptations that ordinary women have to fight against."

" How dare you say that ?—Temptation !—Reckon I know . . . ." A sudden memory of those painful and humiliating moments when she had fought with those strange powers and discontents, made Joanna turn hot with shame. The realization that she had come very close to Ellen's sin in her heart did not make her more relenting towards the sinner—on the contrary, she hardened.

" Anyways, I've said enough to you for to-night."

" I hope you don't mean to say more to-morrow."

" No—I don't know that I do. Reckon you're right, and we don't get any good from ' having things out.' Seemingly we speak with different tongues, and think with different hearts."

She stood up, and her huge shadow sped over the ceiling, hanging over Ellen as she crouched on the bed. Then she stalked out of the room, almost majestic in her turkey-red dressing-gown.

§ 33

Ellen kept very close to the house during the next few days. Her face wore a demure, sullen expression— towards Joanna she was quiet and sweet, and evidently anxious that there should be no further opening of hearts between them. She was very polite to the maids—she won their good opinion by making her bed herself, so that they should not have any extra work on her account.

Perhaps it was this domestic good opinion which was at the bottom of the milder turn which the gossip about her took at this time. Naturally tongues had been busy ever since it became known that Joanna was expecting her back—Sir Harry Trevor had got shut of her for the baggage she was . . . . she had got shut of Sir Harry Trevor for the blackguard he was . . . . she had travelled back as somebody's maid, to pay her fare . . . . she had brought her own French maid as far as Calais . . . . she had walked from Dover . . . . she had brought four trunks full of French clothes. These conflicting rumours must have killed each other, for a few days after her return the Woolpack was saying that after all there might be something in Joanna's tale of a trip with Mrs. Williams—of course everyone knew that both Ellen and the Old Squire had been at San Remo, but now it was suddenly discovered that Mrs. Williams had been there too—anyway, there was no knowing that she hadn't, and Ellen Alce didn't look the sort that ud go to a furrin place alone with a man. Mrs. Vine had seen her through the parlour window, and her face was as white as chalk —not a scrap of paint on it. Mr. Southland had met her on the Brodnyx Road, and she had bowed to him polite and stately—no shrinking from an honest man's eye. According to the Woolpack, if you sinned as Ellen was reported to have sinned, you were either brazen or thoroughly ashamed of yourself, and Ellen, by being neither, did much to soften public opinion, and make it incline towards the official explanation of her absence.

This tendency increased when it became known that Arthur Alce was leaving Donkey Street. The Woolpack held that if Ellen had been guilty, Alce would not put himself in the wrong by going away. He would either have remained as the visible rebuke of her misconduct, or he would have bundled Ellen herself off to some distant part of the kingdom, such as the Isle of Wight, where the Goddens had cousins. By leaving the neighbourhood he gave colour to the mysteriously-started rumour that he was not so easy to get on with as you'd think . . . . after all, it's never a safe thing for a girl to marry her sister's sweetheart . . . probably Alce had been hankering after his old love and Ellen resented it . . . . the Woolpack suddenly discovered that Alce was leaving not so much on Ellen's account as on Joanna's—he'd been unable to get off with the old love, even when he'd got on with the new, and now that the new was off too . . . . well, there was nothing for it but for Arthur Alce to be off. He was going to his brother, who had a big farm in the shires—a proper farm, with great fields each of which was nearly as big as a marsh farm, fifty, seventy, a hundred acres even.

§ 34

Joanna bitterly resented Arthur's going, but she could not prevent it, for if he stayed Ellen threatened to go herself.

"I'll get a post as lady's-maid sooner than stay on here with you and Arthur. Have you absolutely no delicacy, Jo?—Can't you see how awkward it'll be for me if everywhere I go I run the risk of meeting him? Besides, you'll be always plaguing me to go back to him, and I tell you I'll never do that—never."

Arthur, too, did not seem anxious to stay. He saw
that if Ellen was at Ansdore he could not be continually
running to and fro on his errands for Joanna. That
tranquil life of service was gone, and he did not care for
the thought of exile at Donkey Street, a shutting of himself into his parish of Old Romney, with the Kent Ditch
between him and Joanna like a prison wall.

When Joanna told him what Ellen had said, he accepted
it meekly—

" That's right, Joanna—I must go."

" But that ull be terrible hard for you, Arthur."

He looked at her.

" Reckon it will."

" Where ull you go ? "

" Oh, I can go to Tom's."

" That's right away in the shires, ain't it ? "

" Yes—beyond Leicester."

" Where they do the hunting."

" Surelye."

" What's the farm ? "

" Grain mostly—and he's done well with his sheep.
He'd be glad to have me for a bit."

" What'll you do with Donkey Street ? "

" Let it off for a bit."

" Don't you sell ! "

" Not I ! "

" You'll be meaning to come back ? "

" I'll be hoping."

Joanna gazed at him for a few moments in silence,
and a change came into her voice—

" Arthur, you're doing all this because of me."

" I'm doing it for you, Joanna."

" Well—I don't feel I've any call—I haven't any
right . . . . I mean, if Ellen don't like you here, she
must go herself . . . it ain't fair on you—you at Donkey
Street for more'n twenty year . . ."

" Don't you trouble about that. A change won't
hurt me. Reckon either Ellen or me ull have to go and
it ud break your heart if it was Ellen."

" Why can't you both stay ? Ellen ull have to stay
if I make her. I don't believe a word of what she says
about going as lady's maid—she hasn't got the grit—nor

the character neither, though she doesn't seem to think
of that."

" It ud be unaccountable awkward, Jo—and it ud
set Ellen against both of us, and bring you trouble.   Maybe
if I go she'll take a different view of things.   I shan't
let off the place for longer than three year . . . it'll
give her a chance to think different, and then maybe
we can fix up something . . . ."

Joanna fastened on to these words, both for her own
comfort in Arthur's loss, and for the quieting of her con-
science, which told her that it was preposterous that he
should leave Donkey Street so that she could keep Ellen
at Ansdore.   Of course, if she did her duty she would
pack Ellen off to the Isle of Wight, so that Arthur could
stay.   The fact was, however, that she wanted the guilty,
ungracious Ellen more than she wanted the upright,
devoted Arthur—she was glad to know of any terms on
which her sister would consent to remain under her roof
—it seemed almost too good to be true, to think that once
more she had the little sister home . . . .

So she signed the warrant for Arthur's exile, which
was to do so much to spread the more favourable opinion
of Ellen Alce that had mysteriously crept into being since
her return.   He let off Donkey Street on a three years'
lease to young Jim Honisett, the greengrocer's son at
Rye, who had recently married and whose wish to set
up as farmer would naturally be to the advantage of his
father's shop.   He let his furniture with it too . . . .
He himself would take nothing to his brother, who kept
house in a very big way, the same as he farmed . . . .
" Reckon I should ought to learn a thing or two about
grain-growing that'll be useful to me when I come back,"
said Arthur stoutly.

He had come to say good-bye to Joanna on a June
evening just before the quarter day.   The hot scents of
hay-making came in through the open parlour window,
and they were free, for Ellen had gone with Mr. and Mrs.
Southland to Rye for the afternoon—of late she had
accepted one or two small invitations from the neighbours.
Joanna poured Arthur out a cup of tea from the silver
teapot he had given her as a wedding present six years
ago.

" Well, Arthur—reckon it'll be a long time before you and me have tea again together."

" Reckon it will."

" Howsumever, I shall always think of you when I pour it out of your teapot—which will be every day that I don't have it in the kitchen."

" Thank you, Jo."

" And you'll write and tell me how you're getting on ? "

" Reckon I will."

" Maybe you'll send me some samples of those oats your brother did so well with. I'm not over pleased with that Barbacklaw, and ud make a change if I could find better."

" I'll be sure and send."

Joanna told him of an inspiration she had had with regard to the poorer innings of Great Ansdore—she was going to put down fish-guts for manure—it had done wonders with some rough land over by Botolph's Bridge —" Reckon it'll half stink the tenants out, but they're at the beginning of a seven years lease, so they can't help themselves much." She held forth at great length, and Arthur listened, holding his cup and saucer carefully on his knee with his big freckled hands. His eyes were fixed on Joanna, on the strong-featured, high-coloured face he thought so much more beautiful than Ellen's with its delicate lines and pale, petal-like skin . . . . Yes, Joanna was the girl all along—the one for looks, the one for character—give him Joanna every time, with her red and brown face, and thick brown hair, and her high, deep bosom, and sturdy, comfortable waist . . . . why couldn't he have had Joanna, instead of what he'd got, which was nothing ? For the first time in his life Arthur Alce came near to questioning the ways of Providence. Reckon it was the last thing he would ever do for her—this going away. He wasn't likely to come back, though he did talk of it, just to keep up their spirits. He would probably settle down in the shires—go into partnership with his brother—run a bigger place than Donkey Street, than Ansdore even.

" Well, I must be going now. There's still a great lot of things to be tidied up."

He rose, awkwardly setting down his cup. Joanna

rose too. The sunset, rusty with the evening sea-mist, poured over her goodly form as she stood against the window, making its outlines dim and fiery and her hair like a burning crown.

" I shall miss you, Arthur."

He did not speak, and she held out her hand.

" Good-bye."

He could not say it—instead he pulled her towards him by the hand he held.

" Jo—I must."

" Arthur—no ! "

But it was too late—he had kissed her.

" That's the first time you done it," she said reproachfully.

" Because it's the last. You aren't angry, are you ? "

" I ?—no. But, Arthur, you mustn't forget you're married to Ellen."

" Am I like to forget it ?—And seeing all the dunnamany kisses she's given to another man, reckon she won't grudge me this one poor kiss I've given the woman I've loved without clasp or kiss for fifteen years."

For the first time she heard in his voice both bitterness and passion, and at that moment the man himself seemed curiously to come alive and to compel . . . . But Joanna was not going to dally with temptation in the unaccustomed shape of Arthur Alce. She pushed open the door.

" Have they brought round Ranger ?—Hi ! Peter Crouch !—Yes, there he is. You'll have a good ride home, Arthur."

" But there'll be rain to-morrow."

" I don't think it. The sky's all red at the rims."

" The wind's shifted."

Joanna moistened her finger and held it up—

" So it has. But the glass is high. Reckon it'll hold off till you're in the shires, and then our weather won't trouble you."

She watched him ride off, standing in the doorway till the loops of the Brodnyx road carried him into the rusty fog that was coming from the sea.

PART IV

LAST LOVE

§ 1

TIME passed on, healing the wounds of the Marsh. At Donkey Street, the neighbours were beginning to get used to young Honisett and his bride, at Rye and Lydd and Romney the farmers had given up expecting Arthur Alce to come round the corner on his grey horse, with samples of wheat or prices of tegs. At Ansdore, too, the breach was healed. Joanna and Ellen lived quietly together, sharing their common life without explosions. Joanna had given up all idea of "having things out" with Ellen. There was always a bit of pathos about Joanna's surrenders, and in this case Ellen had certainly beaten her. It was rather difficult to say exactly to what the younger sister owed her victory, but undoubtedly she had won it, and their life was in a measure based upon it. Joanna accepted her sister—past and all ; she accepted her little calm assumptions of respectability together with those more expected tendencies towards the "French." When Ellen had first come back, she had been surprised and resentful to see how much she took for granted in the way of acceptance, not only from Joanna but from the neighbours. According to her ideas, Ellen should have kept in shamed seclusion till public opinion called her out of it, and she had been alarmed at her assumptions, fearing rebuff, just as she had almost feared heaven's lightning stroke for that demure little figure in her pew on Sunday, murmuring "Lord have mercy" without tremor or blush.

But heaven had not smitten and the neighbours had not snubbed. In some mysterious way Ellen had won acceptance from the latter, whatever her secret relations with the former may have been. The stories about her grew ever more and more charitable. The Woolpack pronounced that Arthur Alce would not have gone away " if it had been all on her side," and it was now certainly known that Mrs. Williams had been at San Remo . . . . Ellen's manner was found pleasing—" quiet but affable." Indeed, in this respect she had much improved. The Southlands took her up, forgiving her treatment of their boy, now comfortably married to the daughter of a big Folkestone shopkeeper. They found her neither brazen nor shamefaced—and she'd been as shocked as any honest woman at Lady Mountain's trial in the Sunday papers . . . . if folk only knew her real story, they'd probably find . . . .

In fact, Ellen was determined to get her character back.

She knew within herself that she owed a great deal to Joanna's protection—for Joanna was the chief power in the parishes of Brodnyx and Pedlinge, both personally and territorially. Ellen had been wise beyond the wisdom of despair when she came home. She was not unhappy in her life at Ansdore, for her escapade had given her a queer advantage over her sister, and she now found that she could to a certain extent, mould the household routine to her comfort. She was no longer entirely dominated, and only a small amount of independence was enough to satisfy her, a born submitter, to whom contrivance was more than rule. She wanted only freedom for her tastes and pleasures, and Joanna did not now strive to impose her own upon her. Occasionally the younger woman complained of her lot, bound to a man whom she no longer cared for, wearing only the fetters of her wifehood—she still hankered after a divorce, though Arthur must be respondent. This always woke Joanna to rage, but Ellen's feelings did not often rise to the surface, and on the whole the sisters were happy in their life together—more peaceful because they were more detached than in the old days. Ellen invariably wore black, hoping that strangers and newcomers would take her for a widow.

This she actually became towards the close of the year

1910. Arthur did a fair amount of hunting with his brother in the shires, and one day his horse came down at a fence, throwing him badly and fracturing his skull. He died the same night without regaining consciousness —death had treated him better on the whole than life, for he died without pain or indignity, riding to hounds like any squire. He left a comfortable little fortune, too—Donkey Street and its two hundred acres—and he left it all to Joanna.

Secretly he had made his will anew soon after going to the shires, and in it he had indulged himself, ignoring reality and perhaps duty. Evidently he had had no expectations of a return to married life with Ellen, and in this new testament he ignored her entirely, as if she had not been. Joanna was his wife, inheriting all that was his, of land and money and live and dead stock— "My true, trusty friend, Joanna Godden."

Ellen was furious, and Joanna herself was a little shocked. She understood Arthur's motives—she guessed that one of his reasons for passing over Ellen had been his anxiety to leave her sister dependent on her, knowing her fear that she would take flight. But this exaltation of her by his death to the place she had refused to occupy during his life, gave her a queer sense of smart and shame. For the first time it struck her that she might not have treated Arthur quite well . . . .

However, she did not sympathize with Ellen's indignation—

"You shouldn't ought to have expected a penny, the way you treated him."

"I don't see why he shouldn't have left me at least some furniture, seeing there was about five hundred pounds of my money in that farm. He's done rather well out of me on the whole—making me no allowance whatever when he was alive."

"Because I wouldn't let him make it—I've got some pride if you haven't."

"Your pride doesn't stop you taking what ought to have been mine."

"'Ought to' . . . . I never heard such words. Not that I'm pleased he should make it all over to me, but it ain't my doing."

Ellen looked at her fixedly out of her eyes which were like the shallow floods.

" Are you quite sure ?   Are you quite sure, Joanna, that you honestly played a sister's part by me while I was away ? "

" What d'you mean ? "

" I mean, Arthur seems to have got a lot fonder of you while I was away than he—er—seemed to be before."

Joanna gaped at her.

" Of course it was only natural," continued Ellen smoothly—" I know I treated him badly—but don't you think you needn't have taken advantage of that ? "

" Well, I'm beat . . . . look here, Ellen . . . that man was mine from the first, and I gave him over to you, and I never took him back nor wanted him, neither."

" How generous of you, Jo, to have ' given him over ' to me."

A little maddening smile twisted the corners of her mouth, and Joanna remembered that now Arthur was dead and there was no hope of Ellen going back to him she need not spare her secret.

" Yes, I gave him to you," she said bluntly—" I saw you wanted him, and I didn't want him myself, so I said to him ' Arthur, look here, you take her '—and he said to me—' I'd sooner have you, Jo '—but I said ' you won't have me even if you wait till the moon's cheese, so there's no good hoping for that. You take the little sister and please me '—and he said ' I'll do it to please you, Jo.' That's the very thing that happened, and I'm sorry it happened now—and I never told you before, because I thought it ud put you against him, and I wanted you to go back to him, being his wife ; but now he's dead, and you may as well know, seeing the upstart notions you've got."

She looked fiercely at Ellen, to watch the effect of the blow, but was disconcerted to see that the little maddening smile still lingered. There were dimples at the flexing corners of her sister's mouth, and now they were little wells of disbelieving laughter. Ellen did not believe her—she had told her long-guarded secret and her sister did not believe it. She thought it just something Joanna had made up to salve her pride—and nothing

would ever make her believe it, for she was a woman
who had been loved and knew that she was well worth
loving.

§ 2

Both Ellen and Joanna were a little afraid that Arthur's
treatment of his widow might disestablish her in public
opinion. People would think that she must have behaved
unaccountable badly to be served out like that. But
the effects were not so disastrous as might have been
expected. Ellen, poor and forlorn, in her graceful weeds,
without complaining or resentful words, soon won the
neighbours' compassion. It wasn't right of Alce to have
treated her so—showed an unforgiving nature—if only
the real story could be known, most likely folks would
see . . . . There was also a mild scandal at his treatment of Joanna. " Well, even if he loved her all the time
when he was married to her sister, he needn't have been
so brazen about it . . . . Always cared for Joanna
more'n he ought and showed it more'n he ought."

Joanna was not worried by these remarks—she brushed
them aside. Her character was gossip-proof, whereas
Ellen's was not, therefore it was best that the stones
should be thrown at her rather than at her sister. She
at once went practically to work with Donkey Street.
She did not wish to keep it—it was too remote from Ansdore
to be easily workable, and she was content with her own
thriving estate. She sold Donkey Street with all its stock,
and decided to lay out the money in improvements of
her land. She would drain the waterlogged innings
by the Kent Ditch, she would buy a steam plough and
make the neighbourhood sit up—she would start cattle-
breeding. She had no qualms in thus spending the
money on the farm, instead of on Ellen. Her sister
rather plaintively pointed out that the invested capital
would have brought her in a comfortable small income
—" and then I needn't be such a burden to you, Joanna,
dear."

" You ain't a burden to me," said Joanna.

She could not bear to think of Ellen's becoming independent and leaving her. But Ellen was far better contented with her life at home than she wisely let it appear. Ansdore was a manor now—the largest estate not only in Brodnyx and Pedlinge, but on Walland Marsh ; indeed the whole of the Three Marshes had little to beat it with. Moreover, Ellen was beginning to get her own way in the house—her bedroom was no longer a compulsory bower of roses, but softly cream-coloured and purple-hung. She had persuaded Joanna to have a bathroom fitted up, with hot and cold water and other glories, and though she had been unable to induce her to banish her father's Bible and the stuffed owls from the parlour, she had been allowed to supplement—and practically annihilate —them with the notorious black cushions from Donkey Street. Joanna was a little proud to have these famous decorations on the premises, to be indoors what her yellow waggons were outdoors, symbols of daring and progress.

On the whole, this substantial house, with its wide lands, respectable furniture and swarming servants, was one to be proud of. Ellen's position as Squire Joanna Godden's sister was much better than if she were living by herself in some small place on a small income. Her brief adventure into what she thought was a life of fashionable gaiety had discouraged and disillusioned her—she was slowly slipping back into the conventions of her class and surroundings. Ansdore was no longer either a prison or a refuge, it was beginning to be a home— not permanent, of course, for she was now a free woman and would marry again, but a good home to rest in and re-establish herself.

Thanks to Ellen's contrivance and to the progress of Joanna's own ambition—rising out of its fulfilment in the sphere of the material into the sphere of style and manners—the sisters now lived the lives of two well-to-do ladies. They had late dinner every night—only soup and meat and pudding, still definitely neither supper nor high tea. Joanna changed for it into smart, stiff silk blouses, with a great deal of lace and guipure about them, while Ellen wore a rest-gown of drifting black charmeuse. Mene Tekel was promoted from the dairy to be Ansdore's first parlourmaid, and wore a cap and apron, and waited at table. Ellen would have liked to

keep Mene Tekel in her place and engage a smart town
girl, whose hands were not the colour of beetroots and
whose breathing could not be heard through a closed door;
but Joanna stood firm—Mene had been her faithful
servant for more than seven years, and it wasn't right
that she should have a girl from the town promoted over
her. Besides, Joanna did not like town girls—with town
speech that rebuked her own, and white hands that made
her want to put her own large brown ones under the
table.

§ 3

Early the next year Mr. Pratt faded out. He could
not be said to have done anything so dramatic as to die,
though the green marsh-turf of Brodnyx churchyard
was broken to make him a bed, and the little bell rocked
in the bosom of the drunken Victorian widow who was
Brodnyx church steeple, sending a forlorn note out over
the Marsh. Various aunts in various stages of resigned
poverty bore off his family to separate destinations,
and the great Rectory house which had for so long mocked
his two hundred a year, stood empty, waiting to swallow
up its next victim.

Only in Joanna Godden's breast did any stir remain.
For her at least the fading out of Mr. Pratt had been
drama, the final scene of her importance ; for it was
now her task to appoint his successor in the living of
Brodnyx with Pedlinge. Ever since she had found out
that she could not get rid of Mr. Pratt she had been in
terror lest this crowning triumph might be denied her,
and the largeness of her funeral wreath and the lavishness
of her mourning—extinguishing all the relations in their
dyed blacks—had testified to the warmth of her gratitude
to the late rector for so considerately dying.

She felt exceedingly important, and the feeling was
increased by the applications she received for the living.
Clergymen wrote from different parts of the country;
they told her that they were orthodox—as if she had
imagined a clergyman could be otherwise—that they
were acceptable preachers, that they were good with

Boy Scouts. One or two she interviewed and disliked, because they had bad teeth or large families—one or two turned the tables on her and refused to have anything to do with a living encumbered by so large a rectory and so small an endowment. Joanna felt insulted, though she was not responsible for either. She resolved not to consider any applicants, but to make her own choice outside their ranks. This was a difficult matter, for her sphere was hardly clerical, and she knew no clergy except those on the Marsh. None of these she liked, because they were for the most part elderly and went about on bicycles—also she wanted to dazzle her society with a new importation.

The Archdeacon wrote to her, suggesting that she might be glad of some counsel in filling the vacancy, and giving her the names of two men whom he thought suitable. Joanna was furious—she would brook no interference from Archdeacons, and wrote the gentleman a letter which must have been unique in his archidiaconal experience. All the same she began to feel worried—she was beginning to doubt if she had the same qualifications for choosing a clergyman as she had for choosing a looker or a dairy-girl. She knew the sort of man she liked as a man, and more vaguely the sort of man she liked as a parson, she also was patriotically anxious to find somebody adequate to the honours and obligations of the living. Nobody she saw or heard of seemed to come up to her double standard of man and minister, and she was beginning to wonder to what extent she could compromise her pride by writing—not to the Archdeacon, but over his head to the Bishop—when she saw in the local paper that Father Lawrence, of the Society of Sacred Pity, was preaching a course of sermons in Marlingate.

Immediately memories came back to her, so far and pale that they were more like the memories of dreams than of anything which had actually happened. She saw a small dark figure standing with its back to the awakening light and bidding godspeed to all that was vital and beautiful and more-than-herself in her life . . . . "Go, Christian soul"—while she in the depths of her broken heart had cried "Stay, stay!" But he had obeyed the priest rather than the lover, he had gone and not stayed . . . and afterwards the priest had tried to hold him for her in futurity—"think of Martin, pray for Martin," but the lover had let him slip, because she could not think and dared not pray, and he had fallen back from her into his silent home in the past.

The old wound could still hurt, for a moment it seemed as if her whole body was pain because of it. Successful, important, thriving Joanna Godden could still suffer because eight years ago she had not been allowed to make the sacrifice of all that she now held so triumphantly. This mere name of Martin's brother had pricked her heart, and she suddenly wanted to get closer to the past than she could get with her memorial-card and photograph and tombstone. Even Sir Harry Trevor, ironic link with faithful love, was gone now—there was only Lawrence. She would like to see him—not to talk to him of Martin, she couldn't bear that, and there would be something vaguely improper about it—but he was a clergyman, for all he disguised the fact by calling himself a priest, and she would offer him the living of Brodnyx with Pedlinge and let the neighbourhood sit up as much as it liked.

§ 4

Father Lawrence came to see her one April day when the young lambs were bleating on the sheltered innings and making bright clean spots of white beside the ewes' fog-soiled fleeces, when the tegs had come down from their winter keep inland, and the sunset fell in long golden slats across the first water-green grass of spring. The years had aged him more than they had aged Joanna— the marks on her face were chiefly weather marks, tokens of her exposure to marsh suns and winds, and of her own ruthless applications of yellow soap. Behind them was a little of the hardness which comes when a woman has to fight many battles and has won her victories largely through the sacrifice of her resources. The lines on his face were mostly those of his own humour and other people's sorrows, he had exposed himself perhaps not enough to the weather and too much to the world, so that where she had fine lines and a fundamental hardness, he had heavy lines like the furrows of a ploughshare, and a softness beneath them like the fruitful soil that the share turns up.

Joanna received him in state, with Arthur Alce's teapot and her best pink silk blouse with the lace insertion. Ellen, for fairly obvious reasons, preferred not to be present. Joanna was terrified lest he should begin to talk of Martin, so after she had conformed to local etiquette by inquiring after his health and abusing the weather, she offered him the living of Brodnyx with Pedlinge and a slice of cake almost in the same breath.

She was surprised and a little hurt when he refused the former. As a member of a religious community he could not hold preferment, and he had no vocation to settled Christianity.

" I shouldn't be at all good as a country clergyman. Besides, Jo "—he had at once slipped into the brotherliness of their old relations—" I know you ; you wouldn't like my ways. You'd always be up at me, teaching me better, and then I should be up at you, and possibly we shouldn't stay quite such good friends as we are now."

" I shouldn't mind your ways. Reckon it might do the folks round here a proper lot of good to be prayed over same as you—I mean I'd like to see a few of 'em prayed over when they were dying and couldn't help themselves. Serve them right, I say, for not praying when they're alive, and some who won't put their noses in church except for a harvest thanksgiving. No, if you'll only come here, Lawrence, you may do what you like in the way of prayers and such. I shan't interfere as long as you don't trouble us with the Pope, whom I never could abide after all I've heard of him, wanting to blow up the Established Church in London, and making people kiss his toe, which I'd never do, not if he was to burn me alive."

" Well, if that's the only limit to your toleration I think I could help you, even though I can't come myself. I know one or two excellent priests who would do endless good in a place like this."

Joanna suddenly felt her imagination gloat and kindle at the thought of Brodnyx and Pedlinge compelled to holiness—all those wicked old men who wouldn't go to church, but expected their Christmas puddings just the same, those hobbledehoys who loafed against gate-posts the whole of Sunday, those vain hussies who giggled behind their handkerchiefs all the service through—it would be fine to see them hustled about and taught their manners . . . . it would be valiant sport to see them made to behave, as Mr. Pratt had never been able to make them. She with her half-crown in the plate and her quarterly communion need have no qualms, and she would enjoy seeing the fear of God put into other folk.

So Lawrence's visit was fruitful after all—a friend of his had been ordered to give up his hard work in a slum parish and find a country vocation. He promised that this friend should write to Joanna.

" But I must see him, too," she said.

They were standing at the open door, and the religious in his black habit was like a cut paper silhouette against the long streaks of fading purple cloud.

" I remember," he said, " that you always were particular about a man's looks. How Martin's must have delighted you ! "

His tongue did not falter over the loved, forbidden name—he spoke it quite naturally and conversationally, as if glad that he could introduce it at last into their business.

Joanna's body stiffened, but he did not see it, for he was gazing at the young creeper's budding trail over the door.

" I hope you have a good photograph of him," he continued—" I know that a very good photograph was taken of him a year before he died—much better than any of the earlier ones. I hope you have one of those."

" Yes, I have," said Joanna gruffly. From shock she had passed into a thrilling anger. How calmly he had spoken the dear name, how unblushingly he had said the outrageous word " died ! " How brazen, thoughtless, cruel he was about it all !—tearing the veil from her sorrow, talking as if her dead lived . . . she felt exposed, indecent, and she hated him, all the more because mixed with her hatred was a kind of disapproving envy, a re-sentiment that he should be free to remember where she was bound to forget . . . .

He saw her hand clench slowly at her side, and for the first time became aware of her state of mind.

" Good-bye, Jo," he said kindly—" I'll tell Father Palmer to write to you."

" Thanks, but I don't promise to take him," was her ungracious fling.

" No—why should you ? And of course he may have already made his plans. Good-bye, and thank you for your great kindness in offering the living to me—it was very noble of you, considering what your family has suffered from mine."

He had carefully avoided all reference to his father, but he now realized that he had kept the wrong silence. It was the man who had brought her happiness, not the man who had brought her shame, that she was unable to speak of.

" Oh, don't you think of that—it wasn't your doing " —she melted towards him now she had a genuine cause for indignation—" and we've come through it better than we hoped, and some of us deserved."

Lawrence gave her an odd smile, which made his face with its innumerable lines and pouches look rather like a gargoyle's. Then he walked off bare-headed into the twilight.

§ 5

Ellen was intensely relieved when she heard that he had refused the living, and a little indignant with Joanna for having offered it to him.

" You don't seem to realize how very awkward it would have been for me—I don't want to have anything more to do with that family."

" I daresay not," said Joanna grimly, " but that ain't no reason why this parish shouldn't have a good parson. Lawrence ud have made the people properly mind their ways. And it ain't becoming in you, Ellen Alce, to let your own misdoings stand between folk and what's good for 'em."

Ellen accepted the rebuke good-humouredly. She had grown more mellow of late, and was settling into her life at Ansdore as she had never settled since she went to school. She relished her widowed state, for it involved the delectable business of looking about for a second husband. She was resolved to act with great deliberation. This time there should be no hustling into matrimony. It seemed to her now as if that precipitate taking of Arthur Alce had been at the bottom of all her troubles; she had been only a poor little schoolgirl, a raw contriver, hurling herself out of the frying-pan of Ansdore's tyranny into the fire of Donkey Street's dullness. She knew better now—besides, the increased freedom and comfort of her conditions did not involve the same urgency of escape.

She made up her mind that she would not take anyone of the farming classes; this time she would marry a gentleman—but a decent sort. She did not enjoy all her memories of Sir Harry Trevor. She would not take up with that kind of man again, any more than with a dull fellow like poor Arthur.

She had far better opportunities than in the old days. The exaltation of Ansdore from farm to manor had turned many keys, and Joanna now received calls from doctors' and clergymen's wives, who had hitherto ignored her except commercially. It was at Fairfield Vicarage that Ellen met the wife of a major at Lydd camp, and through her came to turn the heads of various subalterns. The young officers from Lydd paid frequent visits to Ansdore, which was a novelty to both the sisters, who hitherto had had no dealings with military society. Ellen was far too prudent to engage herself to any of these boys; she waited for a major or a captain at least. But she enjoyed their society, and knew that their visits gave her consequence in the neighbourhood. She was invariably discreet in her behaviour, and was much reproached by them for her coldness, which they attributed to Joanna, who watched over her like a dragon, convinced that the moment she relaxed her guard her sister would inevitably return to her wicked past.

Ellen would have felt sore and insulted if she had not the comfort of knowing in her heart that Joanna was secretly envious—a little hurt that these personable young men came to Ansdore for Ellen alone. They liked Joanna, in spite of her interference; they said she was a good sort, and spoke of her among themselves as " the old girl " and " Joanna God-dam." But none of them thought of turning from Ellen to her sister—she was too weather-beaten for them, too big and bouncing—over-ripe. Ellen, pale as a flower, with wide lips like rose-leaves and narrow, brooding eyes, with her languor, and faint suggestions of the exotic, all the mystery with which fate had chosen to veil the common secret which was Ellen Alce . . . . She could now have the luxury of pitying her sister, of seeing herself possessed of what her tyrant Joanna had not, and longed for . . . . Slowly she was gaining the advantage, her side of the wheel was mounting while Joanna's went down; in spite of the elder woman's success and substance the younger was unmistakably winning ascendancy over her.

§ 6

Her pity made her kind. She no longer squabbled, complained or resented. She took Joanna's occasionally insulting behaviour in good part. She even wished that she would marry—not one of the subalterns, for they were not her sort, but some decent small squire or parson. When the new rector first came to Brodnyx she had great hopes of fixing a match between him and Jo—for Ellen was now so respectable that she had become a match-maker. But she was disappointed—indeed, they both were, for Joanna had liked the looks of Mr. Pratt's successor, and though she did not go so far as to dream of matrimony—which was still below her horizons—she would have much appreciated his wooing.

But it soon became known that the new rector had strange views on the subject of clerical marriage—in fact, he shocked his patron in many ways. He was a large, heavy, pale-faced young man, with strange, sleek qualities that appealed to her through their unaccustomedness. But he was scarcely a sleek man in office, and under his drawling, lethargic manner there was an energy that struck her as shocking and out of place. He was like Lawrence, speaking forbidden words and of hidden things. In church he preached embarrassing perfections —she could no longer feel that she had attained the limits of churchmanship with her weekly half-crown and her quarterly communion. He turned her young people's heads with strange glimpses of beauty and obligation.

In fact, poor Joanna was deprived of the spectacle she had looked forward to with such zest—that of a parish made to amend itself while she looked on from the detachment of her own high standard. She was made to feel just as uncomfortable as any wicked old man or giggling hussy . . . . She was all the more aggrieved because, though Mr. Palmer had displeased her, she could not get rid of him as she would have got rid of her looker in the same circumstances. " If I take a looker and he don't please me I can sack him—the gal I engage I can get shut of at a month's warning, but a parson seemingly is the only kind you can put in and not put out."

Then to crown all, he took away the Lion and the Unicorn from their eternal dance above the Altar of God, and in their place he put tall candles, casting queer red gleams into daylight . . . Joanna could bear no more ; she swallowed the pride which for the first few months of innovation had made her treat the new rector merely with distant rudeness, and descended upon him in the three rooms of Brodnyx Rectory which he inhabited with cheerful contempt for the rest of its howling vastness.

She emerged from the encounter strangely subdued. Mr. Palmer had been polite, even sympathetic, but he had plainly shown her the indifference (to use no cruder term) that he felt for her as an ecclesiastical authority. He was not going to put the Lion and the Unicorn back in their old place, they belonged to a bygone age which was now forgotten, to a bad old language which had lost its meaning. The utmost he would do was to consent to hang them up over the door, so that they could bless Joanna's going out and coming in. With this she had to be content.

Poor Joanna ! The episode was more than a passing outrage and humiliation—it was ominous, it gave her a queer sense of downfall. With her beloved symbol something which was part of herself seemed also to have been dispossessed. She became conscious that she was losing authority. She realized that for long she had been weakening in regard to Ellen, and now she was unable to stand up to this heavy, sleek young man whom her patronage had appointed. . . . The Lion and the Unicorn had from childhood been her sign of power—they were her theology in oleograph, they stood for the Church of England as by law established, large rectory houses, respectable and respectful clergymen, " dearly beloved brethren " on Sunday mornings, and a nice nap after dinner. And now they were gone, and in their place was a queer Jesuitry of kyries and candles, and a gospel which kicked and goaded and would not allow one to sleep . . . .

§ 7

It began to be noticed at the Woolpack that Joanna was losing heart. " She's lost her spring," they said in the bar—" she's got all she wanted, and now she's feeling dull "—" she's never had what she wanted and now she's feeling tired "—" her sister's beat her and parson's beat her—she can't be properly herself." There was some talk about making her an honorary member of the Farmers' Club, but it never got beyond talk—the traditions of that exclusive body were too strong to admit her even now.

To Joanna it seemed as if life had newly and powerfully armed itself against her. Her love for Ellen was making her soft, she was letting her sister rule. And not only at home but abroad she was losing her power. Both Church and State had taken to themselves new arrogances. The Church had lost its comfortable atmosphere of Sunday beef—and now the State, which hitherto had existed only for that most excellent purpose of making people behave themselves, had lifted itself up against Joanna Godden.

Lloyd George's Finance Act had caught her in its toils, she was being overwhelmed with terrible forms and schedules, searching into her profits, making strange inquiries as to minerals, muddling her with long words.

Then out of all the muddle and welter finally emerged the startling fact that the Government expected to have twenty per cent. of her profits on the sale of Donkey Street.

She was indignant and furious. She considered that the Government had been grossly treacherous, unjust, and disrespectful to poor Arthur's memory. It was Arthur who had done so well with his land that she had been able to sell it to Honisett at such a valiant price. She had spent all the money on improvements, too—she was not like some people who bought motor-cars and took trips to Paris. She had not bought a motor-car but a motor-plough, the only one in the district—the Government could come and see it themselves if they liked. It was well worth looking at.

Thus she delivered herself to young Edward Huxtable, who now managed his father's business at Rye.

"But I'm afraid it's all fair and square, Miss Joanna," said her lawyer—"there's no doubt about the land's value or what you sold it for, and I don't see that you are entitled to any exemption."

"Why not?—If I'm not entitled, who is?"

Joanna sat looking very large and flushed in the Huxtable office in Watchbell Street. She felt almost on the verge of tears, for it seemed to her that she was the victim of the grossest injustice which also involved the grossest disrespect to poor Arthur, who would turn in his grave if he knew that the Government were trying to take his legacy from her.

"What are lawyers for?" she continued hotly. "You can turn most things inside out—why can't you do this? Can't I go to County Court about it?"

Edward Huxtable consulted the Act . . . . "'Notice of objection may be served on the Commissioners within sixty days. If they do not allow the objection, the petitioner may appeal to a referee under the Act, and an appeal by either the petitioner or the Commissioners lies from the referee to the High Court, or where the site value does not exceed £500, to the County Court.' I suppose yours is worth more than £500?"

"I should just about think it is—it's worth something more like five thousand if the truth was known."

" Well, I shouldn't enlarge on that. Do you think it worth while to serve an objection ? No doubt there are grounds on which we could appeal, but they aren't very good, and candidly I think we'd lose. It would cost you a great deal of money, too, before you'd finished."

" I don't care about that. I'm not going to sit down quiet and have my rightful belongings taken from me."

Edward Huxtable considered that he had done his duty in warning Joanna—lots of lawyers wouldn't have troubled to do that—and after all the old girl had heaps of money to lose. She might as well have her fun and he his fee.

" Well, anyhow we'll go as far as the Commissioners. If I were you, I shouldn't apply for total exemption, but for a rebate. We might do something with allowances. Let me see, what did you sell for ? " . . . .

He finally prepared an involved case, partly depending on the death duties that had already been paid when Joanna inherited Alce's farm, and which he said ought to be considered in calculating increment value. Joanna would not have confessed for worlds that she did not understand the grounds of her appeal, though she wished Edward Huxtable would let her make at least some reference to her steam tractor, and thus win her victory on moral grounds, instead of just through some lawyer's mess. But, moral appeal or lawyer's mess, her case should go to the Commissioners, and if necessary to the High Court. Just because she knew that in her own home and parish the fighting spirit was failing her, Joanna resolved to fight this battle outside it without counting the cost.

§ 8

That autumn she had her first twinge of rheumatism. The days of the marsh ague were over, but the dread " rheumatiz " still twisted comparatively young bones. Joanna had escaped till a later age than many, for her work lay mostly in dry kitchens and bricked yards, and she had had little personal contact with the soil, that odorous sponge of the marsh earth, rank with the soakings of sea-fogs and land-fogs.

Like most healthy people, she made a tremendous
fuss once she was laid up. Mene Tekel and Mrs. Tolhurst
were kept flying up and down stairs with hot bricks and
poultices and that particularly noxious brew of camomile
tea which she looked upon as the cure of every ill. Ellen
would come now and then and sit on her bed, and wander
round the room playing with Joanna's ornaments—she
wore a little satisfied smile on her face, and about her was
a queer air of restlessness and contentment which baffled
and annoyed her sister.

The officers from Lydd did not now come so often
to Ansdore. Ellen's most constant visitor at this time
was the son of the people who had taken Great Ansdore
dwelling-house. Tip Ernley had just come back from
Australia ; he did not like colonial life and was looking
round for something to do at home. He was a county
cricketer, an exceedingly nice-looking young man, and
his people were a good sort of people, an old West Sussex
family fallen into straightened circumstances.

On his account Joanna came downstairs sooner than
she ought. She could not get rid of her distrust of Ellen,
the conviction that once her sister was left to herself
she would be up to all sorts of mischief. Ellen had behaved impossibly once and therefore, according to Joanna,
there was no guarantee that she would not go on behaving
impossibly to the end of time. So she came down to
play the dragon to Tip Ernley as she had played the dragon
to the young lieutenants of the summer. There was not
much for her to do—she saw at once that the boy was
different from the officers, a simple-minded creature,
strong, gentle and clean-living, with deferential eyes and
manners. Joanna liked him at first sight, and relented.
They had tea together, and a game of three-handed bridge
afterwards—Ellen had taught her sister to play bridge.

Then as the evening wore on, and the mists crept up
from the White Kemp Sewer to muffle the windows of
Ansdore and make Joanna's bones twinge and ache, she
knew that she had come down too late. These young
people had had time enough to settle their hearts' business
in a little less than a week, and Joanna God-dam could not
scare them apart. Of course there was nothing to fear
—this fine, shy man would make no assault on Ellen Alce's

frailty, it was merely a case of Ellen Alce becoming Ellen Ernley, if he could be persuaded to overlook her " past "— a matter which Joanna thought important and doubtful. But the elder sister's heart twinged and ached as much as her bones. There was not only the thought that she might lose Ellen once more and have to go back to her lonely living . . . . her heart was sick to think that again love had come under her roof and had not visited her. Love . . . love . . . . . for Ellen—no more for Joanna Godden. Perhaps now it was too late. She was getting on, past thirty-seven—romance never came as late as that on Walland Marsh, unless occasionally to widows. Then, since it was too late, why did she so passionately long for it ?—Why had not her heart grown old with her years ?

§ 9

During the next few weeks Joanna watched the young romance grow and sweeten. Ellen was becoming almost girlish again, or rather, girlish as she had never been. The curves of her mouth grew softer and her voice lost its even tones—she had moments of languor and moments of a queer lightness. Great and Little Ansdore were now on very good terms, and during that winter there was an exchange of dinners and bridge. Joanna could now, as she expressed it, give a dinner-party with the best of 'em. Nothing more splendid could be imagined than Joanna Godden sitting at the head of her table, wearing her Folkestone-made gown of apricot charmeuse, adapted to her modesty by means of some rich gold lace ; Ellen had induced her to bind her hair with a gold ribbon, and from her ears great gold ear-rings hung nearly to her shoulders, giving the usual barbaric touch to her stateliness. Ellen, in contrast, wore iris-tinted gowns that displayed nacreous arms and shoulders, and her hair passed in great dark shining licks over her little unadorned ears.

Joanna was annoyed because Ellen never told her anything about herself and Tip Ernley. She wanted to know in what declared relation they stood to each other.

She hoped Ellen was being straight with him, as she was obviously not being straight with her. She did not think they were definitely engaged—surely they would have let her know that. Perhaps he was waiting till he had found some satisfactory job and could afford to keep a wife. She told herself angrily that if only they would confide in her, she would help the young pair . . . they were spoiling their own chances by keeping her out of their secrets. It never struck her that Ernley would rather not be beholden to her, whatever Ellen might feel in the matter.

His father and mother—well-bred, cordial people— and his maiden sister, of about Joanna's age, never seemed to see anything remarkable in the way Ellen and Tip always went off together after dinner, while the others settled down to their bridge. It seemed to Joanna a grossly improper proceeding if they were not engaged. But all Mr. and Mrs. Ernley would say was—"Quite right too—it's just as well when young people aren't too fond of cards." Joanna herself was growing to be quite fond of cards, though in her heart she did not think that for sheer excitement bridge was half as good as beggar-my-neighbour, which she used to play with Mene Tekel, in the old days before she and Mene both became dignified, the one as mistress, the other as maid. She enjoyed her bridge—but often the game would be quite spoilt by the thought of Ellen and Tip in some secluded corner. He must be making love to her, or they wouldn't go off alone together like that . . . . I go no trumps . . . . if they wanted just ordinary talk they could stay in here, we wouldn't trouble them if they sat over there on the sofa . . . . me to play, is it? . . . . I wonder if she lets him kiss her . . . . oh, I beg your pardon, I'm sure . . . .

Joanna had no more returns of rheumatism that winter. Scared and infuriated by her one experience, she took great care of herself, and that winter was drier than usual, with crisp days of cold sunshine, and a skin of ice on the sewers. Once or twice there was a fall of snow, and even Joanna saw beauty in those days of a blue sky hanging above the dazzling white spread of the three marshes, Walland, Dunge and Romney, one huge white plain, streaked with the watercourses black under their ice, like bars of iron. Somehow the sight hurt her; all beautiful things hurt her strangely now—whether it was the snow-laden marsh, or the first scents of spring in the evenings of February, or even Ellen's face like a broad, pale flower.

She felt low-spirited and out of sorts that turn of the year. It was worse than rheumatism . . . . Then she suddenly conceived the idea that it was the rheumatism " driven inside her." Joanna had heard many terrible tales of people who had perished through quite ordinary complaints, like measles, being mysteriously " driven inside." It was a symptom of her low condition that she should worry about her health, which till then had never given her a minute's preoccupation. She consulted " The Family Doctor," and realized the number of diseases she might be suffering from besides suppressed rheumatics —cancer, consumption, kidney disease, diabetes, appendicitis, asthma, arthritis, she seemed to have them all, and in a fit of panic decided to consult a physician in the flesh.

So she drove off to see Dr. Taylor in her smart chocolate-coloured trap, behind her chocolate-coloured mare, with her groom in chocolate-coloured livery on the seat behind her. She intended to buy a car if she won her case at the High Court—for to the High Court it had gone, both the Commissioners and their referee having shown themselves blind to the claims of justice.

The doctor listened respectfully to the long list of her symptoms and to her own diagnosis of them. No, he did not think it was the rheumatism driven inside her . . . . He asked her a great many questions, some of which she thought indelicate.

" You're thoroughly run down," he said at last—" been doing too much—you've done a lot, you know."

" Reckon I have," said Joanna—" but I'm a young woman yet "—there was a slight touch of defiance in her last words.

" Oh, age has nothing to do with it. We're liable to overwork ourselves at all ages. Overwork and worry . . . What you need is a thorough rest of mind and body. I recommend a change."

" You mean I should ought to go away ? "

" Certainly."

" But I haven't been away for twenty year."

" That's just it. You've let yourself get into a groove. You want a thorough change of air, scene and society. I recommend that you go away to some cheerful gay watering-place, where there's plenty going on and you'll meet new people."

" But what'll become of Ansdore ? "

" Surely it can get on without you for a few weeks ? "

" I can't go till the lambing's finished."

" When will that be ? "

" Not till after Easter."

" Well, Easter is a very good time to go away. Do take my advice about this, Miss Godden. You'll never be really well and happy if you keep in a groove. . . ."

" Groove ! " snorted Joanna.

§ 10

She was so much annoyed with him for having twice referred to Ansdore as a " groove " that at first she felt inclined not to take his advice. But even to Joanna this was unsatisfactory as a revenge—" If I stay at home, maybe I'll get worse, and then he'll be coming over to see me in my ' groove ' and getting eight-and-six each time for it." It would certainly be better to go away and punish the doctor by a complete return to health. Besides, she was awed by the magnitude of the prescription. It was a great thing on the Marsh to be sent away for change of air, instead of just getting a bottle of stuff to take three times daily after meals . . . . She'd go, and make a splash of it.

Then the question arose—where should she go ? She could go to her cousins in the Isle of Wight, but they were a poor lot. She could go to Chichester, where Martha Relf, the girl who had been with her when she first took over Ansdore and had behaved so wickedly with the looker at Honeychild, now kept furnished rooms as a respectable widow. Martha, who was still grateful to Joanna, had written and asked her to come and try her accommodation . . . . But by no kind of process could Chichester be thought of as a "cheerful watering-place," and Joanna was resolved to carry out her prescription to the letter.

"Why don't you go to a really good place?" suggested Ellen—"Bath or Matlock or Leamington. You could stay at a hydro, if you liked."

But these were all too far—Joanna did not want to be beyond the summons of Ansdore, which she could scarcely believe would survive her absence. Also, to her horror, she discovered that nothing would induce Ellen to accompany her.

"But I can't go without you!" she cried dismally—"it wouldn't be seemly—it wouldn't be proper."

"What nonsense, Jo. Surely a woman of your age can stop anywhere by herself."

"Oh, indeed, can she, ma'am? And what about a woman of your age?—It's you I don't like leaving alone here."

"That's absurd of you. I'm a married woman, and quite able to look after myself. Besides, I've Mrs. Tolhurst with me, and the Ernleys are quite close."

"Oh, yes, the Ernleys!" sniffed Joanna with a toss of her head. She felt that now was a fitting opportunity for Ellen to disclose her exact relations with the family, but surprisingly her sister took no advantage of the opening thus made.

"You'd much better go alone, Joanna—it won't do you half so much good if I go with you. We're getting on each other's nerves, you know we are. At least I'm getting on yours. You'll be much happier among entirely new people."

It ended in Joanna's taking rooms at the Palace Hotel, Marlingate. No persuasions would make her go farther off. She was convinced that neither Ansdore nor Ellen could exist, at least decorously, without her, and she must be within easy reach of both. The fortnight between the booking of her room and her setting out she spent in mingled fretfulness and swagger. She fretted about Ansdore, and nearly drove her carter and her looker frantic with her last injunctions; she fretted about Ellen, and cautioned Mrs. Tolhurst to keep a strict watch

over her—"She's not to go up to late dinner at Great
Ansdore without you fetch her home." On the other
hand, she swaggered tremendously about the expensive
and fashionable trip she was making. Her room was on
the first floor of the hotel and would cost her twelve-
and-six a night. She had taken it for a week, "But I
told them I'd stay a fortnight if I was satisfied, so reckon
they'll do all they can. I'll have breakfast in bed"—
she added, as a climax.

§ 11

In spite of this, Joanna could not help feeling a little
nervous and lonely when she found herself at the Palace
Hotel. It was so very different from the New Inn at
Romney, or the George at Rye, or any other substantial
farmers' ordinary where she ate her dinner on market
days. Of course she had been to the Metropole at
Folkestone—whatever place Joanna visited, whether
Brodnyx or Folkestone, she went to the best hotel—so
she was not uninitiated in the mysteries of hotel menus
and lifts and hall porters, and other phenomena that alarm
the simple-minded ; but that was many years ago, and
it was more years still since she had slept away from Ansdore, out of her own big bed with its feather mattress
and flowered curtains, so unlike this narrow hotel arrange-
ment, all box mattress and brass knobs.

The first night she lay miserably awake, wishing she
had never come. She felt shy and lonely and scared and
homesick. After the dead stillness of Ansdore, a stillness
which brooded unbroken till dawn, which was the voice
of a thick darkness, she found even this quiet seaside
hotel full of disturbing noise. The hum of the ascending
lift far into the night, the occasional wheels and footsteps
on the parade, the restless heaving roar of the sea, all
disturbed the small slumbers that her sense of alarm
and strangeness would let her enjoy. She told herself
she would never sleep a wink in this rackety place, and
would have sought comfort in the resolution to go home
the next morning, if she had not had Ellen to face, and
the servants and neighbours to whom she had boasted so
much.

However, when daylight came, and sunshine, and her breakfast-in-bed, with its shining dish covers and appetizing smells, she felt quite different, and ate her bacon and eggs with appetite and a thrilling sense of her own importance. The waitress, for want of a definite order, had brought her coffee, which somehow made her feel very rakish and continental, though she would have much preferred tea. When she had finished breakfast, she wrote a letter to Ellen describing all her experiences with as much fullness as was compatible with that strange inhibition which always accompanied her taking up of the pen, and distinguished her letters so remarkably from the feats of her tongue.

When she had written the letter and posted it adventurously in the hotel letter-box, she went out on the parade to listen to the band. It was Easter week, and there were still a great many people about, couples sitting round the bandstand, more deeply absorbed in each other than in the music. Joanna paid twopence for a chair, having ascertained that there were no more expensive seats to be had, and at the end of an hour felt consumedly bored. The music was bright and popular enough, but she was not musical, and soon grew tired of listening to "tunes." Also something about the music made her feel uncomfortable—the same dim yet searching discomfort she had when she looked at the young couples in the sun . . . . the young girls in their shady hats and silk stockings, the young men in their flannels and blazers. They were all part of a whole to which she did not belong, of which the music was part . . . . and the sea, and the sun, and the other visitors at the hotel, the very servants of the hotel . . . . and Ellen at Ansdore . . . . all day she was adding fresh parts to that great whole, outside which she seemed to exist alone.

"I'm getting fanciful," she thought—"this place hasn't done me a bit of good yet."

She devoted herself to the difficult art of filling up her day. Accustomed to having every moment occupied, she could hardly cope with the vast stretch of idle hours. After a day or two she found herself obliged to give up having breakfast in bed. From force of habit she woke every morning at five, and could not endure the long wait

in her room. If the weather was fine she usually went
for a walk on the sea-front, from Rock-a-Nore to the
Monypenny statue. Nothing would induce her to bathe,
though even at that hour and season the water was full
of young men and women rather shockingly enjoying
themselves and each other. After breakfast she wrote
laborious letters to Broadhurst, Wilson, Mrs. Tolhurst,
Ellen, Mene Tekel—she had never written so many letters
in her life, but every day she thought of some fresh thing
that would be left undone if she did not write about it.
When she had finished her letters she went out and listened
respectfully to the band. The afternoon was generally
given up to some excursion or charabanc drive, and the
day finished rather somnolently in the lounge.

She did not get far beyond civilities with the other
visitors in the hotel. More than one had spoken to her,
attracted by this handsome, striking, and probably wealthy
woman—through Ellen's influence her appearance had
been purged of what was merely startling—but they
either took fright at her broad marsh accent . . . .
" she must be somebody's cook come into a fortune " . . .
or the more fundamental incompatibility of outlook kept
them at a distance. Joanna was not the person for the
niceties of hotel acquaintanceship—she was too garrulous,
too overwhelming. Also she failed to realize that all
states of society are not equally interested in the price
of wheat, that certain details of sheep-breeding seem
indelicate to the uninitiated, and that strangers do not
really care how many acres one possesses, how many
servants one keeps, or the exact price one paid for one's
latest churn.

§ 12

The last few days of her stay brought her a rather
ignominious sense of relief. In her secret heart she was
eagerly waiting till she should be back at Ansdore, eating
her dinner with Ellen, sleeping in her own bed, ordering
about her own servants. She would enjoy, too, telling
everyone about her exploits, all the excursions she had
made, the food she had eaten, the fine folk she had spoken

to in the lounge, the handsome amount she had spent
in tips. . . . They would all ask her whether she felt
much the better for her holiday, and she was uncertain
what to answer them. A complete recovery might make
her less interesting ; on the other hand she did not want
anyone to think she had come back half-cured because
of the expense . . . . that was just the sort of thing
Mrs. Southland would imagine, and Southland would
take it straight to the Woolpack.

Her own feelings gave her no clue. Her appetite
had much improved, but, against that, she was sleeping
badly—which she partly attributed to the " noise "—
and was growing, probably on account of her idle days,
increasingly restless. She found it difficult to settle down
to anything—the hours in the hotel lounge after dinner,
which used to be comfortably drowsy after the day of
sea-air, were now a long stretch of boredom, from which
she went up early to bed, knowing that she would not
sleep. The band played on the parade every evening,
but Joanna considered that it would be unseemly for her
to go out alone in Marlingate after dark. Though she
would have walked out on the Brodnyx road at midnight
without putting the slightest strain on either her courage
or her decorum, the well-lighted streets of a town
became to her vaguely dangerous and indecorous after
dusk had fallen. " It wouldn't be seemly," she repeated
to herself in the loneliness and dullness of the lounge,
and went desperately to bed.

However, three nights before going away she could
bear it no longer. After a warm April day, a purple
starry evening hung over the sea. The water itself was
a deep, glaucous gray, holding strange lights besides the
golden path of the moon. Beachy Head stood out purple
against the fading amber of the west, in the east All Hol-
land Hill was hung with a crown of stars, which seemed
to be mirrored in the lights of the fisher-boats off Rock-a-
Nore . . . . It was impossible to think of such an
evening spent in the stuffy, lonely lounge, with heavy
curtains shutting out the opal and the amethyst of night.

She had not had time to dress for dinner, having come
home late from a charabanc drive to Pevensey, and the
circumstance seemed slightly to mitigate the daring of

a stroll.   In her neat tailor-made coat and skirt and black hat with the cock's plumes she might perhaps walk to and fro just a little in front of the hotel.   She went out, and was a trifle reassured by the light which still lingered in the sky and on the sea—it was not quite dark yet, and there was a respectable-looking lot of people about —she recognized a lady staying in the hotel, and would have joined her, but the lady, whom she had already scared, saw her coming, and dodged off in the direction of the Marine Gardens.

The band began to play a waltz from " A Persian Princess."   Joanna felt once more in her blood the strange stir of the music she could not understand.   It would be nice to dance . . . queer that she had so seldom danced as a girl.   She stood for a moment irresolute, then walked towards the bandstand, and sat down on one of the corporation benches, outside the crowd that had grouped round the musicians.   It was very much the same sort of crowd as in the morning, but it was less covert in its ways—hands were linked, even here and there waists entwined . . . .   Such details began to stand out of the dim, purplescent mass of the twilight people . . . . night was the time for love.   They had come out into the darkness to make love to each other—their voices sounded different from in the day, more dragging, more tender . . .

She began to think of the times, which now seemed so far off, when she herself had sought a man's kisses. Half-ashamed she went back to stolen meetings—in a barn—behind a rick—in the elvish shadow of some skew-blown thorn.   Just kisses . . . . not love, for love had been dead in her then . . . .   But those kisses had been sweet, she remembered them, she could feel them on her lips . . . . oh, she could love again now—she could give and take kisses now.

The band was playing a rich, thick, drawling melody, full of the purple night and the warm air.   The lovers round the bandstand seemed to sway to it and draw closer to each other.   Joanna looked down into her lap, for her eyes were full of tears.   She regretted passionately the days that were past—those light loves which had not been able to live in the shadow of Martin's memory. Oh, why had he taught her to love and then made it impossible for her ever to love again?—till it was too late, till she was a middle-aged woman to whom no man came . . . . It was not likely that anyone would want her now—her light lovers all lived now in substantial wedlock, the well-to-do farmers who had proposed to her in the respectful way of business had now taken to themselves other wives. The young men looked to women of their own age, to Ellen's pale, soft beauty . . . . once again she envied Ellen her loves, good and evil, and shame was in her heart. Then she lifted her eyes and saw Martin coming towards her.

§ 13

In the darkness, lit only now by the lamp-dazzled moonlight, and in the mist of her own tears, the man before her was exactly like Martin, in build, gait, colouring and expression. Her moment of recognition stood out clear, quite distinct from the realization of impossibility which afterwards engulfed it. She unclasped her hands and half rose in her seat—the next minute she fell back. " Reckon I'm crazy," she thought to herself.

Then she was startled to realize that the man had sat down beside her. Her heart beat quickly. Though she no longer confused him with Martin, the image of Martin persisted in her mind . . . how wonderfully like him he was . . . . the very way he walked . . . .

" I saw you give me the glad eye . . ." not the way he talked, certainly.

There was a terrible silence.

" Are you going to pretend you didn't ? "

Joanna turned on him the tear-filled eyes he had considered glad. She blinked the tears out recklessly on to her cheek, and opened her mouth to reduce him to the level of the creeping things upon the earth . . . . But the mouth remained open and speechless. She could not look him in the face and still feel angry. Though now she would no longer have taken him for Martin, the resemblance still seemed to her startling. He had the same rich eyes—with an added trifle of impudence under the same veiling, womanish lashes, the same

black sweep of hair from a rather low forehead, the same
graceful setting of the head, though he had not Martin's
breadth of shoulder or deceiving air of strength.

Her hesitation gave him his opportunity.

" You aren't going to scold me, are you ? I couldn't
help it."

His unlovely, Cockney voice had in it a stroking
quality. It stirred something in the depths of Joanna's
heart. Once again she tried to speak and could not.

" It's such a lovely night—just the sort of night you
feel lonely, unless you've got someone very nice with you."

This was terribly true.

" And you did give me the glad eye, you know."

" I didn't mean to." She had found her voice at
last. " I—I thought you were someone else ; at least
I——"

" Are you expecting a friend ? "

" Oh, no—no one. It was a mistake."

" Then mayn't I stay and talk to you—just for a
bit. I'm here all alone, you know—a fortnight's holiday.
I don't know anyone."

By this time he had dragged all her features out of
the darkness, and saw that she was not quite what he had
first taken her for. He had never thought she was a girl
—his taste was for maturity—but he had not imagined
her of the obviously well-to-do and respectable class to
which she evidently belonged. He saw now that her
clothes were of a fashionable cut, that she had about her
a generally expensive air, and at the same time he knew
enough to tell that she was not what he called a lady.
He found her rather difficult to place. Perhaps she was
a wealthy milliner on a holiday . . . . but, her accent
—you could lean up against it . . . . well, anyhow
she was a damn fine woman.

" What do you think of the band ? " he asked, subtly
altering the tone of the conversation which he saw now
had been pitched too low.

" I think it a proper fine band."

" So it is. They're going to play ' The Merry Widow '
next—ever seen it ? "

" No, never. I was never at a play but once, which
they did at the Monastery at Rye in aid of Lady Buller's

Fund when we was fighting the Boers. ' Our Flat ' it was called, and all done by respectable people—not an actor or an actress among 'em."

What on earth had he picked up ?

" Do you live at Rye ? "

" I live two mile out of it—Ansdore's the name of my place—Ansdore Manor, seeing as now I've got both Great and Little Ansdore, and the living's in my gift. I put in a new parson last year."

This must be a remarkable woman, unless she was telling him the tale.

" I went over to Rye on Sunday," he said. " Quaint old place, isn't it ? Funny to think it used to be on the seashore. They say there once was a battle between the French and English fleets where it's all dry marsh now."

Joanna thrilled again—that was like Martin, telling her things, old things about the Marsh. The conversation was certainly being conducted on very decorous lines. She began to lose the feeling of impropriety which had disturbed her at first. They sat talking about the neighbourhood, the weather, and—under Joanna's guidance— the prospects of the harvest, for another ten minutes, at the end of which the band went off for their " interval."

The cessation of the music and scattering of the crowd recalled Joanna to a sense of her position. She realized also that it was quite dark—the last redeeming ray had left the sky. She stood up—

" Well, I must be getting back."

" Where are you staying ? "

" The Palace Hotel."

What ho ! She must have some money.

" May I walk back with you ? "

" Oh, thanks," said Joanna—" it ain't far."

They walked, rather awkwardly silent, the few hundred yards to the hotel. Joanna stopped and held out her hand. She suddenly realized that she did not want to say good-bye to the young man. Their acquaintanceship had been most shockingly begun—Ellen must never know —but she did not want it to end. She felt, somehow, that he just meant to say good-bye and go off, without any plans for another meeting. She must take action herself.

" Won't you come and have dinner—I mean lunch—
with me to-morrow ? "

She scanned his face eagerly as she spoke.   It suddenly
struck her what a terrible thing it would be if he went
out of her life now after having just come into it—come
back into it, she had almost said, for she could not rid
herself of that strange sense of Martin's return, of a second
spring.

But she need not have been afraid.   He was not the
man to refuse his chances.

" Thanks no end—I'll be honoured."

" Then I'll expect you.   One o'clock, and ask for Miss
Godden."

§ 14

Joanna had a nearly sleepless night.   The torment
of her mind would not allow her to rest.   At times she was
overwhelmed with shame at what she had done—taken
up with a strange man at the band, like any low servant
girl on her evening out—My ! but she'd have given it
to Mene Tekel if she dared behave so !   At other times
she drifted on a dark sweet river of thought . . . every
detail of the boy's appearance haunted her with disturbing
charm—his eyes, black and soft like Martin's—his mouth
which was coarser and sulkier than Martin's, yet made
her feel all disquieted . . . .   the hair which rolled like
Martin's hair from his forehead—dear hair she used to
tug . . . .   Oh, he's the man I could love—he's my
sort—he's the kind I like . . . .   And I don't even know
his name . . . .   But he talks like Martin—knows all
about old places when they were new—queer he should
talk about them floods . . . .   Romney Church, you
can see the marks on the pillars . . . .   I can't bear to
think of that . . . .   I wonder what he'll say when
he comes to-morrow ?—Maybe he'll find me too old—
I'm ten year older than him if I'm a day   I
must dress myself up smart—I'm glad I brought my
purple body . . . .   Martin liked me in the old basket
hat I fed the fowls in . . . .   but I was slimmer then
. . . .   I'm getting on now . . . .   he won't like me

as well by daylight as he did in the dark—and properly
I'll deserve it, carrying on like that. I've half a mind
not to be in—I'll leave a polite message, saying " Miss
Godden's compliments, but she's had to go home, owing
to one of her cows having a miscarriage." I'll be wise to
go home to-morrow—reckon I ain't fit to be trusted
alone.

But a quarter to one the next day saw her in all the
splendour of her " purple body," standing before her
mirror, trying to make up her mind whether to wear
her big hat or her little one. The little hat was smarter
and had cost more money, but the big hat put a becoming shadow over her eyes, and hid those little lines
that were straying from the corners. . . . For the first
time Joanna had begun to realize that clothes should
have other qualities besides mere splendour. Hitherto
she had never thought of clothes in any definite relation
to herself, as enhancing, veiling, suggesting, or softening the
beauty which was Joanna Godden. But to-day she chose
warily—her hat for shadow, her shoes for grace, her amber
necklace because she must have that touch of barbarism
which suited her best—an unconscious process this—
and her amber earrings, because they matched her necklace, and because in the mirror she could see the brighter
colours of her hair swinging in them. At the last minute
she changed her " purple body " for one of rich chestnut-
coloured silk. This was so far her best inspiration, for
it toned not only with the amber beads, but with her skin
and hair. As she turned to leave the room she was like
a great glowing amber bead herself, all brown and gold,
with rich red lights and gleams of yellow . . . . then
just as she was going out she had her last and best inspiration of all. She suddenly went back into the room,
and before the mirror tore off the swathe of cream lace
she wore round her throat. The short thick column of
her neck rose out of her golden blouse. She burned to
her ears, but walked resolutely from the room.

Her young man was waiting for her in the lounge,
and she saw his rather blank face light up when she appeared. She had been successful, then . . . the realization gave her confidence, and more beauty. During
the meal which followed, he re-cast a little of that opinion

he had formed of her the night before. She was younger than he had thought, probably only a little over thirty, and far better looking than he had gathered from a first impression. Joanna was that rather rare type of woman who invariably looks her best in sunshine—the dusk had hidden from him her really lovely colouring of skin and eyes and hair ; here at her little table by the window her face seemed almost a condensation of the warm, ruddy light which poured in from the sea. Her eyes, with the queer childlike depths behind their feminine hardness, her eager mouth and splendid teeth, the scatter of freckles over her nose, all combined to hold him in a queer enchantment of youth. There was a curious, delightful freshness about her . . . . and she was a damn fine woman, too.

The night before he had gathered that she was of overwhelming respectability, but now he had his doubts about that also. She certainly seemed of a more oncoming disposition than he had thought, though there was something naïve and virginal about her forwardness. Her acquaintance might prove more entertaining than he had supposed. He fixed his eyes on her uncovered throat ; she blushed deeply, and put her hand up.

Their talk was very much on the same lines as the night before. He discovered that she had a zest for hearing him discourse on old places—she drank in all he had to say about the old days of Marlingate, when it was just a red fishing-village asleep between two hills. He told her how the new town had been built northward and westward, in the days of the great Monypenny, whose statue now stares blindly out to sea. He was a man naturally interested in topography and generally " read up " the places he visited, but he had never before found a woman who cared to listen to that sort of stuff.

After luncheon, drinking coffee in the lounge, they became more personal and intimate. He told her about himself. His name was Albert Hill—his father was dead, and he lived with his mother and sister at Lewisham. He had a good position as clerk in a firm of carpet-makers. He was twenty-five years old, and doing well. Joanna became confidential in her turn. Her confidences mostly concerned the prosperity of her farm, the magnitude of its acreage, the success of this year's lambing and last year's harvest, but they also included a few sentimental adventures—she had had ever so many offers of marriage, including one from a clergyman, and she had once been engaged to a baronet's son.

He wondered if she was pitching him a yarn, but did not think so; if she was, she would surely do better for herself than a three hundred acre farm, and an apparently unlimited dominion over the bodies and souls of clergymen. By this time he was liking her very much, and as he understood she had only two days more at Marlingate, he asked her to go to the pier theatre with him the next evening.

Joanna accepted, feeling that she was committing herself to a desperate deed. But she was reckless now—she, as well as Hill, thought of those two poor days which were all she had left. She must do something in those two days to bind him, for she knew that she could not let him go from her—she knew that she loved again.

§ 15

She did not love as she had loved the first time. Then she had loved with a calmness and an acceptance which were impossible to her now. She had trusted fate and trusted the beloved, but now she was unsure of both. She was restless and tormented, and absorbed as she had never been in Martin. Her love consumed every other emotion, mental or physical—it would not let her sleep or eat or listen to music. It kept her whole being concentrated on the new force that had disturbed it—she could think of nothing but Albert Hill, and her thoughts were haggard and anxious, picturing their friendship at a standstill, failing, and lost. . . . Oh, she must not lose him—she could not bear to lose him—she must bind him somehow in the short time she had left.

There were intervals in which she became uneasily conscious of her folly. He was thirteen years younger than she—it was ridiculous. She was a fool, after all the opportunities she'd had, to fall in love with a mere boy. But she knew in her heart that it was his youth she wanted most, partly because it was Martin's youth, partly because it called to something in her which was not youth, nor yet belonged to age—something which was wise, tender and possessive—something which had never yet been satisfied.

Luckily she had health robust enough to endure the preyings of her mind, and did not bear her conflict on her face when Hill called for her the next evening. She had been inspired to wear the same clothes as before—having once pleased, she thought perhaps she would be wise not to take any risks with the purple body, and as for an evening gown, Joanna would have felt like a bad woman in a book if she had worn one. But she was still guiltily without her collar.

He took her to a small restaurant on the sea-front, where half a dozen couples sat at little rosily lit tables. Joanna was pleased—she was beginning faintly to enjoy the impropriety of her existence . . . dinner in a resty-rong—with wine—that would be something to hold in her heart against Ellen, next time that young person became superior. Joanna did not really like wine—a glass of stout at her meals, or pale ale in the hot weather, was all she took as a rule—but there was a subtle fascination in putting her lips to the red glass full of broken lights, and feeling the wine like fire against them, while her eyes gazed over the brim at Hill . . . he gazed at her over the brim of his, and somehow when their eyes met thus over their glasses, over the red wine, it was more than when they just met across the table, in the pauses of their talk. It seemed to her that he was more lover-like to-night—his words seemed to hover round her, to caress her, and she was not surprised when she felt his foot press hers under the table, though she hastily drew her own away.

After dinner, he took her on the pier. "East Lynne" was being played in the Pavilion, and they had two of the best seats. Joanna was terribly thrilled and a little shocked—she was also, at the proper time, overcome with emotion. When little Willie lay dying, it was more than she could bear . . . poor little chap, it made your heart ache to see him—even though he was called Miss Maidie Masserene on the programme, and when not in bed stuck out in parts of his sailor suit which little boys do not

usually stick out in. His poor mother, too . . . the
tears rolled down Joanna's face, and her throat was speechless and swollen . . . something seemed to be tugging
at her heart . . . she grew ashamed, almost frightened.
It was a positive relief when the curtain came down, and
rose again to show that little Willie had done likewise and
stood bowing right and left in his night-shirt.

Still the tears would furtively trickle . . . what a fool
she was getting—it must be the wine. My, but she had
a weak head . . . she must never take another glass.
Then suddenly, in the darkness, she felt a hand take hers,
pick it up, set it on a person's knee . . . her hand lay
palm downwards on his knee, and his own lay over it—
she began to tremble and her heart turned to water. The
tears ran on and on.

. . . They were outside, the cool sea wind blew over
them, and in the wind was the roar of the sea. Without
a word they slipped out of the stream of people heading
for the pier gates, and went to the railing, where they
stood looking down on the black water.

"Why are you crying, dear?" asked Hill tenderly,
as his arm crept round her.

"I dunno—I'm not the one to cry. But that little
chap . . . and his poor mother . . ."

"You soft-hearted darling." . . . He held her close,
in all her gracious and supple warmth, which even the
fierceness of her stays could not quite keep from him.
Oh, she was the dearest thing, so crude and yet so soft
. . . how glad he was he had not drawn back at the
beginning, as he had half thought of doing . . . she was
the loveliest woman, adorable—mature, yet unsophisticated . . . she was like a quince, ripe and golden red,
yet with a delicious tartness.

"Joanna," he breathed, his mouth close to the tawny,
flying anthers of her hair—"Do you think you could
love me?"

He felt her hair stroke his lips, as she turned her head.
He saw her eyes bright with tears and passion. Then
suddenly she broke from him—

"I can't—I can't. . . it's more than I can bear."

He came after her, overtaking her just before the
gate.

" Darling thing, what's the matter?—You ain't afraid? "

" No—no—it isn't that. Only I can't bear . . . beginning to feel it . . . again."

" Again? "

" Yes—I told you a bit . . . I can't tell you any more."

" But the chap's dead."

" Yes."

" Hang it all, we're alive . . ." and she surrendered to his living mouth.

§ 16

That night she slept, and the next morning she felt calmer. Some queer, submerged struggle seemed to be over. As a matter of fact, her affair was more uncertain than ever. After Albert's kiss, they had had no discussion and very little conversation. He had taken her back to the hotel, and had kissed her again—this time on the warm, submissive mouth she lifted to him. He had said—" I'll come and see you at Ansdore—I've got another week." And she had said—nothing. She did not know if he wanted to marry her, or even if she wanted to marry him. She did not worry about how—or if—she should explain him to Ellen. All her cravings and uncertainties were swallowed up in a great quiet, a strange quiet which was somehow all the turmoil of her being expressed in silence.

The next day he was true to his promise, and saw her off—sitting decorously in her first-class carriage " For Ladies Only."

" You'll come and see me at Ansdore? " she said, as the moment of departure drew near, and he said nothing about last night's promise.

" Do you really want me to come? "

" Reckon I do."

" I'll come, then."

" Which day? "

" Say Monday, or Tuesday."

" Come on Monday, by this train—and I'll meet you at the station in my trap. I've got a fine stepper."

" Right you are. I'll come on Monday. It's kind of you to want me so much."

" I do want you."

Her warm, glowing face in the frame of the window invited him, and they kissed. Funny, thought Hill to himself, the fuss she had made at first, and she was all over him now . . . But women were always like that —wantons by nature and prudes by grace, and it was wonderful what a poor fight grace generally made of it.

Joanna, unaware that she had betrayed herself and womankind, leaned back comfortably in the train as it slid out of the station. She was in a happy dream, hardly aware of her surroundings. Mechanically she watched the great stucco amphitheatre of Marlingate glide past the window—then the red throbbing darkness of a tunnel . . . and the town was gone, like a bad dream, giving place to the tiny tilted fields and century-old hedges of the south-eastern weald. Then gradually these sloped and lost themselves in marsh—first only a green tongue running into the weald along the bed of the Brede River, then spreading north and south and east and west, from the cliff-line of England's ancient coast to the sand-line of England's coast to-day, from the spires of the monks of Battle to the spires of the monks of Canterbury.

Joanna was roused automatically by this return to her old surroundings. She began to think of her trap waiting for her outside Rye station. She wondered if Ellen would have come to meet her. Yes, there she was on the platform . . . wearing a green frock, too. She'd come out of her blacks. Joanna thrilled to a faint shock. She wondered how many other revolutions Ellen had carried out in her absence.

" Well, old Jo . . ." It seemed to her that Ellen's kiss was warmer than usual. Or was it that her own heart was so warm . . . ?

Ellen found her remarkably silent. She had expected an outpouring of Joanna's adventures, achievements and triumphs, combined with a desperate catechism as to just how much ruin had befallen Ansdore while she was away. Instead of which Joanna seemed for the first time in Ellen's experience, a little dreamy. She had but little to say to Rye's one porter, or to Peter Crouch, the groom.

She climbed up on the front seat of the trap, and took the
reins.

" You're looking well," said Ellen—" I can see your
change has done you good."

" Reckon it has, my dear."

" Were you comfortable at the hotel ? "

This, if anything, should have started Joanna off, but
all she said was—

" It wasn't a bad place."

" Well, if you don't want to talk about your own affairs,"
said Ellen to herself—" you can listen to mine, for a change.
Joanna,"—she added aloud—" I came to meet you, because I've got something special to tell you."

" What's that ? "

" Perhaps you can guess."

Joanna dreamily shook her head.

" Well, I'm thinking of getting married again."

" Married ! "

" Yes—it's eighteen months since poor Arthur died,"
sighed the devoted widow, " and—perhaps you've noticed
—Tip Ernley's been getting very fond of me."

" Yes, I had noticed . . . I was wondering why you
didn't tell."

" There was nothing to tell. He couldn't propose to
me till he had something definite to do. Now he's just
been offered the post of agent on the Duke of Wiltshire's
estate—a perfectly splendid position. Of course, I told
him all about my first marriage "—she glanced challeng-
ingly at her sister—" but he's a perfect dear, and he saw
at once I'd been more sinned against than sinning. We're
going to be married this summer."

" I'm unaccountable glad."

Ellen gave her a queer look.

" You take it very calmly, Jo."

" Well, I'd been expecting it all along."

" You won't mind my going away and leaving you ? "

" Reckon you'll have to go where your husband
goes."

" What on earth's happened ? " thought Ellen to
herself—" She's positively meek."

The next minute she knew.

" Ellen," said Joanna, as they swung into the Straight

Mile, " I've got a friend coming to spend the day on Monday—a Mr. Hill that I met in Marlingate."

§ 17

For the next few days Joanna was restless and nervous ; she could not be busy with Ansdore, even after a fortnight's absence. The truth in her heart was that she found Ansdore rather flat. Wilson's pride in the growth of the young lambs, Broadhurst's anxiety about Spot's calving and his preoccupation with the Suffolk dray-horse Joanna was to buy at Ashford fair that year, all seemed irrelevant to the main purpose of life. The main stream of her life had suddenly been turned underground—it ran under Ansdore's wide innings—on Monday it would come again to the surface, and take her away from Ansdore.

The outward events of Monday were not exciting. Joanna drove into Rye with Peter Crouch behind her, and met Albert Hill with a decorous handshake on the platform. During the drive home, and indeed during most of his visit, his attitude towards her was scarcely more than ordinary friendship. In the afternoon, when Ellen had gone out with Tip Ernley, he gave her a few kisses, but without much passion. She began to feel disquieted. Had he changed ? Was there someone else he liked ? At all costs she must hold him—she must not let him go.

The truth was that Hill felt uncertain how he stood— he was bewildered in his mind. What was she driving at ? Surely she did not think of marriage—the difference in their ages was far too great. But what else could she be thinking of ? He gathered that she was invincibly respectable—and yet he was not sure . . . In spite of her decorum, she had queer, unguarded ways. He had met no one exactly like her, though he was a man of wide and not very edifying experience. The tactics which had started his friendship with Joanna he had learned at the shorthand and typewriting college where he had learned his clerking job—and they had brought him a rummage of adventures, some transient, some sticky, some dirty, some glamorous. He had met girls of a fairly good class—

—for his looks caused much to be forgiven him—as well
as the typists, shop-girls and waitresses of his more usual
association. But he had never met anyone quite like
Joanna—so simple yet so swaggering, so solid yet so ardent,
so rigid yet so unguarded, so superior and yet, he told
himself, so lacking in refinement. She attracted him
enormously . . . but he was not the sort of man to
waste his time.

" When do you go back to London ? " she asked.

" Wednesday morning."

She sighed deeply, leaning against him on the sofa.

" Is this all the holiday you'll get this year ? "

" No—I've Whitsun coming—Friday to Tuesday. I
might run down to Marlingate . . . "

He watched her carefully.

" Oh, that 'ud be fine. You'd come and see me here ? "

" Of course—if you asked me ? "

" If I asked you," she repeated in a sudden, trembling
scorn.

Her head drooped to his breast, and he took her in
his arms, holding her across him—all her magnificent weight
upon his knees. Oh, she was a lovely creature . . . as
he kissed her firm, shy mouth it seemed to him as if her
whole body was a challenge. A queer kind of antagonism
seized him—prude or rake, she should get her lesson from
him all right.

§ 18

When he had gone Joanna said to Ellen—

" D'you think it would be seemly if I asked Mr. Hill
here to stay ? "

" Of course it would be ' seemly,' Jo. I'm a married
woman. But would he be able to come ? He's in business
somewhere, isn't he ? "

" Yes, but he could get away for Whitsun."

" Then ask him by all means. But . . . "

She looked at her quickly and teasingly.

" But what ? "

" Jo, do you care about this man ? "

" What d'you mean ? Why should I care ? Or,
leastways, why shouldn't I ? "

" No reason at all. He's a good bit younger than you are, but then I always fancied that if you married it ud be a man younger than yourself."

" Who said I was going to marry him ? "

" No one. But if you care . . . "

" I never said I did."

" Oh, you're impossible," said Ellen with a little shrug. She picked up a book from the table, but Joanna could not let the conversation drop.

" What d'you think of Mr. Hill, Ellen ? Does he remind you of anyone particular ? "

" No, not at the moment."

" Hasn't it ever struck you he's a bit like my Martin Trevor ? "

Her tongue no longer stammered at the name.

" Your Martin Trevor ! Jo, what nonsense, he's not a bit like him."

" He's the living image—the way his hair grows out of his forehead, and his dark, saucy eyes . . . "

" Well, I was only a little girl when you were engaged to Martin Trevor, but as I remember him he was quite different from Mr. Hill. He belonged to another class, for one thing . . . He was a gentleman."

" And you think Mr. Hill ain't a gentleman ? "

" My dear Joanna ! Of course he's not—he doesn't profess to be."

" He's got a good position as a clerk. Some clerks are gentlemen."

" But this one isn't."

" How do *you* know ? "

" Because I happen to be engaged to someone who is."

" That ain't any reason for miscalling my friends."

" I'm not ' miscalling ' anyone . . . Oh, hang it all, Jo, don't let's quarrel about men at our time of life. I'm sorry if I said anything you don't like about Mr. Hill. Of course, I don't know him as well as you do."

§ 19

So Joanna wrote to Albert Hill in her big, cramped handwriting, on the expensive yet unostentatious note-

paper which Ellen had decreed, inviting him to come and
spend Whitsuntide at Ansdore.

His answer did not come for three or four days, during
which, as he meant she should, she suffered many doubts
and anxieties. Was he coming ? Did he care for her ?
Or had he just been fooling ? She had never felt like this
about a man before. She had loved, but love had never
held her in the same bondage—perhaps because till now she
had always had certainties. Her affair with Martin, her
only real love affair, had been a certainty, Arthur Alce's
devotion had been a most faithful certainty, the men who
had comforted her bereavement had also in their different
ways been certainties. Albert Hill was the only man
who had ever eluded her, played with her or vexed her.
She knew that she attracted him, but she also guessed
dimly that he feared to bind himself. As for her, she was
now determined. She loved him and must marry him.
Characteristically she had swept aside the drawbacks of
their different ages and circumstances, and saw nothing
but the man she loved—the man who was for her the return
of first love, youth and spring. A common little tawdry-
minded clerk some might have called him, but to Joanna
he was all things—fulfilment, lover and child, and also a
Sign and a Second Coming.

She could think of nothing else. Once again Ansdore
was failing her, as it always failed her in any crisis of
emotion—Ansdore could never be big enough to fill her
heart. But she valued it because of the consequence it
must give her in young Hill's eyes, and she was impressed
by the idea that her own extra age and importance gave
her the rights of approach normally belonging to the man
. . . Queens always invited their consorts to share
their thrones, and she was a queen, opening her gates to
the man she loved. There could be no question of her
leaving her house for his—he was only a little clerk earn-
ing two pounds a week, and she was Squire of the Manor.
Possibly this very fact made him hesitate, fear to presume . . . Well, she must show him he was wrong, and
this Whitsuntide was her opportunity. But she wished
that she could feel more queenly in her mind—less abject,
craving and troubled. In outward circumstances she was
his queen, but in her heart she was his slave.

She plunged into an orgy of preparation. Mrs. Tolhurst and Mene Tekel and the new girl from Windpumps who now reinforced the household were nearly driven off their legs. Ellen spared the wretched man much in the way of feather-beds—just one down mattress would be enough, town people weren't used to sleeping on feathers. She also chastened the scheme of decoration, and substituted fresh flowers for the pampas grasses which Joanna thought the noblest adornment possible for a spare bedroom. On the whole Ellen behaved very well about Albert Hill—she worked her best to give him a favourable impression of Ansdore as a household, and when he came she saw that he and her sister were as much alone together as possible.

"He isn't at all the sort of brother-in-law I'd like you to have, my dear," she said to Tip, "but if you'd seen some of the men Joanna's taken up with you'd realize it might have been much worse. I'm told she once had a most hectic romance with her own shepherd . . . she's frightfully impressionable, you know."

"Is she really?" said Tip in his slow, well-bred voice. "I shouldn't have thought that."

"No, because—dear old Jo! it's so funny—she's quite without art. But she's always been frightfully keen on men, though she never could attract the right sort; and for some reason or other—to do with the farm, I suppose—she's never been keen on marriage. Now lately I've been thinking she really ought to marry—lately she's been getting quite queer—*détraquée*—and I do think she ought to settle down."

"But Hill's much younger than she is."

"Joanna would never care for anyone older. She's always liked boys—it's because she wants to be sure of being boss, I suppose. I know for a fact she's turned down nearly half a dozen good, respectable, well-to-do farmers of her own age or older than herself. And yet I've sometimes felt nervous about her and Peter Crouch, the groom . . . Oh, I tell you, Jo's queer, and I'll be thankful if she marries Bertie Hill, even though he is off the mark. After all, Tip "—and Ellen looked charming—" Jo and I aren't real ladies, you know."

§ 20

Albert was able to get off on the Friday afternoon, and arrived at Ansdore in time for the splendours of late dinner and a bath in the new bathroom. There was no doubt about it, thought he, that he was on a good thing, whichever way it ended. She must have pots of money . . . everything of the very best . . . and her sister marrying no end of a swell—Ernley, who played for Sussex, and was obviously top-notch in every other way. Perhaps he wouldn't be such a fool, after all, if he married her. He would be a country gentleman with plenty of money and a horse to ride—better than living single till, with luck, he got a rise, and married inevitably one of his female acquaintances, to live in the suburbs on three hundred a year . . . And she was such a splendid creature—otherwise he would not have thought of it—but in attraction she could give points to any girl, and her beauty, having flowered late, would probably last a good while longer. . . .

But——. That night as he sat at his bedroom window, smoking a succession of Gold Flake cigarettes, he saw many other aspects of the situation. The deadly quiet of Ansdore in the night, with all the blackness of the Marsh waiting for the unrisen moon, was to him a symbol of what his life would be if he married Joanna. He would perish if he got stuck in a hole like this, and yet—he thus far acknowledged her queenship—he could never ask her to come out of it. He could not picture her living in streets— she wouldn't fit—but then, neither would he fit down here. He liked streets and gaiety and noise and picture-palaces . . . If she'd been younger he might have risked it, but at her age—thirteen years older than he (she had told him her age in an expansive moment) it was really impossible. But, damn it all ! She was gorgeous—and he'd rather have her than any younger woman. He couldn't make her out—she must see the folly of marriage as well as he . . . then why was she encouraging him like this ? —Leading him on into an impossible situation ? Gradually he was drifting back into his first queer moment of antagonism—he felt urged to conquest, not merely for the gratification of his vanity nor even for the attainment of his desire, but for the satisfaction of seeing her humbled, all her pride and glow and glory at his feet, like a tiger-lily in the dust.

The next day Joanna drove him into Lydd, and in the afternoon took him inland, to Ruckinge and Warehorne. These drives were another reconstruction of her life with Martin, though now she no longer loved Albert only in his second-coming aspect. She loved him passionately and childishly for himself—the free spring of his hair from his forehead, not merely because it had also been Martin's but because it was his—the impudence as well as the soft-ness of his eyes, the sulkiness as well as the sensitiveness of his mouth, the unlike as well as the like. She loved his quick, Cockney accent, his Cockney oaths when he forgot himself—the way he always said " Yeyss " instead of " Yes "—his little assumptions of vanity in socks and tie. She loved a queer blend of Albert and Martin, the real and the imaginary, substance and dream.

As for him, he was enjoying himself. Driving about the country with a fine woman like Joanna, with privileges continually on the increase, was satisfactory even if no more than an interlude. " Where shall we go to-morrow ? " he asked her, as they sat in the parlour after dinner, leaving the garden to Ellen and Tip.

" To-morrow ? Why, that's Sunday."

" But can't we go anywhere on Sunday ? "

" To church, of course."

" But won't you take me out for another lovely drive ? I was hoping we could go out all day to-morrow. It's going to be ever so fine."

" Maybe, but I was brought up to go to church on Sundays, and on Whit Sunday of all other Sundays."

" But this Sunday's going to be different from all other Sundays—and from all other Whit Sundays . . . "

He looked at her meaningly out of his bold, melting eyes, and she surrendered. She could not deny him in this matter any more than in most others . . . She could not disappoint him any more than she could dis-appoint a child. He should have his drive—she would take him over to New Romney, even though it was written " Neither thou nor thine ox nor thine ass nor the stranger that is within thy gates."

§ 21

So the next morning when Brodnyx bells were ringing in the east she drove off through Pedlinge on her way to Broomhill level. She felt rather uneasy and ashamed, especially when she passed the church-going people. It was the first time in her life that she had voluntarily missed going to church—for hundreds of Sundays she had walked along that flat white lick of road, her big Prayer Book in her hand, and had gone under that ancient porch to kneel in her huge cattle-pen pew with its abounding hassocks. Even the removal of the Lion and the Unicorn, and the transformation of her comfortable, Established religion into a disquieting mystery had not made her allegiance falter. She still loved Brodnyx church, even now when hassocks were no longer its chief ecclesiastical ornament. She thought regretfully of her empty place and shamefully of her neighbours' comments on it.

It was a sunless day, with grey clouds hanging over a dull green marsh, streaked with channels of green water. The air was still and heavy with the scent of may and meadowsweet and ripening hayseed. They drove as far as the edges of Dunge Marsh, then turned eastward along the shingle road which runs across the root of the Ness to Lydd. The little mare's chocolate flanks were all a-sweat, and Joanna thought it better to bait at Lydd and rest during the heat of the day.

" You'd never think it was Whitsun," said Albert, looking out of the inn window at the sunny, empty street. " You don't seem to get much of a crowd down here. Rum old place, ain't it ? "

Already Joanna was beginning to notice a difference between his outlook and Martin's.

" What d'you do with yourself out here all day ? " he continued.

" I've plenty to do."

" Well, it seems to agree with you—I never saw anyone look finer. You're reelly a wonder, old thing."

He picked up the large hand lying on the table-cloth and kissed it back and palm. From any other man, even from Martin himself, she would have received the caress quite simply, been proud and contented, but now it brought

her into a strange trouble. She leaned towards him,
falling upon his shoulder, her face against his neck. She
wanted his kisses, and he gave them to her.

At about three o'clock they set out again. The sun
was high now, but the air was cooler, for it had lost its
stillness and blew in rippling gusts from the sea. Joanna
resolved not to go on to New Romney, as they had waited
too long at Lydd ; so she took the road that goes to Ivychurch, past Midley chapel, one of the ruined shrines of
the monks of Canterbury—grey walls huddled against a
white tower of hawthorn in which the voices of the birds
tinkled like little bells.

She was now beginning to feel more happy and self-
confident but she was still preoccupied, though with a new
situation. They had now been alone together for five
hours, and Albert had not said a word about the marriage
on which her hopes were set. Her ideas as to her own
right of initiative had undergone a change. He was in all
matters of love so infinitely more experienced than she
was that she could no longer imagine herself taking the
lead. Hitherto she had considered herself as experienced
and capable in love as in other things—had she not been
engaged for five months ? Had she not received at least
half a dozen offers of marriage ? But Albert had " learned
her different." His sure, almost careless, touch abashed
her, and the occasional fragments of autobiography which
he let fall, showed her that she was a limited and ignorant
recluse compared to this boy of twenty-five. In matters
of money and achievement she might brag, but in matters
of love she was strangely subservient to him, because in
such matters he had everything to teach her.

They stopped for tea at Ivychurch ; the little inn and
the big church beside the New Sewer were hazed over in
a cloud of floating sunshine and dust. She had been here
before with Martin, and after tea she and Albert went into
the church and looked around them. But his interest in
old places was not the same as Martin's. He called things
" quaint " and " rummy," and quoted anything he had
read about them in the guide-book, but he could not make
them come alive in a strange re-born youth—he could not
make her feel the beauty of the great sea on which the
French ships had ridden, or the splendours of the Marsh

before the Flood, with all its towns and taverns and steeples. Unconsciously she missed this appeal to her sleeping imagination, and her bringing of him into the great church, which could have held all the village in its aisles, was an effort to supply what was lacking.

But Albert's attitude towards the church was critical and unsatisfactory. It was much too big for the village. It was ridiculous . . . that little clump of chairs in all the huge emptiness . . . what a waste of money, paying a parson to idle away his time among a dozen people. . . . " How Dreadful is this Place " ran the painted legend over the arches . . . Joanna trembled.

They came out on the farther side of the churchyard, where a little path leads away into the hawthorns of the New Sewer. A faint sunshine was spotting it through the branches, and suddenly Joanna's heart grew warm and heavy with love. She wanted some sheltered corner where she could hold his hand, feel his rough coat-sleeve against her cheek—or, dearer still, carry his head on her bosom, that heavenly weight of a man's head, with the coarse, springing hair to pull and stroke. . . . She put her arm into his.

" Bertie, let's go and sit over there in the shade."

He smiled at the innocence of her contrivance.

" Shall we ? " he said, teasing her—" won't it make us late for dinner ? "

" We don't have dinner on Sundays—we have supper at eight, so as to let the gals go to church.'

Her eyes looked, serious and troubled, into his. He pressed her hand.

" You darling thing."

They moved away out of the shadow of the church, following the little path down to the channel's bank. The water was of a clear, limpid green, new-flushed with the tide, with a faint stickle moving down it, carrying the white, fallen petals of the may. The banks were rich with loosestrife and meadowsweet, and as they walked on, the arching of hawthorn and willow made of the stream and the path beside it a little tunnel of shade and scent.

The distant farmyard sounds which spoke of Ivychurch behind them gradually faded into a thick silence. Joanna could feel Bertie leaning against her as they walked,

he was playing with her hand, locking and unlocking her
fingers with his. Weren't men queer . . . the sudden
way they melted at a touch? Martin had been like that—
losing his funny sulks . . . And now Bertie was just
the same. She felt convinced that in one moment . . .
in two . . . he would ask her to be his wife. . . .

"Let's sit down for a bit," she suggested.

They sat down by the water side, crushing the meadow-
sweet till its sickliness grew almost fierce with bruising.
She sidled into his arms, and her own crept round him.
"Bertie . . ." she whispered. Her heart was throbbing
quickly, and, as it were, very high—in her throat—choking
her. She began to tremble. Looking up she saw his eyes
above her, gazing down at her out of a mist—everything
seemed misty, trees and sky and sunshine and his dear
face. . . . She was holding him very tight, so tight
that she could feel his collar-bones bruising her arms.
He was kissing her now, and his kisses were like blows.
She suddenly became afraid, and struggled.

"Jo, Jo—don't be a fool—don't put me off, now . . .
you can't, I tell you."

But she had come to herself.

"No—let me go. I . . . it's late—I've got to go
home."

She was strong enough to push him from her,
and scrambled to her feet. They both stood facing each
other in the trodden streamside flowers.

"I beg your pardon," he said at last.

"Oh, it doesn't matter."

She was ashamed.

§ 22

She was frightened, too—never in her life had she
imagined that she could drift so far as she had drifted in
those few seconds. She was still trembling as she led the
way back to the church. She could hear him treading
after her, and as she thought of him her heart smote her.
She felt as if she had hurt him—oh, what had she done to
him? What had she denied him? What had she given
him to think?

As they climbed into the trap she could tell that he

was sulking. He looked at her half-defiantly from under his long lashes, and the corners of his mouth were turned down like a child's. The drive home was constrained and nearly silent. Joanna tried to talk about the grazings they had broken at Yokes Court, in imitation of her own successful grain-growing, about her Appeal to the High Court which was to be heard that summer, and the motor-car she would buy if it was successful—but it was obvious that they were both thinking of something else. For the last part of the drive, from Brodnyx to Ansdore, neither of them spoke a word.

The sunset was scattering the clouds ahead and filling the spaces with lakes of gold. The dykes turned to gold, and a golden film lay over the pastures and the reeds. The sun wheeled slowly north, and a huge, shadowy horse and trap began to run beside them along the embankment of the White Kemp Sewer. They turned up Ansdore's drive, now neatly gravelled and gated, and a flood of light burst over the gables of the house, pouring on Joanna as she climbed down over the wheel. She required no help, and he knew it, but she felt his hands pressing her waist; she started away, and she saw him laugh—mocking her. She nearly cried.

The rest of that evening was awkward and unhappy. She had a vague feeling in her heart that she had treated Albert badly, and yet . . . the strange thing was that she shrank from an explanation. It had always been her habit to " have things out " on all occasions, and many a misunderstanding had been strengthened thereby. But to-night she could not bear the thought of being left alone with Albert. For one thing, she was curiously vague as to the situation—was she to blame or was he ? Had she gone too far or not far enough ? What *was* the matter, after all ? There was nothing to lay hold of . . . Joanna was unused to this nebulous state of mind ; it made her head ache, and she was glad when the time came to go to bed.

With a blessed sense of relief she felt the whitewashed thickness of her bedroom walls between her and the rest of the house. She did not trouble to light her candle. Her room was in darkness, except for one splash of light reflected from her mirror which held the moon. She went over to the window and looked out. The marsh swam in a yellow, misty lake of moonlight. There was a strange air of unsubstantiality about it—the earth was not the solid earth, the watercourses were moonlight rather than water, the light was water rather than light, the trees were shadows . . .

" Ah-h-h," said Joanna Godden.

She lifted her arms to her head with a gesture of weariness—as she took out the pins her hair fell on her shoulders in great hanks and masses, golden and unsubstantial as the moon.

Slowly and draggingly she began to unfasten her clothes —they fell off her, and lay like a pool round her feet. She plunged into her stiff cotton nightgown, buttoning it at neck and wrists. Then she knelt by her bed and said her prayers—the same prayers that she had said ever since she was five.

The moonlight was coming straight into the room— showing its familiar corners. There was no trace of Ellen in this room—nothing that was "artistic" or "in good taste." A lively pattern covered everything that could be so covered, but Joanna's sentimental love of old associations had spared the original furniture—the wide feather bed, the oaken chest of drawers, the wash-stand which was just a great chest covered with a towel. Over her bed hung Poor Father's Buffalo Certificate, the cherished symbol of all that was solid and prosperous and reputable in life.

She lay in bed. After she got in she realized that she had forgotten to plait her hair, but she felt too languid for the effort. Her hair spread round her on the pillow like a reproach. For some mysterious reason her tears began to fall. Her life seemed to reproach her. She saw all her life stretching behind her for a moment—the moment when she had stood before Socknersh her shepherd, seeing him dark against the sky, between the sun and moon. That was when Men, properly speaking, had begun for her—and it was fifteen years since then— and where was she now ? Still at Ansdore, still without her man.

Albert had not asked her to marry him, nor, she felt desperately, did he mean to. If he did, he would surely

have spoken to-day. And now besides, he was angry
with her, disappointed, estranged. She had upset him
by turning cold like that all of a sudden . . .   But what
was she saying ? Why, of course she had been quite
right. She should ought to have been cold from the
start. That was her mistake—letting the thing start
when it could have no seemly ending . . . a boy like
that, nearly young enough to be her son . . . and yet
she had been unable to deny him, she had let him kiss
her and court her—make love to her . . .   Worse than
that, she had made love to him, thrown herself at him,
pursued him with her love, refused to let him go . . .
and all the other things she had done—changing for his
sake from her decent ways . . . breaking the Sabbath,
taking off her neck-band. She had been getting irre-
ligious and immodest, and now she was unhappy, and it
served her right.

The house was quite still ; everyone had gone to bed,
and the moon filled the middle of the window, splashing
the bed, and Joanna in it, and the walls, and the sagging
beams of the ceiling. She thought of getting up to pull
down the blind, but had no more energy to do that than
to bind her hair. She wanted desperately to go to sleep.
She lay on her side, her head burrowed down into the
pillow, her hands clenched under her chin. Her bed was
next the door, and beyond the door, against the wall at
right angles to it, was her chest of drawers, with Martin's
photograph in its black frame, and the photograph of his
tombstone in a frame with a lily worked on it. Her eyes
strained towards them in the darkness . . . oh, Martin—
Martin, why did I ever forget you ? . . .   But I never
forgot you . . . Martin, I've never had my man . . .
I've got money, two farms, lovely clothes—I'm just as
good as a lady . . . but I've never had my man . . .
Seemingly I'll go down into the grave without him . . .
but, oh, I do want . . . the thing I was born for . . .

Sobs shook her broad shoulders as she lay there in the
moonlight. But they did not relieve her—her sobs
ploughed deep into her soul . . . they turned strange
furrows . . .   Oh, she was a bad woman, who deserved
no happiness. She'd always known it.

She lifted her head, straining her eyes through the

darkness and tears to gaze at Martin's photograph as if
it were the Serpent in the Wilderness. Perhaps all this
had come upon her because she had been untrue to his
memory—and yet what had so appealed to her about
Bertie was that he was like Martin, though Ellen said he
wasn't—well, perhaps he wasn't . . . But what was
happening now ? Something had come between her and
the photograph on the chest of drawers. With a sudden
chill at her heart, she realized that it was the door opening.

" Who's there ? " she cried in a hoarse angry whisper.

" Don't be frightened, dear—don't be frightened, my
sweet Jo——" said Bertie Hill.

§ 23

She could not think—she could only feel. It was
morning—that white light was morning, though it was
like the moon. Under it the Marsh lay like a land under
the sea—it must have looked like this when the keels of
the French boats swam over it, high above Ansdore, and
Brodnyx, and Pedlinge, lying like red apples far beneath,
at the bottom of the sea. That was nonsense . . . but
she could not think this morning, she could only feel.

He had not been gone an hour, but she must find him.
She must be with him—just feel him near her. She must
see his head against the window, hear the heavy, slow
sounds of his moving. She slipped on her clothes and
twisted up her hair, and went down into the empty, stir-
less house. No one was about—even her own people were
in bed. The sun was not yet up, but the white dawn was
pouring into the house, through the windows, through
the chinks. Joanna stood in the midst of it. Then she
opened the door and went out into the yard, which was a
pool of cold light, ringed round with barns and buildings
and reed-thatched haystacks. It was queer how this
cold, still, trembling dawn hurt her—seemed to flow into
her, to be part of herself, and yet to wound . . . She
had never felt like this before—she could never have
imagined that love would make her feel like this, would
make her see beauty in her forsaken yard at dawn—not
only see but feel that beauty, physically, as pain. Her

heart wounded her—her knees were failing—she went back into the house.

A wooden chair stood in the passage outside the kitchen door, and she sat down on it. She was still unable to think, and she knew now that she did not want to think—it might make her afraid. She wanted only to remember . . . He had called her the loveliest, sweetest, most beautiful woman in the world . . . She repeated his words over and over again, calling up the look with which he had said them . . . oh, those eyes of his—slanty, saucy, secret, loving eyes . . .

She wondered why he did not come down. She could not imagine that he had turned into bed and gone to sleep —that he did not know she was sitting here waiting for him in the dawn. For a moment she thought of going up and knocking at his door—then she heard a thud of foot-steps and creaking of boards, which announced that Mene Tekel and Nan Gregory of Windpumps were stirring in their bedroom. In an incredibly short time they were coming downstairs, tying apron-strings and screwing up hair as they went, and making a terrific stump past the door behind which they imagined their mistress was in bed. It was a great shock to them to find that she was downstairs before them—they weren't more than five minutes late.

"Hurry up, gals," said Joanna, "and get that kettle boiling for the men. I hear Broadhurst about the yard. Mene Tekel, see as there's no clinkers left in the grate ; Mrs. Alce never got her bath yesterday evening before dinner as she expects it. When did you do the flues last ? "

She set her household about its business—her dreams could not live in the atmosphere of antagonistic suspicion in which she had always viewed the younger members of her own sex. She was firmly convinced that neither Nan nor Mene would do a stroke of work if she was not " at them " ; the same opinion applied in a lesser degree to the men in the yard. So till Ansdore's early breakfast appeared amid much hustling and scolding, Joanna had no time to think about her lover, or continue the dreams so strangely and gloriously begun in the sunless dawn.

Bertie was late for breakfast, and came down apologis-

ing for having overslept himself. But he had a warm,
sleepy, rumpled look about him which made her forgive
him. He was like a little boy—*her* little boy . . . she
dropped her eyelids over her tears.

After breakfast, as soon as they were alone, she stole
into his arms and held close to him, without embrace,
her hands just clasped over her breast on which her chin
had fallen. He tried to raise her burning, blushing face,
but she turned it to his shoulder.

§ 24

Albert Hill went back to London on Tuesday, but he
came down again the following week-end, and the next,
and the next, and then his engagement to Joanna was
made public.

In this respect the trick was hers. The affair had
ended in a committal which he had not expected, but his
own victory was too substantial for him to regret any
development of it to her advantage. Besides, he had seen
the impossibility of conducting the affair on any other
lines, both on account of the circumstances in which she
lived and of her passionate distress when she realized that
he did not consider marriage an inevitable consequence
of their relation. It was his only way of keeping her—
and he could not let her go. She was adorable, and the
years between them meant nothing—her beauty had
wiped them out. He could think of her only as the ageless
woman he loved, who shared the passion of his own youth
and in it was for ever young.

On the practical side, too, he was better reconciled.
He felt a pang of regret when he thought of London and
its work and pleasures, of his chances of a " rise "—which
his superiors had hinted was now imminent—of a head
clerkship, perhaps eventually of a partnership and a tight
marriage into the business—since his Whitsuntide visit
to Ansdore he had met the junior partner's daughter and
found her as susceptible to his charms as most young
women. But after all, his position as Joanna Godden's
husband would be better even than that of a partner in
the firm of Sherwood and Son. What was Sherwood's

but a firm of carpet-makers?—a small firm of carpet-makers. As Joanna's husband he would be a Country Gentleman, perhaps even a County Gentleman. He saw himself going out with his gun . . . following the hounds in a pink coat . . . He forgot that he could neither shoot nor ride.

Meantime his position as Joanna's lover was not an unenviable one. She adored him and spoiled him like a child. She poured gifts upon him—a gold wrist-watch, a real panama hat, silk socks in gorgeous colours, boxes and boxes of the best Turkish and Egyptian cigarettes—she could not give him enough to show her love and delight in him.

At first he had been a little embarrassed by this out-pouring, but he was used to receiving presents from women, and he knew that Joanna had plenty of money to spend and really got as much pleasure out of her gifts as he did. They atoned for the poverty of her letters. She was no letter-writer. Her feelings were as cramped as her hand-writing by the time she had got them down on paper; indeed, Joanna herself was wondrously expressed in that big, unformed, constricted handwriting, black yet uncertain, sprawling yet constrained, in which she recorded such facts as " Dot has calved at last," or " Broadhurst will be 61 come Monday," or—as an utmost concession—" I love you, dear."

However, too great a strain was not put on this frail link, for he came down to Ansdore almost every week-end, from Saturday afternoon to early Monday morning. He tried to persuade her to come up to London and stay at his mother's house—he had vague hopes that perhaps an experience of London might persuade her to settle there (she could afford a fine house over at Blackheath, or even in town itself, if she chose). But Joanna had a solid prejudice against London—the utmost she would consent to was a promise to come up and stay with Albert's mother when her appeal was heard at the High Court at the beginning of August. Edward Huxtable had done his best to convince her that her presence was unnecessary, but she did not trust either him or the excellent counsel he had engaged. She had made up her mind to attend in person, and look after him properly.

§ 25

The attitude of Brodnyx and Pedlinge towards this new crisis in Joanna Godden's life was at first uncertain. The first impression was that she had suddenly taken fright at the prospect of old-maidenhood, and had grabbed the first man she could get, even though he was young enough to be her son.

"He ain't twenty-one till Michaelmas," said Vine at the Woolpack.

"She's always liked 'em young," said Furnese.

"Well, if she'd married Arthur Alce when she fust had the chance, instead of hanging around and wasting time the way she's done, by now she could have had a man of her intended's age for a son instead of a husband."

"Reckon it wouldn't have been the same thing."

"No—it would have been a better thing," said Vine.

When it became known that Joanna's motive was not despair but love, public opinion turned against her. Albert's manner among the Marsh people was unfortunate. In his mind he had always stressed his bride's connexions through Ellen—the Ernleys, a fine old county family ; he found it very satisfying to slap Tip Ernley on the back and call him "Ole man." He had deliberately shut his eyes to the other side of her acquaintance, those Marsh families, the Southlands, Furneses, Vines, Cobbs and Bateses, to whom she was bound by far stronger, older ties than any which held her to Great Ansdore. He treated these people as her and his inferiors—unlike Martin Trevor, he would not submit to being driven round and shown off to Misleham, Picknye Bush, or Slinches . . . It was small wonder that respectable families became indignant at such airs.

"What does he think himself, I'd like to know? He's nothing but a clerk—such as I'd never see my boy."

"And soon he won't be even that—he'll just be living on Joanna."

"She's going to keep him at Ansdore ?"

"Surelye. She'll never move out now."

"But what's she want to marry for, at her age, and a boy like that ?"

"She's getting an old fool, I reckon.'

§ 26

The date of the wedding was not yet fixed, though September was spoken of rather vaguely, and this time the hesitation came from the bridegroom. As on the occasion of her first engagement Joanna had made difficulties with the shearing and hay-making, so now Albert contrived and shifted in his anxiety to fit in his marriage with other plans.

He had, it appeared, as far back as last Christmas, arranged for a week's tour in August with the Polytechnic to Lovely Lucerne. In vain Joanna promised him a liberal allowance of " Foreign Parts " for their honeymoon—Bertie's little soul hankered after the Polytechnic, his pals who were going with him, and the kindred spirits he would meet at the chalets. Going on his honeymoon as Joanna Godden's husband was a different matter and could not take the place of such an excursion.

Joanna did not press him. She was terribly afraid of scaring him off. It had occurred to her more than once that his bonds held him far more lightly than she was held by hers. And the prospect of marriage was now an absolute necessity if she was to endure her memories. Marriage alone could hallow and remake Joanna Godden. Sometimes, as love became less of a drug and a bewilderment, her thoughts awoke, and she would be overwhelmed by an almost incredulous horror at herself. Could this be Joanna Godden, who had turned away her dairy-girl for loose behaviour, who had been so shocked at the adventures of her sister Ellen ? She could never be shocked at anyone again, seeing that she herself was just as bad and worse than anyone she knew . . . Oh, life was queer—there was no denying. It took you by surprise in a way you'd never think—it made you do things so different from your proper notions that afterwards you could hardly believe it was you that had done them—it gave you joy that should ought to have been sorrow . . . and pain as you'd never think.

As the summer passed and the time for her visit to town drew near, Joanna began to grow nervous and restless. She did not like the idea of going to a place like London, though she dared not confess her fears to the

travelled Ellen or the metropolitan Bertie. She felt
vaguely that " no good would come of it "—she had lived
thirty-eight years without setting foot in London, and it
seemed like tempting Providence to go there now . . .

However she resigned herself to the journey—indeed,
when the time came she undertook it more carelessly
than she had undertaken the venture of Marlingate. Her
one thought was of Albert, and she gave over Ansdore
almost nonchalantly to her carter and her looker, and
abandoned Ellen to Tip Ernley with scarcely a doubt as
to her moral welfare.

Bertie met her at Charing Cross, and escorted her the
rest of the way. He found it hard to realize that she had
never been to London before, and it annoyed him a little.
It would have been all very well, he told himself, in a shy
village maiden of eighteen, but in a woman of Joanna's
age and temperament it was ridiculous. However, he
was relieved to find that she had none of the manners of
a country cousin. Her self-confidence prevented her
being flustered by strange surroundings ; her clothes were
fashionable and well-cut, though perhaps a bit too showy
for a woman of her type, she tipped lavishly, and was
not afraid of porters. Neither did she, as he had feared
at first, demand a four-wheeler instead of a taxi. On
the contrary, she insisted on driving all the way to Lewisham, instead of taking another train, and enlarged on
the five-seater touring car she would buy when she had
won her Case.

" I hope to goodness you will win it, ole girl," said
Bertie, as he slipped his arm round her—" I've a sort of
feeling that you ought to touch wood."

" I'll win it if there's justice in England."

" But perhaps there ain't."

" I *must* win," repeated Joanna doggedly. " You see,
it was like this . . . "

Not for the first time she proceeded to recount the sale
of Donkey Street and the way she had applied the money.
He wished she wouldn't talk about that sort of thing the
first hour they were together.

" I quite see, darling," he exclaimed in the middle of
the narrative, and shut her mouth with a kiss.

" Oh, Bertie, you mustn't."

" Why not ? "

" We're in a cab—people will see."

" They won't—they can't see in—and I'm not going to drive all this way without kissing you."

He took hold of her.

" I won't have it—it ain't seemly."

But he had got a good hold of her, and did as he liked.

Joanna was horrified and ashamed. A motor-bus had just glided past the cab and she felt that the eyes of all the occupants were upon her. She managed to push Albert away, and sat very erect beside him, with a red face.

" It ain't seemly," she muttered under her breath.

Bertie was vexed with her. He assumed an attitude intended to convey displeasure. Joanna felt unhappy, and anxious to conciliate him, but she was aware that any reconciliation was bound to lead to a repetition of that conduct so eminently shocking to the occupants of passing motor-buses. " I don't like London folk to think I don't know how to behave when I come up to town," she said to herself.

Luckily, just as the situation was becoming unbearable, and her respectability on the verge of collapsing in the cause of peace, they stopped at the gate of The Elms, Raymond Avenue, Lewisham. Bertie's annoyance was swallowed up in the double anxiety of introducing her to his family and his family to her. On both counts he felt a little gloomy, for he did not think much of his mother and sister and did not expect Joanna to think much of them. At the same time there was no denying that Jo was and looked a good bit older than he, and his mother and sister were quite capable of thinking he was marrying her for her money. She was looking rather worn and dragged this afternoon, after her unaccustomed railway journey—sometimes you really wouldn't take her for more than thirty, but to-day she was looking her full age.

" Mother—Agatha—this is Jo."

Joanna swooped down on the old lady with a loud kiss.

" Pleased to meet you," said Mrs. Hill in a subdued voice. She was very short and small and frail-looking, and wore a cap—for the same reason no doubt that she kept an aspidistra in the dining-room window, went to

church at eleven o'clock on Sundays, and had given birth
to Agatha and Albert.

Agatha was evidently within a year or two of her
brother's age, and she had his large, melting eyes, and his
hair that sprang in a dark semicircle from a low forehead.
She was most elegantly dressed in a peek-a-boo blouse,
hobble skirt, and high-heeled shoes.

" Pleased to meet you," she said, and Joanna kissed
her too.

" Is tea ready ? " asked Bertie.

" It will be in a minute, dear—I can hear Her getting
it."

They could all do that, but Bertie seemed annoyed
that they should be kept waiting.

" You might have had it ready," he said, " I expect
you're tired, Jo."

" Oh, not so terrible, thanks," said Joanna, who felt
sorry for her future mother-in-law being asked to keep
tea stewing in the pot against the uncertain arrival of
travellers. But, as it happened, she did feel rather tired,
and was glad when the door was suddenly kicked open
and a large tea-tray was brought in and set down violently
on a side table.

" Cream *and* sugar ? " said Mrs. Hill nervously.

" Yes, thank you," said Joanna. She felt a little disconcerted by this new household of which she found herself a member. She wondered what Bertie's mother and
sister thought of his middle-aged bride.

For a time they all sat round in silence. Joanna covertly
surveyed the drawing-room. It was not unlike the parlour
at Ansdore, but everything looked cheaper—they couldn't
have given more than ten pound for their carpet, and she
knew those fire-irons—six and eleven-three the set at the
ironmongers. These valuations helped to restore her self-
confidence and support the inspection which Agatha was
conducting on her side. " Reckon the price of my clothes
ud buy everything in this room," she thought to herself.

" Did you have a comfortable journey, Miss Godden ? "
asked Mrs. Hill.

" You needn't call her Miss Godden, ma," said Albert,
" she's going to be one of the family."

" I had a fine journey," said Joanna, drowning Mrs.

Hill's apologetic twitter, "the train came the whole of sixty miles with only one stop."

Agatha giggled, and Bertie stabbed her with a furious glance.

"Did you make this tea?" he asked.

"No—She made it."

"I might have thought as much. That girl can't make tea any better than the cat. You reelly might make it yourself when we have visitors."

"I hadn't time. I've only just come in."

"You seem to be out a great deal."

"I've my living to get."

Joanna played with her teaspoon. She felt ill at ease, though it would be difficult to say why. She had quarrelled too often with Ellen to be surprised at any family disagreements—it was not ten years since she had thought nothing of smacking Ellen before a disconcerted public. What was there different—and there was something different—about this wrangle between a brother and sister, that it should upset her so—upset her so much that for some unaccountable reason she should feel the tears running out of her eyes.

On solemn ceremonial occasions Joanna always wore a veil, and this was now pushed up in several folds, to facilitate tea-drinking. She could feel the tears wetting it, so that it stuck to her cheeks under her eyes. She was furious with herself, but she could not stop the tears— she felt oddly weak and shaken. Agatha had flounced off with the teapot to make a fresh brew, Albert was leaning gloomily back in his chair with his hands in his pockets, Mrs. Hill was murmuring—"I hope you like fancy-work—I am very fond of fancy-work—I have made a worsted kitten." Joanna could feel the tears soaking through her veil, running down her cheeks—she could not stop them—and the next moment she heard Bertie's voice, high and aggrieved—"What are you crying for, Jo?"

Directly she heard it, it seemed to be the thing she had been dreading most. She could bear no more, and burst into passionate weeping.

They all gathered round her, Agatha with the new teapot, Mrs. Hill with her worsted, Bertie patting her on the back and asking what was the matter.

" I don't know," she sobbed—" I expect I'm tired,
and I ain't used to travelling."

" Yes, I expect you must be tired—have a fresh cup
of tea," said Agatha kindly.

" And then go upstairs and have a good lay down,"
said Mrs. Hill.

Joanna felt vaguely that Albert was ashamed of her.
She was certainly ashamed of herself and of this entirely
new, surprising conduct.

§ 27

By supper that night she had recovered, and remembered her breakdown rather as a bad dream, but neither
that evening nor the next day could she quite shake off
the feeling of strangeness and depression. She had never
imagined that she would like town life, but she had thought
that the unpleasantness of living in streets would be lost
in the companionship of the man she loved—and she was
disappointed to find that this was not so. Bertie, indeed,
rather added to than took away from her uneasiness. He
did not seem to fit into the Hill household any better
than she did—in fact, none of the members fitted. Bertie
and Agatha clashed openly, and Mrs. Hill was lost. The
house was like a broken machine, full of disconnected
parts, which rattled and fell about. Joanna was used to
family quarrels, but she was not used to family disunion—
moreover, though she would have allowed much between
brother and sister, she had certain very definite notions
as to the respect due to a mother. Both Bertie and Agatha
were continually suppressing and finding fault with Mrs.
Hill, and of the two Bertie was the worst offender. Joanna
could not excuse him, even to her own all-too-ready heart.
The only thing she could say was that it was most likely
Mrs. Hill's own fault—her not having raised him properly.

Every day he went off to his office in Fetter Lane,
leaving Joanna to the unrelieved society of his mother,
for which he apologised profusely. Indeed, she found her
days a little dreary, for the old lady was not entertaining,
and she dared not go about much by herself in so metropolitan a place as Lewisham. Every morning she and

her future mother-in-law went out shopping—that is to say they bought half-pounds and quarter-pounds of various commodities which Joanna at Ansdore would have laid in by the bushel and the hundredweight. They would buy tea at one grocer's, and then walk down two streets to buy cocoa from another, because he sold it cheaper than the shop where they had bought the tea. The late Mr. Hill had left his widow very badly off—indeed she could not have lived at all except for what her children gave her out of their salaries. To her dismay, Joanna discovered that while Agatha, in spite of silk stockings and Merry Widow hats, gave her mother a pound out of the weekly thirty shillings she earned as a typist, Albert gave her only ten shillings a week—his bare expenses.

"He says he doesn't see why he should pay more for living at home than he'd pay in digs—though, as a matter of fact I don't know anyone who'd take him for as little as that, even for only bed and breakfast."

"But what does he do with the rest of the money?"

"Oh, he has a lot of expenses, my dear—belongs to all sorts of grand clubs, and goes abroad every year with the Polytechnic, or even Cook's. Besides, he has lady friends that he takes about—used to, I should say, for, of course, he's done with all that now—but he was always the boy for taking ladies out—and never would demean himself to anything less than a Corner House."

"But he should ought to treat you proper, all the same," said Joanna.

She felt sorry and angry, and also, in some vague way, that it was her part to set matters right—that the wound in her love would be healed if she could act where Bertie was remiss. But Mrs. Hill would not let her open her fat purse on her account. "No, dear; we never let a friend oblige us." Joanna, who was not tactful, persisted, and the old lady became very frozen and genteel.

Bertie's hours were not long at the office. He was generally back at six, and took Joanna out—up to town, where they had dinner and then went on to some theatre or picture-palace, the costs of the expedition being defrayed out of her own pocket. She had never had so much dissipation in her life—she saw "The Merry Widow," "A Persian Princess," and all the musical comedies. Albert did not patronise the more serious drama, and for Joanna the British stage became synonymous with fluffy heads and whirling legs and jokes she could not understand. The late hours made her feel very tired, and on their way home Albert would find her sleepy and unresponsive. They always went by taxi from Lewisham station, and instead of taking the passionate opportunities of the darkness, she would sink her heavy head against his breast, holding his arm with both her tired hands. " Let me be, dear, let me be," she would murmur when he tried to rouse her—" this is what I love best."

She told herself that it was because she was so tired that she often felt depressed and wakeful at nights. Raymond Avenue was not noisy, indeed it was nearly as quiet as Ansdore, but on some nights Joanna lay awake from Bertie's last kiss till the crashing entrance of the Girl to pull up her blinds in the morning. At nights, sometimes, a terrible clearness came to her. This visit to her lover's house was showing her more of his character than she had learned in all the rest of their acquaintance. She could not bear to realize that he was selfish and small-minded, though, now she came to think of it, she had always been aware of it in some degree. She had never pretended to herself that he was good and noble—she had loved him for something quite different—because he was young and had brought her back her own youth, because he had a handsome face and soft, dark eyes, because in spite of all his cheek and knowingness he had in her sight a queer, appealing innocence . . . He was like a child, even if it was a spoilt, selfish child, When she held his dark head in the crook of her arm, he was her child, her little boy . . . And perhaps one day she would hold, through her love for him, a real child there, a child who was really innocent and helpless and weak—a child without grossness to scare her or hardness to wound her—her own child, born of her own body.

But though she loved him, this constant expression of his worst points could not fail to give her a feeling of chill. Was this the way he would behave in their home when they were married ? Would he speak to her as he spoke to his mother ? Would he speak to their children so ? . . . She could not bear to think it, and yet she

could not believe that marriage would change him all
through. What if their marriage made them both miserable?—made them like some couples she had known on
the Marsh, nagging and hating each other. Was she a
fool to think of marrying him?—all that difference in
their age . . . only perfect love could make up for it
. . . and he did not like the idea of living in the country
—he was set on his business—his " career," as he called
it . . . She did not think he wanted to marry her as
much as she wanted to marry him . . . Was it right
to take him away from his work, which he was doing so
well at, and bring him to live down at Ansdore? My,
but he would probably scare her folk with some of his ways.

However, it was now too late to draw back. She
must go on with what she had begun. At all costs she
must marry—not merely because she loved him, but
because only marriage could hallow and silence the past.
With all the traditions of her race and type upon her,
Joanna could not face the wild harvest of love. Her wild
oats must be decently gathered into the barn, even if
they gave her bitter bread to eat.

§ 28

The case of "Godden *versus* Inland Revenue Commissioners" was heard at the High Court when Joanna
had been at Lewisham about ten days. Albert tried to
dissuade her from being present.

"I can't go with you, and I don't see how you can go
alone."

"I shall be right enough."

"Yet you won't even go down the High Street by
yourself—I never met anyone so inconsistent."

"It's my Appeal," said Joanna.

"But there's no need for you to attend. Can't you
trust anyone to do anything without you?"

"Not Edward Huxtable," said Joanna decidedly.

"Then why did you choose him for your lawyer?"

"He's the best I know."

Bertie opened his mouth to carry the argument further,
but laughed instead.

" You *are* a funny ole girl—so silly and so sensible, so hard and so soft, such hot stuff and so respectable . . ." He kissed her at each item of the catalogue—" I can't half make you out."

However, he agreed to take her up to town when he went himself, and deposited her at the entrance of the Law Courts—a solid, impressive figure in her close-fitting tan coat and skirt and high, feathered toque, with the ceremonial veil pulled down over her face.

Beneath her imposing exterior she felt more than a little scared and lost. Godden seemed a poor thing compared to all this might of Inland Revenue Commissioners, spreading about her in passage and hall and tower . . . The law had suddenly become formidable, as it had never been in Edward Huxtable's office . . . However, she was fortunate in finding him, with the help of one or two policemen, and the sight of him comforted her with its suggestion of home and Watchbell Street, and her trap waiting in the sunshine outside the ancient door of the Huxtable dwelling.

Her Appeal was not heard till the afternoon, and in the luncheon interval he took her to some decorous dining-rooms—such as Joanna had never conceived could exist in London, so reminiscent were they of the George and the Ship and the New and the Crown and other of her market-day haunts. They ate beef and cabbage and jam roly poly, and discussed the chances of the day. Huxtable said he had " a pretty case—a very pretty case—you'll be surprised, Miss Joanna, to see what I've made of it."

And so she was. Indeed, if she hadn't heard the opening she would never have known it was her case at all. She listened in ever-increasing bewilderment and dismay.

In spite of her disappointment in the matter of the Commissioners and their Referee, she had always looked upon her cause as one so glaringly righteous that it had only to be pleaded before any just judge to be at once established. But now . . . the horror was, that it was no longer her cause at all. This was not Joanna Godden coming boldly to the Law of England to obtain redress from her grievous oppression by pettifogging clerks—it was just a miserable dispute between the Commissioners of Inland Revenue and the Lessor of Property under the

Act. It was full of incomprehensible jargon about Increment Value, Original Site Value, Assessable Site Value, Land Value Duty, Estate Duty, Redemption of Land Tax, and many more such terms among which the names of Donkey Street and Little Ansdore appeared occasionally and almost frivolously, just to show Joanna that the matter was her concern. In his efforts to substantiate an almost hopeless case Edward Huxtable had coiled most of the 1910 Finance Act round himself, and the day's proceedings consisted of the same being uncoiled and stripped off him, exposing his utter nakedness in the eyes of the law. When the last remnant of protective jargon had been torn away, Joanna knew that her Appeal had been dismissed—and she would have to pay the Duty and also the expenses of the action.

The only comfort that remained was the thought of what she would say to Edward Huxtable when she could get hold of him. They had a brief, eruptive interview in the passage.

"You take my money for making a mess like that," stormed Joanna. "I tell you, you shan't have it—you can amuse yourself bringing another action for it."

"Hush, my dear lady—hush! Don't talk so loud. I've done my best for you, I assure you. I warned you not to bring the action in the first instance, but when I saw you were determined to bring it, I resolved to stand by you, and get you through if possible. I briefed excellent counsel, and really made out a very pretty little case for you."

"Ho! Did you? And never once mentioned my steam plough. I tell you when I heard all the rubbish your feller spoke I'd have given the case against him myself. It wasn't my case at all. My case is that I'm a hard-working woman, who's made herself a good position by being a bit smarter than other folk. I have a gentleman friend who cares for me straight and solid for fifteen years, and when he dies he leaves me his farm and everything he's got. I sell the farm, and get good money for it, which I don't spend on motor-cars like some folk, but on more improvements on my own farm. I make my property more valuable, and *I*'ve got to pay for it, if you please. Why, they should ought to pay me. What's farming coming to, I'd like to know, if we've got to pay for bettering ourselves ? The Government ud like to see all farmers in the workhouse—and there we'll soon be, if they go on at this rate. And it's the disrespectfulness to Poor Arthur, too—he left Donkey Street to *me*—not a bit to me and the rest to them. But there they go, wanting to take most of it in Death Duty. The best Death Duty I know is to do what the dead ask us and not what they'd turn in their graves if they knew of. And poor Arthur who did everything in the world for me, even down to marrying my sister Ellen . . . "

Edward Huxtable managed to escape.

" Drat that woman," he said to himself—" she's a terror. However, I suppose I've got to be thankful she didn't try to get any of that off her chest in Court—she's quite capable of it. Damn it all ! She's a monstrosity—and going to be married too . . . well, there are some heroes left in the world."

§ 29

Bertie was waiting for Joanna outside the Law Courts. In the stillness of the August evening and the yellow dusty sunshine, he looked almost contemplative, standing there with bowed head, looking down at his hands which were folded on his stick, while one or two pigeons strutted about at his feet. Joanna's heart melted at the sight of him. She went up to him, and touched his arm.

" Hullo, ole girl. So here you are. How did it go off ? "

" I've lost."

" Damn ! That's bad."

She saw that he was vexed, and a sharp touch of sorrow was added to her sense of outrage and disappointment.

" Yes, it was given against me. It's all that Edward Huxtable's fault. Would you believe me, but he never made out a proper case for me at all, but just a lawyer's mess, what the judge was quite right not to hold with."

" Have you lost much money ? "

" A proper lot—but I shan't let Edward Huxtable get any of it. If he wants his fees he'll just about have to bring another action."

"Don't be a fool, Joanna—you'll have to pay the costs if they've been given against you. You'll only land yourself in a worse hole by making a fuss."

They were walking westward towards the theatres and the restaurants. Joanna felt that Bertie was angry with her—he was angry with her for losing her case, just as she was angry with Edward Huxtable. This was too much—the tears rose in her eyes.

"Will it do you much damage?" he asked. "In pocket, I mean."

"Oh, I—I'll have to sell out an investment or two, but it won't do any real hurt to Ansdore. Howsumever, I'll have to go without my motor-car."

"It was really rather silly of you to bring the action."

"How, silly?"

"Well, you can't have had much of a case, or you wouldn't have lost it like this in an hour's hearing."

"Stuff and nonsense! I'd a valiant case, if only that fool, Edward Huxtable, hadn't been anxious to show how many hard words he knew, instead of just telling the judge about my improvements and that."

"Really, Joanna, you might give up talking about your improvements. They've nothing to do with the matter at all. Can't you see that, as the Government wanted the money, it's nothing to them if you spent it on a steam plough or on a new hat. As a matter of fact, you might just as well have bought your motor-car—then at least we'd have that. Now you say you've given up the idea."

"Unless you make some money and buy it"—pain made Joanna snap.

"Yes—that's right, start twitting me because it's you who have the money. I know you have, and you've always known I haven't—I've never deceived you. I suppose you think I'm glad to be coming to live on you, to give up a fine commercial career for your sake. I tell you, any other man with my feelings would have made you choose between me and Ansdore—but I give up everything for your sake, and that's how you pay me—by despising me."

"Oh, don't, Bertie," said Joanna. She felt that she could bear no more.

They had come into Piccadilly, and the light was still warm—it was not yet dinner-time, but Joanna, who had had no tea, felt suddenly weak and faint.

" Let's go in there, dear," she said, as they reached the Popular Café, " and have a cup of tea. And don't let's quarrel, for I can't bear it."

He looked down at her drawn face and pity smote him.

" Pore ole girl—aren't you feeling well ? "

" Not very—I'm tired, like—sitting listening to all that rubbish."

" Well, let's have an early dinner, and then go to a music-hall. You've never been to one yet, have you ? "

" No," said Joanna. She would have much rather gone straight home, but this was not the time to press her own wishes. She was only too glad to have Bertie amicable and smiling again—she realized that they had only just escaped a serious quarrel.

The dinner, and the wine that accompanied it, made her feel better and more cheerful. She talked a good deal —even too much, for half a glass of claret had its potent effect on her fatigue. She looked flushed and untidy, for she had spent a long day in her hat and outdoor clothes, and her troubles had taken her thoughts off her appearance —she badly needed a few minutes before the looking-glass. As Albert watched her, he gave up his idea of taking her to the Palace, which he told himself would be full of smart people, and decided on the Alhambra Music Hall—then from the Alhambra he changed to the Holborn Empire. . . . Really it was annoying of Jo to come out with him looking like this—she ought to realize that she was not a young girl who could afford to let things slip. He had told her several times that her hat was on one side, . . . And those big earrings she wore . . . she ought to go in for something quieter at her age. Her get-up had always been too much on the showy side, and she was too independent of those helps to nature which much younger and better-looking women than herself were only too glad to use. . . . He liked to see a woman take out a powder-puff and flick it over her face in little dainty sweeps. . . .

These reflections did not put him in a good humour for the evening's entertainment. They went by 'bus to the Holborn Empire where the first house had already started. Joanna felt a little repulsed by the big, rowdy audience, smoking and eating oranges and joining in the choruses of the songs. Her brief experience of the dress circle at Daly's or the Queen's had not prepared her for anything so characteristic as an English music-hall, with its half-participating audience. "Hurrah for Maudie!" as some favourite took the boards to sing, with her shoulders hunched up to the brim of her enormous hat, a heart-rending song about her mother.

Joanna watched Bertie as he lounged beside her. She knew that he was sulking—the mere fact that he was entertaining her cheaply, by 'bus and music-hall instead of taxi and theatre, pointed to his displeasure. She wondered if he was enjoying this queer show, which struck her alternately as inexpressibly beautiful and inexpressibly vulgar. The lovely ladies like big handsome barmaids, who sang serious songs in evening dress and diamonds, apparently in the vicinity of Clapham High Street or the Monument, were merely incomprehensible. She could not understand what they were doing. The comedians she found amusing, when they did not shock her—Bertie had explained to her one or two of the jokes she could not understand. The "song-scenas" and acrobatic displays filled her with rapture. She would have liked that sort of thing the whole time. . . . Albert said it was a dull show, he. grumbled at everything, especially the turns Joanna liked. But gradually the warm, friendly, vulgar atmosphere of the place infected him—he joined in one or two of the choruses, and seemed almost to forget about Joanna.

She watched him as he leaned back in his seat, singing—

"Take me back to Pompeii—
To Pompey-ompey-i—"

In the dim red light of the place, he looked incredibly young. She could see only his profile—the backward sweep of glistening, pomaded hair, the little short straight nose, the sensual, fretful lips—and as she watched him she was smitten with a queer sense of pity. This was no strong man, no lover and husband—just a little clerk she was going to shut up in prison—a little singing clerk. She felt a brute—she put out her hand and slid it under his arm, against his warm side.

"To Pompey-ompey-i"

sang Bert.

§ 30

The curtain came down and the lights went up for the interval. A brass band played very loud. Joanna was beginning to have a bit of a headache, but she said nothing —she did not want him to leave on her account—or to find that he did not think of leaving . . . She felt very hot, and fanned herself with her programme. Most of the audience were hot.

"Joanna," said Bert, "don't you ever use powder?"

"Powder? What d'you mean?"

"Face-powder—what most girls use. Your skin wouldn't get red and shiny like that if you had some powder on it."

"I'd never dream of using such a thing. I'd be ashamed."

"Why be ashamed of looking decent?"

"I wouldn't look decent—I'd look like a hussy. Sometimes when I see these gals' faces I——"

"Really, Jo, to hear you speak one ud think you were the only virtuous woman left in England. But there are just one or two things in your career, my child, which don't quite bear out that notion."

Joanna's heart gave a sudden bound, then seemed to freeze.

She leaned forward in her chair, staring at the advertisements on the curtain. Bertie put his arm round her —"I say, ole girl, you ain't angry with me, are you?" She made no reply—she could not speak; too much was happening in her thoughts—had happened, rather, for her mind was now quite made up. A vast, half-conscious process seemed suddenly to have settled itself, leaving her quite clear-headed and calm.

"You ain't angry with me, are you?" repeated Bert.

"No," said Joanna—"I'm not angry with you."

He had been cruel and selfish when she was in trouble,

he had shown no tenderness for her physical fatigue, and now at last he had taunted her with the loss of her respectability for his sake. But she was not angry with him. . . . It was only that now she knew she could never, never marry him.

§ 31

That night she slept heavily—the deep sleep of physical exhaustion and mental decision. The unconscious striving of her soul no longer woke her to ask her hard questions. Her mind was made up, and her conflict was at an end.

She woke at the full day, when down on Walland Marsh all the world was awake, but here the city and the house still slept, and rose with her eyes and heart full of tragic purpose. She dressed quickly, then packed her box—all the gay, grand things she had brought to make her lover proud of her. Then she sat down at her dressing-table, and wrote—

" DEAR BERTIE,—When you get this I shall have gone for good. I see now that we were not meant for each other. I am very sorry if this gives you pain. But it is all for the best.—Your sincere friend,

" JOANNA GODDEN."

By this time it was half-past seven by the good gold watch which Poor Father had left her. Joanna's plan was to go downstairs, put her letter on the hall table, and bribe the girl to help her down with her box and call a cab, before any of the others appeared. She did not want to have to face Albert, with inevitable argument and possible reproaches. Her bruised heart ached too much to be able to endure any more from him—angry and wounded, it beat her side.

She carried out her scheme quite successfully as far as the cab itself, and then was betrayed. Poor Father's watch, that huge emblem of worth and respectability, hanging with its gold chain and seals upon her breast, had a rare but embarrassing habit of stopping for half an hour or so, as if to rest its ancient works. This is what it had done to-day—instead of half-past seven, the time was eight, and as the girl and the cabman carried Joanna's box out of the door, Bertie appeared at the head of the steep little stairs.

" Hullo, Joanna ! " he called out in surprise—" Where on earth are you going ? "

Here was trouble. For a moment Joanna quailed, but she recovered herself and answered—

" I'm going home."

" Home ! What d'you mean ? Whatever for ? "

The box was on the taxi, and the driver stood holding the door open.

" I made up my mind last night. I can't stay here any longer. Thank you, Alice, you needn't wait." She put a sovereign into the girl's hand.

" Come into the dining-room," said Albert.

He opened the door for her and they both went in.

" It's no good, Bertie—I can't stand it any longer," said Joanna, " it's as plain as a pike as you and me were never meant to marry, and the best thing to do is to say good-bye before it's too late."

He stared at her in silence.

" I made up my mind last night," she continued, " but I wouldn't say anything about it till this morning, and then I thought I'd slip off quiet. I've left a letter to you that I wrote."

" But why—why are you going ? "

" Well, it's pretty plain, ain't it, that we haven't been getting along so well as we should ought since I came here. You and me were never meant for each other—we don't fit—and the last few days it's been all trouble—and there's been things I could hardly bear. . . . "

Her voice broke.

" I'm sorry I've offended you "—he spoke stiffly—" but since you came here it's struck me, too, that things were different. I must say, Joanna, you don't seem to have considered the difficulties of my position."

" I have—and that's one reason why I'm going. I don't want to take you away from your business and your career, as you say ; I know you don't want to come and live at Ansdore. . . ."

" If you reelly loved me, and still felt like that about

my prospects, you'd rather give up Ansdore than turn me down as you're doing."

" I do love you "—she said doggedly, " but I couldn't give up my farm for you and come and live with you in London—because if I did, reckon I shouldn't love you much longer. These last ten days have shown me more than anything before that you'd make anyone you lived with miserable, and if I hadn't my farm to take my thoughts off I'd just about die of shame and sorrow."

He flushed angrily.

" Reelly, Joanna—what do you mean ? I've given you as good a time as I knew how."

" Most likely. But all the while you were giving me that good time you were showing me how little you cared for me. Oh, it isn't as if I hadn't been in love before and seen how good a man can be. . . . I don't want to say hard things to you, my dear, but there's been times when you've hurt me as no man could hurt a woman he really loved. And I've lived in your home and seen how you treat your poor mother and your sister—and I tell you the truth, though it hurts me—you ain't man enough for me."

" Well, if that's how you feel about me, we had certainly better not go on."

" Don't be angry with me, dear. Reckon it was all a mistake from the start—I'm too old for you."

" Then it's a pity we went as far as this. What'll mother and Agatha think when they hear you've turned me down ? They're cats enough to imagine all sorts of things. Why do you dash off like this as if I was the plague ? If you must break off our engagement, you must, though I don't want you to—I love you, even though you don't love me—but you might at least do it decently. Think of what they'll say when they come down and find you've bolted."

" I'm sorry, Bertie. But I couldn't bear to stick on here another hour. You may tell them any story about me you like. But I can't stay. I must think of myself a bit, since I've no one else to do it for me."

His face was like a sulky child's. He looked at the floor, and kicked the wainscot.

" Well, I think you're treating me very badly, Joanna.

Hang it all, I love you—and I think you're a damn fine woman—I reelly do—and I don't care if you are a bit older —I don't like girls."

" You won't think me fine in another ten years—and as for loving me, don't talk nonsense ; you don't love me, or I shouldn't be going. Now let me go."

Her voice was hard, because her self-control was failing her. She tore open the door, and pushed him violently aside when he tried to stand in her way.

" Let me go—I'm shut of you. I tell you, you ain't man enough for me."

§ 32

She had told the cabman to drive to Charing Cross station, as she felt unequal to the complications of travelling from Lewisham. It was a long drive, and all the way Joanna sat and cried. She seemed to have cried a great deal lately—her nature had melted in a strange way, and the tears she had so seldom shed as a girl were now continually ready to fall—but she had never cried as much as she cried this morning. By the time she reached Charing Cross she was in desperate need of that powder-puff Bertie had urged her to possess.

So this was the end—the end of the great romance which should have given her girlhood back to her, but which instead seemed to have shut her into a lonely and regretful middle-age. All her shining pride in herself was gone—she saw herself as one who has irrevocably lost all that makes life worth living . . . pride and love. She knew that Bertie did not love her—in his heart he was glad that she was going—all he was sorry for was the manner of it, which might bring him disgrace. But he would soon get over that, and then he would be thankful he was free, and eventually he would marry some younger woman than herself . . . and she ? Yes, she still loved him—but it would not be for long. She could feel her love for him slowly dying in her heart. It was scarcely more than pity now—pity for the little singing clerk whom she had caught and would have put in a cage if he had not fluttered so terribly in her hands.

When she arrived at Charing Cross a feeling of desolation was upon her. A porter came to fetch her box, but Joanna—the great Joanna Godden, who put terror into the markets of three towns—shrank back into the taxi, loath to leave its comfortable shelter for the effort and racket of the station. A dark, handsome, rather elderly man, was coming out of one of the archways. Their eyes met and he at once turned his away, but Joanna leapt for him—

" Sir Harry! Sir Harry Trevor! Don't you know me ? "

Only too well, but he had not exactly expected her to claim acquaintance. He felt bewildered when Joanna pushed her way to him through the crowd and wrung his hand as if he was her only friend.

" Oh, Sir Harry, reckon I'm glad to see you! "

" I—I——" stuttered the baronet.

He looked rather flushed and sodden, and the dyeing of his hair was more obvious than it had been.

" Fancy meeting you! " gasped Joanna.

" Er—how are you, Miss Godden ? "

" Do you know when there's a train to Rye ? "

" I'm sorry, I don't. I've just been saying good-bye to my son Lawrence—he's off to Africa or somewhere, but I couldn't wait till his train came in. I've got to go over to St. Pancras and catch the 10.50 for the north."

" Lawrence! "

Thank goodness, that had put her on another scent—now she would let him go.

" Yes—he's in the station. You'll see him if you're quick."

Joanna turned away, and he saw that the tears were running down her face. The woman had been drinking, that accounted for it all . . . well, he wished Lawrence joy of her. It would do him good to have a drunken woman falling on his neck on a public platform.

The porter said there was not a train for Rye for another hour. He suggested that Joanna should put her luggage in the cloak-room and go and get herself a cup of tea—the porter knew the difference between a drunken woman and one who is merely faint from trouble and want of her breakfast. But Joanna's mind was somehow obsessed by the thought of Lawrence—her brother-in-law as she still called him in her heart—she wanted to see him— she remembered his kindness long ago . . . and in her sorrow she was going back to the sorrow of those days . . . somehow she felt as if Martin had just died, as if she had just come out of North Farthing House, alone, as she had come then—and now Lawrence was here, as he had been then, to kiss her and say " Dear Jo " . . .

" What platform does the train for Africa start from ? " she asked the porter.

" Well, lady, I can't rightly say. The only boat-train from here this morning goes to Folkestone, and that's off—but most likely the gentleman ud be going from Waterloo, and the trains for Waterloo start from number seven."

The porter took her to number seven, and at the barrier she caught sight of a familiar figure sitting on a bench. Father Lawrence's bullet head showed above the folds of his cloak ; by his side was a big shapeless bundle and his eyes were fixed on the station roof. He started violently when a large woman suddenly sat down beside him and burst into tears.

" Lawrence ! " sobbed Joanna—" Lawrence ! "

" Joanna ! "

He was too startled to say anything more, but the moment did not admit of much conversation. Joanna sat beside him, bent over her knees, her big shoulders shaking with sobs which were not always silent. Lawrence made himself as large as he could, but he could not hide her from the public stare, for nature had not made her inconspicuous, and her taste in clothes would have defeated nature if it had. Her orange toque had fallen sideways on her tawny hair—she was like a big, broken sunflower.

" My dear Jo," he said gently, after a time—" let me go and get you a drink of water. "

" No—don't leave me."

" Then let me ask someone to go."

" No—no. . . . Oh, I'm all right—it's only that I felt so glad at seeing you again."

Lawrence was surprised.

" It makes me think of that other time when you were kind—I remember when Martin died . . . oh, I can't help wishing sometimes he was dead—that he'd died right at the start—or I had."

"My dear. . . . "

"Oh, when Martin died, at least it was finished; but this time it ain't finished—it's like something broken." She clasped her hands, in their brown kid gloves, against her heart.

"Won't you tell me what's happened? This isn't Martin you're talking about?"

"No. But I thought he was like Martin—that's what made me take to him at the start. I looked up and I saw him, and I said to myself 'That's Martin'—it gave me quite a jump."

The Waterloo train was in the station and the people on the platform surged towards it, leaving Lawrence and Joanna stranded on their seat. Lawrence looked at the train for a minute, then shook his head, as if in answer to some question he had asked himself.

"Look here, Jo," he said, "won't you tell me what's happened? I can't quite understand you as it is. Don't tell me anything you'd rather not."

Joanna sat upright and swallowed violently.

"It's like this," she said. "I've just broken off my engagement to marry—maybe you didn't know I was engaged to be married?"

"No, I didn't."

"Well, I was. I was engaged to a young chap—a young chap in an office. I met him at Marlingate, when I was staying there that time. I thought he was like Martin—that's what made me take to him at the first. But he wasn't like Martin—not really in his looks and never in his ways. And at last it got more'n I could bear, and I broke with him this morning and came away—and I reckon he ain't sorry, neither. . . . I'm thirteen year older than him."

Her tears began to flow again, but the platform was temporarily deserted. Lawrence waited for her to go on—he suspected a tragedy which had not yet been revealed.

"Oh, my heart's broke," she continued—"reckon I'm done for, and there's nothing left for me."

"But, Jo—is this—this affair quite finished? Per-

haps. . . . I mean to say, quarrels can be made up, you
know."

"Not this one," said Joanna. "It's been too much.
For days I've watched him getting tired of me, and last
night he turned on me because for his sake I'd done what
no woman should do."

The words were no sooner out of her mouth than she
was dismayed. She had not meant to say them. Would
Lawrence understand? What would he think of her?
—a clergyman. . . . She turned on him a face crimson
and suffused with tears, to meet a gaze as serene as ever.
Then suddenly a new feeling came to her—something apart
from horror at herself and shame at his knowing, and yet
linked strangely with them both—something which was
tenderer than any shame and yet more ruthless. . . .
Her last guard broke down.

"Lawrence, I've been wicked, I've been bad—I'm
sorry—Lawrence." . . .

"Tell me as little or as much as you like, dear Jo."

Joanna gripped his arm ; she had driven him into the
corner of the seat, where he sat with his bundle on his lap,
his ear bent to her mouth, while she crowded up against
him, pouring out her tale. Every now and then he
said gently—" Sh-sh-sh "—when he thought that her
confession was penetrating the further recesses of Charing
Cross. . . .

"Oh, Lawrence, I feel so bad—I feel so wicked—I never
should have thought it of myself. I didn't feel wicked at
first, but I did afterwards. Oh, Lawrence, tell me what
I'm to do."

His professional instinct taught him to treat the situation with simplicity, but he guessed that Joanna would not
appreciate the quiet dealings of the confessional. He had
always liked Joanna, always admired her, and he liked
and admired her no less now, but he really knew very
little of her—her life had crossed his only on three different
brief occasions, when she was engaged to his brother, when
she was anxious to appoint a Rector to the living in her
gift, and now when as a broken-hearted woman she relieved herself of a burden of sorrow.

"Lawrence—tell me what to do."

"Dear Jo—I'm not quite sure . . . I don't know

what you want, you see. What I should want first myself
would be absolution."

"Oh, don't you try none of your Jesoot tricks on me—
I couldn't bear it.'

"Very well. Then I think there's only one thing you
can do, and that is to go home and take up your life where
you left it, with a very humble heart. 'I shall go softly
all my days in the bitterness of my soul.' "

Joanna gulped.

"And be very thankful, too."

"What for ? "

"For your repentance."

"Well, reckon I do feel sorry—and reckon, too, I
done something to be sorry for. . . . Oh, Lawrence,
what a wicked owl I've been ! If you'd told me six year
ago as I'd ever have come to this I'd have had a fit on
the ground."

Lawrence looked round him nervously. Whatever
Joanna's objections to private penance, she was curiously
indifferent to confessing her sins to all mankind in Charing
Cross station. The platform was becoming crowded
again, and already their confessional had been invaded—
a woman with a baby was sitting on the end of it.

"Your train will be starting soon," said Lawrence—
"let's go and find you something to eat."

§ 33

Joanna felt better after she had had a good cup of
coffee and a poached egg. She was surprised afterwards
to find she had eaten so much. Lawrence sat with her
while she ate, then took her to find her porter, her luggage
and her train.

"But won't you lose your train to Africa ? " asked
Joanna.

"I'm only going as far as Waterloo this morning, and
there's a train every ten minutes."

"When do you start for Africa ? "

"I think to-night."

"I wish you weren't going there. Why are you
going ? "

" Because I'm sent."

" When will you come back ? "

" I don't know—perhaps never."

" I'm middling sorry you're going. What a place to send you to !—all among niggers."

She was getting more like herself. He stood at the carriage door, talking to her of indifferent things till the train started. The whistle blew, and the train began to glide out of the station. Joanna waved her hand to the grey figure standing on the platform beside the tramp's bundle which was all that would go with it to the ends of the earth. She did not know whether she pitied Lawrence or envied him.

" Reckon he's got some queer notions," she said to herself.

She leaned back in the carriage, feeling more at ease than she had felt for weeks. She was travelling third class, for one of Lawrence's notions was that everybody did so, and when Joanna had given him her purse to buy her ticket it had never struck him that she did not consider third-class travel " seemly " in one of her sex and position. However, the carriage was comfortable, and occupied only by two well-conducted females. Yes—she was certainly feeling better. She would never have thought that merely telling her story to Lawrence would have made such a difference. But a great burden had been lifted off her heart. . . . He was a good chap, Lawrence, for all his queer ways—such as ud make you think he wasn't gentry if you didn't know who his father was and his brother had been—and no notion how to behave himself as a clergyman, neither—anyway she hoped he'd get safe to Africa and that the niggers wouldn't eat him . . . though she'd heard of such things. . . .

She'd do as he said, too. She'd go home and take up things where she'd put them down. It would be hard— much harder than he thought. Perhaps he didn't grasp all that she was doing in giving up marriage, the one thing that could ever make her respect herself again. Well, she couldn't help that—she must just do without respecting herself—that's all. Anything would be better than shutting up herself and Albert together in prison, till they hated each other. It would be very hard for her, who had always been so proud of herself, to live without even respecting herself. But she should have thought of that earlier. She remembered Lawrence's words—" I will go softly all my days in the bitterness of my soul " . . . Well, she'd do her best, and perhaps God would forgive her, and then when she died she'd go to heaven, and be with Martin for ever and ever, in spite of all the bad things she'd done. . . .

She got out at Appledore and took the light railway to Brodnyx. She did not feel inclined for the walk from Rye. The little train was nearly empty, and Joanna had a carriage to herself. She settled herself comfortably in a corner—it was good to be coming home, even as things were. The day was very sunny and still. The blue sky was slightly misted—a yellow haze which smelt of chaff and corn smudged together the sky and the marsh and the distant sea. The farms with their red and yellow roofs were like ripe apples lying in the grass.

Yes, the Marsh was the best place to live on, and the Marsh ways were the best ways, and the man who had loved her on the Marsh was the best man and the best lover. . . . She wondered what Ellen would say when she heard she had broken off her engagement. Ellen had never thought much of Bertie—she had thought Joanna was a fool to see such a lot in him ; and Ellen had been right—her eyes and her head were clearer than her poor sister's. . . . She expected she would be home in time for tea—Ellen would be terrible surprised to see her ; if she'd had any sense she'd have sent her a telegram.

The little train had a strange air of friendliness as it jogged across Romney Marsh. It ran familiarly through farmyards and back gardens, it meekly let the motor-cars race it and pass it as it clanked beside the roads. The line was single all the way, except for a mile outside Brodnyx station, where it made a loop to let the up-train pass. The up-train was late—they had been too long loading up the fish at Dungeness, or there was a reaping machine being brought from Lydd. For some minutes Joanna's train stayed halted in the sunshine, in the very midst of the Three Marshes. Miles of sun-swamped green spread on either side—the carriage was full of sunshine—it was bright and stuffy like a greenhouse. Joanna felt drowsy,

she lay back in her corner blinking at the sun—she was
all quiet now. A blue-bottle droned against the window,
and the little engine droned, like an impatient fly—it was
all very still, very hot, very peaceful. . . .

Then suddenly something stirred within her—stirred
physically. In some mysterious way she seemed to come
alive. She sat up, pressing her hand to her side. A flood
of colour went up into her face—her body trembled, and
the tears started in her eyes . . . she felt herself
choking with wild fear, and wild joy.

§ 34

Oh, she understood now. She understood, and she
was certain. She knew now—she knew, and she was
frightened . . . oh, she was frightened . . . now everything was over with her indeed.

Joanna nearly fainted. She fell in a heap against the
window, looking more than ever, as the sunshine poured on
her, like a great golden, broken flower. She felt herself
choking and managed to right herself—the window was
down, and a faint puff of air came in from the sea, lifting
her hair as she leaned back against the wooden wall of
the carriage, her mouth a little open. . . . She felt
better now, but still so frightened. . . . She was done
for, she was finished—there would not be any more talk of
going back and picking up things where she had let them
drop. She would have to marry Bertie—there was no
help for it, she would send him a telegram from Brodnyx
station. Oh, that this should have happened ! . . .
And she had been feeling so much easier in her mind—she
had almost begun to feel happy again, thinking of the old
home and the old life. And now she knew that they had
gone for ever—the old home and the old life. She had cut
herself away from both—she would have to marry Albert,
to shut her little clerk in prison after all, and herself with
him. She would have to humble herself before him, she
would have to promise to go and live with him in London,
do all she possibly could to make his marriage easy for
him. He did not want to marry her, and she did not
want to marry him, but there was no help for it, they

must marry now, because of what their love had given
them before it died.

She had no tears for this new tragedy. She leaned
forward in her seat, her hands clasped between her knees,
her eyes staring blankly at the carriage wall as if she saw
there her future written . . . herself and Albert growing
old together, or rather herself growing old while Albert
lived through his eager, selfish youth—herself and Albert
shut up together . . . how he would scold her, how he
would reproach her—he would say " You have brought
me to this," and in time he would come to hate her, his
fellow-prisoner who had shut the door on both of them—
and he would hate her child . . . they would never have
married except for the child, so he would hate her child,
scold it, make it miserable . . . it would grow up in an
unhappy home, with parents who did not love each other,
who owed it a grudge for coming to them—her child, her
precious child. . . .

Still in her heart, alive under all the fear, was that
thrill of divine joy which had come to her in the first moment
of realization. Terror, shame, despair—none of them
could kill it, for that joy was a part of her being, part of
the new being which had quickened in her. It belonged
to them both—it was the secret they shared . . . joy,
unutterable joy. Yes, she was glad she was going to have
this child—she would still be glad even in the prison-house
of marriage, she would still be glad even in the desert of
no-marriage, every tongue wagging, every finger pointing,
every heart despising. Nothing could take her joy from
her—make her less than joyful mother. . . .

Then as the joy grew and rose above the fear, she knew
that she could never let fear drive her into bondage.
Nothing should make a sacrifice of joy to shame—to save
herself she would not bring up her child in the sorrow and
degradation of a loveless home. . . . If she had been
strong enough to give up the thought of marriage for the
sake of Bertie's liberty and her own self-respect, she could
be strong enough now to turn from her only hope of reputation for the sake of the new life which was joy within her.
It would be the worst, most shattering thing she had ever
yet endured, but she would go through with it for the love
of the unborn. Joanna was not so unsophisticated as to

fail to realize the difficulties and complications of her resolve—how much her child would suffer for want of a father's name ; memories of lapsed dairymaids had stressed in her experience the necessity of a marriage no matter how close to the birth. But she did not rate these difficulties higher than the misery of such a home as hers and Albert's would be. Better anything than that. Joanna had no illusions about Albert now—he'd have led her a dog's life if she had married him in the first course of things ; now it would be even worse, and her child should not suffer that.

No, she would do her best. Possibly she could arrange things so as to protect, at least to a certain extent, the name her baby was to bear. She would have to give up Ansdore, of course—leave Walland Marsh . . . her spirit quailed, but she braced it fiercely. She was going through with this—it was the only thing Lawrence had told her that she could do—go softly all her days—to the very end. That end was farther and bitterer than either he or she had imagined then, but she would not have to go all the way alone. A child—that was what she had always wanted ; she had tried to fill her heart with other things, with Ansdore, with Ellen, with men . . . but what she had always wanted had been a child—she saw that now. Her child should have been born in easy, honourable circumstances, with a kind father—Arthur Alce, perhaps, since it could not be Martin Trevor. But the circumstances of its birth were her doing, and it was she who would face them. The circumstances only were her sin and shame, her undying regret—since she knew she could not keep them entirely to herself—the rest was joy and thrilling, vital peace.

The little train pulled itself together, and ran on into Brodnyx station. Joanna climbed down on the wooden platform, and signalled to the porter-stationmaster to take out her box.

"What, you back, Miss Godden!" he said, "we wasn't expecting you."

"No, I've come back pretty sudden. Do you know if there's any traps going over Pedlinge way?"

"There's Mrs. Furnese come over to fetch a crate of fowls. Maybe she'd give you a lift."

" I'll ask her," said Joanna.

Mrs. Furnese, too, was much surprised to see her back, but she said nothing about it, partly because she was a woman of few words, and partly because they'd all seen in the paper this morning that Joanna had lost her case—and reckon she must be properly upset. Maybe that was why she had come back. . . .

" Would you like to drive ? " she asked Joanna, when they had taken their seats in Misleham's ancient gig, with the crate of fowls behind them. She felt rather shy of handling the reins under Joanna Godden's eye, for everyone knew that Joanna drove like a Jehu, something tur'ble.

But the great woman shook her head. She felt tired, she said, with the heat. So Mrs. Furnese drove, and Joanna sat silently beside her, watching her thick brown hand on the reins, with the wedding ring embedded deep in the gnarled finger.

" Reckon she's properly upset with that case," thought the married woman to herself, " and sarve her right for bringing it. She could easily have paid them missionaries, with all the money she had. But it was ever Joanna's way to make a terrification."

They jogged on over the winding, white ribbon of road—through Brodnyx village, past the huge barn-like church which had both inspired and reproached her faith, with its black, caped tower canting over it, on to Walland Marsh, to the cross roads at the Woolpack—My, how they would talk at the Woolpack ! . . . but she would be far away by then . . . where ? . . . She didn't know, she would think of that later—when she had told Ellen. Oh, there would be trouble—there would be the worst she'd ever have to swallow—when she told Ellen. . . .

§ 35

Joanna saw Ansdore looking at her through the chaffy haze of the August afternoon. It stewed like an apple in the sunshine, and a faint smell of apples came from it, as its great orchard dragged its boughs in the grass. They were reaping the Gate Field close to the house—the hum

of the reaper came to her, and seemed in some mysterious
way to be the voice of Ansdore itself, droning in the sunshine and stillness. She felt her throat tighten, and
winked the tears from her eyes.

She could see Ellen coming down the drive, a cool,
white, belted figure, with trim white feet. From her bedroom window Ellen had seen the Misleham gig turn in at
the gate, and had at once recognized the golden blot beside Mrs. Furnese as her sister Joanna.

" Hullo, Jo ! I never expected you back to-day.
Did you send a wire ? For if you did, I never got it."

" No, I didn't telegraph. Where's Mene Tekel ? Tell
her to come around with Nan and carry up my box. Mrs.
Furnese, ma'am, I hope you'll step in and drink a cup of
tea."

Joanna climbed down and kissed Ellen—her cheek
was warm and moist, and her hair hung rough about her
ears, over one of which the orange toque, many times set
right, had come down in a final confusion. Ellen on the
other hand was as cool as she was white—and her hair lay
smooth under a black velvet fillet. Of late it seemed as if
her face had acquired a brooding air ; it had lost its exotic
look, it was dreamy, almost virginal. Joanna felt her
sister's kiss like snow.

" Is tea ready ? "

" No—it's only half-past three. But you can have it
at once. You look tired. Why didn't you send a wire,
and I'd have had the trap to meet you."

" I never troubled, and I've managed well enough.
Ain't you coming in, Mrs. Furnese ? "

" No, thank you, Miss Godden—much obliged all the
same. I've my man's tea to get, and these fowls to see
to."

She felt that the sisters would want to be alone. Joanna
would tell Ellen all about her failure, and Mene Tekel and
Nan would overhear as much as they could, and tell Broadhurst and Crouch and the other men, who would tell the
Woolpack bar, where Mr. Furnese would hear it and bring
it home to Mrs. Furnese. . . . So her best way of learning the truth about the Appeal and exactly how many
thousands Joanna had lost depended on her going home
as quickly as possible.

Joanna was glad to be alone. She went with Ellen into the cool parlour, drinking in the relief of its solid comfort compared with the gimcrackiness of the parlour at Lewisham.

"I'm sorry about your Appeal," said Ellen—" I saw in to-day's paper that you've lost it."

Joanna had forgotten all about the Appeal—it seemed twenty-four years ago instead of twenty-four hours that she had come out of the Law Courts and seen Bertie standing there with the pigeons strutting about his feet—but she welcomed it as a part explanation of her appearance, which she saw now was deplorable, and her state of mind, which she found impossible to disguise.

"Yes, it's terrible—I'm tedious upset."

"I suppose you've lost a lot of money."

"Not more than I can afford to pay "—the old Joanna came out and boasted for a minute.

"That's one comfort."

Joanna looked at her sister and opened her mouth, but shut it as Mene Tekel came in with the tea tray and Arthur Alce's good silver service.

Mene set the tea as silently as the defects of her respiratory apparatus would admit, and once again Joanna sighed with relief as she thought of the clatter made by Her at Lewisham. . . . Oh, there was no denying that she had a good house and good servants and had done altogether well for herself until in a fit of wickedness she had bust it all.

She would not tell Ellen to-night. She would wait till to-morrow morning, when she'd had a good sleep. She felt tired now, and would cry the minute Ellen began. . . . . But she'd let her know about the breaking off of her engagement—that would prepare the way, like.

"Ellen," she said, after she had drunk her tea—" one reason I'm so upset is that I've just broken off my marriage with my intended."

"Joanna!"

Ellen put down her cup and stared at her. In her anxiety to hide her emotion, Joanna had spoken more in anger than in sorrow, so her sister's pity was checked.

"What ever made you do that ?"

"We found we didn't suit."

" Well, my dear, I must say the difference in your age
made me rather anxious. Thirteen years on the woman's
side is rather a lot, you know. But I knew you'd always
liked boys, so I hoped for the best."

" Well, it's all over now."

" Poor old Joanna, it must have been dreadful for
you—on the top of your failure in the courts, too ; but
I'm sure you were wise to break it off. Only the most
absolute certainty could have justified such a marriage."

She smiled to herself. When she said " absolute certainty " she was thinking of Tip.

" Well, I've got a bit of a headache," said Joanna rising
—" I think I'll go and have a lay down."

" Do, dear. Would you like me to come up with you
and help you undress ? "

" No thanks. I'll do by myself. You might ask the
girl to bring me up a jug of hot water. Reckon I
shan't be any worse for a good wash."

§ 36

Much as Joanna was inclined to boast of her new bathroom at Ansdore, she did not personally make much use
of it, having perhaps a secret fear of its unfriendly whiteness, and a love of the homely, steaming jug which had
been the fount of her ablutions since her babyhood's tub
was given up. This evening she removed the day's grime
from herself by a gradual and excessively modest process,
and about one and a half pints of hot water. Then she
twisted her hair into two ropes, put on a clean night-gown,
and got into bed.

Her body's peace between the cool, coarse sheets seemed
to thrill to her soul. She felt at home and at rest. It was
funny being in bed at that time in the afternoon—scarcely
past four o'clock—it was funny, but it was good. The
sunshine was coming into the room, a spill of misty gold
on the floor and furniture, and from where she lay she could
see the green boundaries of the Marsh. Oh, it would be
terrible when she saw that Marsh no more. . . the tears
rose, and she turned her face to the pillow. It was all
over now—all her ambition, all her success, all the great-

ness of Joanna Godden. She had made Ansdore great and
prosperous though she was a woman, and then she had
lost it because she was a woman. . . . Words that she
had uttered long ago came back into her mind. She saw
herself standing in the dairy, in front of Martha Tilden,
whose face she had forgotten. She was saying: "It's
sad to think you've kept yourself straight for years and
then gone wrong at last. . . ."

Yes, it was sad . . . and now she was being punished
for it; but wrapped up in her punishment, sweetening its
very heart, was a comfort she did not deserve. Ansdore
was slowly fading in her thoughts, as it had always faded
in the presence of any vital instinct, whether of love or
death. Ansdore could never be to her what her child would
be—none of her men, except perhaps Martin, could have
been to her what her child would be. . . . "If it's a
boy I'll call it Martin—if it's a girl I'll call it Ellen," she
said to herself. Then she doubted whether Ellen would
appreciate the compliment . . . but she would not let
herself think of Ellen to-night. That was to-morrow's
evil.

"I'll have to make some sort of a plan, though—I'll
have to sell this place and give Ellen a share of it. And
me—where ull I go?"

She must go pretty far, so that when the child came
Brodnyx and Pedlinge would not get to know about it.
She would have to go at least as far as Brighton . . . then
she remembered Martha Relf and her lodgings at Chichester
—"that wouldn't be bad, to go to Martha just for a start.
Me leaving Ansdore for the same reason as she left it
thirteen year ago . . . that's queer. The mistress who
got shut of her, coming to her and saying—'Look here,
Martha, take me in, so's I can have my child in peace
same as you had yours' . . . I should ought to get
some stout money for this farm—eight thousand pounds
if it's eightpence—though reckon the Government ull want
about half of it and we'll have all that terrification started
again . . . howsumever, I guess I'll get enough of it to
live on, even when Ellen has her bit . . . and maybe
the folk around here ull think I'm sold up because my case
has bust me, and that'll save me something of their talk."

Well, well, she was doing the best she could—though

Lawrence on his blind, obedient way to Africa was scarcely going on a farther, lonelier journey than that on which Joanna was setting out.

"Oh, Martin," she whispered, lifting her eyes to his picture on her chest of drawers—"I wish I could feel you close."

It was years since she had really let herself think of him, but now strange barriers of thought had broken down, and she seemed to go to and fro quite easily into the past. Whether it was her love for Bertie whom in her blindness she had thought like him, or her meeting with Lawrence, or the new hope within her, she did not trouble to ask— but that strange, long forbidding was gone. She was free to remember all their going out and coming in together, his sweet fiery kisses, the ways of the Marsh that he had made wonderful. Throughout her being there was a strange sense of release—broken, utterly done and finished as she was from the worldly point of view, there was in her heart a springing hope, a sweet softness—she could indeed go softly at last.

The tears were in her eyes as she climbed out of bed and knelt down beside it. It was weeks since she had said her prayers—not since that night when Bertie had come into her room. But now that her heart was quite melted she wanted to ask God to help her and forgive her.

"Oh, please God, forgive me. I know I been wicked, but I'm unaccountable sorry. And I'm going through with it. Please help my child—don't let it get hurt for my fault. Help me to do my best and not grumble, seeing as it's all my own wickedness; and I'm sorry I broke the Ten Commandments. 'Lord have mercy upon us and write all these thy laws in our hearts, we beseech thee.'"

This liturgical outburst seemed wondrously to heal Joanna—it seemed to link her up again with the centre of her religion—Brodnyx church, with the big pews, and the hassocks, and the Lion and the Unicorn over the north door—she felt readmitted into the congregation of the faithful, and her heart was full of thankfulness and loyalty. She rose from her knees, climbed into bed, and curled up on her side. Ten minutes later she was sound asleep.

§ 37

The next morning after breakfast, Joanna faced Ellen
in the dining-room.

" Ellen," she said—" I'm going to sell Ansdore."

" You're what ? "

" I'm going to put up this place for auction in September."

" Joanna ! "

Ellen stared at her in amazement, alarm, and some
sympathy.

" I'm driving in to tell Edward Huxtable about it this
morning.　Not that I trust him, after the mess he made of
my case ; howsumever, I can look after him in this business, and the auctioneer, too."

" But, my dear, I thought you said you'd plenty of
money to meet your losses."

" So I have.　That's not why I'm selling."

" Then why on earth . . ."

The colour mounted to Joanna's face.　She looked at
her sister's delicate, thoughtful face, with its air of quiet
happiness.　The room was full of sunshine, and Ellen was
all in white.

" Ellen, I'm going to tell you something . . . because you're my sister.　And I trust you not to let another
living soul know what I've told you.　As I kept your
secret four years ago, so now you can keep mine."

Ellen's face lost a little of its repose—suddenly, for
a moment, she looked like the Ellen of " four years
ago."

" Really, Joanna, you might refrain from raking up the
past."

" I'm sorry, I didn't mean to rake up nothing.　I've
no right—seeing as what I want to tell you is that I'm just
the same as you."

Ellen turned white.

" What *do* you mean ? " she cried furiously.

" I mean—I'm going to have a child."

Ellen stared at her without speaking, her mouth fell
open ; then her face began working in a curious way.

" I know I been wicked," continued Joanna, in a dull,
level voice—" but it's too late to help that now.　The only

thing now is to do the best I can, and that is to get out of here."

"Do you know what you're talking about?" said Ellen.

"Yes—I know right enough. It's true what I'm telling you. I didn't know for certain till yesterday."

"Are you quite sure?"

"Certain sure."

"But——" Ellen drummed with her fingers on the table, her hands were shaking, her colour came and went.

"Joanna—is it Albert's child?"

"Of course it is."

"Then why—why in God's name did you break off the engagement?"

"I tell you I didn't know till yesterday. I'd been scared once or twice, but he told me it was all right."

"Does he know?"

"He doesn't."

"Then he must be told"—Ellen sprang to her feet—"Joanna, what a fool you are! You must send him a wire at once and tell him to come down here. You must marry him."

"That I won't!"

"But you're mad—really, you've no choice in the matter. You must marry him at once."

"I tell you I'll never do that."

"If you don't . . . can't you see what'll happen?—are you an absolute fool? If you don't marry this man, your child will be illegitimate, you'll be kicked out of decent society, and you'll bring us all to ruin and disgrace."

Ellen burst into tears. Joanna fought back her own.

"Listen to me, Ellen."

But Ellen sobbed brokenly on. It was as if her own past had risen from its grave and laid cold hands upon her, just when she thought it was safely buried for ever.

"Don't you see what'll happen if you refuse to marry this man?—It'll ruin me—it'll spoil my marriage. Tip . . . Good God! he's risen to a good deal, seeing the ideas most Englishmen have . . . but now you—you——"

"Ellen, you don't mean as Tip ull get shut of you because of me?"

" No, of course I don't. But it's asking too much of him—it isn't fair to him . . . he'll think he's marrying into a fine family ! "—and Ellen's tears broke into some not very pleasant laughter—" both of us. . . . Oh, he was sweet about me, he understood—but now you—you !—Whatever made you do it, Joanna ? "

" I dunno . . . I loved him, and I was mad."

" I think it's horrible of you—perfectly horrible. I'd absolutely no idea you were that sort of woman—I thought at least you were decent and respectable. . . . A man you were engaged to, too. Oh, I know what you're think-ing—you're thinking I'm in the same boat as you are, but I tell you I'm not. I was a married woman—I couldn't have married my lover, I'd a right to take what I could get. But you could have married yours—you were going to marry him. But you lost your head—like a common servant—like the girl you sacked years ago when you thought I was too young to understand anything about it. And I never landed myself with a child—at least there was some possibility of wiping out what I'd done when it proved a mistake, some chance of living it down —and I've done it, I've won my way back, and now you come along and disgrace me all over again, and the man I love. . . ."

Never had Ellen's voice been so like Joanna's. It had risen to a hoarse note where it hung suspended—anyone now would know that they were sisters.

" I tell you I'm sorry, Ellen. But I can't do nothing about it."

" Yes, you can. You can marry this man, Hill—then no one need ever know, Tip need never know——"

" Reckon that wouldn't keep them from knowing. They'd see as I was getting married in a hurry—not an invitation out and my troossoo not half ready—and then they'd count the months till the baby came. No, I tell you, it'll be much better if I go away. Everyone ull think as I'm bust, through having lost my case, and I'll go right away—Chichester, I'd thought of going to, where Martha Relf is—and when the baby comes, no one ull be a bit the wiser."

" Of course they will. They'll know all about it—everything gets known here, and you've never in your life

been able to keep a secret. If you marry, people won't
talk in the same way—it'll be only guessing, anyhow.
You needn't be down here when the baby's born—and at
least Tip needn't know. Joanna, if you love me, if you
ever loved me, you'll send a wire to this man and tell him
that you've changed your mind and must see him—you
can easily make up the quarrel, whatever it was."

"Maybe he wouldn't marry me now, even if I did
wire."

"Nonsense—he'd have to."

"Well, he won't be asked."

Joanna was stiffening with grief. She had not expected to have this battle with Ellen ; she had been prepared for abuse and upbraiding, but not for argument—
it had not struck her that her sister would demand the re-
habilitation she herself refused.

"You're perfectly shameless," sobbed Ellen. "My
God ! It ud take a woman like you to brazen through a
thing like this. Swanking, swaggering, you've always
been . . . well, I bet you'll find this too much even
for your swagger—you don't know what you're letting
yourself in for. . . . I can tell you a little, for I've
known, I've felt, what people can be. . . . I've had to
face them—when you wouldn't let Arthur give me my
divorce."

"Well, I'll just about have to face 'em, that's all. I
done wrong, and I don't ask not to be punished."

"You're an absolute fool. And if you won't do anything for your own sake, you might at least do something
for mine. I tell you, I'm not like you—I do think of other
people—and for Tip's sake I can't have everyone talking
about you, and may be my own story raked up again. I
won't have him punished for his goodness. If you won't
marry and be respectable, I tell you, you needn't think I'll
ever let you see me again."

"But, Ellen, supposing even there is talk—you and
Tip won't be here to hear it. You'll be married by then and
away in Wiltshire. Tip need never know."

"How can he help knowing, as long as you've got a
tongue in your head ? And what'll he think you're doing
at Chichester ?—No, I tell you, Joanna, unless you marry
Hill, you can say good-bye to me "—she was speaking

quite calmly now—" I don't want to be hard and unsisterly, but I happen to love the man who's going to be my husband better than anyone in the world. He's been good, and I'm not going to have his goodness put upon. He's marrying a woman who's had trouble and scandal in her life, but at least he's not going to have the shame of that woman's sister. So you can choose between me and yourself."

" It ain't between you and myself. It's between you and my child. It's for my child's sake I won't marry Bertie Hill."

" My dear Joanna, are you quite an ass ? Can't you see that the person who will suffer most for all this is your child ? I didn't bring in that argument before, as I didn't think it would appeal to you—but surely you see that the position of an illegitimate child. . . ."

" Is much better than the child of folk who don't love each other, and have only married because it was coming. I'm scared myself, and I can scare Bert, and we can get married—but what'll that be ? He don't love me —I don't love him. He don't want to marry me—I don't want to marry him. He'll never forgive me, and all our lives he'll be throwing it up to me—and he'll be hating the child, seeing as it's only because of it we're married, and he'll make it miserable. Oh, you don't know Bertie as I know him—I don't say as it's all his fault, poor boy, I reckon his mother didn't raise him properly—but you should hear him speak to his mother and sister, and know what he'd be as a husband and father. I tell you, he ain't fit to be the father of a child."

" And are you fit to be the mother ? " Ellen sneered.

" Maybe I ain't. But the point is, I *am* the mother, nothing can change that. And reckon I can fight, and keep the worst off. Oh, I know it ain't easy, and it ain't right ; and I'll suffer for it, and the worst ull be that my child ull have to suffer too. But I tell you it shan't suffer more than I can help. Reckon I shan't manage so badly. I'll raise it among strangers, and I'll have a nice little bit of money to live on, coming to me from the farm, even when I've paid you a share, as I shall, as is fitting. I'll give my child every chance I can."

" Then it's a choice between your child and me. If

you do this mad thing, Joanna, you'll have to go. I can't
have you ever coming near me and Tip—it isn't only for
my own sake—it's for his."

" Reckon we're both hurting each other for somebody
else's sake. But I ain't angry with you, Ellen, same as
you're angry with me."

" I am angry with you—I can't help it. You go and
do this utterly silly and horrible thing, and then instead
of making the best you can of it for everybody's sake,
you go on blundering worse and worse. Such utter ignorance of the world . . . such utter ignorance of your
own self . . . how d'you think you're going to manage
without Ansdore ? Why, it's your very life—you'll be
utterly lost without it. Think of yourself, starting an
entirely new life at your age—nearly forty. It's impossible. You don't know what you're letting yourself in
for. But you'll find out when it's too late, and then both
you and your unfortunate child ull have to suffer."

" If I married Bert I couldn't keep on Ansdore. He
wouldn't marry me unless I came to London—I know
that now. He's set on business. I'd have to go and
live with him in a street . . . then we'd both be miserable, all three be miserable. Now if I go off alone, maybe
later on I can get a bit of land, and run another farm in
foreign parts—by Chichester or Southampton—just a
little one, to keep me busy. Reckon that ud be fine and
healthy for my child. . . ."

" Your child seems to be the only thing you care about.
Really to hear you talk, one ud almost think you were
glad."

" I am glad."

Ellen sprang to her feet.

" There's no good going on with this conversation.
You're quite without feeling and quite without shame.
I don't know if you'll come to your senses later, and not
perhaps feel quite so *glad* that you have ruined your life,
disgraced your family, broken my heart, brought shame
and trouble into the life of a good and decent man. But
at present I'm sick of you."

She walked towards the door.

" Ellen," cried Joanna—" don't go away like that—
don't think that of me. I ain't glad in that way."

But Ellen would not turn or speak. She went out of the door with a queer, white draggled look about her.

"Ellen," cried Joanna a second time, but she knew it was no good. . . .

Well, she was alone now, if ever a woman was.

She stood staring straight in front of her, out of the little flower-pot obscured window, into the far distances of the Marsh. Once more the Marsh wore its strange, occasional look of being under the sea, but this time it was her own tears that had drowned it.

"Child—what if the old floods came again?" she seemed to hear Martin's voice as it had spoken in a far-off, half forgotten time. . . . He had talked to her about those old floods, he had said they might come again, and she had said they couldn't. . . . My! How they used to argue together in those days. He had said that if the floods came back to drown the Marsh, all the church bells would ring under the sea. . . .

She liked thinking of Martin in this way—it comforted her. It made her feel as if, now that everything had been taken from her, the past so long lost had been given back. And not the past only, for if her memories lived, her hopes lived too—not even Ellen's bitterness could kill them. . . . There she stood, nearly forty years old, on the threshold of an entirely new life—her lover, her sister, her farm, her home, her good name, all lost. But the past and the future still were hers.

SHEILA KAYE-SMITH

(1887-1956) was born at St. Leonard's-on-Sea, England, the daughter of a doctor. From an early age she explored the surrounding countryside, studying local customs and dialect. She began writing at the age of fifteen and by the time she had finished school two years later had completed thirteen books: her first published novel, The Tramping Methodist, appeared in 1908. Sheila Kaye-Smith left Sussex in 1909 to live for a time in London where she came to know the Victorian poet Alice Meynell. Later she was to meet numerous literary figures including D. H. Lawrence, Dorothy Richardson and the two authors whose work has been most associated with hers: Mary Webb and Thomas Hardy.

Her first book to attract nationwide attention in England was *Sussex Gorse,* published in 1916. By 1918 she had become a member of the Anglo-Catholic Church, and frequently spoke at meetings. Following the war three more books confirmed her reputation as a Sussex novelist, the most acclaimed being *Joanna Godden* (1921), later to be made into a film starring Googie Withers; but her greatest financial success came with *The End of the House of Alard* (1923).

In 1924, at the age of thirty-seven, she married the assistant priest at St. Stephen's, Gloucester Road: the Reverend Theodore Penrose Fry. Sheila Kaye-Smith left Hastings for London where she continued writing her Sussex novels; in 1929, however, she and her husband were converted to Roman Catholicism. After five years of exile they returned to their beloved Sussex, buying a farm near Northiam where they built a chapel dedicated to St. Thérèse de Lisieux, about whom Sheila Kaye-Smith wrote in her study of four Roman Catholic heroines, *Quartet in Heaven* (1953). Of her fifty published works other notable novels include *The George and the Crown* (1925) and *Susan Spray.* Her last book, *All the Books of my Life,* was published in the year of her death, which occurred at her home three weeks before her sixty-ninth birthday.